THE JAMBUDVEEP SERIES - 1

BHARAT KSHETRA

THE HIDDEN MATRIX

THE JAMBUDVEEP SERIES - 1

BHARAT KSHETRA

THE HIDDEN MATRIX

VIPUL SHAH

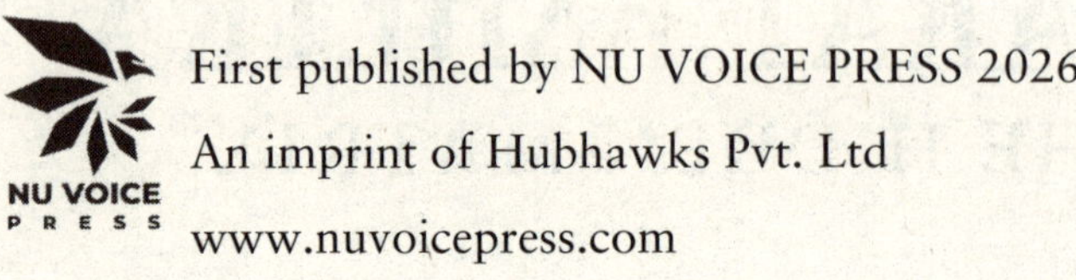

First published by NU VOICE PRESS 2026

An imprint of Hubhawks Pvt. Ltd

www.nuvoicepress.com

This is a work of fiction and all characters and incidents described in this book are the product of the author's imagination. Any resemblance to actual persons, living or dead, is entirely coincidental.

ISBN: 978-81-998993-0-8

Jambudveep Logo Design by Vipul Shah, Nivia Jain, and Kanchan Majithia

Illustrations by Rutvi Pujara

Cover Design by S. Saran and Concept Art by Yasmeen Khan

Typeset by Saanvi Graphics, Noida

Published by Nu Voice Press

For, both my moms, Meena and Mina

Table of Contents

PART 1

THREADS OF DESTINY

CHAPTER 1

Giants of Light and Shadows of Memory

THE DREAM AND FLASHBACK

2012 – Bangalore, Karnataka

Bright, white light overwhelmed every corner of his vision. Pravash instinctively raised a hand to shield his eyes, but the brightness pressed against him relentlessly, as if even shadows radiated light. The air shimmered with an unearthly glow—beautiful yet disorienting—and as he struggled to make sense of it, a realization struck him—he was not alone.

He squinted, his eyes watering as he forced them to adjust. The light softened just enough for the shapes to sharpen. Towering figures—giants, impossibly large, stretching 3000, maybe even 4000 feet tall—moved around him in metrical waves, their sheer size making the sky seem closer than the ground. Each figure emitted a soft, otherworldly glow, halos blurring their forms into delicate, shifting shapes. Their faces were indistinct, hazy, yet somehow alive with purpose. Their expressions flickered—joy, urgency, or something far beyond what human eyes could comprehend. Were they rejoicing? Or running from something unseen?

Pravash strained to follow their movement, craning his neck as if caught between dream and waking. But his gaze kept snapping back to the giants. Their glowing bodies created a living wall so vast, that it hid anything that might have existed beyond it. Each of their steps sent a deep, rhythmic tremor through the ground beneath his feet, the vibrations rippling through his body like distant echoes of thunder.

He felt impossibly small, as though he were an afterthought in their world. Yet, something tugged at him. A deep pull in his chest, subtle but undeniable, like an invisible thread binding him to these beings. He wanted to follow them, to join them in their purpose, whatever it was. But his feet were rooted to the ground, heavy as stone, and a strange ache tightened inside him, a longing so deep, he couldn't name.

Then, one of the giants paused. Slowly, it turned.

Pravash froze as he felt its gaze fall upon him. It wasn't a mere look—it was piercing, searching, like the figure could see into the deepest corners of his soul. His breath hitched as their eyes seemed to lock, the moment suspended in an eternity, he could neither understand nor escape.

And then it all vanished. The light, the tremors, the giants—everything dissolved leaving him standing in a silent, empty void.

Pravash jolted upright in bed, chest heaving, heart pounding fiercely against his ribs. The digital clock beside his bed read October 16, 2012—thousands of miles away, Kolkata was already buzzing vibrantly with preparations, *Durga Puja* merely four days away, and the world would soon shift in ways he couldn't yet fathom. The dim bedroom slowly came into focus, but the dream (or was it something else?) clung to him like smoke. The image of the towering figures and their glowing forms burned into his memory, refusing to fade.

He rubbed his face with slightly trembling hands. *What was that? Who were they? A dream... or something else entirely?* He stayed still, watching the thin light creep through the curtains, the remnants of the vision still wrapped around him.

In the mirror, his reflection stared back—wavy black hair tousled, a 6'1" frame, and the quiet innocence that still softened his face, even after all these years. It was a face that had embraced the chaos of life—savoring the thrill of joy, shouldering the ache of heartbreak, and carrying the silent weight of love and regret—emotions woven into the fabric of his being, unseen by the world.

As he poured himself a cup of tea, inhaling the rich aroma of cardamom mingled with a faint trace of saffron, his thoughts wandered back to the dream, tugging at a quiet corner of his mind. By most measures, his life in Bangalore was steady and predictable. A stable career, a loving wife, **Priyam**, and their lively toddler, **Arya**, who was the source of both boundless joy and chaos. Arya's laughter usually echoed through their home, brightening every corner. Even now, he could hear her humming an off-tune melody to herself, her tiny footsteps pattering across the floorboards. Warmth filled his home, but a restless longing stirred beneath it—something that refused to fade.

Beneath the calm surface of his days, he often found himself thinking of a life he had once imagined—moments of passion and purpose that now felt distant, like whispers from another time. Last nights' vision had cracked something open, a yearning he couldn't name, but couldn't ignore.

He scrolled through the family chat, a stream of messages buzzing with plans for the upcoming Durga Puja celebrations in Kolkata.

Durga Puja was the one time every year when his family had a rare moment when his father and brother would step away from the family business to gather in their hometown. His mother, Meenakshi, the quiet heart of the family had always insisted on it. *No excuses.* For Pravash, these reunions were precious—the crush of crowds around pandals, the scent of incense threading through the air, plates piled high with *bhog*, and nights that hummed with laughter. Even now, he could almost hear the *dhak* rising and falling like a heartbeat, the *city of joy*—Kolkata, glowing and alive in his memory.

His thumb hovered over the date on his screen. Another year had come, yet the emotions surrounding Durga Puja felt as timeless as ever. As he read through the chat, memories of his youth surfaced, uninvited moments that had been buried under the weight of time and responsibility, now rising like gentle waves to the forefront of his mind.

Beneath the lingering echo of his dream and noise of the chat, that same subtle pull returned, sharper this time. A feeling he couldn't name, but one that felt undeniably important.

He sipped his tea, smiling softly to himself as the past unfolded effortlessly within his mind.

It wasn't the first time Puja season stirred old emotions in him. His mind, unanchored, drifted to the earliest ripples of his heart: his first crush at seven, Ismat, her name still bright in his mind after decades. The innocence of that memory had imprinted on him, proof of how easily he gave himself to anyone who showed him kindness. Later came Suhani, whose single, small gesture on a school bus had sparked a silent admiration that stretched over half a decade. Pravash had always been that way—throwing himself wholly and recklessly into anything or anyone who touched his heart.

That same intensity had driven him toward spiritual extremes too. At eleven, deeply inspired by the profound words of a revered Jain monk, he'd nearly renounced everything, ready to walk away from the world entirely. Meenakshi, his mother, had sensed the brewing storm inside him and gently pulled him back, urging him to live the questions rather than rush towards answers too large for his young heart.

But moderation had never held him for long. At fifteen, he fell deeply in love with a girl whose faith made their bond seem impossible. He had stood against everything he knew, defying traditions, boundaries, and family expectations. Even now, years later, a bittersweet smile touched his lips at the thought. How passionately idealistic he had been—and how different he'd become.

He had always chased extremes, relishing the thrill and drama of life's battles, fully aware of the storms his actions could create—and embracing them anyway. He remembered clearly how that rebellious spirit had followed him into his high school years, when he'd single-handedly taken on nine seniors who tried to bully his friend during their first week. That fight had transformed him overnight—from a nobody into someone feared and admired by all. He'd enjoyed every moment of that newfound notoriety, dominating his seniors, basking unapologetically in the spotlight, indifferent to whether it shone positively or negatively upon him.

That was Pravash—always gravitating toward extremes, never content to live quietly. Whether it was love, spirituality, rebellion, or attention, he craved intensity. If he couldn't be the best, he'd gladly become the worst, anything but average. He cherished every wild twist in his past, with one painful exception—his first kiss, a memory he still longed to rewrite in some parallel universe, replacing its hollowness with something sacred and meaningful.

Now, standing in the quiet predictability of his tech-corporate life in Bangalore, he felt a familiar ache. Deep down, Pravash knew he'd trade anything for another taste of that intoxicating unpredictability—another chance to step boldly back into the heart of life's wild thrum.

—⚲✐💻✡—

THE MYSTERIOUS CHARIOTEER

2012 – Kolkata, West Bengal

Two days later, Pravash was swept into the vibrant fervor of Durga Puja in Kolkata. The city pulsed with life, and he savored every moment with his family.

One festive evening, near Victoria Memorial, his family clustered around a roadside *chaat* stall, laughter rising with every *puchka* they ate. It was a lively affair, but amidst the laughter, something strange caught Pravash's attention.

His gaze fell upon a man who rented horse chariots for tourists. Not unusual for Kolkata, yet this one stood apart. He guided his horse with the ease of a seasoned tour guide, but carried himself with a quite, unmistakable dignity. A common charioteer in simple creamy-white clothes, yet he held himself with an air that felt almost regal. A small vertical white tilak on his forehead seemed to glow faintly, as if lit from within. The man turned and smiled. Time stilled. The crowd blurred. For a heartbeat, the world's noise folded into silence, leaving only that warm, familiar smile.

Without breaking his gaze, the mysterious charioteer reached beneath his rough cloth attire and pulled out an enormous white conch shell, polished and glistening like ivory under the twilight. He raised it toward his lips, eyes softening in quiet certainty, and took a deep, unwavering breath.

And then, precisely at 4:39 p.m., he blew.

The sound of the *Panchajanya* erupted—a single note, pure and resonant, louder than thunder, yet as soothing as an ancient lullaby. It surged through the evening air, rolling across the crowded streets, vibrating through walls, through stone, through bone, resonating with every heartbeat in its path.

Beside him, Meenakshi froze. Her hand, midair trembled. She knew that sound, knew its meaning intimately. She bowed her head reverently toward the charioteer, palms pressed together, the gesture small enough to hide in a crowd but powerful enough to crack something open inside her.

In that bow, in that breath, a vision erupted behind her eyelids.

The Ayodhyapuram Adinath Jain Temple in Gujarat, radiant in white stone and eternal silence, waiting. Calling.

She knew instantly: they must go.

Across Kolkata, a hush fell. The bustling city stood still, as the celestial vibration swept through every street, every home, leaving goosebumps on skin and awe in every heart. Children paused in their play; elders closed their eyes in wonder; the entire city held its breath, touched by something otherworldly.

Even far away, beneath the bronze eagle of New York's Grand Central terminal, Frank and Mr. Singh felt the echo of that profound note. Frank staggered slightly, gripping the bench, eyes wide. Mr. Singh closed his eyes softly, whispering a silent prayer, feeling tears of gratitude and reverence tracing familiar paths down his cheeks.

In every realm, from *Devlok* to *Patal Lok*, reality itself seemed to hold its breath, suspended in a sacred silence.

The summons had been sounded. Within seconds, an answer would split another sky.

A declaration, unmistakable and absolute:

We are here.

We are ready to break through the matrix.

Back in Kolkata, as the reverberations faded, Pravash blinked hard, surfacing from the trance.

Their eyes met again.

In that quiet, eternal instant, Pravash felt a deeper question stir within him—one he couldn't yet voice, yet recognized as clearly as his own heartbeat. It was as if his soul recognized something his mind could not yet fully grasp.

The charioteer lowered the Panchajanya, the faint glow of the tilak still visible. He offered one last knowing smile, then turned away, guiding his chariot forward until he dissolved into the color and chaos of the Kolkata streets.

Yet Pravash knew, without a doubt, that their paths would cross again.

A journey had begun.

THE ARRIVAL

2012 – New York, USA

Nine minutes earlier—at exactly 7:00 a.m. on October 18, 2012—halfway across the world on that crisp Autumn morning, two men sat quietly on a bench of cold iron and ages-softened wood beneath the bronze eagle at New York's Grand Central terminal, unaware their reality was moments from cracking open. The station's great clock struck 7:00.

Frank, mid-forties, sharp featured, kept his face half-hidden beneath the brim of a black fedora. His long overcoat hugged his tall frame, its collar turned up against the chill. He held a Starbucks espresso cup in his gloved hand, the espresso inside long gone cold.

Beside him sat Mr. Singh, at least two decades older, with a lean, unhurried presence. His warm-toned complexion, curly, grey-dusted hair, and deep, brown eyes held the calm of someone who had witnessed far more than he would ever speak of. He wore a cream shirt tucked into neatly pressed brown trousers and carried a simple cloth bag on his lap.

"I still don't understand why you insisted on meeting like this," Frank muttered, not looking at him. "We don't do benches, Singh."

Mr. Singh smile was soft, amused. "Sometimes, even the most sacred things hide best in plain sight. We need to reorient and realign our focus. What's happening in academia is not just a trickle. The undercurrents are gathering force."

"Hey, Ind—"

"It's Frank," Frank cut him off sharply, before he could complete the word. "Or Mr. Lewis. You know better."

Mr. Singh nodded. "Very well... Frank. Then listen closely—ancient thought lines, timelines, theories once buried in allegory—they're starting to resurface in paper, ink, and code."

Mr. Singh's jaw tightened.

"Ever since Pakistan, with Abraham's situation. Desiree, Mathew, and Isha are barely holding the line as it is. The *Raktans* and *Ghraaks, their* nests around the Arctic and Antarctic belt keep testing our limits. One breach… and that whole region tears open. We must—"

A sudden chill sliced through the air.

The sky, which had been a gentle autumn blue just moments before, clouded into a charcoal storm front. The mild hum of early morning traffic dulled further, as if the city itself had paused to listen.

And then came the sound.

A sharp, guttural screech—not from any bird of this world. It cracked through the sky like a claw ripping silk.

Both looked up. Something was pushing through the clouds. The beast appeared first.

A colossal white eagle burst through the swirling grey, its wings stretching across the heavens, five hundred feet from tip to tip. Its eyes glowed amber with divine fury, talons as sharp as sculpted obsidian, feathers rippling with streaks of gold that shimmered like lightning. Each beat of its wings shifted the air with such force that even the leaves on the trees around the station trembled.

And then she emerged, riding upon its back.

Not a vision or an imagination. She was a command.

A force of nature wrapped in celestial flesh.

She stood tall and unmoving, poised like the fulcrum of a thousand destinies. Draped in a flowing white *dhoti* bordered in gold, her *Angrakha-style top (An Angrakha-style top is a traditional Indian garment with overlapping front panels tied at the side, offering a graceful, wrap-like elegance),* shimmered with fine embroidery that seemed to flicker with the breath of stars. Her white *mojris*, also rimmed with gold, glinted against the beast's radiant back.

Her long, dark hair cascaded down like a silken waterfall, catching the sunlight that dared peek through the clouds. Upon her brow rested a golden crown, with seven serpent heads rising in an arc, their hoods flared, their forms glowing faintly with divine intelligence.

In her left hand she held it.

The **Gandiv**.

A bow not crafted by mortals. Its body shimmered with celestial alloys—its limbs arched in graceful power, engraved with sacred scripts older than time. Veins of blue light pulsed through its length like the breath of the universe itself. She held the bowstring fully drawn, taut and ready—its curve trembling with the weight of what was to come.

Her gaze was lifted to the heavens, as if seeking permission... or announcing her presence.

Then—

She looked down.

And her eyes met Frank's.

They were deep brown. Infinite. The color of ancient forests and sunlit soil after rain. They held sorrow and storm, mercy and rage, lifetimes of pain and oceans of hope.

Frank's breath locked in his chest.

He staggered back like something had reached inside him and gripped his very soul.

Her gaze was not angry. It was ancient.

The espresso cup slipped from his hand and spilled on the pavement.

Mr. Singh slowly pressed his palm to his forehead. It was not a gesture of fear—it was one of reverence... of regret. Like a man who knew this moment was inevitable but had hoped to delay it just a little longer.

As he looked up at her, tears welled in his eyes—silently, uncontrollably.

And then, as if responding to a silent signal, he rose from the bench and folded his hands in reverence, bowing slightly, letting his tears fall freely now.

The eagle's wings spread even wider, framing the sky like a curtain drawn open for a final act.

She looked back up to the sky.

From a far-off quarter of the world, a single note unfurled—the Panchajanya, pure and resonant. It rolled through cloud and bone alike, a vibration that did not so much travel as simply **arrive**—beneath the bronze eagle, in Frank's ribs, in Mr. Singh's tears. The air itself seemed to understand: the time had been called.

And with one fluid motion, precisely at 7:09 a.m., she released Gandiv's bowstring. What followed was no ordinary thunderclap.

It echoed like the heartbeat of a dying star.

It was a roar that shattered silence across all realms.

A blast louder than any lightning Earth had ever heard. A shockwave so intense it sent flocks of birds flying into spirals. Car alarms erupted. People screamed. Windows trembled. All across the streets in New York, early risers looked up, confused, terrified, searching the skies—but they only saw clouds swirling like a divine whirlpool.

They couldn't see her.

But they heard it.

It sent a pulse through the clouds—a shockwave through the very fabric of the cosmos.

Frank said nothing. He didn't need to. He just stood there, utterly still, his expression suddenly childlike—helpless, vulnerable, stripped of all pretence. It was as if, in that instant, he had finally received an answer to the question he'd carried silently for decades, an answer he had desperately sought—and now wished had remained unknown. He now understood exactly whom he stood against—someone he never wanted to oppose, someone whose power far surpassed his own, someone who felt inexplicably like a mother, even as she confronted him across the expanse of the sky.

The call had gone out.

We are here.

We are ready.

The clouds above Grand Central blazed white.

And just like that—

She vanished.

But the cry of the Gandiv—lingered like the vibration of fate itself.

Frank stood motionless, lips slightly parted, as if the air around him no longer held breath.

Around them, the city resumed—humming, unaware, unchanged.

And deep inside, Frank knew: the matrix had fractured.

And the first arrow had been let loose.

CHAPTER 2
The Pandit and the Immortal

EMERGENCE FROM THE DEPTHS

1982 – Thrikkakara, Kerala

Three decades before the echoes of the Gandiv and the Panchajanya rolled across the cosmos—touching Kolkata, New York, and realms beyond, the story had already begun, quietly, elsewhere.

It was September of 1982.

While Kolkata welcomed the birth of a child whose life would one day shake the fabric of worlds, far to the South, on the quiet shores beyond Thrikkakara, Kerala, another moment of cosmic significance unfolded—one destined to echo across realms and **lifetimes.**

It was a night painted in silver. Moonlight turned the serene backwaters of Thrikkakara into mirrors of the sky; the Arabian Sea breathed gently against the shore, its rhythm as old as the land's myths. Yet the waves carried more than water—they carried destiny.

From the moonlit depths, a figure rose, as if woven from a legend: a man—tall, regal, impossible to mistake for ordinary. He wore a villager's dhoti and a humble shawl, both dripping with seawater. Yet no disguise could hide the royalty that emanated from him.

His beard and moustache framed a face of wisdom and authority, and his eyes held the calm of centuries. Nearly nine feet tall, he moved with silent majesty—measured, purposeful—carrying the quiet authority of one beyond mortal limits. It felt as if the earth itself yielded to his passing. Even the air seemed charged with an older energy, the elements aware of a presence that did not belong to ordinary time.

As he stepped onto the shore, water streamed from his body and sparkled beneath the moon, every droplet a shard of celestial silver. The beads clinging to shawl and dhoti glimmered as though they held fragments of the moon, casting fleeting reflections across the sand. Water, light, and earth appeared to bow to this mysterious figure.

Cradled in his arms lay about a four-month-old infant, wrapped in white cloth. The baby slept with a small, untroubled smile, tiny hands resting against the man's chest. A faint aureole seemed to emanate from him, softening the dark with a gentle light. He breathed so quietly that the night itself seemed to hush around him.

Thrikkakara slept under the whispering palms. The man moved with an ease that spoke of long familiarity, and yet urgency guided his steps. He paused at the edge of the temple grounds, the stone walls breathing sandalwood in the cool air. He looked up at the moon, its light reflecting in his deep eyes—as if seeking confirmation from the sky.

With careful steps he crossed to a modest house beside the temple—the home of Kalaha Dutt, the chief priest and keeper of its ancient wisdom. His shadow stretched long along the planks. A soft knock.

The door opened and warm lamplight spilled across the threshold. Kalaha Dutt, a man in his mid-thirties with keen, knowing eyes, froze—reverence settling over his features at the sight before him: the towering visitor, the radiant child.

Kalaha Dutt's breath hitched. He had sensed the presence even before the knock, but seeing the legend at his threshold humbled him to silence. His gaze settled on the child; awe rose with questions he knew better than to ask.

"My Lord…" he whispered, voice barely audible, trembling with humility and profound reverence. He bowed deeply, forehead nearing the floor, then straightened, his eyes returning softly to the divine child.

The towering figure, still cradling the infant, stepped forward with a grace outside of time. "Please, Kalaha... rise," he said, his voice deep and soothing, steady as a slow river. He lifted a hand gently, eyes reflecting sincere humility. "Do not embarrass me by bowing to one such as **me**. Rather, I seek your blessing. To receive it from you would feel no less than receiving it from Narada-Muni himself—the revered sage whose wisdom traverses the three *lokas*."

Kalaha's lips curled into a gentle, playful smile; mischief glinted in his sharp eyes. "My Lord," he said softly, half-playful, half-reverent, "if I—merely a mortal reflection of Narada—am graced with a bow from one so noble as **you—*Maha-Bali***, the immortal king blessed by Lord Vishnu in his **Vamana Avatar**—what exceptional deed could I have done to deserve such honor? Surely not my love of mischief."

His gaze drifted to the child in Bali's arms. Awe softened his voice. "And yet... you have not come at midnight to merely indulge my vanity. There is purpose in this, is there not?"

Bali inclined his head and stepped into the modest courtyard of Kalaha's home. The open air **nalukettu**—a traditional Kerala-style house—gathered the moonlight, bathing the central *tulsi* in silver.

Kalaha gestured to the chairs by the tulsi. "Come, my King," Kalaha said, voice soft, familiar. "Sit. Let us speak like old friends."

Bali lowered himself with unhurried grace. He adjusted the sleeping infant, cradling him as if the weight of destiny was no weight at all. Kalaha returned with two earthen cups of steaming herbal tea.

"Forgive the simplicity of my offering," Kalaha said humbly, passing a cup. "It is far from the splendor of **Ratna Prabha**."

"Simplicity often reveals truths that grandeur obscures," Bali replied with a warm glance. "Under open skies, the essence of things is clearer than in the radiance of palaces."

Kalaha nodded, his eyes fixed on the child. When he spoke again, his tone had lost its playful edge. "Yet simplicity does not bring you here tonight, my King. Your annual visits for the sacred *Onam* rites, your blessings, the guise of a humble villager admired by the residents—these I know well." Awe touched his features. "Tonight you come bearing an avatar of my beloved Lord—whose forms have walked and guided **Bharat Kshetra** across the ages, whose tales I have sung through eras"

"Indeed, Kalaha," Bali said. "This child is his very avatar, born once more into the currents of destiny. I have brought him in secret from **Adho Lok**—from Ratna-Prabha itself. Neither gods nor demons know he now resides in **Madhya Lok**—only one among the ***Nine*** shares this secret and holds it with reverence. His presence must remain hidden until the day **He** chooses to reveal himself to the world."

Kalaha's eyes widened; exhilaration and gratitude trembled in his voice. "My Lord... through countless ages of this cosmic drama,

I have never known a joy like this. To be entrusted—even for a breath—with the care of my cherished Lord's avatar surpasses every honor I could imagine." Moonlight gentled his expression. "I am small beside his eternal wisdom. Yet, if it pleases you, my King, I shall care for him with quiet devotion—much as **Nanda and Vasudeva** once protected their divine child—until he himself is ready."

Bali's smile deepened. "It is precisely your wisdom, humility, and devotion that bring me to your door. His path ahead is long and difficult, and full of promise."

Kalaha set his cup down; purpose lit his eyes, mischief glinting as ever. "Then trust me, my King—I shall keep him safe, quietly preparing him for the destiny that awaits."

The infant stirred, turning toward Kalaha. For a heartbeat, the aureole around him brightened—as though the cosmos paused to honor the vow between them.

And thus, beneath a sky that listened, an ancient king and an eternal sage wove careful threads of fate—guarding a secret whose revelation would ripple across lifetimes, realms, and destiny itself.

The moon stood sentinel over the courtyard, its silver softening the night into reverence. Kalaha Dutt leaned back, cradling the infant with an ease that belied the moment's weight. He broke the stillness with a playful smile. "My King, your yearly visits have always intrigued the villagers. To them, you're a benevolent traveller—a kind-hearted villager from snowy lands in Europe. How they would marvel to know their humble guest is Mahabali himself, walking between worlds."

Bali chuckled, voice resonant as distant thunder. "Your insight never ceases to amaze me, Kalaha. These visits keep me bound to Bharat Kshetra, honor the *Onam* rites at **Vamana Moorthy**

Temple, and help steady the balance. But tonight is different—the stakes are greater."

Kalaha's gaze drifted to the sleeping child. "This little one," he said softly, awe filling his voice, "will one day trace paths none of us can fully anticipate. The name **Soham**, echo of universal consciousness, suits him. And I, your impish friend, will see he finds wisdom and joy—even in playful disorder. Who better than Narada-Muni to teach with riddles, laughter, and a touch of divine mischief?"

"Indeed, Kalaha," Bali said. "You alone understand that wisdom thrives alongside play; that chaos, tempered, can reveal deeper truths."

The child stirred again, turning toward Kalaha as if recognizing the warmth of his new guardian. When a tiny hand brushed the sage's chest, something indescribable passed through him—a pulse of life and hope, tender as the first light of dawn.

Kalaha's impishness softened; his ancient eyes filled with feeling. Gazing at the boy, he whispered, "In all the eras I've wandered—worlds born and dissolved—I have not known a happiness like this moment. To guard you, little one, even briefly, is the greatest honor and purpose of my existence." He lifted the child slightly, eyes sparkling. "**Narayan! Narayan!** What tales we will create together, Soham!"

Bali rose; shadows shifted as he did. With a final warm look toward Kalaha, he moved to the courtyard's edge and stepped into the night. Just beyond, discreetly kept by his trusted caretaker—the only other soul in Thrikkakara aware of Mahabali's true identity—waited an ordinary wheelchair, a clever veil he had used for years to mute his towering height and regal presence.

Adjusting shawl and dhoti, he seated himself with practiced ease. One last glance toward Kalaha's home, and the immortal king rolled into the sleeping street, the wooden wheels' gentle creak folding into the night.

Kalaha remained beneath the moon, Soham asleep in his arms. Quiet determination mingled with devotion in his chest. A new chapter had begun—guided by karma, by destiny, and by a guardian who had long ago mastered the dance between mischief and wisdom.

Under the vast canopy of stars, the threads of lifetimes intertwined—beginning a story that would ripple across realms, unseen yet felt, awaiting the hour when its true power would be revealed.

Days braided themselves into small rituals—lamps at dusk, jasmine at the threshold, a child learning the world by breath and touch. Two lunar cycles slipped past Thrikkakara's eaves. By then, Soham was six months old.

—✧—

OM SO'HUM

1982 – Thrikkakara, Kerala

Inside the living area of Kalaha Dutt's traditional home, the faint light of oil lamps illuminated the space, casting intricate shadows on the walls carved with ancient designs. The room opened into a courtyard, where the rustling of leaves and the soft chirping of early birds blended seamlessly with the stillness of the morning.

Kalaha Dutt sat on a traditional wooden swing, intricately carved with patterns of flowers and vines. The swing hung gracefully from the ceiling by multiple brass chains, each linked to ornate hooks shaped like an elephant, a horse, a camel, and a peacock. The hooks caught the flicker of the lamp, lending a regal gleam to the room's simplicity.

Kalaha set the swing in a slow, rhythmic motion with one foot, while the other leg was folded on the plank, cradling the head of the infant who rested in his lap. The swing creaked softly, its gentle sway keeping time with the early morning hush.

Soham nestled into the folds of Kalaha's robe, his tiny hands clutching the fabric as if it were an anchor to the world. His serene face, framed by soft curls, seemed to hold a quiet radiance; his small chest rose and fell in even breaths. Kalaha brushed a hand over his head—a touch tender enough to be prayer.

Kalaha brushed his hand gently over Soham's soft, dark curls, his touch filled with a love that words could not express. His lips moved in a steady rhythm, chanting a deep, resonant **"Om.. So'hummm... Om..So'humm... Om..So'hummm..."** Each chant carried a profound vibration, filling the air with a sense of peace and stillness.

Following each Om, he murmured a shloka in a melodic tone, his voice blending with the swing's gentle creaks and the faint rustling of the leaves outside:

"Shantakaram Bhujaga Shayanam Padmanabham Suresham

Vishwadharam Gagana Sadrisham Meghavarnam Shubhangam

Lakshmi Kantam Kamala Nayanam Yogibhih Dhyanagamyam

Vande Vishnum Bhava Bhaya Haram Sarva Lokaika Natham."

The shloka carried the essence of peace and clarity, its rhythmic flow harmonizing with the stillness of the predawn hour. It was as though the words themselves were alive, weaving through the air and casting a protective cocoon around the child. His murmurs carried a quiet plea—a prayer that the chaos and pain of Soham's previous births in Paatal Lok would dissolve into nothingness, leaving the child's path free from the burden of memories too heavy for his young soul to bear. The air itself seemed to resonate with the sacred energy, charged with an ethereal tranquillity.

As the dawn began to break, its faint light filtering through the temple's intricately designed wooden lattice windows, Kalaha Dutt paused and leaned forward, pressing his forehead gently against Soham's. His voice dropped to a whisper, yet it carried the weight of an earnest prayer: "May your mind find peace, my child. May the light within you shine, unburdened by the shadows of the past."

The swing swayed gently, carrying Kalaha's words into the stillness of the morning. The infant stirred slightly, a faint smile curving his lips, as though he understood the love and care being poured into him. Kalaha's heart swelled with tenderness and quiet resolve, his steady hand brushing against Soham's curls once more, as if silently promising to shield him from the chaos of the world.

FIRST LESSON – *NAVAKAR MANTRA*

1985 – Thrikkakara, Kerala

Morning in Thrikkakara unfolded softly, with the sun casting a soft golden glow over the village. In the serene courtyard of his traditional home, Kalaha Dutt sat on a low wooden stool, grinding sandalwood paste with steady, rhythmic motions. The air was filled with the gentle scent of sandalwood, mingling with the freshness of dawn.

Soham, barely three years old, toddled toward him, carrying a small clay bowl filled with water. His tiny steps were unsteady, yet purposeful, as he approached his Appa. He set the bowl down beside Kalaha and plopped onto the ground, crossing his legs in a mimicry of Kalaha's posture. His wide, curious eyes followed every movement of his guru with childlike wonder.

"Appa," he asked, his voice small and filled with innocence, "why do you fold your hands and bow so much? You bow to the sun, to the tree, to the river… even to the ants! What if the sun doesn't shine back at you? Or the river doesn't care? Why do you do it?"

Kalaha paused, his hands halting their steady motion. A spark of amusement danced in his eyes as he looked at Soham, his lips curving into a smile. He had been waiting for a question like this. Setting the sandalwood paste aside, he gestured for Soham to sit closer. The boy obliged, his little legs stretched out before him, his head tilted in curiosity.

"Ah, my little sage," Kalaha said, his tone playful yet thoughtful, "you've asked a question that even the greatest of minds ponder. Why bow when you may not see what you'll get in return? Let me tell you a story."

Soham's face lit up with excitement. He loved Kalaha's stories—they were always magical, filled with laughter and lessons he didn't always understand but loved to hear.

"Once," Kalaha began, "there was a farmer who owned a small piece of land. Every morning, he folds his hands near his heart and bowed to the earth, watered it, and planted seeds, even though the soil looked dry and lifeless. His neighbors mocked him. 'Why waste your time bowing to this barren land?' they said. But the farmer just smiled and replied, 'I bow because it's my way of showing love and respect to the earth. The results are not in my hands.'"

Soham leaned in closer, his eyes wide. "What happened to the farmer?" he asked eagerly.

"Well," Kalaha continued, "days turned into weeks, and the farmer saw no signs of life. His neighbors laughed even more. But he didn't stop. He kept bowing, planting, and watering. Then one day, tiny green shoots appeared, growing into the most abundant field of crops anyone had ever seen. The neighbors were stunned, and the farmer simply smiled and said, 'When you bow without expecting anything in return, the results come in their own time, and they are always right.'"

Soham wrinkled his little brows, deep in thought. "So… bowing makes magic happen?" he asked.

Kalaha laughed, his voice warm and resonant. "Not magic, my boy. When you bow, you're not asking for something in return. You're showing respect, love acknowledging that everything in this universe—big or small—has its place. And when you respect the universe, the universe respects you back, even if you don't see it immediately."

Soham tilted his head, processing his guru's words. "Can I bow too? Will the sun smile at me?"

Kalaha's smile softened. He placed a hand on Soham's small shoulder and said, "You already bow, my child, every time you look at the world with wonder and love. But let me teach you something special—a mantra that will help you bow with your whole heart."

Kalaha lifted Soham into his arms and carried him toward the Shri Bhagawan Mahavir Jain temple. Setting him down before the sacred marble idol of Lord Mahavir (last and 24th Jain Tirthankar), he knelt beside the boy. "Now, repeat after me: Namō Arihantāṇam."

Soham's tiny voice echoed the words as best as he could. "Nammo… Aree… Han-ta-nam."

Kalaha chuckled. "Close enough. Namō Siddhāṇam."

"Namo… Siddha… Nam," Soham repeated, his face scrunched in concentration.

One by one, Kalaha guided him through the entire *Navakar Mantra*. Soham's young voice stumbled and wavered, but his enthusiasm was undeniable. When they finished, Kalaha turned to him with a look of pride. "This mantra is like bowing to everything good in the universe. The Arihants, Siddhas, Acharyas, Upadhyayas, and Sadhus—they didn't bow for rewards but for truth. Now they guide us, asking for nothing in return."

Soham blinked, his little mind trying to grasp the depth of his guru's words. "So... if I bow to everything, everything will be happy?"

Kalaha smiled, his eyes glowing with affection. "Not just happy, Soham. When you bow, you grow. Bowing humbles you, makes you kind and wise—qualities that no one can take away."

Soham nodded solemnly, his tiny hands pressing together in an earnest attempt at Namaste. Kalaha watched him with amusement and pride. "Good," he said, ruffling the boy's dark curls. "Now, my little sage, go bow to that ant over there. He's been waiting for your respect all morning."

Soham giggled and scampered off, his laughter echoing through the courtyard. Kalaha watched him, his heart swelling with gratitude. The boy was young, but the seed had been planted.

And as the morning light bathed the temple in gold, Kalaha murmured the mantra once more, his voice carrying a quiet reverence: "Ēsō Pancha Namōkārō..."

CHAPTER 3
The Lost Worlds and the Divine Legacy

THE RATHORE FAMILY AND THEIR SUNDAY RITUALS

1992 – Kolkata, West Bengal

The Rathore family home was a world within a world, nestled on the second floor of an old colonial building, sprawling over a massive 5000-square-foot flat. It was a place where time seemed to move at its own gentle pace, and every corner of the flat resonated with life. This was not merely a home; it was a sanctuary, a warm cocoon that held together the lives of each family member, their laughter and tears, their joys and sorrows.

At the heart of this household was **Balraj Rathore**, the eldest in the house, a man respected for his wisdom and humility. His wife, **Meenakshi**, was a deep follower of Jainism, a woman whose faith soaked every aspect of her life. Together, they had three children: **Kanchan**, a responsible and diligent sixteen-year-old daughter; **Aakash**, a curious and playful thirteen-year-old son; and the youngest, **Pravash**, just ten years old, with a face filled with wonder and innocence.

Living with them was Balraj's younger brother, **Abhishek**, a man known for his light-heartedness and humor, always ready with a joke to lift spirits. Abhishek's wife, **Prabha**, was a kind and soft-spoken woman, the perfect complement to her husband's vibrant personality. They had two sons, **Prakash**, twelve years old, a serious and studious boy, and **Ankit**, also ten, whose boundless energy matched Pravash's own.

The Rathore household was a lively tapestry of family bonds, a blend of personalities woven together by love and tradition. Each morning began with the aroma of spices and the clinking of pots in the kitchen as Meenakshi and Prabha prepared breakfast, their soft laughter filling the space as they exchanged stories and whispered secrets. Balraj and Abhishek would sit in the living room, sipping their morning tea, discussing everything from politics to family matters, while the children, half-dressed in school uniforms, raced through the hallways, their laughter echoing through the corridors.

But Sundays held a special place in the Rathore household. It was a day of rest, a day when the family would gather in the living room to indulge in their shared ritual—the weekly television broadcast of the Mahabharata. At exactly 10:00 a.m., the family would settle into their places, cushions and chairs arranged in a semicircle around the old television set, as if they were preparing for a sacred event. The atmosphere was one of admiration, for the Mahabharata was no ordinary show; it was a window into the world of gods, heroes, and cosmic battles.

Young Pravash would sit cross-legged on the floor, his gaze fixed on the screen, his eyes wide with anticipation as the opening chants of the Mahabharata began. The slow, rhythmic music filled the room, casting a spell over everyone present. It was as though the boundaries of their home dissolved, and they were transported to the ancient world of **Kurukshetra**, where *dharma* (righteousness) and *adharma* (unrighteousness) clashed in an eternal struggle.

As the episodes unfolded, depicting the lives and tribulations of the **Pandavas** and **Kauravas**, the Rathores found themselves lost in the epic. Balraj would occasionally explain a particular scene, his voice filled with awe and admiration for the characters. When Bhishma took his vow of celibacy, Balraj's voice trembled with awe, explaining the gravity of sacrifice and duty. And when Krishna delivered the Bhagavad Gita to a conflicted Arjuna, the family listened in hushed silence, absorbing the timeless wisdom.

For Pravash, these moments were more than just entertainment; they were lessons, stories that planted seeds of curiosity and introspection in his young mind. The epic battles, the intricate relationships, and the moral dilemmas of the Mahabharata fascinated him, leaving him with questions about life, fate, and the nature of the soul. It was during these Sundays that Pravash's love for ancient stories and spiritual teachings began to take root, shaping the foundation of his beliefs.

When the episode ended, the spell broke. Solemnity dissolved into laughter as they switched to "Dekh Bhai Dekh," a comedy show that depicted the quirks and mishaps of an Indian joint family. The Rathores saw themselves in the characters onscreen—the misunderstandings, the sibling rivalries, the shared love and laughter. They laughed heartily, sometimes even harder than the show's punchlines warranted, because the humor felt personal, relatable.

Abhishek, always quick with a joke, would mimic the characters, causing another round of laughter. He would often nudge Balraj, saying, "Bhai, that character is just like you!" Balraj would respond with a mock-serious frown, causing the children to giggle even more. It was a time of togetherness, of pure joy, and Pravash would look around the room, feeling a warmth that seeped into his heart. These Sundays became memories etched in his soul—a reminder of a time when life was simple, bound by love and the magic of shared experiences.

In the evenings, after the television shows had ended, the family would gather once more in their home temple, a small, serene space where idols of Jain Tirthankaras were enshrined. Meenakshi would light a diya (oil lamp), its soft glow illuminating the marble idols, while Balraj sang Jain devotional songs, nearly hitting the right notes. The children would join their hands in silent prayer, absorbing the peaceful energy of the moment.

Pravash, even as a young boy, felt a deep connection to this sacred space. He would gaze at the idols, especially the serene face of Lord Parshvanath, the 23rd Tirthankara, and feel a quiet sense of admiration.

These Sundays, filled with epic stories, laughter, and quiet moments of devotion, were the threads that wove the Rathore family together. They were more than just rituals; they were expressions of love, shared wisdom, and a collective journey through life's lessons. For Pravash, these were the days that would become memories—moments that he would carry with him long after he left the confines of his childhood home.

A MOTHER'S TALE – THE STORY OF LORD PARSHVANATH

The small temple in the Rathore household was a tranquil sanctuary, where the soft glow of a diya mingled with the faint scent of sandalwood incense. Marble idols of the Jain Tirthankaras stood in silent grace, their serene expressions inviting devotion. Among them, the figure of Lord Parshvanath, protected by the hood of a multi-headed serpent, caught young Pravash's attention one evening.

Curiosity danced in his wide eyes as he turned to his mother, who was seated beside him, lost in prayer. "Maa," he whispered, tugging gently at her saree, "why is there a snake above Lord Parshvanath? Is it protecting him?"

Meenakshi smiled gently and placed a hand on his shoulder. "Yes, *beta*. That serpent is Padmavati Maa, the goddess who protected Lord Parshvanath. But there's a story behind it—a story of lifetimes, where forgiveness triumphed over resentment and compassion over revenge."

Pravash leaned closer as Meenakshi's voice took on the gentle rhythm of wisdom passed down through generations.

"Before he became a Tirthankara, Parshvanath was known as Marubhuti in one of his previous lives," Meenakshi explained. "In their very first life, Marubhuti and Kamath were born as half-brothers to a brahmin priest serving a royal family. Marubhuti was a scholar, the embodiment of kindness and virtue. The king adored him, and his gentle heart earned him the love of all. But Kamath, his elder half-brother, carried jealousy in his veins. He envied Marubhuti's grace, his goodness, and the love the world showered upon him."

Meenakshi gently stroked Pravash's hair, whispering softly, as though sharing an eternal truth, "Hatred festers when envy goes unchecked, beta."

"One day, Kamath's resentment turned into an act so vile that it shattered the bond of their family. While Marubhuti was away attending courtly duties, Kamath approached Marubhuti's wife, attempting to harm her honor—violating not just her trust, but the sacred bond of family itself. The news reached Marubhuti when he returned."

"Heartbroken, Marubhuti confronted his brother. His eyes were filled not with anger, but with sorrow—a sorrow that pierced deeper than any sword could.

'You are my brother,' Marubhuti said, his voice trembling. 'Why do you carry such darkness in your heart? I forgive you, Kamath. Let us not let hatred poison what little bond we have left.'

"But Kamath saw Marubhuti's forgiveness as an insult. Instead of feeling remorse, his envy deepened into rage. In his eyes, Marubhuti's virtue mocked him—his forgiveness humiliated him. He could not bear the weight of Marubhuti's compassion.

"Consumed by his rage, Kamath followed Marubhuti into the forest one evening. Marubhuti, seeking solace, had gone to meditate under an ancient tree, hoping to calm the storm within his heart.

"As the moon cast its pale light on the forest floor, Kamath crept toward him, a heavy rock in his hand. Marubhuti sensed his presence and opened his eyes, his expression serene and filled with love. 'Kamath, let go of this hatred,' he whispered, his heart, even in that moment, held no fear—only compassion.

"But Kamath's ears were deaf to reason. He lifted the rock high above his head, his eyes filled with rage, and brought it crashing down on Marubhuti's skull.

"In that instant, as pain seared through him, Marubhuti's calm shattered. His eyes, once filled with forgiveness, flashed with anger and disbelief. For a fleeting moment, he saw not a brother but a murderer—and in that moment, anger stained his soul. His final breath was not one of peace but of pain and fury.

"The forest fell silent. Kamath stood alone, the rock stained with his brother's blood. But victory brought him no peace. As he fled deeper into the woods, the weight of his actions consumed him. He died a lonely death, tormented by malice and guilt.

"Marubhuti, too, was bound by his final anger. Though his life had been one of compassion, his soul could not escape the karmic chain created by his last moment of rage."

Meenakshi's voice softened, her gaze distant, as though she could see the tragedy unfold in the quiet forest. "And so, Pravash, the bond of karma was forged. Their destinies became entwined, their souls locked in a cycle of pain and retribution. Marubhuti's anger cursed him to be reborn, and Kamath's resentment chained him to lifetimes of darkness."

Pravash, who had been listening in rapt silence, asked softly, "What happened in their next lives, Maa?"

Meenakshi's voice carried a grave weight as she continued.

"In the next life, Marubhuti's soul was reborn as a **mad elephant**—a creature of immense strength but blinded by uncontrollable rage. His anger from the moment of his death, followed him like a shadow. This elephant roamed the forest, attacking anything and anyone that crossed its path. Travelers, innocent animals, even towering trees were not spared his fury. The forest became a place of terror, and his once noble soul was now chained by the anger that consumed him."

Pravash's brow furrowed. "But why was he so angry, Maa? Was it because of what Kamath did?"

Meenakshi nodded gently. "Yes, my son. The anger he felt in his final breath poisoned his soul. Though he was once a prince of virtue, his death in rage cursed him to a life of violence. He became a beast, unable to see reason or compassion."

She paused briefly before continuing, her voice softening with hope.

"But one day, a **Jain Muni**, a wandering sage, entered the forest. The sage radiated peace, his mere presence calming the chaos around him. The villagers warned him of the mad elephant, but the Muni walked calmly to the riverbank, where the elephant had come to drink.

"The elephant charged at the sage, its eyes wild and bloodshot, but the Muni raised his hand, his voice steady and filled with kindness.

'My brother,' the Muni said, 'do you not remember who you are?'

"The elephant froze, its massive body trembling. Something in those words stirred the depths of its soul, breaking through the fog of rage. The sage continued,

'In your past life, you were Marubhuti—noble, compassionate, and beloved by all. You were betrayed, yes, but your anger does not serve you. Let go of this rage. Remember the peace you once carried.'

"The elephant let out a mournful cry, as though releasing lifetimes of anguish. Slowly, it bowed before the sage, its eyes softening with understanding. From that day on, the elephant ceased its violence and lived a life of peace, protecting the very forest it had once terrorized."

Pravash's eyes widened. "He remembered? Just because of the sage's words?"

"Yes," Meenakshi said, "because truth awakens even the deepest memories. His soul began its journey back to compassion. But Kamath... he had taken another path.

"In that same life, Kamath was reborn as a **vicious snake** with **wings of fire**, a creature of pure malice. The snake slithered across the same forest, poisoning every creature it encountered. Birds, deer, even other predators fell lifeless under his bite.

"One day, the snake came upon the elephant at the riverbank. Its jealousy, its hatred from their first life, flared up once more. As the elephant drank peacefully, the snake struck—its venom sinking deep into the elephant's flesh.

"But this time, Marubhuti's soul held no anger. The elephant looked at the snake with quiet sorrow, as if to say, 'I forgive you.' He fell to the ground, breathing his last breath with peace in his heart. The snake, however, writhed in its own hatred, unable to let go. Kamath's soul, burdened by anger, burned itself further into darkness. He too died shortly after, consumed by his own venom and hatred."

Meenakshi's voice grew steadier as she carried the tale forward.

"And so, Pravash, the wheel of karma bound them tightly across lifetimes. In another birth, Marubhuti was born a prince later turned sage, cut down by Kamath—this time as a hunter, then as a lion, then again as serpent. Each time Kamath struck, carrying hatred through every rebirth. And each time Marubhuti's soul, though tested, rose a little higher—his compassion deepening, his forgiveness more unshakable. The cycle repeated again and again, Kamath sinking deeper into darkness, Marubhuti climbing closer to liberation."

Meenakshi's voice grew reverent, her words carrying the weight of the tale as she recounted the final chapter of Marubhuti's soul and Kamath's long cycle of hatred.

"In his final birth, Marubhuti was born as Parshvanath, the crown prince of Kashi—noble, compassionate, and devoted to dharma. From a young age, his heart was drawn to the path of non-violence, wisdom, and truth. Parshvanath's presence radiated a calm strength, and his love for all living beings was boundless.

"But Kamath's soul, still chained by rage, was reborn as Meghamali, a powerful sorcerer and an accomplished master of dark yagnas and rituals. Meghamali's heart burned with ambition—he sought power over the celestial forces themselves, and his pride knew no bounds.

"One day, a great crowd gathered near a massive yagna Meghamali had arranged. The fire roared like a consuming beast, and the air hummed with mantras chanted to summon celestial energies. People watched in awe as Meghamali sat at the center of it all, clad in dark robes, his face twisted with pride and obsession.

“It was then that Parshvanath, the young prince, happened upon the scene. His gaze fell on the blazing fire, and in an instant, his sharp intuition revealed the cruelty hidden within the ritual. He sensed the cries of two souls—two serpents, burning alive beneath the wood of the sacrificial pyre.

“Parshvanath raised his hand, his voice calm yet firm, cutting through the noise of the yagna.

‘Stop this immediately!’ he commanded.

“The crowd fell silent, startled by the authority in the prince’s tone. Meghamali looked up, his eyes narrowing. ‘Who dares interrupt my yagna?’ he growled.

‘There are two living beings trapped in this fire,’ Parshvanath declared. ‘You must stop this ritual before their lives are lost.’

“The crowd murmured in disbelief, but Meghamali’s face twisted in defiance. ‘You are mistaken, Prince. This is a sacred ritual for celestial blessings—your interruption is sacrilege!’

“But Parshvanath stepped forward, unwavering. ‘No ritual that causes harm can be called sacred. Stop this now, or I will intervene myself.’

“Meghamali refused, his anger boiling. Parshvanath, seeing no other way, ordered his men to extinguish the fire. The flames hissed and died, revealing two scorched snakes, barely alive, their bodies blackened by the heat.

“The crowd gasped, their reverence for Parshvanath swelling. Gently, Parshvanath knelt beside the snakes, his heart heavy with compassion. He recited the ***Navakar Mantra***, his voice soothing and filled with divine energy. As the sacred syllables flowed from his lips, the snakes' pain eased, their souls lifted peacefully from their broken bodies.

"The entire crowd erupted in praise of Parshvanath, but Meghamali's heart darkened with jealousy and humiliation. His power, his spectacle—shattered by the prince.

'You will regret this,' Meghamali whispered to himself, his voice venomous.

"Consumed by anger, Meghamali left the gathering and retreated deep into the forests. There, he began intense penances, performing dark rituals and yagnas to gain more power. His hatred for Parshvanath burned brighter than ever, driving him to achieve mastery over forces that no mortal should wield.

"Years passed, and Parshvanath, having renounced his royal life, began his journey as a **sage**. He abandoned all material pleasures and devoted himself to the path of enlightenment, seeking liberation from the cycle of birth and death.

"It was during one of his deep meditations that Meghamali—now a sorcerer of tremendous power—discovered him. Enraged at the sight of Parshvanath's serene form, Meghamali vowed to break him, to shatter his peace.

"With his dark sorcery, Meghamali summoned illusions of **ferocious animals**—lions, tigers, scorpions, and venomous serpents. They emerged from the shadows of the forest, roaring and hissing, their claws and fangs glinting in the dim light. The earth shook as they charged toward Parshvanath.

"But Parshvanath sat unmoved, his mind anchored in the sacred ***Samayak***, his meditation deep and unbreakable. The animals snarled and circled him, but as they drew closer, their rage dissolved. One by one, they turned and slinked back into the forest, as though their very being had been calmed by his presence."

Pravash's eyes widened. "They didn't harm him?"

"No," Meenakshi said, her voice steady. "Because true peace cannot be touched by hatred."

"Seeing his magic fail, Meghamali's fury exploded. He **summoned a storm**, more violent than any the world had seen. Black clouds swallowed the sky. Lightning slashed across the heavens, and deafening thunder rolled like the voice of an angry god. Torrential rain poured down in sheets, threatening to drown everything in its path.

"Parshvanath, seated in meditation, remained still. The storm lashed at him, the wind roaring, the waters rising—but he did not move.

"It was then that the **two divine protectors**—Padmavati Maa and Dharanendra Dev, appeared.

"Padmavati Maa, radiant and fierce, manifested around Parshvanath, her **serpent form** coiling protectively around him, raising him above the rising waters. Dharanendra Dev, a thousand-headed serpent, spread his hoods wide like a celestial canopy, shielding Parshvanath from the storm's wrath.

"The storm raged on, but it could not touch the sage. Meghamali watched in disbelief, his power crumbling before the divine light.

"It was then that Padmavati Maa turned to Meghamali, her voice resonating like thunder itself.

'Meghamali,' she said, her tone both stern and compassionate, 'do you not remember who you are? Why do you carry this hatred through lifetimes? You and he are bound not by revenge, but by love—a bond you refuse to see.'

"Meghamali fell to his knees, trembling. The storm quieted, and the weight of his actions bore down on him.

'Forgive me,' he whispered, tears streaming down his face. 'I have carried this hatred for too long. What must I do to atone?'

"Padmavati Maa's gaze softened. 'Let go of your anger. Seek forgiveness. Free yourself from this burden.'

"Overwhelmed, Meghamali turned to Parshvanath, who had opened his eyes, his face radiant with peace.

'Brother,' Meghamali sobbed, 'forgive me. I was blind… lifetimes wasted in hatred. Show me the path to redemption.'

"Parshvanath, his voice calm and filled with grace, spoke:

'Let your soul heal. Seek peace, and your suffering will end.'

"Meghamali wept, his heart finally released from its hatred. Padmavati Maa and Dharanendra Dev withdrew, their divine light fading. Meghamali, now humbled, left to atone for his deeds."

"So, he didn't need to forgive Kamath again?" Pravash asked, his voice thoughtful.

Meenakshi shook her head gently. "No, my child. Parshvanath had forgiven him long ago, in their second lifetime of enmity. His forgiveness remained constant, unmoved by Kamath's hatred. And when Parshvanath attained liberation, the karmic bond between them finally dissolved."

Pravash felt a swell of awe and devotion as Meenakshi's words sank in. "So, Maa, the snake on top of Lord Parshvanath… it's Dharanendra Dev?"

"Yes," Meenakshi said, her smile returning. "And Padmavati Maa. Together, they symbolize the protection Parshvanath earned through his selflessness, his ability to forgive, and the purity of his soul."

Pravash turned his gaze to the idol of Lord Parshvanath, his heart brimming with admiration. The divine serpent, once a mere carving in marble, now felt alive with meaning. He could see the unwavering serenity in Parshvanath's face, a reflection of a soul untouched by hatred or fear.

Meenakshi's voice softened further, her words carrying the essence of Jain teachings. "Remember this, Pravash—compassion and forgiveness are not just virtues; they are strengths. They have the power to transform even the darkest hearts and dissolve the deepest hatreds. Just as Parshvanath triumphed over Kamath's hatred with his compassion, so can we overcome the challenges in our own lives."

Pravash nodded slowly, his young mind absorbing every word deeply. Beneath the gentle glow of the diya, he sensed a profound connection to something timeless—a path of compassion, forgiveness, and spiritual resilience. Though unaware at the time, this moment quietly planted seeds within him that would one day awaken, guiding him toward a destiny he could not yet comprehend.

THE JAIN PATHSHALA AND THE STORY OF BHARAT KSHETRA AND ITS SURROUNDING WORLDS

A few days after hearing the remarkable story of **Lord Parshvanath** from his mother, young Pravash found himself at the ***Jain Pathshala***, surrounded by other children eager to learn. His mother had suggested he attend, mentioning that the pathshala would deepen his understanding of Jain teachings, the lives of the Tirthankaras, and the ancient wisdom that shaped their family's faith.

Inside the small classroom, sunlight gently filtered through windows, illuminating rows of eager faces. At the front stood Lata Ma'am, a gentle yet knowledgeable teacher, welcoming Pravash with a kind, encouraging smile. After explaining some foundational principles of Jainism, she asked if anyone had questions. Pravash, unable to contain his curiosity, raised his hand.

"Ma'am," he began, his voice filled with eagerness, "could you tell us more about **Lord Parshvanath** and his family? I heard he came from a noble lineage."

Lata Ma'am nodded. "Yes, Pravash. Lord Parshvanath was a member of the ***Ikshvaku*** **dynasty**, a lineage known for producing noble kings and righteous leaders who upheld dharma in ***Bharat Kshetra***."

"The Ikshvaku dynasty was held in great respect in Bharat Kshetra for its unparalleled legacy of dharma and nobility," Lata Ma'am continued, her voice steady with admiration. "Among its most celebrated figures is **Lord Ram**, known as **Maryada Purushottam.** Lord Ram stands as an eternal symbol of virtue and righteousness—a king who ruled with wisdom, fairness, and an unyielding commitment to truth."

The students perked up at the mention of Lord Ram. Many of them had become familiar with his story through the popular television series on the **Ramayan**, one of the few programs broadcast widely in India at the time.

Lata Ma'am's eyes glimmered as she spoke of other luminaries from the Ikshvaku lineage. "There were many noble kings in this line," she said. "**King Sagar**, remembered for his devotion and perseverance; **King Harishchandra,** whose commitment to truth and integrity remained unshaken even in the face of unimaginable hardship; **Bahubali**, who epitomized spiritual strength and renunciation; and **King Bharath,** after whom Bharat Kshetra itself is named. These rulers weren't just kings—they were custodians of dharma, guiding their kingdoms with justice, wisdom, and a deep sense of responsibility."

Pravash felt a connection to these noble figures, a sense that their virtues still lingered in the world, guiding people toward righteousness.

"Now, Bharat Kshetra," Lata Ma'am continued, "is just one world inside something much bigger."

She turned and tapped the large illustrated map on the wall. Under the tubelight glow, the shapes of mountains, rivers and strange concentric lands seemed almost alive.

"Think of **Jambudveep** as a great islandworld," she said. "Not only a vast-cosmic-island surrounded by water and lands beyond, but an island of *realms*. Different kshetras, each with their own laws of life, time and karma."

Pravash leaned forward on his wooden bench, eyes wide and curious.

Her finger settled near the lower part of the map. "Here is only one *khand* or part among the six *khands of* Bharat Kshetra—the world we think of as *the* world—some also called it *Arya Khand*."

She traced a circle around it.

Bharat Kshetra

"Bharat is a vast, flat stretch of land," she said softly, "surrounded on all sides by towering walls of ice. Imagine a great white ring, higher than any mountain you've ever seen, going all the way around us. That ring is our boundary. Our prison. Our protection."

A murmur went through the room.

Pravash forgot to blink. He could almost see it: a flat land, all the countries and oceans he knew, held in a bowl of impossible ice.

"These ice walls aren't just frozen water," Lata Ma'am went on. "They are *maryada*—a divine limit. They keep the worlds from crashing into each other before it's time."

She lowered her voice a notch.

"And Jain scriptures whisper that somewhere along this wall, there is a narrow passage. A hidden opening. A doorway to the outer regions of Bharat Kshetra."

"Can anyone go through it?" Pravash breathed.

Lata Ma'am smiled knowingly. "Perhaps, someone with divine powers can only, but those stories are for another day. For now, know this: Bharat Kshetra is covered by a celestial dome, a protective shield that guards it from the unknown forces beyond."

"According to Jain teachings," Lata Ma'am said, "the sky—*akasha*—is formless and colorless. The blue you see is a useful illusion, a dance of light with fine particles, filtered through senses shaped by karma. Even eclipses speak in this language of shadow. Above Jambudvipa, two Suns and two Moons revolve—perhaps beyond the transparent dome—and their rhythms are shaped by Rahu and Ketu, the nodes of shadow and release. Light and dark aren't enemies; they are partners. Their balance reminds us to look past appearances to what is true."

She gestured gracefully, her voice steady with astonishment. "The Sun represents light, vitality, and enlightenment, while the Moon symbolizes peace, introspection, and calm. Rahu and Ketu, though often seen as shadowy forces, play an essential role in maintaining balance. They remind us that light and dark, action and rest, are not opposites but complementary forces working together to sustain harmony in Bharat Kshetra."

Lata Ma'am concluded with a serene smile. "In Jain teachings, such phenomena remind us to reflect on the illusory nature of the world around us. The blue sky, the eclipses, and even the interplay of light and shadow are all part of *Maya* (illusion). They urge us to look beyond what our senses perceive and seek the eternal truths hidden beneath these layers of existence."

Pravash felt a shiver of awe as he visualized the skies above Bharat Kshetra. The image of two Suns and two Moons, moving in perfect synchrony, casting complementary light over the land, resonated deeply within him. It was not just a vision of the heavens but a metaphor for life—a reminder that balance is essential, that light and dark, activity and rest, must coexist in harmony.

"Bharat Kshetra," Lata Ma'am began, her voice steady and reverent, "is the world we live in. It is a realm surrounded by other kshetras, each distinct yet interconnected. Jambudveep, as a whole, is a vast cosmic structure—far beyond what mortal eyes can comprehend. At its center lies **Mahavideh Kshetra**, a realm of unparalleled spiritual significance. Surrounding it are kshetras like **Ramyak, Hiranyavanta, Airavat, Harivarsa, Nilavanta,** and **Himavanta**—all serving unique roles in the karmic journey of the soul."

"Bharat Kshetra is surrounded by Himavanta Kshetra," she explained, her hand moving to trace the edges of the **Himalayas** on the map.

"Himavanta is not just a mythical realm—it exists in dimensions we cannot perceive with mortal eyes. The great mountain ranges we know, like the Himalayas, are deeply connected to Himavanta. This kshetra spans regions that intertwine with the Himalayas, extending into the unseen and intersecting with Bharat Kshetra at points we barely understand."

She gestured to the towering peaks depicted on the map, their snow-capped summits glinting with light. "The **Vaitadhya** and **Himavant** mountains dominate Himavanta Kshetra, reaching heights unimaginable. Rivers like **Sindhu, Ganga, Rohitamsa,** and **Rohit** trace paths that often vanish into realms hidden from our sight, only to reemerge miles away in a form that seems otherworldly."

Her voice softened as she pointed to shimmering bodies of water etched into the map. "Himavanta is also home to immense lakes like **Padma** and **Mahapadma.**"

She shifted her attention to the northern regions of the map. "Beyond Himavanta lies Harivarsa Kshetra, a realm bordered by the **Nisadh mountains**. Rivers like **Harikanta, Rohit**, and **Harit** flow through Harivarsa, nurturing its lands and sustaining its beings. The major lake, **Tingichha,** is a shimmering oasis, surrounded by landscapes so vibrant they appear to glow."

Her hand moved back to the map's center. "Mahavideh Kshetra," she said, her tone deepening, "lies at the very heart of Jambudveep. It is the spiritual epicentre, home to the **Meru Parvat**, a golden mountain that stands as a beacon of enlightenment. Mahavideh is a realm untouched by the trials of Bharat Kshetra. Here, the cycle of enlightenment remains unbroken. Tirthankaras walk among the beings, guiding them with teachings that lead directly to liberation."

She traced the golden river lines flowing across Mahavideh. "Rivers like **Sita** and **Sitoda** bring life to this kshetra."

"Beyond Mahavideh lies Ramyak Kshetra, bordered by the **Nilavanta** and **Rukmani mountains**. This kshetra is closest to Mahavideh in proximity and influence.

She paused to point out the river Narakanta, which connected to the massive Lake Kesar. "Ramyak has only one major river, **Narakanta,** which flows directly into **Kesar.**"

Jambudveep Map

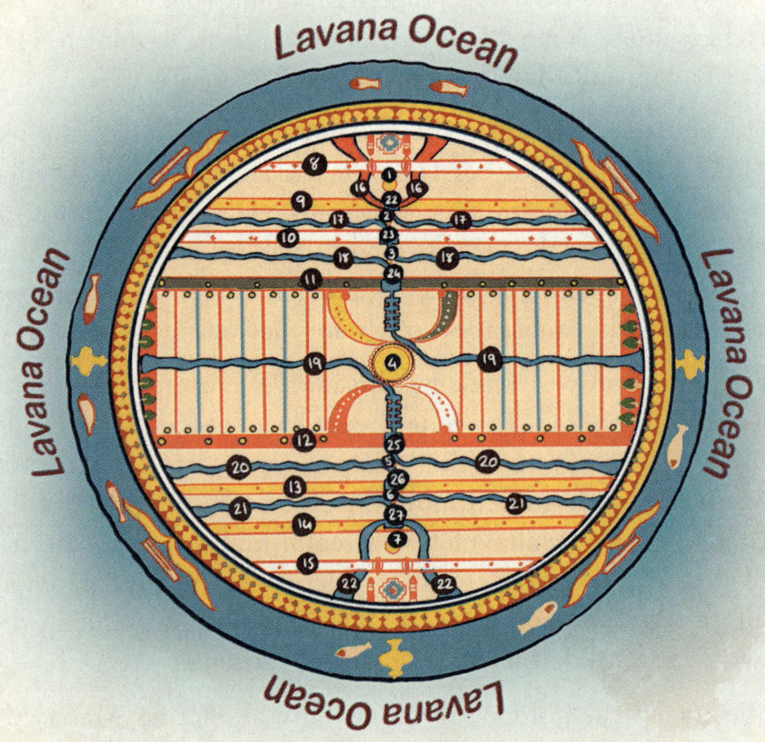

A.Continets

1)Airavat Kshetra
2)Hiranyavanta Kshetra
3)Ramyak Kshetra
4)Mahavideh Kshetra
5)Harivarsha Kshetra
6)Haimavanta Kshetra
7)Bharat Kshetra

B.The Main Mountain Ranges

7)Vaitadhya
8)Sikharin Parvat
9)Rukmani Parvat
10)Nilavanta Parvat
11)Nishadh Parvat
12)Maha - himavanta Parvat
13)Himavanta Parvat
14)Vaitadhya

C.The Main Rivers

15)Raktoda, Rakta
16)Rupyakula,Suvarnakula
17)Narakanta, Nari
18)Sitoda,Sita
19)Harikanta, Harit
20)Rohitamsa,Rohit
21)Sindhu,Ganga

D.The Lakes

22)Pundarika
23)Mahapundarika
24)Kesar or Kesarin
25)Tingiccha
26)Mahapadma
27)Padma

Her fingers traced the jagged **Shikharin Mountains** to the east. "Far beyond lies Airavat Kshetra, the furthest kshetra from Bharat. This is a land of extremes, where the karmic cycles of *Avsarpini* and *Utsarpini* are similar to Bharat Kshetra but magnified in intensity. *Avsarpini* marks a period of decline, where morality, life span, and spiritual awareness diminish. *Utsarpini*, in contrast, is a period of ascension, bringing growth, enlightenment, and renewal."

She pointed to the rivers flowing from Airavat. "**Raktoda, Rakta, Suvarnakula**—these rivers carry hues as vivid as their names, winding through the kshetra before feeding into the massive Lake **Pundarika.**"

"Between Airavat and Ramyak lies Hiranyavanta Kshetra, bordered by the **Rukmani Mountains**. Hiranyavanta is a realm of golden beauty, where rivers like **Nari** and **Rupyakula** carve their way through the shimmering land."

She gestured again to the Nilavanta Mountains. "These mountains form the boundary between Ramyak and Mahavideh, linking the realms with their celestial energy. The landscapes of Ramyak and Hiranyavanta both draw from the spiritual brilliance of Mahavideh, creating a balance that sustains life across Jambudveep."

Pravash's heart stirred at the remembrance of the passage beyond Bharat Kshetra. Could such a gateway truly exist? The idea of stepping beyond the confines of Bharat Kshetra into the realms of Himavanta or Mahavideh filled him with both awe and longing. What kind of divine power, he wondered, was needed to traverse these mysterious lands?

Lata Ma'am's voice softened as she addressed the students. "These realms remind us of the vastness of existence. The beings in each kshetra may look different from us, but their journey is the same—they, too, are striving for growth, understanding, and liberation. Each kshetra offers a unique perspective on life, a chance to experience existence through a different lens. And ultimately, all paths lead toward the same goal: the realization of the soul's true nature."

As she stepped back from the map, her explanation complete, Pravash felt a deep sense of awe settle over him. The teachings of Jainism, which had always seemed profound yet abstract, now felt tangible and alive. Jambudveep was no longer a distant concept—it was a living, breathing structure, a cosmic tapestry of realms interwoven with purpose and meaning.

The seed of curiosity planted in his heart began to take root, its tendrils reaching toward something he could not yet name. For the first time, Pravash felt a connection to something far beyond himself, a pull toward a journey that neither he nor anyone else around him could yet foresee.

As the lesson came to an end, Pravash felt an unfamiliar but undeniable yearning awaken within him—a quiet yet insistent desire to understand, to see, and perhaps, even to explore the worlds beyond Bharat Kshetra. The thought of a secret doorway within the towering ice walls stirred something deep within his young heart. It was as if a veil had been lifted, revealing a glimpse of a universe far greater than he had ever imagined.

Walking out of the pathshala that day, the world seemed both unchanged and yet entirely new. The sounds of the bustling streets, the fragrant whispers of incense floating from the temple, and the laughter of children playing nearby all felt like echoes of something larger, as though they were faint ripples of a much grander design. Bharat Kshetra, he now realized, was not just the world he lived in—it was one piece of a vast cosmic structure. And somewhere within that divine boundary, hidden in the icy walls that encircled it, was a passage—a secret path that only the chosen could traverse.

As Pravash made his way home, his imagination painted vivid pictures of the realms Lata Ma'am had described. He envisioned luminous beings in Mahavideh, radiating peace and wisdom; resilient figures in snowy Himavanta, their voices blending with the whistling winds; majestic, elephant-like beings in Airavat, embodying strength and grace; and glowing figures in the forests of Harivarsa, guardians of nature's delicate balance. Each realm felt alive in his mind, as though he could almost reach out and touch them.

A peculiar warmth stirred in his chest, an unnameable pull toward something just beyond his reach. It was not longing, nor was it fear—it was something simpler, purer: curiosity. Innocent, unfiltered curiosity.

As he approached his home, Pravash paused on the doorstep, a strange sensation washing over him—a fleeting moment of déjà vu. For a heartbeat, the familiar world blurred around him, and suddenly he stood beneath different skies, in another time or place entirely. He closed his eyes, trying to hold onto the feeling, and in that stillness, an image flickered across his mind.

He saw himself standing before an enormous wall of ice, its surface gleaming in the light of twin Suns. The wall stretched endlessly in both directions, towering above him like a celestial fortress. Beyond the wall, a soft, golden light beckoned, its glow gentle yet impossibly radiant. It felt like a call, an invitation to step beyond the boundaries of the world he knew.

And then, just as suddenly as it appeared, the vision vanished, leaving Pravash trembling slightly, wide-eyed and breathless, a profound sense of awe lingering in his chest.

What was that? he thought, his young mind trying to make sense of the fleeting glimpse. *Was it real, or merely my imagination?*

Yet somehow, deep within, Pravash knew the answer mattered—perhaps more than he could yet understand.

Pravash shook his head, a mix of excitement and confusion bubbling within him. It had been only a flash, a fleeting moment, but it felt so vivid, so real. It lingered in his thoughts as he stepped inside his home, a spark that refused to fade.

That night, as he lay in bed, the stories from the pathshala replayed in his mind, weaving themselves into his dreams. He imagined the two Suns and two Moons moving gracefully across the sky, casting their complementary light over Bharat Kshetra. He saw the towering ice walls surrounding the land, shielding it from the unknown. And beyond them, he pictured the distant realms Lata Ma'am had described—lands filled with beings whose lives were as real as his own, yet impossibly far away.

Questions began to form in his mind, though he didn't yet have the words to fully express them. *Why are there ice walls? What lies beyond them? Could I, someday, find the path through them and see those other worlds for myself?*

The thought of such a journey filled him with a quiet thrill, the kind of wonder only a child could feel. It wasn't a yearning for answers or an urge to escape—it was simply the pure, uncontainable curiosity of someone just beginning to glimpse the vastness of existence.

As he drifted into sleep, the image of the ice wall and the light beyond it lingered in his dreams. The question remained, persistent and unspoken, a seed planted deep within his heart. And though its meaning was not yet clear, that seed was planted deeply, destined to grow—quietly, steadily—leading him toward a future that neither he nor anyone around him could have foreseen.

CHAPTER 4
The Divine Protector

WRATH OF DIVINE

1992 – Ghaggar-Nagar, Rajasthan; Thrikkakara, Kerala; Shikharjee-Bihar

As dawn broke over the holy hills of **Shikhajee**, a revered Jain pilgrimage near Parasnath in Jharkhand, the Rathore family stirred with purpose, their hearts filled with devotion as they prepared to embark on their sacred journey to the peak of the Parshvanath Temple, the sacred site where the 23rd Tirthankara had attained Moksha. Completely unknown to them, far away, somewhere in Rajasthan, on the banks of the **Ghaggar-Hakra River**, events of divine and disturbing significance were unfolding—events that would ripple through their lives and intertwine with a destiny they could not yet imagine.

In the early days of May 1992, monsoon had arrived early that year, awakening the dried banks of the Ghaggar-Hakra River, believed by some to be the remnants of the sacred Saraswati. The river's renewed flow had brought life back to the region, and the air carried a faint scent of wet earth and blooming flora. The district of Ghaggar-Nagar, Rajasthan, lay nestled near this ancient river. Its sleepy streets stirred only faintly in the pre-dawn hours.

Near the riverbank, beneath the canopy of a towering peepal tree, a baby girl no older than three years sat, her tiny frame was adorned with a red *Angrakha*-style top tied with golden tassels at the side, and a matching dhoti skirt. Her dark curls framed her glowing, cherubic face as she fidgeted playfully with the soft edges of the fabric. Her large, curious eyes darted around, catching the shimmering glow of the water under the faint moonlight. Every now and then, her tiny hands clapped together in delight, reacting to the sounds of chirping crickets and the rustling leaves. Her soft laughter broke the quiet stillness of the riverbank, filling the air with a childlike innocence that seemed almost otherworldly.

But as serene as the scene appeared, a sense of unease lingered. The air grew heavier, charged with a foreboding presence.

A drunk man, stumbling through the darkness, had made his way to the child. Somewhere in his late twenties, the man was tall and wiry, his tattered t-shirt and jeans clinging to a frame that swayed under the weight of alcohol. His face, partially shadowed by a ragged beard and a horseshoe moustache. His bloodshot eyes darted around as he muttered incoherently some song to himself.

His gaze fell upon the baby, a monstrous smile twisted his lips. His unsteady steps quickened as he approached, his breath growing heavier with evil anticipation. The innocence and glow of the child were lost on him, his darkened soul seeing only an opportunity to satiate his monstrous urges.

He crouched down, his rough, calloused hand reaching out to touch the child. But as his fingers brushed the fabric, the little girl recoiled instinctively, letting out a soft, startled cry. Her tiny hands moved defensively to push him away, her innocent protests mingling with giggles as though she mistook his approach for play. The man, emboldened, leaned closer…

At that precise moment, thousands of kilometres away, Soham in Thrikkakara, Kerala—awoke with a scream that pierced the silence of the night. His small hands clutched his chest as he doubled over in pain, his face contorted in agony. It felt as though an unseen force was tearing at his very soul, pulling it out from the center of his being. His cries echoed through the house, waking Kalaha Dutt, who rushed to his side.

"Soham! What happened?" Kalaha Dutt asked, his voice laced with panic as he placed a comforting hand on the boy's trembling shoulder.

"I don't know…" Soham gasped, tears streaming down his face. "It hurts… it feels like something is pulling me from the inside…" His voice broke into sobs as the pain intensified, his small frame shaking uncontrollably.

And back at the riverbank, the drunk man, oblivious to the ripples his actions were causing across realms, leaned closer, his intentions darkening with every passing second. As he reached out again, this time with both hands, the child screamed—a piercing, heart-wrenching sound that shattered the stillness of the riverbank. But before he could react, the air around him grew heavy, charged with an unseen force…

Far from the riverbank, in the lush hills of Shikhajee, the Rathore family had just begun stirring to life, Pravash, still rubbing the sleep from his eyes, was caught up in the affectionate chaos of cousins and siblings packing last-minute essentials. The warm scent of breakfast wafted through the air as Meenakshi, his mother, called out for everyone to hurry. Amid the rush, Pravash suddenly froze.

A strange, searing sensation rushed through his body, beginning at the base of his spine and shooting upward with alarming intensity. His chest tightened, his breath caught, and before he could process the feeling, he felt a blinding pain behind his eyes.

"Ma! Ma! I can't see! I can't see anything!" Pravash screamed, his voice laced with panic.

He clutched his face, his small hands pressing against his eyes as if to force the pain away. It felt as though all the blood in his body had surged toward his head, burning behind his eyelids, making him certain he had lost his sight. The sharp ache was relentless, as if something unseen was clawing at his very soul, trying to pull it out through his eyes.

The family rushed to his side, voices filled with alarm. Meenakshi knelt, gripping his trembling shoulders. "Pravash! Pravash, look at me! What's wrong?"

Pravash's voice faltered, his breathing uneven as tears streamed down his face. "It hurts... my eyes... I can't..."

In Parasnath, amidst the serene slopes of Shikhajee, the pain was incomprehensible, as if his body were responding to something beyond his understanding, something far away yet inexplicably connected to him.

At the banks of Ghaggar-Hakra River, the drunk man felt a sudden chill race down his spine. Before he could react, the silence of the riverbank was shattered by a piercing screech. From above, an eagle descended, its sharp talons shining in the moonlight. Behind it came another, and another, until the sky was filled with a swarm of eagles, their cries slicing through the stillness.

The man stumbled backward, his eyes widening in terror. But his nightmare was far from over. The calm waters of the Ghaggar-Hakra began to ripple violently, and from its depths emerged hundreds of snakes. Their scales shimmered like liquid metal under the faint light, their hoods flaring as they slithered with impossible speed. Most were cobras, their fangs bared, their movements fluid yet deliberate as they encircled the man.

The man's blood ran cold as he looked into the unblinking eyes of the cobras. The eagles circled above him, their talons gleaming like daggers in the faint light. The man's terror was evident, his breath quickening as the realization of his doom dawned upon him. The creatures seemed to find joy in his fear, their collective gaze radiating an almost supernatural intelligence. They did not strike immediately; instead, they savored the moment, as though drawing satisfaction from the terror etched into his face. For a brief moment, the eagles and the snakes paused, their collective gaze fixed on the man. The drunkard's eyes started rushing wildly, his breath uneven as panic overtook him. It was as though they were feeding on the fear etched into his face.

Then, with a coordinated ferocity, they attacked.

The first cobra struck, sinking its fangs deep into the man's leg. His scream tore through the air, but it was only the beginning. The eagles swooped down, their talons ripping into his flesh, starting with his genital area.

The eagles aimed for his limbs, their sharp beaks and talons tearing through flesh with savage efficiency. One eagle dove directly at his face, its beak gouging out his eye. The snakes coiled around his legs, biting into his flesh repeatedly, their venom spreading through his body like fire.

It was not a quick death. The eagles and snakes seemed intent on making him suffer, their attacks methodical, almost vengeful. The man's screams echoed through the empty riverbank, growing weaker with each passing moment.

The child, no longer serene, sat upright amidst the chaos. Yet, she was not terrified. Her large, innocent eyes watched the scene with an expression that defied comprehension—an awareness far beyond her years. There was no fear in her gaze, only an air of quiet acceptance, as though she understood the justice of what was unfolding before her. Her expression held the purity of divine innocence mingled with a satisfaction that was neither vengeful nor cruel, but profound in its fairness.

Not far from the carnage stood a lone witness—a rishi (sage) dressed in saffron robes, his forehead adorned with a thick paste of sandalwood and vermilion. The holy man, who had been rushing to save the child, stopped dead in his tracks. His hands folded instinctively in prayer, his eyes wide with awe. It was not fear that rooted him to the spot, but a profound sense of wonder. He watched in silent reverence, his lips murmuring prayers as though he were witnessing a divine act unfold before his very eyes.

ECHOES OF DIVINE FURY

To the rishi, the scene was unlike anything he had ever witnessed. The sound of flapping wings, the hissing of snakes, and the man's fading screams seemed to blend into a haunting symphony. In the distance, he thought he heard the faint ringing of temple bells, as though the heavens themselves were acknowledging the sanctity of the moment.

At that same moment, in Parasnath, where Pravash's earlier cries of pain and panic, now transformed as if the bells carried a divine assurance, soothing the boy's anguish, the sound of temple bells erupted, echoing through the mountains like a sacred call. It was unlike anything anyone had experienced before—every bell in the vicinity seemed to come alive, ringing with a force and rhythm that left the family in awe.

Pravash, still clutching his mother's arm for support, felt an inexplicable relief wash over him. His vision began to clear, the burning in his eyes subsided, and his breath evened out. "Mumma... the pain... it's gone," he whispered, his voice shaky but filled with a mixture of awe and confusion.

Meenakshi, who had been on the verge of tears, let out a long breath of relief, holding Pravash tightly. The family exchanged glances, their earlier panic dissolving into a reverent silence as the bells continued to chime. It was as though the entire mountain itself was rejoicing, celebrating something far beyond their understanding.

The hushed chatter of the cousins and relatives resumed, filled with wonder rather than fear, and the family continued their preparations to begin their journey toward the sacred peak of Parshvanath Temple. Suddenly, Meenakshi's elder sister, Vidu, came rushing into the room, her face flushed with excitement, her breath uneven from running. She grabbed Meenakshi's arm and leaned close, speaking in a hurried whisper, her voice trembling with awe.

"Meenakshi... something miraculous has happened!" Vidu said excitedly. "In the new part of the temple, the newly consecrated idols of Lord Parshvanath and Padmavati Maa are shedding tears of *ami!*"

Meenakshi froze, her eyes widening in astonishment. "Ami?" she repeated softly, her voice filled with devotion. Her hand instinctively covered her mouth as the significance of Vidu's words sank in. Ami—the divine tears, considered one of the rarest and most miraculous blessings in Jainism. Only a handful of souls in a lifetime are fortunate enough to witness such an event, a divine occurrence that signifies the boundless compassion of the Tirthankaras.

"Yes," Vidu confirmed, her voice trembling as her eyes glistened with unshed tears. "The priests are saying it started just a few moments ago. They've gathered to pray and chant, but... Meenakshi, this is unlike anything I've ever seen."

Without another word, Meenakshi turned to her family, her voice low but firm. "We must go. This is a blessing beyond words—we cannot let this moment pass without offering our prayers."

As they entered the new section of the temple, they were greeted by the sight of the idols—majestic figures of Lord Parshvanath, carved from pristine white marble, their serene expressions unchanged even as tears of ami glistened and rolled down their cheeks. The air was thick with the scent of sandalwood and incense, the faint hum of the priests' chanting *Navakar Mantra,* an atmosphere of divine sanctity.

The Rathore family folded their hands in prayer, their heads bowing low. Meenakshi's eyes filled with tears as she whispered a quiet prayer, her heart overwhelmed by the sheer magnitude of the moment. Pravash, still reeling from the earlier pain and confusion, found himself drawn to the sight of the idols. The tears of ami, shimmering like liquid light, seemed to carry with them a message he could not yet decipher but felt deeply in his soul.

Each family member took out their puja cloth—a sacred handkerchief tied around their mouths and noses to prevent their breath from touching the idols—and carefully collected a few drops of ami. The priests, standing nearby, nodded approvingly, their own faces reflecting a deep sense of wonder and gratitude for the miracle unfolding before them.

Far to the south in Thrikkakara, where Kalaha Dutt sat by Soham's bedside, the sudden, resounding bells of the temple broke through the stillness of the night. The sound was so profound and persistent that it seemed to carry across every corner of the village. Soham, whose face had been filled with pain moments ago, let out a soft sigh and calmed. His small, trembling body relaxed, and his breathing returned to its gentle, rhythmic pace. The tension on Kalaha Dutt's face melted into a tender smile as he brushed the boy's hair with his fingers, humming a soothing hymn under his breath.

"It's alright now, my child," he murmured softly. "Rest... you are safe."

Soham's eyelids fluttered shut as he drifted back into a peaceful sleep, his small hands clutching at the corner of his blanket. Kalaha Dutt sat there quietly, his eyes glancing toward the distant temple bells that seemed to have rung with an almost otherworldly zeal. He closed his eyes briefly, whispering a prayer under his breath.

The bells continued to ring for a few moments longer before their echoes faded into the stillness of the early dawn. It was as though the divine forces that had intervened at the riverbank had sent ripples across realms, their resonance felt by those who were inexplicably connected to the child thousands of kilometres away.

Back in Parasnath, the Rathore family began their climb up the sacred mountain, the incident with Pravash left as an unspoken question lingering in their hearts. In Thrikkakara, Kalaha Dutt continued to keep watch over Soham, his mind quietly pondering the mysterious bond between the boy and the extraordinary events unfolding in distant lands.

Back on the banks of the Ghaggar-Hakra River, the rishi stood motionless, his hands folded in prayer. His eyes remained fixed on the serene glow of the child, undiminished and perfect amidst the remnants of chaos. The eagles and snakes, their divine task complete, retreated. The cobras slithered back into the river, their hoods lowering as they disappeared beneath the surface. The eagles soared into the sky, their cries fading into the distance until silence blanketed the riverbank once more.

The rishi, his heart filled with awe, whispered a silent prayer. He had witnessed the divine—an act of justice so profound that it would echo through lifetimes. And as he looked upon the child's peaceful expression, he knew she was no ordinary being. She was a vessel of divine innocence and power, a presence that would ripple through the realms in ways no one could yet comprehend.

—❀—

THE DESCENT OF LIGHT

As the eagles and snakes retreated, a deafening silence fell upon the riverbank. The air, thick with the weight of what had just transpired, seemed to hold its breath, as if bracing for what was to come. Then, with a crack that split the heavens, the world above seemed to shatter—a sound so sharp and powerful, it felt as though the very glass of the sky had been torn open.

A massive thunderclap echoed through the valley, and rain began to pour in torrents, each drop heavy and cold, drenching the earth in moments. The river roared with renewed ferocity as lightning illuminated the darkened skies, each flash revealing a presence descending from above. The sound of enormous wings cutting through the stormy air grew louder, accompanied by an almost melodic cry, one that spoke of both fury and grace.

From the fractured sky emerged a sight that could humble the bravest of warriors and silence the most eloquent of poets. A massive **Garuda** (Eagle), its wings pure white—spanning nearly 500-feet and radiant as freshly fallen snow, cut through the air with a power that seemed to shake the earth. The bird's feathers shimmered with a divine glow, their purity a stark contrast to the darkness of the storm. Its presence radiated an aura of majesty and peace, silencing the chaos below. The sight was both humbling and awe-inspiring, a force of nature made flesh, its every movement a testament to the divine.

From the light that enveloped the Garuda, a goddess began to emerge—a radiant being whose glow was so brilliant, so pure, that it momentarily turned the darkness of the pre-dawn hour into the full brilliance of sunrise. For miles around, the land bathed in her light, casting away shadows and revealing every leaf, every droplet of rain, in vivid clarity. She sat poised on the back of the Garuda, her regal form both commanding and serene, a presence that seemed to bridge divinity and mortal understanding.

The goddess was a vision of divine grace and strength. Her crown, wrought of gold and adorned with seven serpent heads rising protectively above her, shimmered with an otherworldly brilliance. Her attire, a flowing garment of reddish pink saree intricately embroidered with golden threads, seemed to ripple with its own life, as if woven from strands of celestial light. Her hair cascaded behind her like a river at night, caught in the wind and glowing faintly in the halo of her aura. Her eyes, fierce yet tender, scanned the riverbank with an intensity that pierced through all pretence, as if she could see directly into the hearts of those below.

As she descended closer to the earth, she gazed at the sage, who still stood rooted in place, his hands folded in reverence. Recognizing the Garuda and the crown she wore, he instantly understood her divine origin. His lips quivered as he whispered to himself, "Hey Maa!" He bowed deeply, his forehead almost touching the ground, his entire being trembling with awe and gratitude.

The goddess, still seated upon the Garuda, inclined her head toward the sage, returning his gesture with a gentle *pranam* of her own—a bow of respect and acknowledgment. The sage's heart swelled with humility; this divine being, this celestial force, had honored him, a mere mortal, with her gesture.

"Rise, O Sage," the goddess spoke, her voice resonating like the harmonious notes of a veena, both melodious and commanding.

"Do not lower yourself before me, for it is I who seek your assistance."

The sage stood, his hands still clasped, his lips quivering with words that failed to escape. He simply nodded, his breath caught in his chest, as her luminous gaze turned towards the child.

"This child..." she began, her voice softening as her eyes lingered on the girl, who remained serene amidst the chaos that had unfolded around her. "She is not an ordinary mortal, nor is she a rebirth of any goddess or soul you might know. She is me—a fragment of my essence, given form to fulfil a purpose that lies beyond the understanding of mortals."

The sage's eyes widened in astonishment, his gaze shifting between the goddess and the child. He opened his mouth to speak, but words failed him in the enormity of the moment. As if sensing the weight of the conversation

The goddess continued, her tone carrying a hint of sorrow, as though she bore the weight of an unseen burden. "In this form, she will live as any child of Bharat Kshetra would—unaware of her origins, innocent to her powers. She will grow, stumble, and learn as mortals do. She will laugh and love, and yet she will face trials that would break even the strongest of souls. And still, she will endure—for she must."

The sage finally found his voice, though it trembled with reverence. "What is her purpose, Divine One?" he asked, his eyes now resting on the child, who had begun to tug gently at the edge of her crimson dress, her expression a blend of distraction and quiet contentment. The moment her fingers brushed the hem of her garment, however, she froze, as if remembering something unspoken. Her tiny hands stilled, and her gaze once again locked onto the radiant figure of the goddess, her small frame emitting a quiet calm.

The goddess's expression turned resolute, her words imbued with purpose. "When the shadow of destruction looms over Bharat Kshetra, she will be its light. When the forces of chaos threaten the delicate balance of existence, she will rise to restore it. Hers will not be an easy path, but through her trials, she will spread the light of truth and hope to all who believe in her."

The child tilted her head slightly, her brows furrowing in a way that seemed almost thoughtful, as though the goddess's words resonated in her small, divine heart. Her lips, though parted in an innocent smile, quivered briefly, as if caught between her mortal form's fragility and something far greater dwelling within her.

The goddess's gaze softened as it fell upon the sage. "But for now, she is simply a child. She must be protected, nurtured, and guided. I entrust this sacred duty to you, O Sage. You shall raise her with wisdom and love, just as **Maharishi Bhrigu** once took care of me."

The sage, moved beyond words, nodded reverently. He watched as the child reached out toward the goddess with a trembling hand, her fingers brushing at the cascading light that surrounded the celestial figure. Though her gesture was small and hesitant, it carried an undeniable innocence, as though she already felt a pull toward the divinity she carried within herself.

"I am honored beyond measure," the sage said finally, his voice steadying. "She shall be my own, and I shall protect her as fiercely as I would my very soul."

The goddess's lips curved into a faint smile. "You shall call her **Tejomayi**, for she will carry the light of the universe within her, even in this mortal form."

The sage whispered the name softly, his voice imbued with love. "Tejomayi…" he murmured, his heart swelling with a mixture of pride and humility. The child, upon hearing her name, tilted her head curiously and gave a small, hesitant laugh—an innocent sound that cut through the tension like sunlight piercing a storm.

The goddess's expression hardened momentarily as her gaze shifted to the lifeless body of the drunkard. "Do not mourn his fate," she said with quiet finality. "His karma was long overdue. The sins he carried—violence, depravity, and the corruption of innocence—bound him to this end. Even the depths of Narak Lok may not suffice to cleanse his soul."

The sage nodded solemnly, his eyes briefly flicking to the man's body before returning to the child.

"I shall honor her name and her purpose," the sage vowed, his resolve firm.

The goddess inclined her head, a look of gratitude crossing her radiant features. "I know you will." She turned her gaze skyward, her expression once again calm and resolute. "And now, I must return. Her time will come, but until then, protect her. Guide her as you would your own soul."

As the Garuda spread its vast, pure white wings, the goddess's light enveloped it in brilliance. The rain ceased, and the clouds began to part as the divine bird ascended, its ascent marked by a soft, melodic cry that echoed across the valley. The goddess, her form shimmering with the golden glow of dawn, disappeared into the heavens, leaving behind a world that felt forever changed.

The sage remained motionless for a long moment, his eyes fixed on the sky as the celestial light faded. The child, now standing on her small, unsteady legs, tugged gently at his robes, her face filled with a quiet curiosity. He looked down at her, and a tender smile broke across his face.

"Come, Tejomayi," he said softly, kneeling to take her small hand in his. Her fingers, warm and trusting, wrapped around his own as she followed him without hesitation. Together, they began the journey to his hermitage, the first rays of the morning sun painting their path in hues of gold and amber.

And so, with the dawn of a new day, Tejomayi's mortal journey began!

CHAPTER 5
The Unshackled Scholar

A PRODIGY IN THE MAKING

1988 – Thrikkakara, Kerala

By the time Soham turned six, he had blossomed into a child who seemed to radiate an effortless charm that drew people toward him. His long, dark curls framed his angelic face, most tied into a small bun atop his head, so no strands obscured his fair, glowing complexion. Slightly chubby cheeks lent him a soft, innocent appeal, while bright, curious eyes held a warmth that felt unspoken but unmistakable. A healthy build and graceful movements added to the quiet magnetism he carried—an ease that made people, without quite knowing why, want to linger near him.

In the village, Soham was adored in a way few children ever were. Elders often found themselves overcome with affection whenever they saw him. They couldn't help but place their hands on his head in blessing, murmuring heartfelt wishes for his well-being. And even after they uttered their prayers, their hands would linger, as though reluctant to break the moment of connection. The mere act of touching his forehead seemed to fill them with a sense of peace and fulfilment, as though Soham carried with him an energy that soothed their worries and softened their hearts.

The women of the village often spoke of him with a sense of wonder, calling him "Hridaya Bala" (the child of hearts), for he had the uncanny ability to win over anyone with his soft smile and gentle words. Even the men, often reserved in their displays of affection, would pat his shoulder or ruffle his curls, their stern faces melting into expressions of fondness. Children his age were equally drawn to him—not because he was the smartest among them, but because there was something comforting about his presence, as if being around Soham made everything feel just a little brighter.

Yet, for all the love and admiration he received, Soham remained blissfully unaware of his effect on others. To him, the world was a vast garden of questions waiting to be answered, a place where learning and play went hand in hand. Kalaha Dutt, observing the way Soham brought joy and warmth to those around him, would often smile to himself, quietly thanking the heavens for such a child. "Love surrounds you, my son," he would say, resting his hand on Soham's head. "Cherish it, and let it guide your path."

Kalaha Dutt had devoted himself entirely to Soham's upbringing, serving as both his **Appa** and **Guruji.** Soham's days were filled with lessons, but not the kind most children received. Kalaha ensured that Soham's mind was enriched with the teachings of the Vedas and Puranas, the fundamentals of mathematics, science, astronomy, and an understanding of world religions through literature. From ancient Vedas, Puranas to Jain scriptures to modern scientific principles, Kalaha nurtured Soham's boundless curiosity and intellect. Soham grasped it all with ease, his extraordinary memory allowing him to recall even the smallest details with flawless precision.

His recall bordered on eidetic—verses, diagrams, and images settled in him as naturally **as breath**. He could recite complex Sanskrit verses after hearing them only once, solve intricate puzzles with ease, and explain philosophical concepts with a depth far beyond his years. Kalaha often watched in amazement as Soham breezed through lessons that would challenge even the most learned scholars.

Yet, despite his brilliance, Soham remained a child at heart—playful, curious, and full of questions. One sunny morning, as they sat in the temple courtyard, Soham looked up from a book he had been reading and asked, "Guruji, why do I always remember everything I read or see? Is everyone like this?"

Kalaha set aside the scroll he had been studying and looked at Soham with a fond smile. "No, my child, not everyone is like this. Your memory is a gift, one that sets you apart. But it is also a responsibility. The knowledge you carry must be used to help others, to bring light to the world."

Soham tilted his head, considering his Guruji's words. "But, Guruji, what if I remember things that make me sad or scared?"

Kalaha reached out and gently adjusted the bun on Soham's head, his touch calming and steady. "Soham, everything you remember—good or bad—has its purpose. Sadness helps you understand the value of happiness. Without bad, you would never recognize the good. If there is light, then there would be shadow. The world exists in balance, and so must you. Hold on to both joy and sorrow, for together they will help you grow and understand life's deeper truths." Soham pondered his Guruji's words, his young mind processing the profound lesson. "So even sad memories are important?"

"Yes," Kalaha replied, placing a gentle hand on Soham's head. "They are the roots that nourish the tree of your wisdom." Kalaha's voice softened, yet carried the depth of a lesson he wanted Soham to hold close. "Learn from them," he said, his words deliberate, "and you will understand that the true value lies not in the destination, but in the journey." He paused, letting the meaning settle before adding, a playful smile tugging at his lips, "Or should I say, *pravaash*"—he emphasized the Sanskrit word for journey "for it is within the journey that you will discover the significance of *tejo* (light) and *chhaayaa* (shadow)."

His tone grew reflective, layering the words with wisdom. "Shadows are not always darkness, my child. At times, they shelter us from the scorching heat of the Sun. To truly live, you must understand and embrace both—light and shadow, joy and sorrow. Only by experiencing both sides of emotion will you come to know the depth of life."

—⚲✒▭✡—

BAL-NARADA

The children in the village often teased him, calling him "Guruji's shadow" or "the boy who lives in books." Most of the time, Soham ignored their taunts, but one afternoon, a group of older boys, led by a boy named Veeraj, decided to trouble him.

The boys, aged eight to ten, blocked Soham's path in the temple courtyard. "Hey, bookworm!" Veeraj jeered. "What are you doing here? Come to recite another boring shloka?"

Soham stopped, his calm gaze meeting Veeraj's. "I'm here for the same reason you are—to enjoy the day."

Veeraj smirked. "Enjoy the day? You don't even know how to have fun."

The other boys laughed, but Soham remained unbothered. Instead, he walked away, heading toward Kalaha, who was seated under the shade of a banyan tree. "Appa," Soham said softly, "the boys are bothering me again. What should I do?"

Kalaha glanced at the group of boys in the distance, then back at Soham. His expression was calm but thoughtful. "Do not fight them, my child. Use your mind. Guide them to where they need to be, and let their own actions reveal their flaws. It's like chess—your move will influence theirs, and in the end, they will set their own trap."

Soham's lips curled into a mischievous smile. He immediately understood what his Appa meant. Turning back toward the boys, Soham approached them with an air of innocence. "Don't you like sweets?" he asked, his tone casual.

The boys exchanged excited glances. "Sweets? Where?" Veeraj demanded.

"At the southern courtyard," Soham said, pointing. "But you'll have to hurry before the poor kids eat it all."

Without a second thought, the boys dashed toward the south courtyard. Soham watched them leave, his mischievous smile widening as he walked back to Kalaha.

In the south courtyard, Veeraj and the other boys rushed to the front of the line, pushing aside the smaller children. "Move! Today's my birthday!" Veeraj declared loudly, puffing out his chest. His arrogance was met with confused stares, but Veeraj didn't notice. He was too busy reaching for the sweets.

Just then, Veeraj's mother appeared from behind the distribution table, her face stern and disapproving. "Veeraj!" she scolded, grabbing his ear and pulling him aside. "What are you doing here? And what nonsense is this about your birthday? Today is your grandfather's death anniversary! We're distributing food in his memory, not celebrating anything!"

Veeraj's face turned bright red as his mother continued to berate him. "You're supposed to be helping distribute food, not pushing other children and making a fool of yourself!"

The other parents and children stared, some stifling laughter, while Veeraj's mother grabbed his ear and dragged him aside, scolding him loudly in front of everyone. "Have you no shame? Your father will hear about this! And you two," she pointed at the other boys, "get out of the line! —Veeraj! Of all the days to act like this! If your grandfather were alive, he'd want to die again seeing you today!"

Soham and Kalaha, standing at a distance, burst into laughter. Kalaha placed a hand on Soham's shoulder, his eyes twinkling with amusement. "You see, my child, all you had to do was arouse Veeraj's greed for sweets. Knowing him, it was clear he would act on it without thinking. And because you already knew why the sweets were being distributed, you anticipated the outcome."

Soham nodded, his young face glowing with understanding. "It's like chess, Appa. I made one move, and it influenced Veeraj's moves."

His pride and joy returned as they walked back to the temple, their laughter deepening the bond between them.

TEACHER OF TEACHERS

1989-1990 – Thrikkakara, Kerala

The late summer of 1989 marked a pivotal moment in Soham's young life. At the tender age of seven, he had already established himself as an extraordinary child. His brilliance and charm left an indelible impression on everyone he met, drawing them in with his articulate speech, graceful demeanor, and sharp intellect. Fluent in English, Sanskrit, and several regional languages, Soham had mastered the fundamentals of science, mathematics, astronomy, and religious scriptures under Kalaha Dutt's meticulous guidance. Yet, despite his vast knowledge, he carried himself with the humility and curiosity of a child eager to explore the world.

A year prior, Kalaha Dutt had realized that Soham needed exposure to a broader environment to truly flourish. While Kalaha's teachings had laid a strong foundation, he believed that experiencing different cultures and traditions firsthand would enrich Soham's understanding. He decided to enroll him in St. Thomas School, a Catholic institution just outside Thrikkakara village, known for its discipline and holistic approach to education. Though Soham had memorized the teachings of the Bible and could quote them fluently, Kalaha wanted him to experience Catholic values, the culture of the school, and the sense of community it nurtured.

The day of Soham's admission interview arrived. As they stood before the principal, Sister Mary Agnes—a sharp yet compassionate nun with a presence that commanded respect—asked Soham a series of questions. His responses were thoughtful, articulate, and laced with an innocence that belied the depth of his intellect.

"And why do you want to study here, Soham?" she asked, her tone curious.

Soham, standing straight with his hands clasped respectfully, replied, "I want to get closer to the teachings of the Lord, Sister, and experience His way of love and kindness."

His sincerity brought a faint smile to Sister Mary Agnes's face. "You speak well for a child your age," she said. After asking a few more questions, it became clear that Soham's knowledge far exceeded expectations. Though he was only six, she recommended he skip the 1st standard and begin directly in the 2nd standard.

Kalaha, standing quietly nearby, gave Soham an approving nod. He had always taught Soham to let his actions and words speak for him rather than flaunt his knowledge. As they left the school that day, Kalaha's heart swelled with pride. Little did either of them know that the journey ahead would be far from ordinary.

For Soham, adapting to school life was easy—almost too easy. The *ICSE* (India Certificate of Secondary Education Board) curriculum, with its structured approach to subjects, presented no challenge to him. Whether it was mathematics, science, or literature, Soham breezed through the lessons with an ease that left his teachers astounded. Yet, despite his brilliance, he never flaunted his intelligence. He was respectful and humble, though his natural curiosity sometimes led him to question his teachers—a habit that would soon make him both admired and resented.

His classmates, though initially in awe of him, began to see him as someone they could look up to. But for his teachers, Soham's questions often presented a challenge. It wasn't that he intended to embarrass them; his questions stemmed from a genuine desire to understand. Yet, there were moments when his intellect overshadowed theirs, leaving them flustered.

By the time Soham entered the 3rd standard, his reputation had spread throughout the school. Teachers admired his brilliance but were wary of his habit of correcting them. It wasn't pride—it was an inability to ignore inconsistencies in what he was taught. And then came the day that cemented his reputation as a "Teacher of Teachers."

It was a bright afternoon, and the 3rd standard class was learning about the solar system. Mr. Ray, an experienced but traditional teacher, stood before the blackboard, explaining the heliocentric model. He drew the nine planets (Pluto still included in 1989) in circular orbits around the Sun and paused dramatically before saying, "And Venus, as the second planet from the Sun, always revolves inside Earth's orbit. That's why we see it as the morning or evening star."

Soham, seated in the middle row, raised his hand. His classmates exchanged knowing glances, some stifling giggles. Soham's questions had become the talk of the class—some found them amusing, others admired his fearlessness. Mr. Ray hesitated, already familiar with Soham's tendency to ask questions that often-left teachers fumbling, but he nodded reluctantly.

"Sir," Soham began, his tone calm and respectful, "if Venus revolves inside Earth's circular path, how can we see Venus more than halfway up the horizon at 10:51 p.m. here in India?"

The class fell silent, and the playful smirks vanished. All eyes turned to Soham, their attention riveted. Mr. Ray froze, momentarily unsure of how to answer. Soham, sensing the hesitation, stood up. "May I explain, sir?" he asked politely.

Before Mr. Ray could respond, Soham walked to the blackboard. Picking up a piece of chalk, he drew concentric circles representing Earth's orbit (A) and Venus's orbit (B). His small hand moved with precision, the chalk making clean, confident lines. "If Venus's orbit is closer to the Sun and Earth is here"—he pointed to a specific position— "then the tangent of sight from A to B wouldn't allow Venus to appear so high above the horizon during the night. It would only be visible at dawn or dusk. Then we add the complexity of curvature drop of 0.08 meters per kilometre. Will it create the bulge blocking the line of sight?"

The room was utterly still, the silence broken only by the faint scratching of chalk on the board. Soham continued, his voice steady. "For Venus to be visible halfway up the horizon at 10.51 p.m., the angular deviation in our line of sight must account for more than just its position relative to Earth's orbit. The current heliocentric model doesn't explain this properly."

He paused, turning to face the class. "The fact that we see Venus high in the night sky suggests that its orbital path isn't as simple as we're being taught. The tangent we draw doesn't logically align with the observed position."

Using basic geometry, Soham calculated the tangent and angular deviation (θ) to prove his point. The blackboard filled with neat diagrams and equations, the kind of precision and clarity no one expected from a 3rd standard student.

The classroom erupted—not with noise, but with an almost tangible awe. Soham's classmates stared, wide-eyed and slack-jawed. Some murmured softly among themselves, their whispers filled with amazement.

"Is he serious?" a girl whispered to her friend.

"How does he know all this?" another boy muttered, his voice tinged with a mixture of confusion and admiration.

A boy in the back row, unable to suppress his awe, exclaimed, "That's crazy! Even my older brother doesn't know this stuff!"

As Soham turned back to the board, one of his friends whispered, "He's like a mini-Einstein."

Even those who didn't fully grasp the complexity of Soham's explanation could sense the magnitude of what he had just done. The confidence with which he spoke, the precision of his drawings, and the way he seamlessly connected concepts left them all spellbound. For the first time, they truly realized that Soham wasn't just smart—he was extraordinary.

Mr. Ray, however, didn't share their admiration. His face turned red with humiliation as he struggled to comprehend the argument Soham had presented. His frustration boiled over. "That's enough, Soham!" he barked. "Return to your seat immediately!"

"But, sir, the tangent—" Soham began, only to be cut off.

"Quiet!" Mr. Ray's voice was sharp and final. "Your behavior is disruptive and disrespectful. Come with me to the principal's office." Before leaving, Mr. Ray angrily wiped the blackboard clean, erasing every trace of Soham's work.

The expressions of amazement on Soham's classmates' faces still lingered as he followed Mr. Ray quietly to the principal's office. The silence between them was heavy, broken only by the sound of their footsteps. Once there, Kalaha was called, and when he arrived, he found Mr. Ray fuming and Sister Mary Agnes seated with a pensive expression.

"Soham has been repeatedly disruptive in class," Mr. Ray complained. "Today, he humiliated me in front of the entire class. His behavior is unacceptable."

Sister Mary Agnes turned to Kalaha, her tone measured but firm. "Kalaha Dutt, we admire Soham's brilliance, but his repeated corrections of teachers are being seen as indiscipline. After today's incident, we must ask that you withdraw him immediately. This environment cannot hold him."

Kalaha listened silently, his expression unreadable. He turned to Soham, who stood with his hands clasped, his gaze steady. "Come, my child," Kalaha said softly. "Let's go."

As they walked home, Kalaha broke the silence. "Soham, do you know why this happened?"

Soham looked up at him, his voice thoughtful. "Because I asked too many questions?"

Kalaha smiled faintly, placing a hand on Soham's shoulder. "No, my child. It happened because knowledge is powerful, but it must be shared with wisdom. Not everyone is ready to hear certain truths. Your questions were valid, but how you present them matters. Knowledge alone doesn't make a scholar—humility does."

Soham nodded slowly, his young mind absorbing the lesson. Though he had been expelled from school, he felt no resentment—only a quiet determination to continue his journey of learning.

—⚬✎▭✡—

THE CROSSROADS OF FATE

Kalaha Dutt sat quietly in the dimly lit sanctum of the Shri Vaman Moorthy Temple, the faint scent of sandalwood lingering in the air like an unspoken prayer. The temple bells, which had earlier resonated with their sonorous chants, now lay silent, leaving only the gentle rustle of leaves in the courtyard. Thrikkakara had been his home for over a decade, a place where his earthly role as a Pandit intertwined with a divine purpose. Yet Kalaha knew the time had come for him and Soham to leave. What filled his heart was not sadness but a profound sense of fulfilment—a recognition that this chapter of the divine tapestry was complete, and the next thread awaited.

Soham's expulsion from St. Thomas School was not a setback but a marker of destiny, a gentle nudge from the cosmic order to guide them forward. Kalaha understood this with the clarity of one who walked the line between the mortal and the divine. His human form had not aged like others; his sharp features, lean frame, and unchanging appearance stood as a quiet testament to his celestial origins. He had long accepted that his role as a Pandit in Thrikkakara was a temporary station, one that had now run its course.

As he moved through their modest home, gathering belongings under the soft glow of an oil lamp, Kalaha allowed himself a moment of reflection. In this human incarnation, he had come to understand the intricate threads of his purpose. He was not merely here to guide the villagers or teach the scriptures. His true role had been to act as a bridge, ensuring that Mahabali could bring Soham into Bharat Kshetra—the mortal plane of middle-earth. A faint smile crossed Kalaha's face as he thought of his real self in Swarg Lok—the celestial realm—likely plucking the strings of his veena to play the next note in the music of destiny, setting the necessary events into motion.

Kalaha's gaze wandered to the few belongings he had packed: scrolls, clothes, and a collection of ancient texts that Soham cherished. The act of leaving did not weigh on him. This role, this village, and this life had been but a fragment of his greater purpose. As long as this incarnation persisted, he would remain by Soham's side, guiding him through the twists and turns of his journey.

Their next destination was Goa, where Kalaha hoped to immerse Soham in a new cultural environment among Christians. He planned for them to live as Catholics, blending into the local community on the outskirts of Calangute. Yet, even as he made these plans, a quiet unease lingered at the edges of Kalaha's mind.

The Hidden Kingdom lay not far from Goa's shores—a place where echoes of Soham's forgotten lifetimes could stir. Memories that, once awakened, might unravel the delicate fabric of his present journey.

The proximity gnawed at him, raising fears of what might come to light.

As the night deepened, Kalaha knelt before the small shrine in their home, offering a silent prayer. The divine plan had brought them this far, and he trusted it would continue to guide them. Rising, he glanced at Soham, who lay peacefully asleep, his face serene in the moonlight filtering through the window. Kalaha's heart swelled with a mixture of love and resolve. Together, they would move forward, one step closer to the destiny that awaited them.

As Kalaha rose from his prayer, he heard Soham stir behind him. The boy sat up, rubbing his eyes, the moonlight catching the curious tilt of his head.

"Appa," Soham's voice was soft, tinged with drowsiness, "why are we leaving? And where will we go?"

Kalaha turned to face him, his ever-present smile deepening as he walked to sit beside Soham. He reached out, ruffling the boy's hair gently.

"Ah, my curious little sparrow," Kalaha began, his tone playful yet warm, "have you ever watched a river, how it flows without staying in one place? It doesn't question why it must leave the mountains to meet the plains, or why it journeys to the sea. It simply flows, because it trusts that each bend holds a purpose."

Soham frowned slightly, trying to make sense of the words. "But... we're not a river."

Kalaha chuckled, the sound low and musical, as if it carried the echoes of another world. "No, but we are part of its song. Our journey is like a melody—each note must be played in its time, no matter how much we may wish to linger. If we stay too long in one place, Soham, we risk losing the rhythm."

Soham's eyes brightened with understanding, though a flicker of hesitation remained. "And where will this melody take us next?"

"To a land where the sea sings its own tune," Kalaha said, his voice softening. "We will blend into its symphony and learn to listen. Trust me, Soham, the path ahead is not just ours to walk—it is written in the stars and carried by the winds."

Soham looked up at him, his face a mixture of acceptance and wonder. "Will you be with me, Appa?"

Kalaha leaned forward, resting a hand on Soham's shoulder. "Always, my boy. Even the river carries the reflection of the moon, no matter where it flows."

Soham nodded, a small smile spreading across his lips as he lay back down, this time with a quiet peace in his eyes. Kalaha watched him for a moment longer before rising, the faint echo of his own words lingering in the room like the veena's final note.

By dawn a westbound bus would carry them along the Konkan coast, and with every mile the sea would begin to teach the boy a different kind of scripture.

CHAPTER 6
Disguised Shadows in Goa

LIFE IN GOA

1990-1991 – Calangute, Goa

Their journey brought them to the serene outskirts of Calangute, where the coastal air carried the faint scent of salt and earth. It was here that Kalaha, now **Mathew Francis**, took up his new role at the local branch of a government bank. The move was not one of necessity but strategy. Over the years, Mathew had quietly built a web of connections, enough to create a history that could withstand scrutiny. Documents, IDs, and records—everything had been meticulously fabricated to craft a believable past for himself and Soham, now called **Leo Francis**. Though wealth was not a concern, this role provided them with the perfect cover.

Leo's arrival in the town quickly became a talking point. His unruly curls, made even wilder by the coastal humidity, framed a face so full of innocence and charm that even the most uptight villagers found themselves smiling in his presence. The way his curious eyes seemed to absorb every detail, paired with the effortless kindness in his voice, made him the beloved boy of the neighborhood. "There's something special about that child," the bakery owner's wife often murmured to her husband, watching Leo pass by their shop.

Having spent a year at St. Thomas School, Leo was no stranger to Christian traditions, but Goa offered him a deeper lens into the culture. Enrolled in Don Bosco School, he learned not just through books but by observing the lives around him. It was not the sermons or rituals that fascinated him the most, but the simple, unspoken values that guided the community.

Every Sunday morning, Mathew and Leo would make their way to the **Church of St. Alex in Calangute**, one of the oldest and most beautiful churches in the region. The elegant white facade, framed by twin towers and a large dome, stood as a beacon of faith against the backdrop of swaying coconut palms. The faint smell of incense mingled with the salty breeze from the sea, creating an air of serenity that even Leo, as young as he was, found deeply comforting.

Leo loved the Sunday Mass, especially the music. The hymns sung by the choir seemed to resonate with his very soul. He would sit quietly beside Mathew, his hands clasped in prayer, but his ears and heart tuned to the melodic notes that filled the church. Each note seemed to dance in the air, weaving a tapestry of divine harmony. By the time the service ended, Leo would find himself humming the tunes as if he had memorized every rise and fall of the melody.

"He has an ear for music," the choir conductor once remarked to Mathew after the service, watching Leo hum along perfectly to a hymn. "He picks up notes like they're second nature to him. Have you thought about having him join the choir?"

Mathew smiled and gently declined. "Thank you, but he already has too many books calling his name. Let him hum his way through life for now."

Leo, however, carried these melodies in his heart, often singing softly to himself as he played or helped Mathew with household errands. The songs became a source of solace and joy, connecting him to the community in a way that transcended words.

One evening, the storm raged through the night. The skies turned an ominous shade of grey as thunder cracked like a whip, reverberating through the air. The winds howled, shaking windowpanes and lashing against the fragile wooden doors. Rain fell in torrents, a relentless hammering that echoed through their small home. Inside, Leo sat by the window, his small hands pressed against the cool glass. He watched as the flickering streetlights struggled against the onslaught of the storm, their glow dimming and flaring like a battle cry. The smell of wet earth seeped in through the cracks, mingling with the salty tang of the ocean. Among those affected was their neighbor, a fisherman whose nightly catches were his family's only source of income. By morning, it was evident that the storm had robbed him of his livelihood for the night.

While Goa nurtured their days with quiet lessons and unwavering kindness, Thrikkakara's sacred pull was inescapable, a thread of destiny woven tightly into their journey.

The next day, on his way back from school, Leo noticed the fisherman's shop was still closed. Concern etched across his young face, he asked Mathew,

"Appa, is something wrong with our neighbor? Are they alright? Should we visit them to see if they need help?"

Mathew smiled knowingly. "Patience, Leo. Step outside with me, and you will see the magic of compassion."

Together, they walked to their doorstep. Across the street, they saw the baker's wife carrying a tray of bread and cakes to the fisherman's home, her husband following close behind with a pot of steaming soup. Leo stood in silent awe, the simplicity of the act striking a chord deep within him.

After a long moment, he turned to Mathew. "Appa, this reminds me of the Gospel of Luke. The priest in St. Thomas said Jesus showed compassion to the poor, and that we must do the same. These people… they may not know the Bible by heart... but they definitely live it."

Mathew rested a hand on Leo's shoulder. "That, my child, is the power of faith in action. True compassion does not wait for recognition or reward. It flows naturally, like the air we breathe, becoming a part of who we are."

Leo nodded, the moment etching itself into his memory like a sacred lesson.

KARMIC BALANCE

The evening breeze carried the scent of the ocean as Leo sat cross-legged on the floor near Mathew, who was arranging scrolls on a small wooden desk. The house was quiet, save for the occasional murmur of distant waves and the creak of the ceiling fan. Leo's face was pensive, his brows furrowed as if trying to untangle a knot of thoughts.

"Appa," Leo began hesitantly, his voice soft but firm. "I've been thinking... isn't fishing also a sin? The fish suffer so much before they die, gasping for breath. Shouldn't the fisherman suffer too, since it's just one life compared to the hundreds he takes every day?"

Mathew paused, his hand lingering on an old scroll. He looked at Soham, a faint smile tugging at his lips. The boy's eyes, so full of innocence and conviction, reminded him of the delicate balance between empathy and understanding that he, too, had once struggled to master.

"Leo," Mathew said gently, setting the scroll aside, "your heart is full of compassion, and that is a gift. But compassion, when it's one-sided, can blind us to the larger picture. What you feel now is not wrong—it's your soul reacting to the pain you perceive. But pain is not the whole story."

Leo tilted his head, his confusion evident. "But Appa, doesn't their suffering matter more? Hundreds of fish die, while the fisherman only loses his livelihood for a day. Isn't one life suffering less than many?"

Mathew chuckled softly, a deep warmth in his voice. "You speak as though suffering can be measured in numbers, my son. But life isn't so simple. Think of the fisherman's family—his children who wait for their father to bring home food. If he cannot fish, they too will suffer. Karma is not a ledger where one life's pain can be balanced against another's. It is a web, intricate and unyielding, where every thread is connected."

His frown deepened, his young mind struggling to grasp the complexity. "Then why does it hurt so much, Appa? Every time I see a fish struggling to breathe, or any life in pain, it feels like... like it's happening to me."

Mathew's gaze softened, his heart swelling with both pride and sorrow. He knelt beside Leo, placing a reassuring hand on his shoulder. "That is because, my child, you are connected to every life around you. Your soul feels their pain because it recognizes them as part of the same divine whole. But remember, we are in *Karma Bhoomi*—the land of action, the middle realm where every being must balance its deeds."

He paused, letting the words settle before continuing. "Not all suffering is reserved for Pataal Lok, the realm of punishment. Often, karmic burdens are carried out here, in Bharat Kshetra, where we exist between the extremes of Swarg Lok and Pataal Lok. This is the only place where beings can truly understand both sides of karma and grow from it."

Soham's eyes filled with tears, his small hands clutching his knees. "But Appa, what if my pain doesn't help them? What if it's all for nothing?"

Mathew smiled gently, brushing a strand of hair from Leo's forehead. "Your pain is not for nothing, my son. Every time your heart aches for another's suffering, you release a part of their karmic burden. The Tirthankaras themselves have walked this earth, enduring pain and hardship to free not only themselves but all who crossed their paths. Your pain is a reflection of your purity, a reminder that you are here to bring light, even if you don't see the results immediately."

Soham looked down, his lips quivering. "I still don't understand, Appa. Why does it have to be this way?"

Mathew sighed, his tone growing lighter. "Ah, my dear Leo, that is a question for **Chitragupt**, the divine accountant of deeds. He keeps track of every being's karma, ensuring the balance is never tipped. Let us leave these matters to him, for if everyone could free themselves from their karmic cycles so easily, wouldn't Moksha be a rather crowded place?"

Soham blinked, his tears drying as a faint smile tugged at his lips. He knew his Appa was trying to make him laugh, but the question still lingered in his heart, unanswered. "I'll find the answer one day, won't I?"

Mathew nodded, ruffling Soham's hair. "You will, my son. When the time comes, you will see the threads of this web more clearly. Until then, let your compassion guide you, but don't let it consume you. Even the strongest flame must burn steadily to light the way."

As the evening deepened, Soham sat quietly beside his Appa, the weight of his questions pressing softly against his young heart.

He didn't have the answers yet, but he knew that this was just the beginning of his journey.

—⚲✎💻✡—

WHISPERS OF NEW CHAPTER

1992 – Ghaggar-Nagar, Rajasthan; Thrikkakara, Kerala; Shikharjee-Bihar

Every year during *Onam*, Kalaha and Soham returned, disguised as humble pilgrims. The Vaman Moorthy Temple, vibrant with the colors of the festival, stood as a beacon of devotion. They blended effortlessly into the throng of worshippers, their steps measured, their movements inconspicuous.

Kalaha, however, ensured that they maintained their distance from Mahabali, who would descend to the temple during this sacred festival. It was not time for them to cross paths again—not yet.

The air in Thrikkakara carried both nostalgia and unease for them. The whispers of destiny seemed louder here, like an invisible current tugging at their souls, urging them forward. Yet he trusted that every step was part of a design far greater than his understanding.

The year 1992 brought an unshakable sense of anticipation to Kalaha. For reasons he could not yet articulate, he felt an undeniable pull to visit Thrikkakara during Vishu, a time they had never chosen before. Trusting the signs, he and Soham arrived at the quiet village, blending into the community as they always did. The visit seemed uneventful at first, the peaceful rhythms of the village lulling them into a sense of calm. Yet Kalaha could feel it—an invisible thread tugging at the edges of their lives, a whisper of something yet to unfold.

It was late one night during their stay when the atmosphere shifted. Kalaha had been sitting by the faint glow of an oil lamp, engrossed in quiet meditation, while Soham slept soundly in the adjacent room. The stillness of the hour was broken only by the occasional chirp of a cricket or the rustle of palm leaves swaying in the night breeze.

Without warning, Soham's pained cry pierced the silence. Kalaha rushed to his side, his heart racing as he saw the boy clutching his chest, his small body writhing as though some unseen force was trying to rip his soul away.

"Soham! What happened?" Kalaha asked, his voice laced with panic.

"I don't know, it hurts... it feels like something is pulling me from the inside..." Soham gasped, his voice trembling as tears streamed down his face.

Kalaha gathered him into his arms, whispering words of reassurance, though his own thoughts were a storm of concern. The child's agony was palpable, and Kalaha could feel that this was no ordinary pain—it was something deeper, something that resonated far beyond their current reality.

"Breathe, Soham," he murmured, his voice steady despite the chaos in his mind. "You are safe. I am here."

Far away, in another corner of India, Ghaggar-Nagar, Rajasthan, a sinister act was unfolding. A drunkard stumbled upon the divine child Tejomayi, her radiant form exuding an ethereal light even in the darkness of night. His unsteady hands reached out to touch her, and in that moment, Soham's pain intensified. It was as if their souls were connected by a thread stretched across realms; someone with ghastly intentions attempting to harm her was enough to hurt Soham.

Kalaha held Soham tightly, murmuring prayers under his breath, and then, suddenly, it stopped. The resounding bells of the temple broke through the stillness of the night. The sound was so profound and persistent that it seemed to carry across every corner of the village.

Soham, whose face had been filled with pain moments ago, let out a soft sigh and calmed. His small, trembling body relaxed, and his breathing returned to its gentle, rhythmic pace. The tension on Kalaha's face melted into a tender smile as he brushed the boy's hair with his fingers, humming a soothing hymn under his breath.

"It's alright now, my child," he murmured softly. "Rest... you are safe."

Soham's eyelids fluttered shut as he drifted back into a peaceful sleep, his small hands clutching at the corner of his blanket. Kalaha sat there quietly, his eyes glancing toward the distant temple bells that seemed to have rung with an almost otherworldly zeal. He closed his eyes briefly, whispering a prayer under his breath.

Repeated for continuation from Chapter – The Divine Protector

As the boy slept, Kalaha's thoughts raced. He rose and went to the attic of their old, rarely visited home, pulling down a dust-covered chest that had remained untouched for years. Even in their secretive visits, Kalaha had ensured that the house remained undisturbed, its treasures hidden from prying eyes. Inside, among relics of their past, he found what he sought: an ancient parchment rolled tight and sealed with a faded thread.

His hands trembled slightly as he unrolled the aged parchment, its surface worn and delicate, revealing faded ink that seemed to hold the weight of centuries. The words, written in the cryptic style of ancient sages, carried a prophecy Kalaha now realized had manifested before him:

जब घंटानां घोषो मधुरो भवेत्,
तस्याः आगमनं समयं कथयेत्।
प्रत्येक मारुते गीतं वहति,
तिमिरं दूरं कृत्वा ज्योतिर्जहाति।
यो तस्यं पूर्णं करोति आगता,
वर्तमानं चिकित्स्य, भूतं जागृता।
- इति व्यासवचनम्

In English Script

Jab ghaṇṭānāṁ ghoṣo madhuro bhavet,
Tasyāḥ āgamanaṁ samayaṁ kathayet.
Pratyeka mārute gītaṁ vahati,
Timiraṁ dūraṁ kṛtvā jyotirjahāti.
Yo tasyaṁ pūrṇam˙ karoti āgatā,
Vartamānam˙ chikitsya, bhūtaṁ jāgṛtā.
- Iti Vyāsavacanam

English Translation goes like...

When the bells sing in joyous chime,
Her presence will mark the passage of time.
Through every breeze, a hymn shall flow,
Her light revealed where shadows grow.
The one who completes him has come at last,
To heal the present and awaken the past.
– Thus spoke Vyasa

The distant tolling of the temple bells seemed to echo the prophecy, their profound resonance carrying across the quiet village. Kalaha knew with unwavering certainty: a chapter in their journey had concluded, and the next was now unfolding.

Cont.. from Chapter – The Divine Protector. Meanwhile, in Parasnath, after the Rathore family had collected Ami (joyous tears of God) and were walking back to their rooms at the Dharamshala, Meenakshi halted at a side corridor. ***A white marble idol of Saraswati Maa*** *stood there—serene, unmistakable—its plinth carrying a* ***short Gujarati verse*** *etched in vivid red. She read the lines once and then again; the words seemed to sing themselves into memory.*

The marble bore the following verses in Gujarati:

આ ગીતને ભૂલશો નહીં,
સામાન્ય તોફાન સમજીને.
હવા અને ઘંટની તાલ,
એ ગાય છે તેનું સ્વાગત કાલ.
જેણે તેના દુઃખને અનુભવું છે,
તેના માટે આ બધું અનુમૂલ્ય છે.
પ્રેમ અને કૃપાનું પ્રતીક જે,
કાળના કડકમાં રક્ષણ કરશે હમેશા તે.

In English script

Ā gīt nē bhūlsho nahī,

Sāmānya tōfān samajīnē.

Havā ane ghanṭ nī tāl,

Ē gāy chē tēnū svāgat kāl.

Jēṇē tēnā duḥkh nē anubhavyū chē,

Tēnā māṭē chē ā badhū anumūlya chē.

Prēm ane kṛpānū pratīk jē,

Kāḷnā kaḍakmā rakṣaṇ karśē hameshā tē.

English Translation goes like..

Do not mistake this song,
For a regular storm.
The air and bells belong.
They sing her welcome near,
To the one who felt her tear.
The icon of love and grace,
Who will guard him through time's embrace.

"I'll ask the priest on our way back," she whispered, letting the family tug her forward toward the climb to Parshvanath's peak.

They returned hours later, legs aching and spirits light. Meenakshi retraced her steps to the same corridor—only to find bare stone where the idol had stood. The niche was empty, the air ordinary.

She approached a senior priest near the doorway. "The Saraswati murti by the new section—the one with the Gujarati verse on the base—where has it been moved?"

He frowned, then shook his head slowly. "There is no such idol here now. There was a Saraswati idol long ago in that wing, but it was shifted to a temple in Madhya Pradesh. Not in my tenure."

Meenakshi stared at the corridor again. She could still see the letters—fresh and red—as if carved before her eyes this very moment. A shiver ran through her; the memory was not memory at all, but presence.

Meenakshi's heart stirred as the text lingered in her mind, its message resonating deeply within her. She couldn't help but wonder about its meaning and the precise timing of its revelation. The distant tolling of bells seemed almost deliberate, as if the divine itself bore silent witness to an unfolding story yet untold. Saraswati Maa, the embodiment of wisdom and grace, seemed to whisper an assurance—though laced with a shadow of doubt—that this moment was intricately tied to a greater plan, one destined to shape both Pravash and the world beyond.

A FAREWELL TO GOA

1992 – Calangute, Goa

Returning to Goa after their visit to Thrikkakara, Kalaha knew the time had come to leave. Soham's connection to the divine had been more than a sign—it was a herald of the next chapter in their journey. Goa, which had served as a sanctuary for them, was no longer where their destinies aligned. The whispers of fate were clear; they had to move forward.

Soham, now ten years old, had become the heart of Calangute. His laughter rang through the streets, a melody that lifted even the weariest spirits. From the fishermen to the baker's family, everyone spoke of Leo with fondness. His unruly curls and infectious smile had made him a beacon of light, leaving an indelible mark on the lives he touched. Yet Kalaha, ever the seer of unseen threads, knew that the boy's destiny lay far beyond the sunlit shores of Goa.

One evening, as the sun dipped below the horizon, painting the Arabian Sea in hues of gold and crimson, Kalaha sat with Soham on their veranda. The salty breeze carried the faint hum of distant waves. "Leo," he began, his voice calm yet resolute, "we must leave Goa. I've taken a job in Kolkata."

Soham's eyes lit up with curiosity, a flicker of excitement mingling with understanding. "Why, Appa?" he asked, though a part of him seemed to already know the answer.

Kalaha smiled faintly, his gaze distant, as though he were looking past the present into what lay ahead. "My child, it is simply time. Kolkata will be our next home, a place where you will learn the ways of another faith. Just as you embraced the culture of Christianity here, you will now come to understand the Islamic way of living."

Soham nodded slowly, his trust in Kalaha unwavering. Yet a quiet curiosity lingered in his young mind. He could sense there was more to his Appa's decision than he was being told. Across the nation, tensions between Hindus and Muslims simmered like an unseen storm, but for Kalaha, this unrest was more than mortal strife. He could feel the subtle ripples of disrupters—beings from other Kshetras, banished souls slipping through the dimensions of space and time. Their actions threatened the delicate balance of Bharat Kshetra, feeding chaos into an already divided world. These forces, Kalaha knew, were often abetted by celestial beings intent on keeping humanity distracted from their higher potential.

Their new home would be on **Zakaria Street**, nestled in the heart of Kolkata and home to the grand **Nakhoda Mosque**. Revered as the largest mosque in Eastern India and one of the most significant in the entire country, the Nakhoda Mosque stood as a beacon of faith, culture, and history. Its towering minarets and intricate architecture would now become part of Soham's daily life, a backdrop to his exploration of the stories behind a new faith.

As they packed their belongings under the dim light of their modest home, Kalaha whispered a silent prayer, his thoughts focused on the road ahead. The time had come to leave Goa behind and step into the unknown—a place where destiny awaited, its threads pulling tighter with every passing moment.

CHAPTER 7
Disguised Shadows in Kolkata

LIFE IN KOLKATA – THE ARRIVAL AND NEW BEGINNINGS

1992 – Kolkata, West Bengal

The train whistled as it slowed down, the rhythmic clatter of wheels against the tracks announcing their arrival in Kolkata. Soham, now known as **Asif Ali**, pressed his small face against the window, his dark curls framing wide, wonder-filled eyes. The verdant green landscapes they had passed on their journey gave way to busy urban scenes as they approached Howrah Station. For Asif, this journey had been nothing short of enchanting—a symphony of colors, smells, and sights unlike anything he had ever seen.

Stepping off the train with his father, now **Mirza Baig Ali**, Asif's gaze darted in every direction, drinking in the sights of the station. Vendors hawked their wares, porters balanced heavy loads, and a cacophony of voices filled the air. The moist breeze that greeted them carried a hint of the Hooghly River, mingling with the scent of coal smoke and fried snacks. It was chaotic, yet somehow welcoming.

Their contact, **Ariful Khan**, a stout man with a greying beard and kind eyes, met them outside the station, a warm smile spreading across his face. "*Assalamu Alaikum*, Baig Sahab," he greeted with a slight bow, his voice carrying the lilting accent of the region, to which Baig greeted gracefully "*Wa Alaikum Assalam*, Ariful Bhai." "Welcome to Kolkata."

As they crossed the iconic **Howrah Bridge**, Asif leaned out of the rickshaw, marvelling at the sprawling river below and the hum of life all around them. The bridge itself, a marvel of colonial-era engineering, seemed to breathe with the rhythm of the city, its metal glowing in the setting sun as if it held the stories of every life crossing its span.

Asif took a deep breath, the air here feeling different—laden with history, culture, and something he couldn't quite name. It felt both heavy and welcoming, like an old story waiting to be told.

Their destination, Zakaria Street, was a world of its own. The entrance was overwhelming, a sensory overload of vibrant sights and sounds. Narrow alleys bustled with life, vendors shouting to advertise their goods, and the heady aroma of spices mingled with the sweetness of fresh fruits. The towering Nakhoda Mosque, with its majestic domes and intricate facade, loomed over the street, its presence commanding respect.

Mirza Baig Ali had been meticulous in choosing their residence and shop. The house, arranged by Ariful, was situated away from butcher shops, ensuring that Asif wouldn't be exposed to anything that might disturb his sensitive nature. The home itself, a classic **middle-to-rich Muslim household,** was both modest and elegant. The entrance opened into a small, tiled courtyard surrounded by whitewashed walls adorned with intricate latticework. A tall neem tree stood in one corner, its leaves swaying gently in the breeze, casting dappled shadows.

Inside, the rooms were spacious yet simple, with high ceilings and arched doorways. Asif's room was small but cozy, with a wooden bed draped in crisp white linens and a low, carved desk by the window. A bookshelf lined one wall, its shelves already beginning to fill with books in Arabic, Urdu, and English—his father's gift to nurture his ever-growing hunger for knowledge. The window offered a view of the bustling street below, the mosque's minarets visible in the distance.

Living next to Ariful Khan's family, Asif quickly became part of their daily life. Ariful, a fruit vendor with a sharp wit and a generous heart, took an immediate liking to the boy. Asif often accompanied him to the mosque, learning the rhythm of life in a religious Muslim community. He joined Ariful and his sons in performing Namaz five times a day at the mosque, where he effortlessly blended into the congregation.

The Imam of the Nakhoda Mosque, a man of great wisdom and authority, noticed Asif early on. The boy's earnestness and quiet humility stood out, as did his surprising knowledge of Islam for someone so young. Asif recited verses from the Quran with clarity and understanding that contradicted his years, though he carefully avoided showing the full extent of his intellect, remembering the lessons learned in Thrikkakara.

Ariful's family, consisting of his wife and three children, treated Asif like one of their own.

They admired his politeness, his eagerness to help, and the natural warmth he brought to their home. Yasmeen, the youngest of Ariful's children, had taken a special liking to Asif. One evening, as the family gathered in the courtyard, she tugged at his kurta, insisting he tell her the story of the hidden nations—*Yajuj* and *Majuj* once more. "Bhai-Jaan, you tell it better than anyone! Are they the same as *Gog* and *Magog*?" she asked, her bright eyes wide with anticipation.

Even as Asif integrated seamlessly into this new life, he couldn't shake an inexplicable heaviness in his heart, especially during quiet moments. Their house was just a street away from

Tarachand Dutta Street, where the **Rathore family** resided, though neither he nor Mirza Baig Ali knew of this connection yet. On their first night in Zakaria Street, as Asif lay on his bed, the weight on his chest seemed to echo the faint creak of the neem tree outside, as though the winds carried whispers of a connection he had yet to uncover.

Kalaha, ever perceptive, noticed Asif's unease but chose not to address it. He knew that the threads of fate were weaving themselves tighter, pulling them inevitably toward the next chapter of their journey. For now, he focused on building their new life, aware that the rushing streets of Kolkata were only the beginning of what lay ahead.

SHADOWS OF DIVISION

By late 1992, Baig and Asif had settled seamlessly into the busy life of Zakaria Street. Their fruit shop had become a familiar fixture in the neighborhood, drawing regular customers who appreciated Baig's warm demeanor and Asif's polite charm. Asif, now a favorite of both the Imam and their neighbors, moved through the vibrant streets with ease, his youthful energy blending effortlessly with the rhythm of the community.

Yet, as their lives flourished within their small world, a shadow began to creep across the nation. Tensions between Hindu and Muslim communities, simmering for decades, began to rise with alarming intensity. Whispers of unrest reached Zakaria Street, carried by newspapers and hushed conversations. The unease turned into fear on **6th December 1992**, when news broke that the **Babri Masjid** in Ayodhya had been demolished. The act triggered a wave of communal riots across India, the most devastating of which unfolded in Bombay, where thousands lost their lives. Images of burning homes, looted shops, and streets stained with blood dominated the newspapers, though many deaths were left unreported. The nation was gripped by chaos, curfews were imposed, and the fragile thread of harmony seemed irreparably severed.

In Zakaria Street, families huddled in their homes, their prayers mingling with the distant echo of police sirens. Mirza Baig Ali and Asif, too, remained indoors, their fruit shop shuttered as the streets emptied of life. The once-bustling neighborhood now felt like a ghost town, the vibrant energy of the markets replaced by an oppressive stillness.

Asif sat cross-legged on the floor of their modest home, the faint flicker of a kerosene lamp casting long shadows on the walls. He clutched a book in his lap, though his wide, troubled eyes betrayed his inability to focus. Finally, he broke the silence. "Appa," he began hesitantly, his voice trembling, "why don't people love each other? Don't Hindus and Muslims both believe in Adam... or Manu... whatever we call him? Aren't we all the same?"

Baig looked up from where he was seated, his sharp features softened by the lamplight. He set aside the Qur'an he had been reading and leaned forward, his expression both tender and grave. "Ah, Asif," he said softly, "you ask what many wise men have struggled to answer. Yes, at our core, we are all one. Adam, Manu—they are the same ancestor, the root of the vast tree of humanity. But over time, people forgot their roots and began to focus only on their branches."

"Why did they forget?" Asif asked, his young voice filled with frustration. "Why can't we just live together?"

Baig sighed, his gaze distant. "Because some people thrive on division, my son. They realized long ago that power can be gained by setting one community against another. They build walls in our hearts and minds, so we forget our shared humanity. And this isn't new. It has happened for centuries."

"But why does God allow it?" Asif's voice cracked with emotion. "Doesn't God want us to be happy?"

Baig's lips curved into a faint, bittersweet smile. "Gods have their reasons, Asif. Long ago, humans were united in strength, so much so that they began to challenge the heavens themselves. Ravan, for instance—he was no ordinary man. His power shook even the Swarg Lok. The gods feared mortals would grow too strong, so they salted the earth with doubt, and we forgot the root for the branches. They wanted us to stay busy fighting among ourselves, so we would never again threaten the balance of the cosmos."

Asif blinked, his young mind trying to process the weight of Baig's words. "So... even the gods are against us?"

Baig shook his head. "Not against us, Asif. They protect their realms, just as we protect our homes. But it's not only the gods. There are other forces—beings from far-off realms, exiled from their own kshetras. They have found their way here, hiding in high places, manipulating minds, and creating chaos. They thrive on our conflicts, feeding on the negativity they spread."

Asif shivered, clutching his book tighter. "Is that why the riots happened? Because of those beings?"

Baig's expression grew solemn. "The riots happened because humans allowed hatred to fester in their hearts. These beings might fan the flames, but the fire starts with us. The destruction of the Babri Masjid was a spark, but the kindling had been there all along, waiting for the right moment to ignite."

Asif looked down, his small hands trembling. "But Appa, what if the fighting comes here? What if it happens in our street?"

Baig placed a reassuring hand on Asif's shoulder, his voice steady. "Then we will do what we've always done, my son. We will hold on to love, to kindness, to each other. Remember, Asif, the greatest power lies not in strength, but in understanding. When you understand, you cannot hate."

Outside, the call to prayer echoed faintly in the distance, a reminder of the faith that bound their small community together. Asif closed his eyes, trying to find solace in his father's words, though the unease in his heart remained.

The curfew lifted days later, and the streets of Zakaria Street began to stir once more. Yet, the shadow of those days lingered in Asif's mind, shaping his thoughts and understanding of the world. Though he was too young to fully grasp the complexities of what had happened, he held on to one certainty: love and kindness were the only weapons that could stand against hatred.

THE CRY THAT SHOOK THE COSMOS

1993 – Kolkata, West Bengal; Ghaggar-Nagar District, Rajasthan

By early 1993, life in Kolkata had started to regain its rhythm. The curfews were lifted, the streets filled again with the hum of rickshaws, hawkers, and the chatter of people. Though the scars of the riots lingered in hushed conversations and wary glances, the city's spirit remained unbroken. Zakaria Street, with its vibrant hustle, was no exception. Mirza Baig Ali and his son Asif, now well-settled in their fruit business, had become part of this close-knit Muslim community. Asif, with his earnestness and quiet charm, was adored by neighbors and mosque-goers alike. Baig's reputation as a kind and fair merchant had also earned him respect.

Across the lane, life on Tarachand Dutta Street was returning to its own sense of normalcy. Ten-year-old Pravash Rathore, unaware of the intricate threads weaving their way through his life, was more concerned with the simple joys of childhood. The end of curfews meant he could once again meet his friends at the video game parlor near the intersection of the two streets—a shared space that linked two very different worlds.

One such evening, Pravash stepped out of the dimly lit parlor, his heart still racing from the excitement of the games. His friends followed, their laughter echoing through the alley as they discussed strategies and bragged about high scores. At the corner, Pravash spotted his mother speaking with a neighbor near a small grocery shop. He froze for a moment, realizing he had told her he was going to play cricket at Mohammed-Ali. A lie.

Not wanting to be caught, Pravash quickly decided to take an unfamiliar route home—one that led through Zakaria Street. The idea made him uneasy. He had heard hushed conversations at home and on the street about the recent riots, the distrust and tension between Hindus and Muslims still palpable. But his fear of being scolded by his mother outweighed his hesitation.

As Pravash turned onto Zakaria Street, the atmosphere shifted. The narrow lanes bustled with life, the air rich with the aroma of spices, grilled meats, and fresh produce. The towering minarets of Nakhoda Mosque loomed over the street, their intricate details catching the fading light of the evening. Vendors called out to passersby, their voices mingling with the occasional honk of a rickshaw. It was a world so different from his own that Pravash couldn't help but glance around in fascination.

But his fascination quickly soured. As he passed a butcher's shop, though not directly in his path, the sight of meat hanging on hooks and the faint metallic scent of blood jolted him. Memories of the riots and the stories he had overheard bubbled to the surface. Anger, fear, and prejudice he didn't fully understand surged within him, and without thinking, he muttered under his breath: **"Bloody Muslims!"**

The words carried venom he didn't comprehend but resonated loudly enough for nearby ears to catch. One of those ears belonged to Mirza Baig Ali, who was buying vegetables at a small stall just across the lane. He turned instinctively toward the voice, and his eyes fell on the boy who had spoken.

In that moment, time itself seemed to pause for Baig. His celestial essence stirred, unlocking a sight mortals could never perceive. As his gaze fixed on Pravash, the boy's face became a tapestry of lives lived before. Baig saw glimpses of his past lifetimes—moments of triumph and conflict—as if the boy's soul itself laid bare its journey. In the present, fragments of Pravash's life so far floated before him, like pieces of a puzzle waiting to be arranged.

And then, amidst the shifting tapestry of lifetimes, a presence emerged—a familiar soul, her radiance as unyielding as the morning sun breaking through a storm. She had walked through Pravash's past lives before—shaping him, breaking him, guiding him. And now, her return was inevitable, a silent thread tying the past to the present.

Baig's breath stilled as realization dawned upon him; this was the one Vyasa had spoken of, the soul whose essence would intertwine with Pravash's destiny and Soham's path. Though her form in this lifetime remained veiled, her essence sang to him with a resonance no mortal heart could miss. It was unmistakable—as familiar as a forgotten poem reawakened by the wind, its verses echoing through time.

Baig's eyes softened, filling with reverence as he looked upward. His arms opened slowly, and his face shone with a profound satisfaction, as though the universe had whispered a long-awaited truth into his ear. He closed his eyes, his lips trembling with quiet ecstasy as tears welled up unbidden. "***Narayan... Narayan...***" he murmured softly, the words flowing like a prayer born of acceptance and gratitude.

In that silent moment, he knew. The incident at Thrikkakara had been her announcement—a ripple across time and space, heralding the arrival of a force that would change everything. The past and the present were converging, and the future, though still cloaked in mystery, felt as inevitable as the rising of the sun.

And then, with a fleeting glimpse into the threads of the future, the face of the boy became clear—Pravash was destined to play a pivotal role in Soham's life. The connection between them, though distant, was undeniable, and Baig now understood why their journey had brought them to Kolkata. A purpose had been served.

For Pravash, the silence was unbearable. Baig's intense gaze unnerved him, and he interpreted the man's look as anger. His heart pounding, he turned abruptly and bolted, his friends following closely as their hurried footsteps echoed through the crowded lane.

Baig's lips curled into a knowing smile, one that carried the mischievous hint of Narada's divine playfulness. He closed his eyes and whispered a silent prayer, a prayer that carried the weight of his insight:

"Hey Narayan, let this child grow beyond the walls of hatred that bind him. Even if suffering must pave his path, let him discover love for all communities, for all beings. Let the fire within him burn away prejudice, and let his heart awaken to the unity that transcends all division."

Then, with a quiet solemnity, Baig whispered with soft smile, "*Wa 'asa an takrahu shai'an wa huwa khayrun lakum, wa 'asa an tuhibbu shai'an wa huwa sharrun lakum, wallahu ya'lamu wa antum la ta'lamoon*," the verse from Surah Al-Baqarah (2:216). Its meaning lingered in the air like a divine echo: "*At times, what you may dislike is actually good for you, and what you may love is harmful to you. Trust in him, for He knows, and you do not.*"

As Baig's voice faded, the world around him seemed to pause. The street fell silent, the distant hum of life dimming as though the divine itself leaned closer to listen. Time stretched, its fabric thinning, until every breath felt heavy with sacred stillness. For a fleeting moment—one that felt eternal—the universe held its breath alongside him.

And then, with a soft sigh, the world resumed its rhythm. A gentle breeze stirred the hem of his kurta, carrying his words skyward, as though delivering them to realms beyond mortal sight. The air seemed lighter, the weight of the prayer lifted, and Baig's heart rested in quiet certainty—his plea had been heard.

As Baig approached the entrance of their building, a sound like no other pierced the air. It was a cry, raw and guttural, as though it came from the depths of one's soul. It was Asif. Baig's heart clenched—he had never heard him cry like this before. The sound was unbearable, a scream of pain that seemed to set the very air ablaze. Dropping his bags, he rushed toward the source, his steps quick and frantic.

At the base of the stairs, Baig froze. Asif was on the ground, clutching a cow as though it were his lifeline, his small arms wrapped around its neck, his face buried in its side. The cow stood trembling, its large eyes filled with confusion and fear. Baig's neighbor, Ariful, stood nearby, his face a mask of helplessness.

"Asif found out that this cow is going to be slaughtered," Ariful explained breathlessly. "I don't know how, but he found out. He won't let go."

Baig knelt beside Asif, his voice firm but calm. "Asif, let go. Let her go, my son. You cannot stop what is written."

But Asif clung tighter, his small frame trembling with the force of his sobs. "No, Appa!" he screamed, his voice raw. "She's innocent! She's done no wrong!"

Baig tried to pull him away, but it was as though Asif's strength had multiplied tenfold. He held on, unyielding, his cries echoing through the narrow stairwell. And then, suddenly, he screamed—a sound so loud and powerful it felt as though it reverberated through the three lokas.

"Wa mā min dābbatin fī al-arḍi wa lā ṭā'irin yaṭīru bijanāḥayhi illā umamun amthālukum; mā farratnā fī al-kitābi min shay'in; thumma ilā rabbihim yuḥsharūn!" (Quran, Surah Al-An'am, 6:38) *'There is not a moving creature on the earth, nor a bird that flies with its two wings, but are communities like you. We have neglected nothing in the Book. Then unto their Lord they (all) shall be gathered.'*

As the last word left his lips, his chest heaved with effort, his tear-streaked face contorted with grief. And then came the second cry—a piercing, guttural scream that transcended words, shaking the very essence of everything around him. It was as though the cry itself was a curse, a lamentation of unbearable pain and fury, raw and untamed.

"Man lā yarḥam lā yurḥammmm!!!!"

('Whoever does not show mercy will not be shown mercy.')

This scream tore through the air, rising like an inferno that could burn the heavens themselves. The earth seemed to tremble as his voice carried across the realms. Birds took flight in alarm, dogs howled, and even the crowded Zakaria Street fell silent for a fleeting moment, as though the world itself held its breath.

The sheer force of the cry seemed to rip through the fabric of existence. It reached beyond the mortal plane, touching hearts, minds, and souls. In distant corners of Bharat Kshetra, celestial beings paused, their gazes shifting as though they had heard a call they could not ignore.

Asif's body convulsed, and then he collapsed against the cow. His tiny frame crumpled, his hands sliding off the animal's neck as he fainted, his strength finally spent, as though the scream had drained every ounce of life from him. Baig caught him just in time, pulling him into his arms as he whispered frantically, "Asif, my child! Open your eyes!" his heart pounding as he cradled the boy's unconscious form.

At that very moment, hundreds of miles away in the serene courtyard of a hermitage, Tejomayi woke with a start. Her scream mirrored Asif's, as though the pain of his cry had reached her across space and time. Her guardian, Sage Paramarishi, looked on in alarm as Tejomayi clutched her chest, gasping as if she herself were burning. Without a word, she ran toward the nearby lake, her feet barely touching the ground, and threw herself into the water.

"Tejomayi!" the Paramarishi shouted, rushing after her. He dived into the lake, pulling her unconscious form to the shore. His heart raced as he laid her on the grass, his mind struggling to understand what had just transpired. Who or what had caused such a reaction in the girl he had vowed to protect?

Meanwhile, on Tarachand Dutta Street, Pravash climbed the stairs to his home, his mind preoccupied. The world seemed to tilt, and suddenly his legs gave way beneath him. He fell hard, his head striking the edge of a step with a sickening thud. Blood pooled around him as the world faded into darkness.

By the time his family found him, Pravash was unresponsive. Rushed to the hospital, he underwent emergency surgery to address a minor injury to the sensitive area at the back of his head. Though he survived, the trauma resulted in temporary memory loss, leaving his family grappling with the uncertainty of what lay ahead.

Soham's eyes fluttered open in the stillness of the night. The faint glow of an oil lamp cast long shadows on the walls, and the sound of Kalaha's soft chanting filled the air. Kalaha sat by his side, his eyes filled with a mixture of worry and tenderness. He had not left Soham's side for even a moment, his presence a constant anchor through the turbulent storm that had overtaken the child.

The moment Soham regained consciousness, tears welled up in his eyes. A heart-wrenching cry escaped his lips, a sound so raw and filled with grief that it pierced Kalaha's soul. It was a cry of loss, as if Soham had been separated from his very essence, a cry so profound it mirrored the sorrow of a child who had lost his mother.

Kalaha placed his hand gently on Soham's chest, steadying him. "Soham," he whispered, his voice calm yet firm, "breathe, my child. Breathe. Let the pain flow through you, but do not let it consume you. I am here."

Soham clung to Kalaha, sobbing into his chest, his small frame trembling like a leaf caught in a storm. Kalaha held him close, stroking his curls, murmuring soothing words that seemed to calm the chaos within him. Soham's breathing eventually slowed, the sobs ebbing into soft breaths.

"Come," Kalaha said gently, his hand warm on Soham's shoulder. "There is something I want you to see."

He helped Soham to his feet, his movements slow and deliberate, as though coaxing a wounded animal back to trust. Together, they descended the stairs in silence, the cool night air brushing against their skin. In the courtyard below, bathed in pale moonlight, the cow lay on a bed of straw, peaceful and unafraid. Her large, gentle eyes reflected a calm that felt almost divine.

Soham froze. Tears welling up again, but this time they were tears of relief. He ran to the cow and wrapped his arms around her neck. His sobs returned, quieter now, laced with a sigh of profound solace. It felt like finding something he had already mourned.

Kalaha watched, his own heart swelling with a quiet sense of fulfilment. He stepped closer, placing a reassuring hand on Soham's shoulder.

"She is safe now, my child," he said. "I have made arrangements. At first light, she will be sent to a cow shelter where she will be cared for. You have done your part."

Soham looked up at him, his eyes still glistening with tears, but there was a newfound light in them. "Thank you, Appa," he whispered, his voice trembling with gratitude.

Kalaha nodded, a faint smile touching his lips. "Our purpose here is served, Soham. Now, it is time for us to move forward. *Onam* will arrive in a few months, and as always, we will travel to Thrikkakara to pay our respects to Lord Vaman."

Soham's expression softened, the weight of the night beginning to lift. "And after that?" he asked quietly.

Kalaha's smile deepened, a twinkle of mischief in his eyes. "After that, we start a new journey. But first, I may have a small task for you. The final step of our disguise. A little fun, a little preparation, and something to set certain things in motion."

Soham tilted his head, curiosity sparking. "What kind of work, Appa?"

Kalaha chuckled, his voice warm and knowing. "Patience, my child. All will be revealed in time. For now, rest. The morning will bring new light, and with it, new purpose."

As they returned to their room, Soham felt a quiet resolve settle within him. The night's events had left an indelible mark, but they had also taught him a profound lesson about compassion, purpose, and the delicate threads of fate. And as he lay down to sleep, the cow's gentle presence in the courtyard below filled his heart with a peace he hadn't known before.

Kalaha remained awake, watching over him. His thoughts had already turned to what lay ahead. The threads of destiny were tightening. The next chapter was about to unfold.

—◊⁄□✡—

SYMPHONY OF SHADOWS

1993 – Chennai, Tamil-Nadu

The train ride to Chennai marked the opening move of another of Kalaha Dutt's carefully crafted plans.

Soham, now ten-years-old boy with a charm that could disarm kings, every new city was a mystery waiting to unfold. By the time they arrived into Chennai, Kalaha had already set the stage: a modest room in the heart of the city and, through old contacts, a curious role for Soham as a "tea boy" in a well-known music studio.

Soham didn't question it. To him, Kalaha's plans, always carried a purpose that revealed itself in time. When handed a small tray and dressed in clothes worn from many washes—a simple white shirt, now tinged faintly yellow at the edges, paired with faded blue trousers—he simply accepted it. His old white slippers, marked with traces of mud and wear, slapped softly against the studio's gleaming floors as he moved. To those around him, he was just another tea boy—unassuming, quiet, and easy to overlook.

Yet there was something about Soham that set him apart.

It wasn't just the way his soulful eyes seemed to carry an unspoken understanding or how his smile lit up his face like the gentle glow of an oil lamp—it was his demeanor, humble and sincere, that wove him effortlessly into the rhythm of the studio. Wherever he went, he greeted everyone with a soft, heartfelt **"Vanakkam, Anna"** or a gentle **"Good morning, Sir,"** his tone as genuine as the innocence in his gaze. Even the most irritable of technicians—men who grumbled over tangled wires or snapped at misplaced equipment—found themselves pausing, their expressions softening as they returned his greeting with a reluctant yet inevitable smile.

No one in the studio ever asked for his real name. To them, he simply became "Tambi"—the Tamil word for "younger brother" spoken with affection. It was a name born from habit but carried with warmth, one that nestled itself into Soham's daily routine like a familiar song. Though he remained quiet most of the time, his presence was felt everywhere. Each morning, before the studio's hum of activity began, Soham ensured that the newspapers were placed carefully at the reception desk and in every recording room. The crinkle of the pages under his small hands, the scent of fresh ink mingling with the faint aroma of tea—these became part of the studio's rhythm, unnoticed yet indispensable.

And then, one day, the headlines screamed louder than the music itself.

The **1993 Bombay Blasts**—the coordinated attacks that shattered the nation's financial capital—spread across the front pages like dark clouds gathering over the land. The name **Dawood Ibrahim** appeared in bold letters, whispered in hushed tones across the studio halls. The world seemed to pause, recoiling from the weight of what had happened—**257 lives lost, over a thousand critically injured**—the chaos of senseless violence shaking India's soul once again.

Soham's hands paused on one of the newspapers as he placed it on the recording table. The grim, glaring headlines burned into his mind, a stark contrast to the harmony that surrounded him. For a brief moment, the walls of the studio—his sanctuary—felt heavier, as if it, too, mourned.

And yet, inside those walls, life continued.

It was as though Soham belonged to the very pulse of the place, the flow of creation running through him as he moved from room to room. He was there when musicians strummed their first chords, when singers rehearsed their scales, and when the studio fell silent in awe of a perfect take. Tambi—this boy with his old clothes and worn slippers—had become a thread in the fabric of their days, so seamlessly woven that no one stopped to wonder where he came from.

To Soham, the studio breathed. The walls vibrated with melodies that resonated deep within his being, as though the very essence of the music sought him out. Every hum of a string, every tap on a drumhead, every pause where silence dared to linger—it all whispered secrets only he could hear. Day after day, as he moved between rooms serving steaming cups of tea to musicians and technicians, Soham absorbed it all like a sponge, his ears tuned not just to music but to meaning.

Kalaha had trained him well—mastering instruments like the veena, piano, and flute—but here Soham learned something deeper. Music was something to be felt, to be lived. Kalaha, revered as though he were a child of Maa Saraswati, the goddess of knowledge and music herself, had nurtured in Soham an understanding of music that transcended notes and scales. Kalaha had often told Soham, "*Music is the language of the universe, the heartbeat of creation itself. It is through sound that we connect to the divine.*"

To Soham, these words were no longer just teachings; they were truths that echoed through the studio's walls. Music, for him, was the pulse of creation—a force older than time, alive and breathing through every instrument, every voice, every silence. As he walked the corridors carrying trays of tea, his heart swelled with quiet joy, even as the weight of the world outside lingered at the edge of his consciousness, carried in the ink-stained newspapers he set down each morning.

One afternoon, as Soham quietly moved through the studio carrying a tray of steaming tea, a sound stopped him mid-step.

It struck like the first thunderclap of a summer storm—raw, wild, and untamed. The thrum of Sivamani's drums roared through the recording room, reverberating off the walls with an energy that felt alive. It was not just sound—it was the earth's pulse itself, unleashed and unbound.

Soham froze, his breath caught in his chest, the beats stirring something deep and primal within him. Slowly, as though guided by an unseen force, he placed the tray on a side table. His eyes fell on a wooden flute nearby, forgotten and waiting. A red ribbon with golden lace tied neatly to its end shimmered faintly under the studio lights, almost as if it recognized him.

The room remained oblivious to his quiet steps. Sivamani was a storm, his hands a blur, his rhythms like a torrent flooding the space. The sound was chaos—formless, furious, and glorious. And then, through that chaos, came the first note of Soham's flute.

Soft, so soft it could have been mistaken for a breath of wind. It rose tentatively, delicate yet unwavering, like the first light of dawn breaking against the storm. It was the *Sa* note in G Scale—a note so pure it seemed to cut through the chaos and silence the very air.

Sivamani's hands faltered for the barest of moments, his gaze snapping toward the sound, only to find himself pulled back in. The storm had been met with a guiding wind, and instinctively, he surrendered to it.

Then Soham played.

The melody flowed like liquid gold, winding its way through the untamed rhythm. It didn't fight the drums; it danced with them. It was the harmony that fire finds in the wind, the wild given shape and purpose. Sivamani's furious beats no longer roared—they sang, following the flute's quiet command.

To those who looked on, the music took on a visible form. It shimmered in the air like waves of light, vibrating in colors no one could truly see but all could feel. Red and gold rose from the thunder of Sivamani's drums, swirling with the blues and greens that poured from Soham's flute. The room was no longer a space—it was a canvas, alive with invisible strokes of music that touched every soul present.

Sivamani, once playing to impress, now found himself led like a pilgrim following a divine call. His hands moved as though possessed by the very rhythm of creation, his spirit bending to the child's tune. And there stood Soham, eyes closed, his expression serene as the notes poured from him like a song sung straight from the heart of the universe.

To Soham, this was not performance—it was his soul speaking in the only language it knew. Music was not art; it was life.

Time itself seemed to hesitate. In that room, nothing existed but sound and silence, sorrow and joy, creation and peace.

And then—

The door swung open with a thud, the sound shattering the spell like glass. "Mani Ratnam sir has arrived," an assistant's voice rang out, mundane and jarring against the symphony that had held the room captive.

The spell shattered.

Silence fell. The last flute note lingered, then vanished.

Sivamani's hands fell silent. The last note of Soham's flute hovered in the air for a heartbeat longer before vanishing, as if it had never existed.

The studio room stood still. Musicians and engineers, stunned and disoriented, glanced at each other as though waking from a shared dream.

Sivamani turned toward the spot where Soham had stood, his chest rising and falling with the weight of what had just passed. But there was no sign of the boy. The flute lay where it had been before, untouched, its ribbon trailing like a quiet echo of the magic that had just been.

"Was that... the tea boy?" someone whispered, afraid to break the silence.

Sivamani wiped his brow, his hands still trembling, his voice hoarse with awe. "I don't know," he whispered. "But I swear... I felt like... I was playing for the gods."

Outside, Soham walked toward Kalaha, who stood waiting in the soft shade beyond the studio doors. The faint noise of the city swirled around them, unnoticed. Kalaha met Soham's gaze, a smile tugging at his lips as he took the boy's hand into his own.

"Come, Soham," Kalaha said softly, his voice carrying both calm and purpose. "The last step awaits."

He handed Soham an old, slightly crumpled newspaper.

TOLL OF THOUGHTLESS VOILENCE IN BOMBAY

Soham frowned as he traced the words with his small fingers. "This is an old paper, Appa."

Kalaha smiled., his eyes twinkling with a knowing mischief rarely seen. He ruffled Soham's curls affectionately. "Sometimes, old truths must awaken new hearts. Go, Tambi,"—he said, the word rolling playfully off his tongue, unusual coming from him—"place this in the recording room. Quietly, and leave before anyone notices you."

Soham, though puzzled, obeyed as always. Slipping into the recording room like a quiet breeze, he placed the newspaper delicately on the console table where Mani Ratnam and AR Rahman sat, immersed in their work. The soft rustle of paper went unnoticed amidst the faint hum of machines and conversations. With the same silent steps, Soham vanished into the corridors of the studio, the act complete.

Minutes later, Mani Ratnam, adjusting his chair to reach for a sheet of notes, caught sight of the paper. The headline struck him—its bold, harrowing letters freezing him mid-motion. He picked it up slowly, his eyes narrowing as he scanned the words, the weight of the violence and sorrow unfolding in his mind like a slow, heavy wave.

Rahman noticed Mani's stillness and turned. "Everything alright?"

Mani didn't respond immediately. The paper crinkled softly in his hands as he leaned back, his brow furrowed, his thoughts far away. Finally, he spoke, his voice low, yet filled with a quiet urgency that commanded attention.

"Rahman," he said, his words measured, "we need to do something about this."

Rahman's curiosity sparked. "What are you talking about?"

Mani lifted the newspaper slightly, tapping the headline with a finger. "This. *This* cannot be forgotten. A story like this—it cannot be ignored. People need to feel it, to see the human side of this destruction."

Rahman's gaze sharpened, his mind already spinning as inspiration took hold. "What kind of story do you have in mind?"

Mani's fingers began to tap rhythmically on the console, almost absentmindedly, his voice gaining momentum. "A story of unity—love and pain amidst the ruins. Something to wake hearts, to remind people that beyond religion, beyond hatred, we are all human. *That* is the story we need to tell."

In the days that followed, whispers of the locked-room miracle spread through the studio like an unfinished melody. Those few who had been there—the percussionists, the sound engineers—spoke in hushed voices, their words failing to capture what their hearts had felt.

"It was like nothing I've ever heard," murmured one of the engineers, his voice still trembling with awe. "Like the rhythm of the earth itself."

"Did you at least record it?" asked others, hungry to hear the sound that had stunned them. The engineer could only shake his head. He had forgotten to press *record*. "It was supposed to be a simple jam session—nothing worth saving. I didn't think..." His voice trailed off, eyes distant, as though he still stood in that room, surrounded by the music that would never be heard again.

Sivamani remained the most shaken. "We weren't playing the music," he told his colleagues one evening, his hands still trembling as they hovered over his drums. "It was playing us. I don't know who that boy was... but that sound—*his sound*—it will never leave me."

No one saw Tambi again. He was gone as suddenly as he had come, leaving behind a silence that felt louder than the music itself. Those who had witnessed it tried to move on, yet they carried with them the weight of something divine—a brief moment where the ordinary had touched the extraordinary.

Kalaha had seen it too. When his gaze met Pravash's on that street in Kolkata, the connection had been undeniable—a fleeting moment that stretched into eternity. It was then that Kalaha had known why they had been called to Kolkata, why they had walked those streets, and why Soham's path had led them here. The threads of fate were tightening, binding lives and souls together, pulling them toward something neither the mortal world nor the gods could yet comprehend.

THE UNINVITED RAIN IN WASHINGTON DC

1993 – Washington DC, USA

A few months ago, when the echoes of Soham's cry in Kolkata still rippled through unseen realms, it had torn through time and space. It touched Tejomayi, Pravash, and—on the other side of the world—it woke a man from his deep sleep.

The rain came uninvited. It fell from the sky in heavy sheets, pattering against the windows of the White House and soaking the empty streets in an unseasonal deluge. The kind of rain that did not belong to Washington D.C.—as though summoned from elsewhere, pulled into existence by the quiet turmoil of a single man.

A figure stepped out from the pristine gates of the White House. The streetlights flickered faintly as if straining to hold his shadow. He was a man of quiet authority—early forties, well-built, and immaculate in appearance. His sharp features were framed by a black overcoat and a hat pulled low, shielding his eyes from the downpour. But even the rain could not mask the tension etched into his brow, a tension that seemed to weigh heavier than the storm itself.

The Secret Service SUV waited for him, its black frame glistening under the rain's relentless assault. Without a word, he climbed into the back seat. The driver didn't ask questions. This was routine—a man who required no explanations, only silence.

The SUV glided through the empty streets, the windshield wipers battling against the sheets of rain. Seven miles passed before the man raised his hand, a single gesture that halted the car. The driver stopped near a corner where an old **public telephone booth** stood—its faded paint peeling, its glass fogged by condensation.

The man stepped out, his black boots splashing into a shallow puddle. The rain lashed at him mercilessly, but he walked unfazed, his coat flaring behind him as though the storm itself bowed to his presence. The clouds above seemed to roil, their fury mirroring the quiet storm in his mind.

He paused briefly at the telephone booth, his gloved hand brushing against the glass. The soft hum of the storm seemed to falter for just a moment—as though waiting.

Pulling the door shut behind him, the man stood in the narrow, dimly lit space, the scent of rain and rust thick in the air. Droplets fell from the brim of his hat, sliding down the glass in uneven trails. He reached into his pocket and pulled out a coin—small, silver, and etched with symbols too old for this world.

Clink.

The coin fell into the slot. The rotary dial turned slowly under his gloved fingers, each click cutting through the muffled sound of the rain. The connection crackled to life, static hissing softly on the other end of the line.

He spoke.

His voice was deep—commanding, yet calm—like thunder rumbling far in the distance. Words carefully measured, deliberate, as though each carried a weight too great to bear.

"*Something has stirred.*"

The silence on the other end was palpable, heavy with anticipation. He closed his eyes for a moment, rain dripping from his hat onto the floor, his breath slow and deliberate.

"A vibration tore through the air tonight. I felt it—powerful enough to wake me. Powerful enough to shake... everything."

The static crackled louder, as though the line itself were alive, waiting for him to continue.

"This should not have happened." His grip on the receiver tightened. *"If something this strong exists, we should have known. But we did not. Something this powerful, hidden from us... might threaten what we have been protecting for thousands of years."*

He paused, as if piecing his thoughts together, then his voice dropped—quieter now, almost like a whisper meant only for the storm to hear.

"Someone is hiding it. Someone... or something."

The rain outside intensified, pounding against the glass walls of the booth, matching the sharp tension in his words.

His final statement came, low and resolute.

"It's time for the Nine to meet."

With that, he returned the receiver to its place, the soft *click* echoing unnaturally loud. For a moment, the man stood still, the rain outside blurring the glass, making him a shadow amidst shadows.

He stepped back into the storm, his overcoat trailing behind him. The waiting SUV pulled forward again, and he climbed in without looking back.

As the black vehicle vanished into the night, the rain began to slow—its purpose, it seemed, fulfilled.

PART 2

ECHOES OF ETERNITY

CHAPTER 8

Shadows to Sanctuary

EVIL BABA!!

1994 – Ghaggar-Nagar, Rajasthan

Nearly a year after Paramarishi had settled in a quiet hermitage on the outskirts of **Ghaggar-Nagar** in Rajasthan. The villagers whispered tales of the mysterious death of Vikram—the son of the region's notorious MLA and liquor mafia head—**Gurpreet Kandola**. None could explain what had happened that night. Meanwhile the hermitage where Tejomayi and Paramarishi were living in its isolated walls, shaded under ancient banyan trees, kept them untouched by the chaos of the outside world.

Paramarishi, however, was not at peace.

The incident by the lake still haunted him—the moment Tejomayi, seized by a cry that tore through her very being, had leapt into the water. He had pulled her out unconscious, her small frame gripped by something he could not yet fathom. To soothe her heart and perhaps distract her mind, Paramarishi decided to take her to Ghaggar-Nagar's **Gauri-Shankar Temple** for the Mahashivratri celebrations.

On the eve of Mahashivratri, however, that peace dissolved into vibrant celebration. The temple courtyard had transformed into a sea of colors and sounds, drawing thousands from neighboring villages. Stalls lined the fairgrounds like rows of jewels—vibrant bangles shimmering under lantern light, embroidered shawls and sarees glowing in hues of crimson and gold, and fragrant flower garlands swaying gently in the evening breeze. The air carried the tempting aroma of deep-fried sweets and savory *samosas*, mingling with the heady scent of marigold and incense.

Children darted about squealing with joy, their hands clutching kites, wooden toys, and spinning tops. Elders strolled leisurely, savoring the festive air with nostalgic smiles, their voices mingling with the distant clang of temple bells. The entire town seemed to hum with a rhythm of devotion and revelry—an unspoken promise of divine blessings on the sacred night ahead.

Amidst this jubilance, Paramarishi and Tejomayi made their way through the swamp. Tejomayi, her tiny feet kicking up dust, clutched Paramarishi's hand as her wide eyes drank in the colors and chaos. Dressed in a simple white frock with golden embroidery, she stood out, her innocent laughter like music among the temple bells.

The evening before the great night of Mahashivratri, the temple grounds hosted a special *pravachan* by an influential guru—known to the villagers as *Baba Maheshwaranand*. The courtyard transformed into an audience hall, where thousands—farmers, mothers, children, and merchants—sat spellbound, their eyes locked on the grand stage.

The Baba, clad in elaborate **saffron robes** embroidered with gold, was a master of spectacle. His voice boomed through the microphone, a tone drenched in authority and charisma. Beside him, young women draped in **saffron sarees** and men in orange kurtas served as his "devoted staff," moving about the stage with choreographed precision.

"Bring forth your problems, and Lord Shiva's blessings shall cure you!" the Baba declared, spreading his arms wide.

The crowd erupted into chants of *"Jai Shiv Shambhu!"*, their voices thundering back to him in hypnotic unison.

On stage, one by one, "miracles" unfolded. A limping man approached, leaning heavily on a staff. The Baba placed a hand on his forehead, murmured a mantra, and—**as if by magic**—the man dropped his staff, walking without aid to wild applause.

A woman in tears sobbed about her runaway husband who'd stolen her jewellery. With a dramatic wave of his hands, Baba summoned an assistant who produced the very jewellery she had described. "Take this, my child," he said, his voice dripping with false compassion. "Shiva has blessed you with freedom from your sorrow."

Every act ended with his triumphant cry of *"Jai Shiv Shambhu!"* echoed by thousands.

Among the sea of faces in the crowd, Tejomayi's curious gaze landed on a peculiar man near the front. He stood out—not for his reverence but his strange appearance. His paralyzed lips twisted sideways into a permanent sneer, and beneath his dhoti, a tied-up leg hinted at a missing limb. His other foot turned oddly outward, adding to his grotesque gait.

To Tejomayi, his unmoving expression seemed deliberate, as though mocking her. Anger flashed in her eyes. *Is he teasing me?*

The man's face didn't change. Annoyed, she stuck out her tongue at him in playful retaliation—but still, he didn't respond.

When two men helped him to the stage—presumably seeking Baba's "miracle"—Tejomayi's frustration bubbled over. Without a word, Tejomayi slipped free. The crowd closed after her like water.

The stage buzzed with excitement as the Baba began his act. The strange man sat at the center, his crooked face and "missing leg" drawing sympathetic gasps from the audience. Baba raised his arms theatrically, signalling the crowd to chant.

From behind, unseen by anyone, a tiny figure crept onto the stage. Tejomayi, small and determined, approached the man and pinched his hidden "paralyzed" leg.

The result was instantaneous and explosive.

The man let out a yelp of pain, jumping to his feet. The tied-up leg sprang free, both feet now planted firmly on the ground. His crooked mouth straightened as he cried out, his face contorted not with paralysis but with shock.

The crowd froze in stunned silence.

Tejomayi, oblivious to the gravity of what she had done, raced to the microphone like any gleeful child discovering a new toy. She gripped it with both, her voice ringing through the speakers—

"Jai Shiv Shambhu!!"

The crowd roared back, laughter spilling into their chants. They thought it was part of the act.

Baba froze for a moment when Tejomayi's laughter rang through the microphone—a sound innocent and pure, yet so wildly out of place amidst his orchestrated solemnity. His calculating mind spun into action as he caught the crowd's stunned, uncertain gazes. He could feel their faith teetering on the edge of doubt, a fragile thing that could shatter at any moment.

Then, with the flair of a seasoned performer, He dramatically dropped to his knees, his saffron robes pooling around him like molten gold. His face contorted into an expression of utter awe as he raised his trembling hands toward Tejomayi.

"*Hey Maa*!" he cried, his voice booming with desperation and reverence. "You have come in this child's form! I knew it—I knew today you would descend!"

The audience gasped as though the earth itself had shifted beneath them. A wave of whispers rippled through the crowd:

"Is it true?"

"Maa Durga has come?"

"Baba ji had foretold this!"

Baba's voice rose above the growing murmurs, loud and commanding, yet steeped in trembling awe. He gestured wildly to the sky as though communing with the heavens.

"*Today, Maa Durga*—the mother of the universe—has graced us with her presence! And I… I had kept a temple ready for you, *Maa*, at my humble *Minai Ashram*!"

The name struck like a gong through the crowd: *Minai Ashram*—a place shrouded in rumors, a sprawling compound about 450 KMs away from Ghaggar-Nagar, in outskirts of Jodhpur, Rajasthan.

"Only yesterday," Baba continued, his voice breaking in feigned emotion, "I decorated your temple, knowing you would come. Minai Ashram was built for you, Maa—for your divine refuge, where you shall reside and bless your children!"

As the crowd erupted into chants of *"Jai Shiv Shambhu! Jai Mata Di!"*, Baba gave a subtle signal with his eyes to his attendants standing in the shadows.

On stage, Tejomayi blinked in confusion as Baba fell at her feet. The sight of a grown man bowing to her was so absurd that she giggled—a bright, bubbly laugh that echoed across the temple grounds. Her tiny hands reached instinctively to push at the man's hunched shoulders as though shooing him away, but Baba seized this gesture as a blessing.

"See! Maa has blessed me!" he shouted, pointing to the little girl, his voice vibrating with false ecstasy. The crowd roared louder, their doubts swept away by the tide of Baba's theatrics.

Two saffron-draped women hurried forward, their faces solemn, their movements rehearsed. One of them knelt beside Tejomayi and gently placed a saffron shawl—silken and heavy—over her small shoulders. Its ends trailed down her back, far too large for her frame.

"Maa, this is your robe," the woman whispered, her voice syrupy and soothing, as though speaking to a divine being. "Wear it, and let us serve you."

Tejomayi, still caught in the excitement, let out another giggle as she spun in place to make the shawl swirl. Her innocence only deepened the illusion to the crowd. They gasped, pointing and bowing. Some began to weep openly, pressing their foreheads to the dusty ground in worship.

At the edge of the crowd, Paramarishi felt his blood turn cold.

He saw her—on the stage.

"Tejomayi!" he shouted, forcing his way forward.

Shoving past villagers, Paramarishi reached the edge of the stage. "Stop this madness!" he shouted hoarsely, his voice drowned by the chants of "*Jai Mata Di! Jai Shiv Shambhu!*"

Baba noticed him immediately. His sharp, predatory gaze narrowed. With a slight flick of his wrist, he signalled to his guards—hulking men in saffron kurtas, their eyes cold and unfeeling.

Two guards pushed through the crowd and grabbed Paramarishi roughly.

"Careful, brother," one sneered, his breath reeking of liquor. "You don't want to disrupt Babaji's blessings."

"I said—let her go!" Paramarishi cried, struggling against their grip.

A well-aimed elbow to his ribs sent him stumbling to the ground. The impact stole the breath from his lungs. Another guard delivered a sharp blow to his head. Blood trickled down Paramarishi's temple as he watched helplessly, his vision swimming.

From the stage, Baba's voice rang out louder than ever:

"Maa Durga! The temple at Minai Ashram awaits you! Let me take you there, where you can bless all of humanity!"

The crowd erupted again, drowning out Paramarishi's broken cries.

Meanwhile, two attendants ushered Tejomayi gently but firmly toward the back of the stage. "Come, Maa," one said softly, holding her hand. "We have sweets for you, and your temple awaits."

They led her behind the curtains, away from the crowd's eyes. One of the women knelt and offered her a small silver tray filled with brightly colored candies, their sugary scent wafting into the air.

"Here, Maa," she cooed. "Take these. You must be tired."

Tejomayi, still basking in the excitement and unaware of the danger, smiled as she reached for a sweet.

From the ground, Paramarishi watched as Tejomayi disappeared from view. Rage and desperation surged through him, giving him strength to rise, his voice hoarse and broken:

"Tejomayi!"

The guards shoved him back again, laughing cruelly.

"Go home, old man," one sneered. "Goddess has chosen her place."

Paramarishi staggered, blood mixing with the dust at his feet. His gaze locked on the stage—now empty of the girl he had sworn to protect. His mind raced, heart pounding as realization sank in.

THE LAST DARSHAN

1994 – Ghaggar-Nagar, Rajasthan

The morning sun spilled lazily over Ghaggar-Nagar, but for Paramarishi, the world had gone dark. He stumbled into the village police station, messy and desperate. His voice trembled as he pleaded with the constables.

"My daughter... My child has been kidnapped," Paramarishi gasped, his face streaked with dust and tears.

The constable behind the counter leaned back lazily, unimpressed. "Who took her?"

"Baba Maheshwaranand!" Paramarishi cried. "He took her! He's claiming she's Maa Durga. She's not *Maa*! She's just a child—my child!"

The name froze the room. The constable exchanged a glance with his colleague, his expression turning smug. He stood and patted Paramarishi's shoulder as if speaking to a delusional man.

"*Baba ji* hasn't taken your daughter. Maa Durga has descended to bless us all," he said smoothly. "You should be proud—you're the chosen one. Now go back. Forget her. She belongs to all of us now."

"No!" Paramarishi shouted, his fists slamming against the counter. "She's *my daughter*! Help me!"

"Chal, *baba,* don't create a scene," one of the officers sneered, grabbing Paramarishi by his arms. "You're lucky—most men would beg to be the father of a goddess."

"I'll take this to someone else!" Paramarishi screamed as they pushed him out onto the dusty street. A final shove sent him sprawling to the ground. One of the officers spits near him, muttering, "Go home, old man. You're wasting everyone's time."

For the entire day leading up to the *Last Darshan*, Tejomayi lay in an unnatural slumber, drugged by the sweets fed to her backstage. Her tiny frame had been dressed in layers of crimson silk, her small wrists adorned with golden bangles that clinked softly as she breathed. She had been positioned on an elaborate throne-like chair, surrounded by garlands of marigold flowers and incense so thick it hung in the air like a fog.

The *Last Darshan* had been announced—a chance for thousands of devotees to seek blessings from the divine child who had "descended as Maa Durga" before she leaves for Minai Ashram.

From morning until dusk, a river of humanity wound its way to the temple. People carried trays of flowers, incense, milk, and coins. Mothers wept openly, begging for blessings to cure their sick children. Fathers whispered prayers for prosperity and salvation.

Tejomayi, asleep and unaware, was fanned constantly by two attendants who murmured soft praises in her ear. Occasionally, her head lolled to the side, and the devotees gasped in reverence as though it was a sign.

"See? Maa is listening to us!" someone cried. "She is smiling in her sleep!" wailed another.

Paramarishi stood in the endless queue, unrecognizable. His face was swollen, his beard stained with blood from earlier blows, his torn clothes caked with mud. To anyone watching, he looked like a beggar, a man crushed under the weight of loss.

As he inched closer to the stage, his gaze fixed on Tejomayi. Tears welled in his eyes as he whispered, "Tejomayi..."

When Paramarishi finally reached the steps of the stage, the crowd was deafening. Baba Maheshwaranand stood at the front, hands raised in triumph. "See, my children! Maa Durga sits before us!" he proclaimed, his voice thundering through the speakers. "Her blessings are upon you all!"

The chants of *"Jai Mata Di! Jai Shiv Shambhu!"* grew louder, drowning Paramarishi's broken cries. The guards flanking Baba sneered as they spotted him, grabbing his arms before he could set foot on the stage.

"*Baba ji* has chosen her. You have no claim here!" one of them hissed, shoving Paramarishi back.

"Tejomayi!" Paramarishi screamed.

The sound of his voice broke through the fog of Tejomayi's drugged stupor. Her heavy eyelids fluttered open, her vision blurry. For a moment, she could only see the bright orange robes of Baba Maheshwaranand standing in front of her. But then—through the sea of faces—her gaze locked onto a familiar figure.

"Baba!" she cried, her voice cutting through the chants like lightning.

The chants faltered. Gasps rippled outward.

Baba Maheshwaranand's face twisted with fury as he stepped in front of her, blocking her view. "I am your Baba now," he hissed, his voice low and threatening.

But Tejomayi's gaze remained fixed beyond him. She saw Paramarishi's pained face and the guards holding him back. A surge of emotion—fear, anger, and instinct—coursed through her tiny body. Without realizing what she was doing, she reached forward and grabbed Maheshwaranand's leg.

The crowd fell silent.

The massive man wavered.

Before he could react, Tejomayi pulled with a strength no child could possess. Baba Maheshwaranand toppled backward, landing with a thunderous crash that silenced the temple grounds.

Gasps echoed like ripples across the crowd. People froze in disbelief, their eyes wide.

Tejomayi stood over the fallen guru, her small frame shaking with fury. Her eyes burned with a light that none could explain. Without hesitation, she lifted her tiny foot and brought it down onto his face.

CRACK!!

The sound of Maheshwaranand's skull cracking reverberated like a death knell. Blood pooled around his lifeless body, his face shattered beyond recognition.

For one unbearable heartbeat, the world stopped.

Then a scream tore through the crowd.

"*Baba ji is dead!*"

Panic erupted. People screamed and scattered in every direction. The stage trembled as devotees tripped over each other in their rush to flee. Dust swirled in the air, blending with the acrid scent of blood and incense.

Paramarishi, taking advantage of the chaos, broke free from the guards. He scrambled onto the stage, his trembling hands reaching for Tejomayi.

"Baba!" she cried again, tears streaking down her face as he scooped her into his arms.

"I've got you," he whispered hoarsely, holding her close as he pushed through the madness.

No one stopped them. The crowd was too consumed by fear, disbelief, and the sight of the lifeless Baba.

As Paramarishi carried Tejomayi away, her small hands clung to his torn kurta. "Baba, don't cry," she whispered, her voice soft and tired. "I'm here…"

Together, they disappeared into the narrow alleyways, the dust of Ghaggar-Nagar swallowing them whole. Behind them, the temple lay in ruin—its false god dethroned, its devotees left to wonder whether they had witnessed divinity… or judgment.

THE ROAD TO SOLAN

1994 – Hidden Forest in Solan district, Himachal Pradesh

Paramarishi's steps were heavy, but his grip on Tejomayi's small hand remained firm as they boarded the bus that would carry them far from Ghaggar-Nagar. The vehicle groaned to life, its engine roaring against the stillness of dawn. Tejomayi, cradled at his side, pressed her face against the window, her wide, curious eyes absorbing the world beyond.

The narrow, winding roads of Himachal Pradesh snaked through the mountains like ancient veins, each bend revealing landscapes untouched by time. Valleys opened like vast green carpets, snow-capped peaks gleamed on distant horizons, and rivers cut through the hills like silver threads. The air turned crisp and pure, carrying the scent of pine needles, wildflowers, and a hint of cool mist.

Tejomayi gasped softly, her face alight with wonder. "Baba, look!" she whispered, pointing toward a family of langurs leaping across a rocky ledge. Her voice brought a faint smile to Paramarishi's lips, though his eyes remained clouded with thoughts he did not speak aloud. He simply nodded, his mind fixed on the place they were seeking—one far removed from the chaos they had left behind.

Hours later, the bus slowed and stopped. Paramarishi stood, gathering their small bundle of belongings. "Come, child," he said softly, taking her hand.

They stepped down onto a small stretch of highway, isolated except for the faint hum of wind and distant bird calls. Around them, the world seemed untouched—dense forests lined on one side of the road, their canopies casting shadows that danced with the breeze. Solan, nestled in the folds of Himachal, was a quiet, hidden world far removed from the chaos they had left behind.

Paramarishi turned to Tejomayi, his voice gentle. "We must walk from here. It isn't far."

They left the highway behind and descended onto a narrow trail that led into the heart of the forest. The path, worn by time and feet long forgotten, was cloaked in shadows cast by towering deodar and oak trees. Their branches wove together like an ancient embrace, filtering the sunlight into dappled patches. Tejomayi walked quietly, her small steps matching Paramarishi's. The air grew cooler as they walked, filled with the rustling of leaves and the distant murmur of flowing water. The rhythmic murmur of a river grew louder with every turn, pulling them forward as though it were calling them home.

The dense forest opened suddenly into a clearing, and before them lay a small, serene house—hidden, yet waiting. Its walls, darkened by time and damp with moss, seemed as much a part of the earth as the rocks and trees surrounding it. A stone pathway, worn smooth, led to the entrance, shaded by the gnarled arms of an ancient tree whose branches stretched protectively above.

To the left of the house, nestled against the roots of the old tree, stood a temple no larger than a humble room. Its spire rose quietly into the sky, and the faint fragrance of incense drifted toward them. Within the temple, a three-foot stone idol of Maa Durga sat serenely, her form simple yet powerful. Though the ceiling above her was low and weathered, the idol's presence seemed ageless, a stillness so profound it touched the heart.

Just beyond the house, the Saraswati River flowed like liquid crystal, its gentle song mingling with the whisper of the forest. The water shimmered in the sunlight, curling around smooth stones and carrying secrets only the mountains knew.

A cow grazed peacefully by the entrance, her pale coat tinged with patches of earth. She lifted her head briefly, meeting Tejomayi's gaze, before lowering it again to the grass.

From within the house, voices stirred. Seven sages stepped into the light, their forms clad in simple, flowing dhotis. Their faces—weathered yet calm—carried an ancient wisdom that seemed to ripple outward like the river itself. There was something about them, an unspoken reverence that made Paramarishi's breath catch.

He let go of Tejomayi's hand and bowed low—his forehead nearly touching the earth. The act was one of pure, unwavering devotion, as though he had stepped into the presence of something divine.

"Blessings, Gurus," he murmured, his voice trembling with humility. "I bring her here, seeking refuge and guidance."

The sages said nothing. They exchanged glances, their expressions serene, as though they had been waiting for this moment. Their eyes lingered on Tejomayi, who clung to Paramarishi's side, her own gaze curious yet unafraid.

One of the sages stepped forward, his voice as gentle as the river. "Come, Paramarishi. You and the child are welcome here."

The house was simple and humble, its single hall serving as both a living and resting space. Pots lined the walls, and scriptures lay stacked in corners, their spines worn from use. At the back of the house, a small bedroom stood—bare save for a low wooden bed and a single window that looked out onto the river. It was given to Paramarishi and Tejomayi, a space they could call their own.

Tejomayi peeked through the window, her eyes lighting up at the view of the flowing water. The soft light of dusk painted everything gold, and for the first time in days, she felt a quiet joy settle within her.

Paramarishi sank to the floor, his shoulders finally releasing their burden. He looked up at the sages, his eyes glistening with gratitude. He did not need to say it aloud; they knew what he was thinking. They had always known.

The seven sages returned his gaze with a quiet understanding—one that transcended words. Outside, the Saraswati River continued its endless journey, and the winds whispered through the trees, carrying the promise of peace.

Tejomayi turned to Paramarishi, her voice a soft murmur. "Baba, is this our home?"

Paramarishi looked at her, a faint smile tugging at the corner of his lips. "It is, my child. It is."

And as the sun disappeared behind the hills, the hermitage became a sanctuary—guarded by the earth, the river, and the seven sages who watched over it.

THE COW, THE RIVER, AND THE GUARDIANS

1994 – Hidden Forest in Solan district, Himachal Pradesh

Life in the serene hermitage began to flow like the Saraswati River itself—gentle and unhurried, yet carrying something timeless within its course. The hermitage, hidden amidst the hills of Solan, became a small world unto itself, untouched by the chaos of men.

From the very first day, Tejomayi was drawn inexplicably to the lone cow grazing outside. The sages had named her **Surabhi,** but to Tejomayi, she was more than a mere animal—she was a friend, a silent confidant.

Every morning, before even the first glimmers of dawn touched the river, Tejomayi would tiptoe out of the house. Clutching a small basket—filled with fresh grass or grains she had gathered the evening before—she would whisper soft secrets into Surabhi's ear. *"You'll eat first, won't you?"* she would coo, her tiny hands brushing lovingly against the cow's warm flank. And when no one was watching, she would throw her arms around Surabhi's neck and bury her face in the comforting warmth, seeking something that words could never explain.

The sages often found her asleep in the haystack beside Surabhi, the afternoon sun warming her curls as she dozed peacefully. Her face, nestled against the cow's side, wore an expression of such innocent joy that it softened even the sternest hearts. "Khindni," the sages began to call her—one who scatters things everywhere. It was a name born of affection, for she had a habit of tossing books, slippers, and even prayer beads into odd places before dashing to hide behind Maa Durga's idol in the small temple.

The river Saraswati flowed like never before. Normally dry this time of year, its waters now danced tirelessly over stones and roots, weaving prosperity into the fields it touched. Villagers downstream marvelled at their bountiful harvests—golden wheat swaying under the sun, and green fields stretching far as the eye could see. Whispers of divine intervention drifted through the air, though no one knew of the little girl hidden in the forested hills.

It wasn't just the river that seemed to bend in reverence. Eagles—majestic and watchful—circled the skies more frequently, their cries echoing like omens. At night, serpents glided silently toward the hermitage, their calm presence an unspoken acknowledgment of something sacred. The sages noticed these signs, exchanging glances, but they spoke little. They already knew who Tejomayi was and chose not to question the cosmic forces at work.

It was on a quiet night, with the moon hanging low in the sky, that Tejomayi stirred in her sleep. Outside the hermitage, hushed voices broke the stillness. Paramarishi stood near the base of the ancient banyan tree, the faint light of the river dancing nearby. Opposite him, Sage Vashishth leaned against the trunk, his arms folded, eyes serene.

"I found this in the market today," Paramarishi murmured, holding out a crumpled newspaper. The headline glimmered faintly under the moonlight:

"Second Mystical Death Baffles Ghaggar-Nagar: No Witnesses Speak."

Vashishth unfolded the paper and scanned it, his brow lifting ever so slightly.

"The article mentions Baba Maheshwaranand's death. No witnesses, no suspects. Even the police refuse to speak of it, as if—" He paused, his voice trembling. "As if they truly believe it was Maa Durga's wrath."

Vashishth was calm as ever, but his gaze darkened slightly when Paramarishi continued.

"And there's more." Paramarishi's voice tightened, barely containing his anger. His hands shook as he gestured to the crumpled newspaper. "The women from Baba's ashram... they've come forward." His words were heavy, each one carrying the weight of their unspoken pain. "Young girls—helpless, innocent—kidnapped or sold by their families. Trapped in that wretched place for years, exploited, abused, silenced. They were too terrified to speak while Baba was alive, but now the truth is spilling out."

He paused, his voice dropping into a low tremor. "And it doesn't end there, Guru Vashishth. The article says Maheshwaranand used the ashram as a front for massive drug trafficking. His evil ran deeper than we could imagine."

Sage Vashishth let out a quiet sigh, his calm demeanor unbroken. "Yes. And now?"

"Now they've spoken of him as a monster. A demon hiding behind saffron robes." Paramarishi's voice broke with grief and disgust. "But no one saw what happened that day. They say Maa Durga herself punished him. That's what they believe."

Vashishth smiled faintly, though it did not reach his eyes. "You already know the truth, Paramarishi. What troubles you is not their belief—it's your fear."

Paramarishi turned to him sharply. "She's too small, Guru Vashishth. Too innocent for powers like this. I led her into danger. I failed as her guardian..."

Vashishth raised a hand, his voice calm yet resolute, "Your fears are not misplaced, Paramarishi, but remember—her path is already written, and so is her greatness. We know who she is, and though she is still young, she is not alone. We are here, all of us, to guide her and protect her until the time arrives when she must embrace what she is destined to become."

"And besides," Vashishth added, a soft smile tugging at his lips as he turned toward the temple of Maa Durga, its small spire glowing faintly in the moonlight, "she is Khindni, isn't she? Always scattering our belongings like leaves in the wind. Just this morning, I caught her slipping mangoes from our stock—so discreetly, you'd think she was a master thief—only to feed them to Surabhi like an honored queen."

Paramarishi's lips curled into a faint smile, but his thoughts lingered on another question. "What is her connection to Surabhi, Guru Vashishth? I've never seen her so attached to any animal before."

The sage's expression turned contemplative. "Surabhi is no ordinary cow, Paramarishi. She was meant to die—a fate sealed by human hands for their hunger. But someone intervened, someone whose love and sorrow left an imprint on her very soul. That bond still lingers, and Tejomayi feels it—because she is who she is, eternally bound to the one who saved Surabhi."

Paramarishi's eyes widened, realization dawning slowly. "You mean… *he* is already here?"

Vashishth's voice was soft, yet certain. "Yes. Sometimes, love leaves echoes in the simplest of beings. And when the time is right, those echoes call out and lead us to our paths."

For a long moment, silence reigned. The river murmured softly, its flow a steady companion to their thoughts. Overhead, an eagle soared through the moonlit sky, its cry sharp and clear, as though acknowledging the truth.

Inside the hermitage, Tejomayi slept peacefully. Tomorrow, she would scatter their belongings, feed Surabhi, and hide behind Maa Durga's idol. Tomorrow, she would ask the idol her childish questions again.

But tonight, the sages watched over her, their hearts burdened with knowledge and softened by love.

CHAPTER 9
The Nine

THE MEET

1994 – Trinity Island, Antarctica

Jan 1994 - The Southern Atlantic roared with an untamed ferocity, its waves crashing and curling under a sky heavy with storm clouds. Through the chaos, a sleek white yacht surged forward at an unrelenting speed of 90 knots, its hull slicing through the waters with precision. Behind it trailed a froth of white foam, the storm's dark clouds chasing as though unable to keep pace.

At the bow of the yacht, a symbol stood boldly etched into the gleaming surface: three equilateral triangles symmetrically arranged around a central point. The triangles rotated evenly, their design forming nine distinct outer vertices—a geometry so precise it felt almost divine, or ominous. The symbol carried no name, yet it radiated an unspoken authority.

Standing at the forefront was a man, his tall figure shrouded in a large black overcoat buttoned tightly against the biting wind. The high collar obscured part of his face, but what was visible spoke volumes. His features were sharply defined, his piercing blue eyes fixed ahead with unwavering intensity. A storm mirrored in his gaze—anger, tension, and a calculation that seemed almost mechanical. The silver strands in his neatly combed hair caught the yacht's lights, glinting against the backdrop of darkness.

The man's presence was as commanding as the vessel he rode. His gloved hands rested behind his back, their grip firm as though holding the weight of the world—or worlds—together. The cold Atlantic wind whipped against him, but he stood unmoving, an unyielding figure in a sea of chaos.

As the yacht neared a critical point—roughly 20 kilometers from Antarctica's Deception Island—shadows began to emerge from the distance. Polar patrol ships, their lights faint but deliberate, approached from all directions, converging on the lone vessel like a swarm of predators circling prey.

The crew aboard the yacht exchanged uneasy glances. Yet, the man at the bow remained motionless, his expression unchanged. The guard ships closed in, their sleek forms cutting through the water with practiced precision. Their intent was clear: no one went beyond this point without scrutiny.

But then, something changed.

The guards aboard the ships turned their gaze to the yacht's prow, their eyes catching the intricate symbol etched into its surface. A silence seemed to fall over them, even amidst the crashing waves and howling wind. One by one, the guard ships slowed, their engines rumbling to a near halt. A moment later, they began to peel away, turning back into the storm as though repelled by an unseen force.

The yacht pressed on, undeterred. Its speed barely faltered as it tore through the waves, leaving the now-distant guards behind.

Just little ahead, Deception Island loomed, shrouded in the icy mist of Antarctica, its secrets hidden within its harsh expanse. But the yacht had no intention of going there—not yet.

The vessel slowed as it approached Trinity Island, little ahead of Deception Island, its jagged cliffs rising from the icy waters like the remnants of a forgotten world. Small and desolate, the island seemed to exist outside the bounds of time and place. The vessel's engine hummed to a softer cadence as it docked beside another white yacht bearing the same symbol.

The man descended from the bow to the main deck, his boots clicking against the polished surface with deliberate, measured steps. As the yacht glided into the island's shadow, he stepped onto the narrow platform that connected the vessel to the shore.

The biting cold of the Antarctic air seemed to welcome him, wrapping around him like a second skin. He paused briefly, his eyes scanning the rugged terrain ahead. His jaw tightened, and for the first time, his expression softened—not in relief, but in anticipation.

The terrain shifted from jagged rock to a vast expanse of flat, snow-covered ice. Ahead, hidden in plain sight, lay a helipad—a black surface barely discernible against the white landscape, known only to those who sought it. Resting upon it was a black helicopter, its sleek form marked with the same symbol as the yachts.

In his mind, the man thought grimly: *Three have already reached.*

His eyes scanned the area—the helicopter, the yachts. *Jay and Vijay by air… Karthik by sea,* he figured.

As he moved further inland, a stark white structure emerged from the mist—a bunker, unassuming but fortified. Its small, airtight gate was fitted with a military-grade coded lock. Without hesitation, the man keyed in a sequence, and the door hissed open. He descended a narrow staircase into the depths below.

The bunker opened into a vast, sterile space of gleaming white walls and glasspanelled rooms—functional yet oddly luxurious, a hidden sanctuary. A cafeteria sat to one side, its shelves neatly stocked with essential food packets, coffee, and tea. Beyond were several meeting rooms, some with frosted glass that obscured their interiors.

The man headed to the cafeteria first, pouring himself a cup of coffee. The aroma mingled with the faint hum of the bunker's generators. With his coffee in hand, he moved purposefully toward an opaque conference room.

Inside, the room was stark yet elegant, furnished with a long table and high-backed chairs. Inside, waiting for him, another man in a black suit stood in the corner like a dark sentinel. His sharp, angular jawline was clean-shaven, his wavy hair slicked back with a subtle elegance, giving him an aura of fierce commander. His deep-set eyes, the color of molten amber, seemed to glow under the harsh white light, carrying both the weight of untold battles and an allure that was impossible to ignore. His presence was magnetic, a figure carved straight from myth and legend but cloaked in modern sophistication.

It was not just his looks that commanded attention—it was the sheer intensity in his gaze, as if he could see right into the soul of anyone who dared meet his eyes. Every movement he made, no matter how small, was deliberate, calculated, and yet effortless, betraying the confidence of a man who knew he held the reins to unimaginable power. This was Karthik, whose name, whispered among circles of influence, carried both reverence and fear.

Seated at the head of the table was Ved Vyas, the eternal scholar. His slightly curly, shoulder-length hair had streaks of grey that seemed to shimmer like silver threads, adding a timeless grace to his lean, weathered face. His warm, dark brown eyes were deep pools of knowledge, exuding a quiet wisdom that belied the storms he had weathered across lifetimes. A simple shawl was draped over his shoulders, and he carried himself with the humility of a sage and the quiet authority of a kingmaker. His every word seemed to resonate with the weight of ancient scriptures, each syllable laden with meaning.

The moment he entered, Indra's sharp gaze flicked toward Ved, his voice clipped but laced with a respect he rarely showed. "When did you get here?" he asked, his tone a blend of curiosity and authority, like a commander demanding a report from his most trusted general.

Ved glanced up from his steaming cup of tea, his expression calm and inscrutable. "I joined Karthik from Cape Town," he replied evenly, the words rolling off his tongue with the unhurried precision of someone who knew the importance of pacing—of revealing just enough, never too much.

Jay and Vijay sat opposite each other at the table, their contrasting appearances reflecting the dualities they represented. Jay, with his clean-shaven face and meticulously styled silver hair, had the air of a seasoned diplomat—charming yet intimidating when needed. His light grey eyes flickered with a quiet cunning as he sipped his coffee, his posture upright, exuding the polished demeanor of a man who could bend the law itself to his will.

Vijay, on the other hand, was ruggedly stylish, with a salt-and-pepper French beard that gave him a worldly allure. His dark grey eyes sparkled with a mischievous edge, a stark contrast to the seriousness of his brother. Dressed in a fitted navy blazer and an open-collared shirt, Vijay carried a casual charm, as though he could be just as comfortable negotiating billion-dollar deals as he could be sharing a drink at an exclusive club. Yet beneath that exterior lay a mind as sharp as a blade, always calculating, always two steps ahead.

The door opened again, admitting three more figures. First was a woman whose very presence seemed to draw every eye in the room. Anasuya, dressed in a tailored coat of ivory and gold accents, walked in with the grace of a queen. Her chestnut-brown hair cascaded in soft waves over her shoulders, framing her flawless, wheatish complexion. Her warm brown eyes held a motherly kindness, yet there was a steel-like resolve in her gaze that reminded everyone she was not to be underestimated. She carried the aura of someone who could cradle a child in one hand and command the stars with the other.

Behind her was Vishwakarma, his imposing frame clad in a rugged brown biker's jacket and a scarf that hinted at his practical, hands-on nature. His broad shoulders and weathered face, with a strong chevron moustache, gave him the look of a warrior who had traded battlefields for blueprints. His light brown eyes glinted with a sharp intellect, and his movements were deliberate, as though every step was part of a larger design. The scent of earth and iron seemed to follow him, a reminder of the worlds he had built—and destroyed.

The last to enter was Chitragupt, whose towering figure seemed to fill the room with a quiet, almost divine authority. His long, wavy hair framed his fair, angular face, and his deep black eyes, like twin abysses, seemed to pierce through layers of illusion to see the truth beneath. His white shirt and tailored black trousers were understated yet impeccably fitted, hinting at a meticulousness that extended to every aspect of his being. He carried himself with an unshakable calm, as though he alone held the ledger of life and death, and with it, the ultimate power.

Indra—watched as the last figure took their place at the table. His steely eyes swept over the room, lingering on each face. The tension in the air was palpable, the storm outside mirroring the storm brewing within.

"Shall we start?" Karthik's deep, resonant voice broke the silence. He remained in his corner, arms still folded, his gaze piercing. "Why was this meeting called so urgently?"

Jay glanced at the clock on the wall before responding, his voice measured but firm. "Let's give her a few more minutes before we begin."

Indra's jaw tightened, his patience visibly thinning. "No. She should have been here by now. We cannot all be in the same place for too long."

As if on cue, the door swung open, and a gust of cold air followed the final arrival. Menaka entered, her presence instantly captivating every man in the room. Her long, jet-black hair was tied in a sleek ponytail, accentuating her high cheekbones and perfectly sculpted face. Her fitted burgundy trench coat hugged her hourglass figure, and her thick-framed black glasses added an intellectual allure to her striking beauty. She was a vision of sophistication and charm, radiating a magnetism that made her the object of desire for anyone who crossed her path.

"I'm so sorry," she said, her voice warm yet commanding. "I had to finalize media and communication rights for the upcoming cable TV expansion in India." She smiled, the kind that disarmed even the harshest critics.

Indra's stern expression didn't waver. "Let's not get distracted by you turning the conversation to your world, as usual. Take your seat."

Menaka smirked, unfazed by the rebuke, and gracefully took her place at the table.

Indra began, his voice cutting through the tension like a blade. "How did this happen? Something powerful is rising. I felt a shift—a force that shook the very core of my being. It's unknown to me. Karthik, Jay, Menaka... use your networks to uncover any abnormal activity."

Before he could continue, Ved Vyas interjected, his tone calm but deliberate. "Abnormal activity happens every day, Indra. How do you expect us to sift through the noise to find this one thing?"

Indra's eyes flashed, but he managed a thin smile. "Do I need to remind each of you of your capabilities? Do I need to spell out what kind of abnormality I'm talking about?"

Ignoring Ved, he turned to Anasuya. "Check your satellites. If there's anything out of the ordinary, I want to know."

Anasuya leaned forward, her voice calm and methodical. "We've already picked up increased Ghraak and Raktan activities around the Arctic Circle, especially during the polar night. It seems they're exploiting the extended darkness. We need to secure and possibly close the North Pole portal immediately."

Jay's brow furrowed. "Has anyone been able to track them? If they keep spreading, we'll have chaos on our hands."

Karthik nodded. "My contacts in the northern military bases are already trying to contain sightings and mitigate panic, but they're elusive. Once captured, we'll send them back to the Isles of Rakta River, in north of Jambudveep. But containment must improve."

Indra shifted his gaze to Menaka. "Bermuda Triangle speculations are also rising again. The public is getting suspicious. Menaka, create compelling stories to distract and control these narratives. Keep them in the realm of myths and conspiracies."

Menaka smiled confidently, jotting down notes with a sleek pen. "Consider it done. Public fascination is my domain. They will stay entertained and confused enough."

Vijay leaned back in his chair, thoughtful. "Also, we have another minor irritant—the so-called Flat Earth Society. They're surprisingly close to deciphering some key geographical and mathematical discrepancies in our maps. While not a huge threat yet, we should keep a close eye on them."

Indra's eyes narrowed. "Ensure they remain fringe elements, ridiculed as conspiracy theorists, cranks, anti-social groups. They must never be taken seriously by mainstream academics or the media."

Menaka added, "Our technological advancements should help. If needed, I'll discreetly influence academic institutions and publishing houses. They'll remain a laughingstock."

Vijay nodded approvingly. "Good. It's under control then."

Ved leaned forward again, his tone measured. "And what of Kalaha? Narada lives by the name of Kalaha Dutt now. He's close to Mahabali, meeting him every *Onam*."

Indra smirked. "Kalaha. He's always been creative with names. Vedji, meet him. Find out what he's up to."

After several more discussions, each detailing their plans and concerns, Indra finally stood. He nodded at them all, acknowledging the gravity of every issue discussed—from demons in the Arctic to the Flat Earth murmurs, and the portals stirring rumors across the globe. But then he paused, his eyes darkening with something far deeper.

"All of these... yes, they're important," he said, his voice dropping an octave, more to himself than the others. "But what I felt—it wasn't just a threat. It was something else entirely. Older. More potent, far more powerful. It hasn't given me a moment of peace."

He swept his gaze across the room.

"Stay alert. The stakes are too high."

As they departed, Karthik lingered behind, his voice soft but firm. “I won’t let this slip again.”

Indra’s reply was equally quiet. “I know you won’t.”

Ved Vyas was the last to leave, his hand lingering on the table for a moment. His simple, earthy-toned attire reminded all of the humility that accompanied true knowledge. He paused at the door and turned to Indra. “Remember,” he said, his voice soft but steady, “it’s not always power that disrupts the balance. Sometimes, it’s faith.”

The bunker’s lights dimmed, and one by one, the Nine ascended to the surface and disappeared into the white expanse—yachts, rotors, and footfalls swallowed by snow—leaving only shadows behind.

SHADOWS AWAKEN

1994 – Ngari, Tibet

Year 1994 – Early February—The winds swept across the Tibetan plateau—sharp, cold, and laden with ancient whispers. Somewhere outside *Ngari*, Tibet, a small wooden house stood solitary against the snow-laden stillness, a quiet refuge where time seemed to pause. From its doorstep, *Mount Kailash* loomed a few kilometres away—majestic and radiant, its peaks shimmering like a divine sentinel under the soft glow of the fading winter sun.

Inside the house, the air carried faint murmurs—low, urgent, and cautious, as though the walls themselves could listen. Kalaha sat near the hearth, his face composed, his eyes reflecting a depth that seemed older than the room itself—a thousand unspoken thoughts held in their stillness. Across from him, a man cloaked in heavy, woollen garments sat, his posture slightly hunched.

The stranger's round spectacles caught the flickering firelight, momentarily obscuring his deep brown eyes—eyes that carried the weariness of millennia. His gaunt frame and weathered face told tales of time endured, yet his presence exuded both quiet wisdom and an unnamed tension.

"Nine has met, Kalaha," the unfamiliar voice murmured, soft yet tense, as if the very mountains outside might overhear. "They have seen the signs… and now they are alert. You need to be careful."

Kalaha remained still, his calm gaze fixed on the speaker, his silence a quiet acknowledgment of the weight of those words. Then, breaking the fragile stillness, the sound of footsteps crunching through snow reached their ears.

The wooden door creaked softly as Soham entered, an armful of firewood cradled in his arms. His cheeks were flushed pink from the cold, and snowflakes clung stubbornly to his dark hair. As he stepped inside, the warmth of the room embraced him, but his steps faltered.

He had heard it— *"Nine… signs… careful."*

Soham paused for just a heartbeat, his young mind racing to piece together fragments of a conversation not meant for him. Then, as he pushed the door fully open, the murmurs ceased. The two men turned toward him.

Kalaha's face softened, as steady as always, yet his silence felt heavier than usual. The stranger, however, froze mid-sip, a small cup of *po-cha*—Tibetan butter tea—hovering in his hand.

Their eyes met.

For a breathless moment, the world seemed to stand still.

The stranger's gaze lingered on Soham, dark eyes welling with an emotion that seemed to pierce through the veil of time itself.

Tears glistened at the corners of his eyes, catching the dim firelight like fleeting stars. It was not sorrow. Nor joy. It was reverence—an affection so profound it defied words.

Soham shifted, uneasy under the stranger's tearful stare. His brows furrowed, and he glanced toward Kalaha, silently seeking answers. Kalaha, however, remained motionless—his expression unreadable, as though letting the moment play out untouched.

The stranger set the cup down with deliberate care, his hands trembling slightly. Rising to his feet, he stepped toward Soham, his gaze never wavering. Then, with the gentleness of a father's blessing, he placed his hand softly atop Soham's head.

The touch lingered, a wordless benediction that left Soham more bewildered than before.

"Mmm..." the stranger murmured under his breath, his voice barely audible and trembling as though burdened by what he could not say. He exhaled sharply, grounding himself, and then stepped back.

Soham opened his mouth—questions bubbling to the surface—but the man turned abruptly toward the door, his movements swift and final. The door creaked as it opened, the frigid air rushing in to greet him. Then, without another word, he vanished into the night, his footsteps swallowed by the howling wind.

For a long while, Soham stood frozen in place, staring at the door through which the strange man had disappeared. The fire crackled softly behind him, the only sound breaking the tension that lingered like frost in the room.

Finally, he turned to Kalaha, his face etched with confusion. "Appa, who was he? And... why was he crying?"

Kalaha's calm gaze met Soham's, as steady as the mountains themselves. He held the boy's curious eyes for a moment before speaking.

"Come, Soham. Let's sit outside by the fire."

Soham hesitated but didn't press further. He followed Kalaha out into the crisp evening air. Outside, the night had fallen, and Mount Kailash stood bathed in moonlight, its silver silhouette rising against the velvet sky. Kalaha struck a fire, its flames crackling and dancing as the two sat side by side, sipping on the warmth of their own butter tea.

THE TALE OF KINGS, BARRIERS, AND NINE GUARDIANS

The fire crackled steadily, sending flickers of light dancing against the dark sky. The cold night in Ngari pressed in around them, but its chill was no match for the warmth of the fire and the reverence in Kalaha's voice. Soham sat cross-legged beside him, his hands wrapped around the small earthen cup of butter tea. The faint silver glow of Mount Kailash loomed in the distance, as though it, too, was listening.

Kalaha's face remained serene, though his eyes held a weight that only those who have seen beyond time can carry. He took a slow sip of tea before he began.

"Long ago, Soham," he said, his voice deep and measured, "there was a time when great kings and extraordinary beings walked upon *Bharath Kshetra*—the land we live in. Bharath Kshetra was named after King *Bharath*, the first *Chakravarti*—a global ruler—who was the son of Lord Adinath, the first Tirthankara. Bharath's brother, *Bahubali*, was a being of such immense strength and virtue that he could have conquered Swarg Lok itself if he had wished."

Soham listened in awe, the firelight reflecting in his wide eyes.

Kalaha continued, "But Bahubali was not the only one who was that powerful though he never disturbed the peace in Dev Lok, but then there were others—*Ravan*, *Hiranyakashipu*, *Mahabali*, and *Indrajit*. Each of them, through relentless penance and unwavering devotion, acquired powers that made even the *Devas* tremble. Some, like Indrajit, went so far as to conquer Dev Lok, the realm of Indra, the king of the heavens."

Kalaha nodded. "As you know, the Devas, though celestial, were not invincible. Whenever such a being—what we call a *Prati-Vasudev*—arose to challenge the heavens, it was always Vasudev, Lord Vishnu, who intervened. He is the protector, the preserver of balance."

The fire crackled louder as the tale grew heavier. Kalaha's voice dropped slightly, as if sharing a forbidden truth.

"But then came a time when Indra grew restless. He was weary of humans and Asuras achieving such power—always through boons granted by Mahadev (Lord Shiva) or Brahma. He knew that their determination and faith made them a force even the heavens could not contain.

One day, Indra went to Narayan and said, 'I cannot allow this any longer. I need to create a barrier between *Madhya Lok*—the earthly realms—and Swarg Lok so they can never reach us again.'"

Soham's brows furrowed. "What did Narayan say?"

Kalaha's lips curved faintly, his gaze steady. "Vishnu smiled at Indra's desperation. 'Do you truly believe,' Vishnu asked him, 'that a barrier will stop those who earn boons from Mahadev himself? What power of yours can stand against such devotion?'

Indra was perplexed. Frustrated. So he made another declaration. 'Then I will go to Madhya Lok myself,' he said. 'I will ensure no one looks up to the heavens to gain such power. I will lead them and make sure they are distracted enough not to gain such power ever again.'

Narayan's smile faded. His voice grew stern. 'Madhya Lok is not for you to lead or rule, Indra,' he said. 'If you try to block humans from their divine connection, you will become the reason for leading them into the darkness of *Dukham-Dukham*—an age of decline in this current *Avsarpini* cycle. Spirituality will erode, and the world will suffer.'"

Kalaha paused for a moment, letting the words settle into the silence. Soham's heart raced as he absorbed the gravity of what was being said.

"And yet," Kalaha continued, "Indra persisted. 'I will not rule them,' he said, 'but I will ensure they do not rise to great power. I will take eight others with me—together, we will influence the leaders of Madhya Lok. From the shadows, we will guide them to prevent any threat from rising against Swarg Lok.'"

Kalaha's tone darkened, a shadow falling over his face. "At this, Vishnu finally agreed, but he set forth *rules*—laws that Indra should not defy."

THE RULES SET BY VISHNU

Kalaha counted the rules on his fingers, his voice solemn as though reciting ancient commandments.

1. **Human Form:** "You must live like humans. Though you will be invincible in body, you will inherit all the weaknesses of human emotion—love, anger, sorrow, and longing. These will test you in ways power cannot."

2. **One from Madhya Lok**: "Among the nine, one must be chosen from *Madhya Lok*—someone who understands humanity. You may choose from *Ved Vyas*, *Parshuram*, *Hanuman*, *Kripacharya*, or *Vibhishana*. Others, like Mahabali, cannot leave *Ratna Prabha*, and *Ashwatthama* is bound until my *Kalki* avatar calls for him."
3. **No Control Over Free Will**: "You cannot take control of humanity's free will. Influence only. Choice remains theirs."
4. **Identities**: "Even though you will be immortal in Madhya Lok, you must remain hidden. You cannot stay in one place for more than nine years and must keep shifting identities, so no generation recognizes you from the past."
5. **Delegate Your Celestial Duties**: "While you live in Madhya Lok, others must assume your celestial roles. One of the other 63 Indras will continue your duty in Dev Lok, with all 63 agreeing."
6. **Rule Through Influence, Not Power**: "You cannot rule Madhya Lok directly. You must operate from shadows, pulling strings through influence, never force."
7. **Return**: "You will return immediately if you become the reason for pushing Madhya Lok toward Dukham-Dukham—the final stage of decline in this cycle."

Soham sat speechless, the enormity of the tale sinking into him like the cold around them. "And Indra agreed?"

Kalaha nodded gravely. "Yes. Indra chose his eight carefully. '*Karthik, Menaka, Anasuya, Vishwakarma, Jay, Vijay, Ved Vyas,* and…'" Kalaha paused, as if echoing Indra's own hesitation, "'Yammm… mmm.. no.. Chitragupt, I will go with Chitragupt as ninth.'"

Kalaha stared into the fire, his voice softer now. "Vishnu smiled faintly, for he saw the truth Indra could not yet comprehend. By trying to save Dev Lok with mere threats, Indra had unknowingly planted the seeds for the rise of *Kali*—the *Prati-Narayan*, the darkness that would consume Bharath Kshetra before its ultimate reset."

Soham's heart raced, his thoughts swirling in the stillness of the night. "And the man today?"

Kalaha looked at him gently, his expression unreadable yet calm. "The man you saw was Ved Vyas. He knows everything about your previous lives, Soham. That is why his eyes filled with tears."

Soham bowed deeply, his hands folded in reverence toward the path Ved Vyas had taken. The title "The Great" felt inadequate to describe the weight of the man's presence.

As the fire crackled steadily between them, Soham sat back and stared into the flames. Its flickering glow mirrored the swirl of unease and curiosity in his young eyes. The cold wind carried the hum of Mount Kailash in the background, its silver outline now more imposing under the moonlight.

Finally, he broke the silence, his voice tentative yet determined. "Appa… the Nine. Who are they now? What are they doing in Adho Lok today?"

Kalaha's gaze shifted toward Mount Kailash, as though the sacred peak was answering on his behalf. For a moment, he was silent, his thoughts wandering to places Soham could not follow.

"They live among us," Kalaha began softly, his voice carrying the gravity of a seer. "Hidden but not absent. They guide from behind the veil, shaping the world in ways mortals cannot imagine."

He straightened, his tone taking on a deliberate weight as he spoke of each one.

"**Karthik** ensures the strength of nations, their defence and military."

"**Menaka** controls the distractions of the modern world—media, entertainment, sports, games and illusions that captivate humanity."

"**Anasuya** governs the realms of science and space, ensuring that humanity's reach into the unknown does not tip the scales of balance."

"**Vishwakarma,** the eternal architect, shapes the physical world. From towering cities to intricate machines, he blends ancient wisdom with innovation."

Kalaha's voice sharpened slightly, as though cutting through the veil of ignorance that hid these truths.

"**Jay** ensures justice prevails, guiding the systems of law and order to keep chaos at bay. And **Vijay** balances wealth and power."

"**Ved Vyas**, as you saw today, remains the eternal keeper of knowledge. His wisdom flows through the scriptures, guiding the dharma in Bharath Kshetra. It is interwoven into every sacred text and tradition, shaping humanity's understanding of the eternal truths. Recognizing the diversity of human minds and cultures, he ensured knowledge was shared in many forms and traditions, allowing each individual to find their own path to enlightenment. However, in doing so, he also saw the unintended consequence of division. The very traditions meant to unite often became reasons for barriers among brothers. He is the architect of language itself, crafting words that could bridge worlds, yet he remained quietly in the shadows, letting others take the stage.

Over centuries, as his teachings passed through time and translations, he observed with both pride and sorrow how they were sometimes misinterpreted or wielded for power by others. Yet, Ved Vyas's role remains unchanged—to inspire humanity toward understanding, even amidst the complexity of interpretations."

"And Chitragupt?" Soham asked, his voice barely above a whisper.

Kalaha's gaze darkened slightly, the shadows from the fire playing across his face. "**Chitragupt** where he tallied the lives of Adho Lok, ensuring that every action is weighed against karma. Now, his role is to record the balance between life and death, through medicine, health and wellness, a responsibility that carries the weight of the entire cycle itself."

Soham shivered, not from the cold but from the profound realization that these nine were not just stories but active architects of the world he lived in.

Kalaha's gaze turned upward to the heavens, his voice soft yet laced with power. "Together, they do more than lead. They not only protect Bharath Kshetra, but also the heavens above."

His eyes glimmered with a knowing light as he continued. "Above Bharath Kshetra lies a dome, an invisible barrier crafted by the Nine. It separates us from the greater cosmos, shielding us from forces that could disrupt the balance. The stars, the moon, the sun—all move just outside this dome, their light reaching us but never their presence."

Soham's gaze instinctively followed Kalaha's to the sky. The idea of an invisible dome enclosing Bharath Kshetra was overwhelming, its implications monumental. "But... there must be a way out?"

Kalaha's voice dropped to a whisper, carrying the weight of hidden truths. "There is. The mountain before you—Mount Kailash—is not just sacred. It is the gateway. It is the first of the eight peaks of *Ashtapad*. The others remain hidden, veiled by dimensions beyond mortal comprehension. Through Kailash lies one of the paths beyond the dome, a way to go beyond Bharath Kshetra."

The words hung in the air like a prophecy. Soham's eyes locked onto the radiant peak, its divine glow now infused with an aura of mystery and purpose.

"And one day," Kalaha said, his gaze meeting Soham's with quiet intensity, "you will have to walk that path."

Kalaha rose slowly, his robes brushing the cold earth. For a moment, he stood in silence, his gaze fixed on Mount Kailash. The fire flickered behind him, its light casting long shadows that stretched toward the sacred peak.

Without a word, he turned and stepped back into the small wooden house, leaving Soham alone under the vast expanse of the dome-covered sky.

Inside, Kalaha moved with quiet purpose. He opened an old chest tucked into the corner of the room. From within its depths, he retrieved a satellite phone, its surface worn but functional.

He pressed a sequence of buttons, his face calm but resolute. The faint hum of the connection echoed in the silence.

A voice crackled faintly on the other end, distorted but familiar.

Kalaha's voice was low and firm, carrying the weight of unspoken plans. "It's time," he said simply. "Begin preparations for the cruise line to Antarctica via the Indian Ocean. The tourism project must start."

CHAPTER 10
Whispers of Love

THE FACE IN THE WARFIELD

1993 – Kolkata, West Bengal

The air reeked of blood and dust.

Pravash stood in the heart of a battlefield—a vast, endless warfront where the earth itself seemed to tremble under the weight of death.

The clash of metal on metal, the war cries of warriors, and the wails of the fallen merged into a terrifying crescendo. Banners lay torn, swords buried in flesh, and arrows streaked like fire across the smoke-choked sky.

His chest heaved as his trembling hands gripped the hilt of an enormous sword, the weapon heavy with a burden he couldn't comprehend. Around him, shadows of warriors loomed—hulking figures with faceless helmets, their movements precise and unrelenting, as though puppets under an unseen hand.

Then he saw her.

Across the chaos, through smoke and bodies, she rose into view. She wore a crown of *seven golden serpent heads,* their jewelled eyes flickering as they swayed. Her lower half wound into a serpent's form, molten scales shimmering and shifting like liquid gold as they struck the dust in rhythmic coils. The upper half of her body radiated a glow that seemed both maternal and destructive, dressed in a pinkish-red saree tied like a warrior's drape. Across her chest hung golden chain-links fashioned into war armor, glimmering with the sheen of blood and dust.

Her face—terrifyingly beautiful—was streaked with blood and marred by small scratches, yet it bore the glow of an unshakable resolve. Wavy black hair flowed wildly behind her, caught in the gusts of war, a tempest answering her command. Her grey eyes, deep as eternity itself, burned with anguish and wrath—eyes that spoke of love and pain far beyond mortal understanding.

"*Mahendra! Look back!*"

The words tore from her throat—a cry so fierce, so desperate that it cleaved through the chaos like a blade of thunder.

Pravash's heart seized.

The name she shouted—*Mahendra*—clawed into him like an old scar being torn open. His body froze as the sound echoed in his bones, a part of him recognizing it, knowing it, though his mind failed to place it.

Before he could move, a sudden pain struck him from behind—an arrow piercing through his chest. His breath caught, his gaze still locked on her radiant figure. *Her cry. Her face.*

He stretched out his trembling hands toward her, as if reaching for something already lost. But then—

A blow struck the back of his head—silent and unseen.

A blinding white light consumed everything. His senses dissolved into nothingness as his voice erupted, raw and desperate.

"*Maaa! MAAAA!*"

The white light shifted into a harsh glare.

Pravash's eyes snapped open, his breath ragged and his body trembling.

Above him, surgical lamps blazed like miniature suns, their sterile brightness making him squint. Pain roared at the back of his head—a deep, pulsing ache where he could feel the faint tug of stitches.

"Maaa... Maa..." he muttered, his voice cracked, hoarse with panic.

"Pravash!"

The voice—soft yet urgent—cut through his confusion. His eyes darted wildly before fixing on the face leaning over him: *Meenakshi*. His mother's eyes, wide with worry, brimmed with unshed tears. Her trembling hands hovered over his damp hair, brushing it gently as if to reassure herself that he was still there.

"Where—where am I?" His voice scraped his throat. "What happened?"

Meenakshi's voice trembled as she spoke, though she tried to steady herself. "You're safe, beta. Don't worry. You slipped near the stairs yesterday... remember? You hit your head badly. The doctors are stitching you up now, just a few stitches. It's nothing serious."

Pravash frowned. *Stairs?*

The word didn't fit. Fragments flashed in his head —serpents, blood, that voice calling his name. *"Mahendra! Look back!"*

The cry still echoed faintly in his ears. He looked at his mother helplessly. "How... how did I fall?"

Meenakshi forced a smile that didn't quite reach her eyes. "It's all right, Pravash. You'll be fine. Just rest." Her voice carried the warmth of comfort, but Pravash felt the storm still churning inside him.

The hum of medical equipment buzzed faintly in the room as the doctors finished stitching his wound. He stared at the white ceiling, his heart racing, questions pounding louder than the throb at the back of his head.

Who was she? Why did she call him *Mahendra*? Why did her voice feel like it had travelled lifetimes to find him?

As he lay there, his mother's hand holding his gently, Pravash closed his eyes, trying to steady his breath. But behind the darkness of his eyelids, he still saw her—the warrior with the serpent crown, the pain in her grey eyes, and the scream that had shattered something deep inside him.

Outside the operation room, the wind whispered as if carrying secrets across time. Somewhere in the vast cosmos, threads that had long remained hidden began to pull tighter, weaving a story that had only just begun.

THE DIVIDE AND THE DEVOTION

1994 – Kolkata, West Bengal

Pravash didn't return from the hospital unchanged.

The stitches healed. The doctors reassured them. Life, on the surface, resumed. But something in the house had already begun to crack—and once it did, it spread fast.

The first sign came one evening when Pravash returned from a cricket match, bat slung over his shoulder, shoes still dusted red. As he approached the courtyard, he froze. Angry voices erupted from inside the house—louder, sharper than he had ever heard before. Balraj, his father, and Abhishek, his uncle, were in the midst of a heated argument. Words slammed into walls that had once echoed with jokes and evening prayers. Meenakshi and

Prabha stood between them, pleading, trying to slow the fire, but the argument only sharpened. Pravash stood still, unseen, listening as something fundamental broke. By the next morning, everything had changed.

The house no longer felt like one. Invisible lines split it cleanly down the middle. On one side lived Balraj, Meenakshi, and their children—Kanchan, Aakash, and Pravash. On the other side, Abhishek, Prabha, and their sons Prakash and Ankit.

The business that had bound the family together was also split in half, the divide running as deep as the hearts it tore apart.

Silence replaced laughter. The cousins avoided each other under strict instruction. Meals were eaten in separate corners, the clink of utensils filling the space where conversation used to live. Pravash often looked across the divide, catching a cousin's eye, only to look away again.

It wasn't long before Balraj made a decision.

Late one night, as the silence smothered the house like a heavy fog, Balraj quietly packed their belongings. By morning, the family had moved to a new house—small and humble—next to the Parshvanath Jain Temple in Kolkata.

The distance eased the tension. It did not lift the weight.

In the months that followed, Pravash drifted toward the temple—not out of discipline, but refuge.

The Parshvanath Jain Temple became his second home. Its serene atmosphere, the quiet chants of monks, and the fragrance of sandalwood and incense wrapped around him like a comforting embrace.

It was here that he first heard Acharyashri Padmasagar.

Acharyashri was no ordinary sage. His presence commanded silence. His voice carried wisdom not just in words but in the space between them, as though the universe itself whispered through him. When Pravash first sat among the crowd, a reluctant eleven-year-old, he had expected boredom. But instead, Acharyashri's words struck him like lightning.

"*How many days from your life can you truly remember?*" the sage had asked, his voice rippling through the temple like a gentle wave. "*Why do we let life slip by, unnoticed and uncherished? Why do we live as though the days are infinite, when every moment is a gift to be lived fully?*"

Pravash sat transfixed. The sage's words seeped into his very soul.

He began visiting the temple every day, sitting quietly among the disciples of Acharyashri, listening, learning, absorbing the teachings of the Tirthankaras. While other boys played cricket in dusty fields or laughed over stories of movies and games, Pravash spent hours in the temple, his small frame sitting still as stone, his mind wandering through realms of thought too vast for his age.

His siblings and mother began to notice the change. He no longer joined his classmates for idle games. At night, when other children returned home with scraped knees and dirty hands, Pravash would still be in the temple, lost in prayers and conversations with sages.

"*Pravash, it's late—come home,*" Meenakshi would call softly each night. She often found him sitting quietly at the feet of Acharyashri Padmasagar, his head bowed in contemplation.

"*Just a little longer, Maa,*" Pravash would reply.

Meenakshi watched her youngest son with a mixture of pride and unease. Pravash had always been a thoughtful, curious child, but his days at the temple were changing him in ways she hadn't anticipated.

At first, it was Acharyashri Padmasagar's speech on life—how each day must hold meaning, how moments define the essence of our journey. Pravash had returned home that night with a quiet determination, whispering those words to himself like a secret prayer.

But what began as a spark of inspiration grew into something far deeper. Pravash became engrossed in Jain teachings, devoring everything he could learn about the Tirthankaras, their lives of renunciation and wisdom. He sat for hours listening to stories of those who had attained moksha, learning about *Pratikraman*—the practice of introspection and repentance—and memorizing ancient Sanskrit shlokas and scriptures with astonishing ease.

His interests shifted dramatically. Subjects that once thrilled him—Maths and Science—began to feel secondary compared to his new obsession. He would talk endlessly about Swarg Lok, the divine realms of gods and goddesses, and the intricate workings of karma. Words like *nirvana*, *soul purification*, and *non-attachment* became part of his everyday vocabulary, his young mind grappling with concepts far beyond his years.

Initially, Meenakshi found comfort in his devotion, proud that her son was walking a path of knowledge and righteousness. But the unease in her heart grew when Acharyashri Padmasagar visited their home one afternoon.

It was a day like any other. Meenakshi had prepared food for the sage, as part of *Dharm Laabh*—the Jain tradition of offering food to Jain Sages, who live a material-free life. Pravash sat nearby, his eyes bright with reverence as Acharyashri entered the home, his presence filling the small space with serenity.

Meenakshi served him with devotion, her hands steady but her mind already restless.

"*Meenakshi-ji,*" he said, his voice teasing but layered with meaning, "*You've served me well today. But instead of food, why not give me your son? Let him live a life without possession, without attachment and walk the path of ultimate truth.*"

Pravash's eyes lit up at the words, his small face beaming with excitement.

Meenakshi, however, felt her heart drop. Acharya's words, though spoken in jest, struck a chord of fear deep within her. She realized, then and there, how far Pravash's mind had wandered from the world of childhood joys. If this path continued, she knew she would lose him to a life of renunciation far too soon.

That evening, Meenakshi sat beside Pravash as he pored over an old scripture, his finger tracing the lines of the shlokas. She placed a gentle hand on his book, forcing him to look up.

"*Pravash,*" she said softly, her voice steady but firm, "*you are too young to carry the weight of these teachings. They are beautiful, yes, but you need to live your life first—to play, to laugh, to be a child.*"

The next day, Meenakshi took matters into her own hands. She encouraged Pravash to join his friends for cricket matches, even taking him herself to a nearby cricket coaching class. She clapped for him when he practiced his shots, cheered when he bowled with precision.

At first, Pravash was reluctant, his thoughts drifting back to the temple and the tranquil words of the sages. But as time passed, his youthful spirit began to stir again. The joy of hitting a ball clean across the field, the cheerful moments with friends, and the thrill of competition slowly worked their way into his heart.

THE SPARKS OF AFFECTION

1995 – Kolkata, West Bengal

Year 1995. A year that etched itself into the cultural memory of India, as Mani Ratnam dared to bring to life a story that no one had ever tried to tell before. The release of *Bombay*—a film that unflinchingly depicted the conflict between two major communities, Hindus and Muslims—sent ripples across the nation. It laid bare the anguish of the Bombay riots, yet wove within it a tale of love and hope, embodied through the tender bond of a Hindu boy and a Muslim girl who defied the world for their love.

The response was immediate—and violent.

Across the country, theatres screening the movie became targets of violence. Protestors, outraged at its audacity, attacked cinemas in the initial days, shattering windows and setting fire to posters. Theatres became battlegrounds, and the government was forced to intervene, placing guards and police at entrances to protect both the audience and the story they had come to witness.

It was amidst this charged atmosphere that Pravash—now stepping into his teenage years—went to watch *Bombay* with his family. The excitement of the film's controversy only made him more eager to see it, his mind racing with curiosity about the events he had overheard adults whisper of.

Sitting in the dark theatre, the flicker of the screen illuminating his face, Pravash was swept into the world Mani Ratnam had created. He watched the riots, the destruction, and the pain with wide, unblinking eyes. But what struck him most was not the violence—it was the love.

The hero of the movie, a young Hindu man, stood firm against the world for the girl he loved, a Muslim. He defied family, society, and circumstance, determined to bridge the chasm of faith and prejudice with nothing but his love. Pravash felt his heart pound with admiration. *This... he thought, this is the kind of love, a life should have.*

The movie had lit a fire inside him. Love, he realized, wasn't soft or fragile. It was defiant. Brave. Worth standing alone for. His view of the Muslim community shifted—not through ideology, but through empathy.

Walking out of the theatre that evening, Pravash barely spoke. His mind replayed the scenes of the movie again and again. The hero's struggle to be with his beloved felt more thrilling than any cricket match, more meaningful than anything he had known so far.

Pravash, just thirteen, wanted to feel that kind of love—something so deep it could rewrite destinies. He wanted a girlfriend, someone whose presence would make his heart race, someone he could protect against the world like the hero in *Bombay*.

And yet, even as his heart brimmed with these newfound dreams, he couldn't bring himself to act on them. The image of Suhani flashed through his mind—Suhani, the girl who had once handed him a glass of water on a school bus when he had been quietly crying.

For years, Suhani had remained an anchor of silent admiration in Pravash's life. Her smile, her voice—it was all etched into his heart. Yet, despite how much she meant to him, Pravash could never gather the courage to speak to her.

He remembered the ache of watching her from a distance, of feeling a thousand unspoken words crowding his throat but never finding a voice. Even now, as thoughts of *Bombay* filled his mind with ideas of love and rebellion, he couldn't break past his shyness.

So he returned to what asked nothing of him.

Cricket didn't demand confessions. Only focus. Timing. The clean sound of a bat meeting ball.

But the fire that *Bombay* had ignited within him refused to die. Pravash began to look at the world differently—at love, at people, at life. Somewhere deep down, he promised himself that one day he would experience that kind of love, that kind of purpose.

THE FIRST BRUSH WITH LOVE

1995-1998 – Kolkata, West Bengal

For the next few years, Pravash's world revolved around cricket. His days were spent perfecting his shots, sweating it out on the dusty school playgrounds, and dreaming of standing on the field with his idol—*Sachin Tendulkar*. To him, Sachin was not just a cricketer; he was a god, a beacon of what greatness looked like. Pravash would hang posters of Sachin on his walls, imitate his batting stance in the mirror, and imagine himself smashing boundaries under roaring stadium lights.

But the road to watching a live match in a stadium, where Sachin's genius unfolded, was nearly impossible for a boy from a middle-class family in those days. Tickets were like gold dust, and Pravash's parents could barely keep up with his cricket obsession. Yet, this passion fuelled him. Over the next two years, Pravash's game reached new heights, and he earned a spot in the state-level school tournaments.

Unfortunately, his focus on cricket came at a cost. Studies, which had once been a priority, faded into the background. Pravash's report cards plummeted, and his teachers grew increasingly exasperated. Almost every other day, he stood outside the classroom as punishment, the weight of missed homework or failed tests hanging over him.

Yet, amidst this chaos, something unexpected happened—something that would forever change the boy who was too shy to speak to a girl.

One afternoon, Pravash stood outside his classroom again, his arms crossed, eyes fixed on the ground, avoiding any glance from passersby. He had grown used to the humiliation—until a sound broke through his sulking silence. Laughter. Not the cruel laughter of classmates mocking him, but something far sweeter.

He looked up.

Across the corridor, outside another classroom, stood a girl. She looked like an *angel*. Her cheeks were soft and slightly chubby, giving her face a round, cherubic sweetness. Her brown eyes gleamed with mischief and warmth, and her smile—it dripped with an innocence so pure, it almost seemed unreal. Her long, wavy hair cascaded down her shoulders, catching the sunlight as if she were surrounded by a golden halo.

Pravash froze, captivated.

She was laughing with her friends, her face aglow with joy. And then, she turned to him. Her gaze held his, and she waved playfully, teasing him with a mischievous grin. Pravash's face burned red. His heart hammered against his chest, and he quickly looked away, pretending to inspect the cracks in the corridor floor.

"Who is she?" he thought, his mind racing. He had never spoken to a girl, let alone received a smile like that.

Her name was *Saira*. He would learn this soon enough during a school recess when their mutual friend Shyam casually introduced them. It was an ordinary handshake, but to Pravash, it was electric. The moment Saira's hand touched his, a current seemed to jolt through his entire body. He had never felt anything like it before.

Saira was everything Pravash wasn't—bubbly, outgoing, and fearless. She teased him often, flashing that same mischievous smile that had first caught his attention. Her best friend, Yasmeen, quickly became a friend to Pravash as well. Yasmeen and Pravash shared a bond that was unique—she became like a sister to him, someone who could read his emotions even when he stayed silent. Her understanding, her quiet strength, and her teasing banter made her an anchor in Pravash's life.

Over time, Shyam, Saira, Yasmeen, and Pravash became an inseparable group.

But for Pravash, it was never just friendship. Saira's laughter, her sparkling eyes, and her easy kindness captured his heart completely. Whenever she came to watch his cricket matches, Pravash would feel his hands tremble on the bat. He would glance toward the sidelines to see her cheering him on, and no matter how nervous he felt, he made sure to play his best—for her.

Yasmeen, perceptive and caring, noticed the way Pravash looked at Saira. One day, when they sat together after school, she told him gently, "I know you like Saira. But... she's in love with someone else. Yusuf."

The words struck Pravash like a blow to the chest. He blinked, trying to mask his pain. *Yusuf...* He knew Yusuf—a fellow cricketer on the school team, someone he had always shared casual friendship with.

Days later, Pravash found the courage to confront Saira. He admitted to her that he loved her, his voice shaking with nervous honesty. "I know you don't feel the same," he added quickly, "and that's okay. I just... don't want this to affect our friendship."

Saira had said nothing in response, only offering him a small, sad smile. Pravash left with his heart heavier than before.

Yet, even in his heartbreak, Pravash remained Saira's silent supporter. He watched Yusuf closely, and in an unexpected moment of candor, he asked, "Do you have feelings for Saira?" Yusuf, unaware of Pravash's own emotions, nodded but added bitterly, "It doesn't matter. Her family wouldn't let it happen. My family won't either. Shia-Sunni differences... they'd never allow it."

Somewhere in his sorrow, Pravash felt an odd sense of relief. *Even Yusuf won't be with her...* the thought crept into his mind, and though it brought a flicker of selfish comfort, it also deepened his respect for Saira's pain.

Months passed. Pravash carried his silent love like a quiet flame, never letting it burn out but keeping it hidden.

Then, one night, everything changed.

The landline phone rang in the Rathore house. Aakash, Pravash's elder brother, picked it up. "Hello?" A pause. A sly grin crept onto Aakash's face. "Pravash!" he called loudly. "It's Saira!"

The name alone was enough to send a jolt through Pravash's body. He stumbled forward, half-believing his brother was joking. "Stop lying, bhai!"

"I'm serious. She's on the phone," Aakash said, barely hiding his smirk.

Heart pounding, Pravash grabbed the receiver. "Hello?"

"Pravash?" came Saira's voice—soft, nervous, yet somehow sure.

"Yes... Saira?"

There was a silence on the line, as if she were gathering her courage. Then, she spoke the words Pravash had longed to hear.

"Pravash... I think... I think I love you."

For a moment, time stopped. Pravash's mind went blank. Did he hear her right? Was this real? His heartbeat roared in his ears, and his face broke into an uncontrollable smile. He couldn't believe it.

That night, unable to contain his excitement, Pravash rushed to the bathroom and picked up his father's razor. His hands shook as he shaved for the first time in his life, leaving small cuts on his cheeks. He didn't care. Sleep was impossible.

19th March 1998—a date Pravash would never forget. At dawn, he was the first to reach school. His heart raced with anticipation as he waited near the gate. And then he saw her.

Saira stood there, shy yet radiant, her eyes meeting his. She walked up to him slowly, her cheeks flushed pink. For the first time, Pravash saw her hesitate—her usual confidence replaced by a quiet tenderness.

Finally, she whispered the words he had waited so long to hear.

"I love you."

Pravash's world shifted. His heart, which had carried so much longing, felt as though it might burst. *This*—this was the feeling he had seen in movies, dreamed of during sleepless nights, and imagined every time he saw her smile.

In that moment, beneath the morning sun, life itself seemed to stretch into eternity.

THE SCAR OF BETRAYAL AND THE FLIGHT TO SAIRA

1998 – Kolkata, West Bengal; Vadodara, Gujarat

In early May 1998, Pravash experienced a new world—one of stolen glances, shy smiles, and the kind of love that made time itself pause. He sat beside Saira in a dimly lit theatre, the screen glowing with scenes of romance and heartbreak from *Titanic*, the movie that had already captured hearts across the globe. Jack and Rose's story of impossible love mirrored something within them—pure, innocent, and untouched by the cruel realities of the world.

For the first time, Pravash held her hand in his trembling fingers, his heart racing. He felt her soft palm clasp back, as if sealing an unspoken promise. Their bond, so tender and unworldly, made the crowded theatre disappear into nothingness. At the film's most touching moments, Pravash stole glances at Saira's face—her chubby cheeks glistening with tears, her brown eyes wide with emotion, her sweetness radiating like the warmth of a sunrise.

From that day on, their love blossomed in the quiet corners of cafés and during long walks under Kolkata's dusty skies. They talked for hours—about their dreams, their fears, and sometimes nothing at all. Words weren't always necessary. Pravash would kiss her forehead every time they said goodbye, as though reassuring her, *I'll always be here.*

It was a love so pure that even their friends Yasmeen and Shyam admired it. Yasmeen, who shared a sister-like bond with Pravash, often teased him about his endless blushing whenever Saira was near. At times, Saira, Yasmeen, and Shyam would visit Pravash's home, laughing and chatting over endless cups of chai. Meenakshi, unlike many parents of the time, never once judged Saira's background. She treated her with the same warmth she showed Yasmeen—just friends, she believed, nothing more.

One evening, during dinner, Aakash couldn't resist teasing his younger brother. "Mark my words, Ma—your son is going to repeat *Bombay*'s story," he said with a playful grin.

Meenakshi shot him a sharp look. "Stop filling his head with nonsense," she scolded, though her voice carried pride. "My Pravash knows his boundaries. He won't cross them."

But soon enough, the illusion of calm shattered.

It was a Sunday. Pravash, Saira, Yasmeen, and Shyam sat outside the apartment, laughing and teasing one another, completely unaware of the storm brewing. Shyam slipped into the house, his face tense, and found Balraj sitting in the living room.

"Uncle," Shyam said, hesitating, "I think... I think Pravash is in trouble. He's deeply in love with Saira, and I'm scared he'll take some extreme step."

Balraj's face darkened. He rose abruptly and hurried outside, his hands trembling. What he saw broke him—Saira, standing beside his son, laughing innocently. Without a word, Balraj folded his hands before Saira and bowed his head. His voice was hoarse, trembling with both pain and desperation.

"Please," he said, barely above a whisper. "Leave my son alone. I beg you—go away from his life."

Saira froze, tears springing to her eyes. She looked at Pravash, confused and hurt, before turning to run. Yasmeen followed, calling her name, while Pravash stood rooted to the ground, numb.

His eyes darted to Shyam, who lingered behind his father, unable to meet his gaze. *You...* Pravash thought, his heart breaking. The betrayal seared into his soul, leaving a scar that would never heal. In that moment, he vowed never to trust anyone so completely again. He would draw his boundaries, walls no one could cross.

That same night, Balraj and Meenakshi decided to send Pravash away. By that same evening, he was on a flight to Vadodara, Gujarat, to live with Meenakshi's cousin.

Vadodara was a city unknown to Pravash, but it offered a clean slate. Within weeks, he became the heartthrob of his new school. His talent in cricket earned him a place as the team's opening batsman, and his quiet charm intrigued everyone.

When asked why he had joined mid-term, Pravash told his story—his love for Saira, the pain of being torn apart, and the betrayal he could not forgive. The girls listened in awe, their admiration deepening. Many of them said they had never met a boy who could feel so deeply for someone. Pravash became their hero—a lover, a fighter, a boy whose heartbeat was louder than his fears.

Amidst all this, three friends stood by him—Chaitali, Metali, and Hetali. Chaitali, especially, became a confidant, almost a best friend, though Pravash kept his emotional walls intact. He liked her company but refused to let her or anyone else become too close.

But love, like a fire, cannot be extinguished so easily. Pravash missed Saira every moment. His allowance, small and restricted, was never enough to make the costly outstation calls from PCO back to Kolkata. So he began stealing small amounts of money from his cousin's home, desperate for just a few minutes to hear her voice.

When they couldn't speak, the agony consumed him. Inspired by the dramatics of Bollywood, Pravash would cut his arms, hoping physical pain could ease the torment in his heart. Chaitali grew deeply worried for him, her concern evident in her eyes every time she saw the faint scars on his arms.

But trouble followed him here too. Chaitali, pretty and strong-willed, attracted unwanted attention from boys with dangerous connections. They saw her friendship with Pravash as a threat.

"You stay away from her," one of them growled, flashing a sword at Pravash. Another day, a revolver gleamed under his nose as they dragged him into a hostel, threatening unspeakable horrors if he didn't "make her his sister" or disappear.

Pravash said nothing. He couldn't afford to attract attention, not when he was secretly planning to reunite with Saira.

When Chaitali found out, her anger was swift and fierce. One afternoon, during recess, she stormed up to the boy who had threatened Pravash and slapped him across the face in front of the entire school. Her voice rang like thunder. "If you *ever* talk to Pravash again, I promise you it'll be your last day."

The incident only added to Pravash's turmoil. He knew this was spiralling out of control. *I have to leave.*

One night, with only 400 rupees in his pocket, Pravash scribbled a note and left it on his cousin's desk. It was a suicide note—his way of ensuring no one would search for him immediately. Then he slipped out of the house, his heart pounding, his mind set on one goal:

Reunite with Saira.

The train to Kolkata was waiting, and so was the girl who had promised him her love.

THE CALL FROM KOLKATA

1998 – Ayodhyapuram-Vallabhipur, Gujarat

The evening sun dipped behind the horizon of Ayodhyapuram, Gujarat, where the sound of bells reverberated softly through the temple courtyard. Though still under construction, the **Adinath Jain Temple** carried an air of quiet reverence, its partially completed spires standing tall—a testament to patience and faith.

Kalaha Dutt—now known as Vasudev in Ayodhyapuram—moved with practiced ease between the idols in the temple's sanctum, his voice carrying the low, melodic rhythm of the *aarti*. A **diya** flickered in his steady hands as he circled it before the marble idols, their serene faces catching the light in a glow of divinity. The incense smoke curled around him like whispers of ancient blessings, as laborers and visitors watched the modest priest lost in his quiet devotion.

The day's labor had wound to an end when a voice broke the calm.

"Ohh, Vasudev bhai! Telephone for you—from Kolkata!"

The diya stilled in his hands. For a moment, the only sound was the faint rustle of wind brushing against temple walls. Vasudev carefully placed the diya on the altar and walked briskly across the courtyard to the office.

Inside, he lifted the receiver, his expression unreadable, his tone measured. "Yes?"

"It's me," came Ariful's voice—urgent, clipped with worry. "Bhai... Pravash is gone."

Vasudev's jaw tightened, his fingers curling around the phone. "Tell me everything."

Ariful exhaled sharply, his voice trembling despite its control. "He's been missing since this morning. He left Vadodara, Vasudev bhai. They found a note... a *suicide note.*"

The words settled heavily, yet Vasudev's composure did not falter. "Where did you hear this?"

"*Yasmeen*," Ariful admitted, his tone softening when he spoke her name. "She still keeps in touch with his friends there. She heard it first. Pravash's family is in chaos—police are already involved, both in Vadodara and Kolkata. Balraj Rathore has pulled every string, but no one knows where the boy is. Some of Pravash's friends from Bharuch are also missing—they're hostel kids, Vasudev bhai. Yasmeen's scared. She's..." He hesitated, searching for words. "She always saw Asif in Pravash, you know? After you and Asif left Kolkata..."

The mention of **Asif**—Soham in those days—brought a flicker of something unspoken to Vasudev's eyes.

"And now?" Vasudev prompted gently, pulling Ariful back to the present.

"That's all she said," Ariful continued, regaining his composure. "She's praying for him, Vasudev bhai, like we all are. His family's desperate. They've checked every corner—every friend, every contact. Even the cops are at a loss."

Vasudev nodded to himself, his mind already racing—calculating timelines, routes, and possibilities with the precision of a man who left nothing to chance. Finally, he spoke, his words carrying the weight of quiet certainty.

"Don't worry, Ariful," he said firmly. "I'll take care of it from here. Tell Yasmeen not to speak of this to anyone. Not yet."

"Understood," Ariful replied, unquestioning as ever.

Vasudev placed the receiver down and paused, the faint sound of bells lingering like a distant echo. For a brief moment, his thoughts drifted to Ariful—an ally he had trusted forever. Before they left Kolkata, Baig had tasked Ariful to keep an eye on Pravash. And though Ariful had never asked why or how Vasudev foresaw what he did, he followed every instruction with the unwavering faith of a man who knew Kalaha Dutt's words carried far more than they revealed.

Vasudev wasted no time. Picking up the receiver again, he dialled a number only he knew. When the line connected, he spoke without introduction.

"You need to visit Balraj Rathore's home tonight," Vasudev instructed, his voice calm yet unyielding. "Tell him you are an astrologer. Say you've heard troubling news through his close relatives."

The man on the other end hesitated. "What news, Guruji?"

"Pravash is missing," Vasudev replied evenly. "But you will tell them this—the boy will return to Kolkata in four days. He will be on the Howrah Express."

A tense silence followed. "And the family?"

"Make sure you say this clearly—his mother must be at the station." Vasudev's voice sharpened.

The man's voice wavered. "What if they question me? What if they don't believe—"

"They won't," Vasudev cut in, his tone brooking no doubt. "Speak with conviction. Tell them the stars have revealed it to you. Use whatever words you must, but deliver the message. Trust me—you will not be questioned."

The man exhaled, his voice resigned. "As you say, Guruji. I'll go tonight."

"*Jai Jinendra!*" Vasudev said simply, then hung up.

The temple had grown quiet under the cover of night. Outside, the workers had left their tools—hammers and chisels glinting under the faint moonlight—while the wind stirred gently through the hills.

Vasudev returned to the sanctum, his steps soundless as he entered the half-finished shrine. The idol of Adinath Bhagwan stood at the center, the diya Vasudev had lit earlier still glowing faintly at its base. He placed another diya beside it, bowing low as he whispered softly into the silence.

"*He is not alone.*"

CHAPTER 11
The Call of Balance

TWILIGHT IN SNOW

1994 – Styrsö Bratten Island-Gothenburg, Sweden

Mid 1994 - The air was sharp and bracing, carrying the unmistakable scent of the North Sea. Pumpkin Peaches Point, nestled on the tranquil Styrsö Bratten Island in Sweden's Gothenburg archipelago, was a place of rare stillness in the heart of winter. The rocky coastline jutted out into the icy waters, each stone and crevice partially dusted with snow, while the waves lapped gently against the shore. The horizon seemed endless, blending into the pale, overcast sky, as though earth and heavens had conspired to shroud the moment in quiet introspection.

Karthik stood at the edge of the point, his tall, commanding silhouette framed against the muted light of twilight. Dressed impeccably in a sleek black suit with a matching black shirt and tie, he exuded authority and restraint. His gelled hair, neatly combed, barely moved in the cold wind, and his sharp brown eyes stared into the horizon, reflecting the weight of his thoughts. His broad shoulders and well-built frame radiated strength, but his stillness betrayed an inner turmoil.

The icy breeze tugged at the edges of his suit, chilling the air around him. Yet he stood unmoving, his hands buried deep in the pockets of his coat. His angular features, typically calm and decisive, now seemed etched with a quiet unease. The solitude of the island mirrored the storm within him, its wintry expanse a perfect canvas for his unrest.

The faint crunch of snow behind him pulled him from his thoughts. Before he could turn, soft, warm hands slipped beneath his arms, wrapping around his chest with a tenderness that reached deeper than the chill. A familiar scent—gentle, comforting, and filled with love—washed over him like a hearth's embrace.

Devasena.

Her embrace was a calming tide, easing the tempest inside him.

She leaned her cheek lightly against his back, her voice soft as a whisper of spring. "You're here with us now," she murmured, her words weaving warmth into the icy expanse. "Let us take care of you, my love. Leave your worries to the wind. Just feel me—feel us—and let everything else go."

Her words reached places no strategy or command could. He closed his eyes, leaning into her embrace as though her presence alone could ground him.

Devasena's radiance was a serene contrast to the stark, snow-covered landscape. Her small, delicate features carried the warmth of a Nordic winter sun. Dark brown hair framed her fair complexion, which was touched with the pink blush of the cold. She wore a white and pink high-neck sweater under a long black overcoat, her brown high-ankle boots leaving faint marks in the snow as she stepped closer. Her calmness was a perfect counterpoint to Karthik's storm.

"Rudra has grown so much, now as tall as you." she said gently, her voice carrying a note of loving pride. "He's become as handsome as his father. And Usha..." She smiled, her words tinged with a gentle pride. "She's blossomed into a beautiful young woman. I see so much of you in her, Karthik. It's been so long since they've had you close. They've missed you. We've missed you."

Karthik let out a long breath, his voice heavy with the weight of his thoughts. "It's your father," he said quietly, his tone filled with reverence and restraint. "He's troubled. He felt something—a disturbance. Everything we've done to keep Dev Lok safe... I don't know how many karmas we've tied ourselves to in the process. And now, he believes it's all in danger. I have the power of the world's defences at my command, Devasena, and yet I missed it. How could I miss it?"

Her arms slid down to take his hands, her fingers threading through his as she stepped beside him. Her touch carried the promise of solace, her words the wisdom of ages. "You carry so much on your shoulders, my love," she said softly. "But even you can't carry the weight of the cosmos alone. You've done everything with the purest intention of preserving peace. That matters more than you realize. And sometimes, no matter how powerful we are, the karmas of others unfold in ways we cannot control. Their burdens are theirs to bear, not yours. You can only guide, not dictate. Let go, Karthik. Let the universe play its course. You're here, with me, with us."

She lifted her head to meet his gaze, her tender eyes steadying him. "For now, let the universe take care of itself. You're now with me, with us. Walk with me. Let me hold your hand and take you home."

The tension in his body eased as he took her hand. Together, they walked along the snow-dusted path, the sea's gentle whispers fading as they moved inland. The narrow lanes of Styrsö were silent, save for the soft crunch of their boots on snow and the occasional rustle of Devasena's coat as she leaned her head on his shoulder.

Ahead, their modest Swedish cottage came into view, nestled amidst pristine white lawns. Its steeply pitched roof, framed windows, and golden glow spilling from within offered a perfect picture of warmth and comfort. From the lawn, the playful sounds of laughter echoed—Rudra and Usha teasing each other, their voices filled with youthful joy.

Devasena's smile deepened, her eyes alight with love as she glanced at Karthik. "Do you hear them?" she said softly, a playful lilt in her tone. "They're back to their little arguments. Let's go in before they wake the neighbors—or break something."

Her words lingered in the crisp air as they stepped through the snow-covered lawn toward the house. Snowflakes fell gently around them, settling softly as they walked into the light and warmth of their home.

WHISPERS IN THE HERMITAGE

1994 – Solan District, Himachal Pradesh

In autumn of 1994, Solan, with its mist-cloaked valleys and snow-draped peaks, had become a haven of divine purpose. The Saptarishis, sages of unmatched wisdom and mastery, had turned their hermitage by the Saraswati River into a cradle of spiritual and cosmic knowledge. Here, in the serenity of nature's embrace, Tejomayi had found a home unlike any other. Now fondly called Khindni, a name born of her playful mischief, she flourished under their guidance.

The Saraswati River, flowing beside the hermitage, seemed to embody the vitality of this sacred place. Its waters sparkled like a silver ribbon under the sunlight, carrying with them the essence of purity and life. Wherever the Saraswati flowed, it left behind a trail of prosperity—fields blooming with abundance, forests thriving with vibrant life, and villages rejuvenated by the availability of clean, life-giving water. It was said that the river's unbroken flow brought not just sustenance but also a divine harmony that blessed the lands it touched.

Amid this harmony, Tejomayi found her dearest companion in Surabhi, the snow-white cow whose coat shimmered like moonlight. From the moment they met, an unspoken bond formed between them, as if their destinies were intertwined. Surabhi followed Tejomayi with quiet devotion, her gentle eyes reflecting an understanding far beyond words. And Tejomayi, in turn, refused to let anyone else care for Surabhi.

Each morning, she would rise with the first light of dawn and hurry to Surabhi's side. The cow greeted her with a soft moo, and Tejomayi would smile, her hands already reaching for the comb she used to groom Surabhi's silken coat. "You're the most beautiful, Surabhi," she would whisper, leaning her cheek against the cow's warm side. Her hands moved with gentle precision, brushing her tail and feeding her fresh grass plucked from the nearby meadows. No task was too small or mundane when it came to caring for her beloved companion.

One morning, as the sunlight filtered through the pine trees, casting dappled patterns on the ground, Tejomayi rested her small head against Surabhi's flank. The river's soft murmur blended with the rustling of the wind, creating a melody of peace. "Surabhi," she murmured, her voice filled with innocent wonder, "do you think Maa Durga hears me when I talk to her? Maybe you hear her instead."

Surabhi answered with a gentle moo. Tejomayi giggled, her laughter light and carefree, like the tinkling of bells. Her voice carried the innocence of a child who believed in magic. Surabhi, as if understanding, nudged her gently, making Tejomayi laugh even more.

The sages often watched this bond from a distance, their hearts warmed by the purity of the connection. At night, when the hermitage grew quiet, Tejomayi could often be found curled up beside Surabhi, whispering stories about the stars or humming lullabies. The cow's steady breaths were like a heartbeat in the stillness, and under the vast blanket of stars, they seemed to belong to a world untouched by sorrow.

The Saraswati River, ever-flowing and ever-nurturing, was a silent witness to these moments. Its waters mirrored the moonlight as it wound its way through the valley, a constant reminder of the divine blessings that sustained this sacred place. Its flow brought not just life but a profound sense of peace and renewal, as if the river itself carried the whispers of the universe.

The hermitage, nestled by the Saraswati River, was a place of unparalleled beauty, as if nature itself had conspired to create a paradise. The river's waters flowed with an almost musical cadence, their crystal clarity mirroring the vibrant blue of the sky. Around the hermitage, fields of wildflowers bloomed in a riot of colors—golden marigolds, delicate daisies, and vivid violets swayed gently in the mountain breeze. Pine trees stood like sentinels, their emerald-green needles glistening with morning dew. The air carried a freshness that invigorated the spirit, mingled with the sweet fragrance of blossoms and the earthy scent of the riverbanks.

The animals of the region, as if drawn by the tranquillity of the place, roamed freely and without fear. Birds of every hue flitted among the trees, their songs harmonizing with the murmuring river. Rabbits darted through the meadows, and even the occasional deer was spotted grazing peacefully. It was as though the entire valley pulsed with life, a living mirage of divine harmony.

At the heart of this paradise was Surabhi, whose presence seemed as ethereal as the Saraswati herself. She roamed the meadows with a regal grace. To Tejomayi, Surabhi was more than a companion—she was a confidant, a guardian, and a source of unending joy.

It was during these early days in Solan that Tejomayi's life grew richer with the arrival of two extraordinary companions.

The first came on a brisk afternoon, as she practiced archery under Vishwamitra's watchful eye. Her bow, a finely crafted piece, was drawn taut as she aimed at a distant tree. Just as she released the arrow, a fierce cry split the air, and a baby eagle descended from the sky, perching on her outstretched arm as if it had chosen her. Its feathers were pure white, shimmering like freshly fallen snow, and its eyes held a sharp, knowing intelligence far beyond that of an ordinary bird.

Tejomayi looked at Vishwamitra with wide, amazed eyes. "Guruji, did you see that?" she asked, cradling the eagle gently in her arms.

Vishwamitra smiled, a rare softness in his otherwise stern demeanor. "This is no ordinary eagle, Khindni," he said. "It is a symbol of strength, courage, and loyalty—a companion worthy of a warrior."

Her eyes shone. "You brought him for me, didn't you?"

Vishwamitra chuckled and nodded. "His name is Tarkshya." He stepped closer, his voice brimming with pride. Tejomayi's brow furrowed slightly in curiosity. "Tarkshya?"

"Long ago," Vishwamitra continued, resting a steady hand on her shoulder. "Tarkshya served Vishnu himself, carrying him across the heavens in his divine battles. He is no ordinary eagle but a symbol of strength, courage, and loyalty. I brought him to you because I see in you the same qualities that he embodies. Just as he once carried Vishnu, he will now be your guardian, your protector."

Tejomayi looked back at the eagle, now resting calmly on her arm. His presence felt fierce yet comforting, like a silent promise of unyielding loyalty. "Tarkshya," she murmured, testing the name on her lips. Then she smiled, wide and bright. "It suits him perfectly. Thank you, Guruji."

Vishwamitra watched her bond with the eagle take root, pride glowing in his eyes. Tarkshya fluttered onto her shoulder, his young but sturdy wings spreading briefly before folding neatly against his sides.

A week later, another gift arrived, this time from Vashishth.

Tejomayi was sitting by the Saraswati River, watching Tarkshya hop and flap playfully along the water's edge, when she saw Vashishth approaching. He carried a small, white bundle in his arms, cradled like something precious.

Tejomayi stood, her curiosity piqued. "What is that, Guruji?" she asked, running up to him.

Vashishth knelt slightly to meet her gaze, his serene smile lighting up his face. Slowly, he unwrapped the cloth, revealing a tiny white owl. Its feathers were downy and soft, and its luminous eyes seemed to hold the wisdom of ages.

"This, Khindni," he said, placing the owl gently in her hands, "is Uluka. She is a symbol of wisdom and foresight, gifts that you must cherish and cultivate. While Tarkshya is your strength, Uluka will be your guide. She will teach you patience, understanding, and the importance of silence in the face of chaos. And one day…" He paused, his smile deepening. "One day, you may even ride her."

Tejomayi's mouth fell open in awe as she held Uluka close, the owl blinking up at her with unhurried grace. "Ride her?" she asked, her voice filled with wonder.

"Indeed," Vashishth said with a knowing nod. "But for now, she is your reminder that wisdom must always balance strength."

From a distance, Vishwamitra chuckled, unable to resist a playful jab. "Wisdom and patience are all well and good, Vashishth, but when the time comes for battle, I think we both know who will prove more useful." He gestured toward Tarkshya, who was now perched proudly on a rock, watching the exchange with keen eyes.

Vashishth, ever composed, raised an eyebrow. "Strength without wisdom is a blunt blade, Vishwamitra. When the time comes, it will be Uluka who devises the strategy Tarkshya will follow."

Tejomayi laughed, clutching Uluka closer as she glanced between the two sages. "I love them both," she said with earnest delight. "Tarkshya and Uluka—they're perfect together."

As months turned into years, Tarkshya and Uluka grew at an astonishing pace. Tarkshya's wings stretched nearly ten feet, his regal presence commanding the skies. Uluka, though smaller and quieter, was no less impressive. Her silent flight and penetrating gaze held an otherworldly grace that captivated everyone. The two creatures, so different in temperament, complemented each other perfectly—Tarkshya bold and fierce, Uluka calm and deliberate.

But they were not the only ones drawn to the hermitage. Snakes of various kinds began appearing in greater numbers, their sinuous forms gliding through the meadows and coiling around the rocks. Despite their natural instincts, Tarkshya never attacked them, and Uluka observed them with a quiet respect. It was as though an unspoken truce existed among the creatures, a harmony that reflected the divine balance of the place.

Surabhi, Tarkshya, Uluka, and the snakes became an inseparable part of Tejomayi's world. The sages, watching this growing circle, marvelled at the divine forces at play. "Even nature itself bends to her presence," Vashishth remarked one evening, his voice filled with quiet reverence.

"And yet," Vishwamitra added, his tone light but sincere, "it is Tarkshya who watches over her most fiercely."

Tejomayi, oblivious to their banter, stood in the meadow with Tarkshya perched proudly on one shoulder and Uluka settled calmly on the other. Surabhi grazed nearby, her tail swishing contentedly. As the wind rustled through the wildflowers and the Saraswati's waters sparkled in the sunlight, Tejomayi laughed—a sound so pure and unburdened that it seemed to echo through the valley, carrying with it the promise of a world in harmony.

As Tejomayi settled into life at the hermitage, the Saptarishis began her training in earnest, each imparting their unique wisdom to her growing mind and spirit. She wore a simple yet striking outfit for her training sessions—a baggy white dhoti paired with an Angrakha-style top adorned with golden lace. The attire, loose and flowing, moved with her as she leapt and spun, her hair dancing in the wind like dark flames.

Vashishth, the keeper of Dharma and spiritual knowledge, taught her morality, wisdom, and the delicate balance of cosmic order. His lessons were like gentle ripples on a tranquil lake, centering her restless energy and grounding her fiery enthusiasm. Yet, despite her respect for his teachings, her mischievous nature often led her to abandon his lessons halfway.

It usually began innocently enough. Vashishth would sit with her under the shade of a large tree, reciting ancient shlokas with serene patience. Tejomayi would listen, her fingers tracing patterns in the soil, until a sudden movement in the distance caught her eye. Vishwamitra, standing just within her line of sight, would silently hold up a gleaming bow, an arrow notched and ready to fire. Other times, he would wave a sword with a flourish, the metal glinting tantalizingly in the sunlight.

Her discipline dissolved instantly. "Guruji, I'll be back in a moment!" she'd exclaim, springing to her feet. "Tejomayi!" Vashishth would call after her, shaking his head in exasperation. "Wisdom cannot be wielded like a weapon, child!"

Vishwamitra, grinning with smug satisfaction, would mutter under his breath as she approached, "Wisdom has its place, but a sharp sword speaks louder in battle."

Of all the sages, it was Vishwamitra who became her favorite. His lessons were electrifying, designed to test her potential and unveil the power within her. Under his guidance, she learned to move with a grace and agility that could rival the most skilled gymnast. Her body flowed like water as she practiced ancient martial arts, her movements precise yet imbued with raw energy.

One day, Vishwamitra handed her a sword to test her strength. The blade was blunt, intended for practice, yet it felt alive in her hands. He led her to a large, weathered boulder, its surface scarred by centuries of wind and rain.

"Show me your strength, Khindni," Vishwamitra said, his voice steady but expectant.

Tejomayi tightened her grip, her hair falling in waves around her determined face. With one fluid motion, she swung the sword, its edge connecting with the stone in a deafening crack. When the dust cleared, the boulder stood split cleanly in two, the pieces resting neatly on either side.

Silence fell over the hermitage.

Even Vishwamitra stood stunned. "Extraordinary," he murmured at last. "But power without control is dangerous."

That lesson fell to Jamadagni. Master of discipline and inner fortitude, he guided her in emotional stability and the importance of restraint. One afternoon, he led her to the riverbank, where a massive stone sat half-buried in the soil.

"Lift it, Khindni," he instructed.

Tejomayi stepped forward, wrapping her hands around the stone's edges. She lifted it effortlessly, her small frame belying the sheer force she wielded. But as she moved, a crack echoed through the ground, the sheer power of her grip splitting the stone beneath her feet. Startled, she let go, her eyes wide with confusion.

Jamadagni approached her, placing a steady hand on her shoulder. His voice, though gentle, carried the weight of his wisdom. "Strength without control is destruction," he said. "But strength with discipline... that is creation. You have the potential to shape worlds, Tejomayi, but only if you learn to master yourself first."

His words rooted themselves deep within her heart. Though she relished the thrill of her growing power, she began to understand the importance of balance—a lesson that would guide her as she continued her journey.

Bharadvaja's lessons on science and innovation brought a different perspective to her training. He taught her the logic of solving problems, often explaining the mysteries of space and the interconnectedness of all things. Atri introduced her to the healing properties of cosmic light, while Gautama's philosophy sessions delved into the complexities of human nature and ethical decision-making.

Kashyapa, the sage of creation, opened her eyes to the delicate balance of life forces. “Every creature, every element, is part of a greater whole,” he explained one evening, pointing to the flowing Saraswati. “Protecting that balance is the greatest duty of all.”

Winter, with its snow-covered peaks and crisp air, became Tejomayi’s favorite season. She would trek alongside Vishwamitra to the higher altitudes, their footprints the only marks on the untouched snow. The world seemed to hold its breath at these heights, where the silence was profound, and the views stretched endlessly into the horizon.

One such trek led them to the summit of a small peak. The air was so thin that their breaths formed clouds, and the sky above was a tapestry of fading sunlight. Sitting cross-legged on a rocky ledge, they chanted the Gayatri Mantra together, their voices harmonizing with the winds.

As the chant ended, Vishwamitra turned to her, his expression distant. “Do you know, Khindni,” he said softly, “there was a time when I trusted the world completely. Then Indra… and Menaka…” His voice faltered, his pain raw even after centuries.

Tejomayi, her young heart brimming with empathy, reached out to him. “Guruji,” she whispered, “Did she betray you?”

“She was sent to break me,” Vishwamitra said, his gaze fixed on the horizon. “By Indra, who feared my penance. She succeeded, and I… I lost my path. It took everything to find it again.”

Tejomayi listened silently, her hand resting on his arm. She didn’t fully understand the depth of his pain, but she felt it, and in her innocence, she vowed to never let anyone break her resolve.

By the time Tejomayi turned nine, her days were filled with a blend of adventure, training, and introspection. Her favorite retreat was a small temple near the hermitage, where a statue of

Maa Durga stood resplendent. The temple became her sanctuary, a place where she could speak her heart without reserve.

One evening, as the sun dipped below the horizon, she sat before the idol, her knees drawn to her chest. "Maa," she began, her voice trembling with emotion, "why don't you talk to me? I miss you so much. When will you come to see me?"

Tears glistened in her eyes as she continued. "I want to feel your hand on my head, like Paramarishi does when I'm sad. I want you to stroke my hair and make me sleep. Are you angry with me, Maa? Please don't be. I just want to see you."

Her words echoed softly in the stillness of the temple, carrying with them the purest yearning of a child's heart. The sages, who sometimes overheard her prayers, remained silent, knowing that this bond was something far beyond their understanding.

Outside, the Saraswati River flowed as vibrantly as ever, its waters carrying not just life but whispers of something greater—something that would one day change the world.

THE RUNAWAY

1998 – Vadodara-Bharuch-Ahmedabad, Gujarat

1998-Gujarat, four years after the quiet winters of Sweden and Solan, in the heat and dust of Gujarat, a different storm was gathering.

The morning sun cast a faint glow over the streets of Vadodara as Pravash stepped out of Meenakshi's sister's house, his heart pounding with a mix of fear and determination. The weight of the suicide note he had left behind lingered in his mind, but he pushed the thought away. All that mattered now was reaching Saira, the girl who had captured his heart and given him a reason to dream.

He knew he couldn't leave from Vadodara station; his uncle's influence and connections made it too dangerous. Bharuch, a town about 100 kilometers away, seemed like the safer choice.

Two of his closest friends accompanied him, their scooter wobbling under the weight of three teenage boys. The roads stretched endlessly before them, the cool morning air brushing against their faces as they rode in silence. Pravash clung to his emotions, using the image of Saira's innocent smile as fuel for his journey.

By the time they reached Bharuch, the sun had dipped low, casting long shadows over the quiet town. Exhausted from the ride, the trio sought refuge in an unfinished building on the outskirts. They climbed to the terrace, where the bare cement walls stood exposed to the night. Lying under the open sky, Pravash gazed at the stars, his thoughts consumed by Saira.

The air was cool, and the sounds of distant traffic mingled with the chirping of crickets. His friends eventually drifted to sleep, but Pravash remained awake, his heart heavy with worry and longing.

The first light of dawn brought with it a sense of urgency. Pravash and his friends made their way to the Bharuch station, the air buzzing with the sounds of porters and passengers. The station was alive with activity, yet Pravash felt like a ghost moving through it, unseen and unnoticed. He boarded the first train to Ahmedabad, his heart racing as he realized he didn't have a ticket.

As the train lurched forward, Pravash slipped into the toilet, locking the door behind him. The small, cramped space reeked of rust and urine, but he ignored it, pressing his ear against the door to listen for the footsteps of the ticket collector. Every time the train stopped, he braced himself, his heart hammering against his ribs. The minutes dragged into hours, each moment a battle against his rising panic.

By the time the train pulled into Ahmedabad in the late afternoon, Pravash was drained—physically and emotionally. He stepped onto the platform, his legs shaky from crouching for hours, his clothes damp with sweat. The sprawling station felt overwhelming, its chaotic energy a stark contrast to his weary state.

He wandered through the station, asking passengers and staff about the next train to Kolkata. "Tomorrow morning," they told him. The words sank heavily into his chest. He had barely 200 rupees in his pocket and no place to stay.

As night fell, Pravash found a corner of the platform to settle in. He pulled his bag close, resting his head on it as he stretched out on the cold stone floor. Around him, other travellers huddled together, their quiet murmurs blending with the distant rumble of trains.

But peace was short-lived. Around 10 p.m., a group of police officers stormed the platform, their voices harsh and commanding. They began clearing the area, shouting at the sleepers to leave. One officer swung his *lathi* indiscriminately, striking people to force them up. Pravash felt the sharp sting of the stick on his back, and a cry escaped his lips before he scrambled to his feet, clutching his bag.

Fear gripped him as he ran, his thin frame darting through the chaos. Tears stung his eyes, but he didn't dare stop. The officers' shouts faded as he burst through the station's exit and into the night. His chest heaved as he stood on the darkened street, his hands trembling from the adrenaline coursing through his veins.

He was a mere fifteen-year-old boy, alone in a city that felt vast and indifferent. But even in the depths of his fear and despair, one thought burned brightly in his mind: Saira. Her name was a lifeline, a fragile thread that kept him moving forward. "For her," he whispered to himself, his voice barely audible in the stillness. "I have to keep going."

The streets outside Ahmedabad station were dimly lit, the flickering streetlights casting uneven shadows on the cracked pavement. Pravash wandered aimlessly, his stomach gnawing with hunger, his heart heavy with loneliness. The faint aroma of frying pakoras reached his nostrils, drawing him toward a small hawker stall illuminated by a single yellow bulb. The vendor, a wiry man with sharp features and a quick smile, was busy serving customers, his hands moving deftly as he dipped battered vegetables into sizzling oil.

Pravash hesitated before stepping closer. The few coins in his pocket felt insignificant, but hunger pushed him forward. The vendor noticed him and paused, wiping his hands on a greasy cloth. His eyes, quick and observant, scanned Pravash from head to toe.

"You look different, boy," the vendor said, his voice curious but kind. "Polished. Like you come from a good family. What are you doing here, wandering around like this?"

Pravash, overwhelmed by the man's words and his own exhaustion, felt tears welling up in his eyes. Before he could stop himself, they spilled over, and his voice cracked as he replied, "I've run away from home. I'm on my way to meet someone... someone I love."

The vendor's eyebrows lifted, and he leaned slightly forward. "Run away, huh?" he said, his tone shifting to one of feigned concern. "Must have been something serious for a boy like you to leave a family like that." He handed Pravash a plate of pakoras, the golden pieces glistening with oil. "Here, eat. Don't worry about money. Sit and tell me everything."

Pravash, his hunger overcoming his hesitation, took the plate gratefully and began to eat. The vendor, who introduced himself as Nagesh, sat beside him on a low stool, his eyes sharp with calculation as he listened.

"I'm going to Kolkata," Pravash said between bites, his voice soft but filled with determination. "I'll meet Saira there, and then... then everything will be fine." His words tumbled out in a mix of hope and fear, his innocence laid bare before a stranger.

Nagesh nodded slowly, his mind working quickly. He saw in Pravash a golden opportunity. The boy's innocence, coupled with his polished demeanor, would fetch a high price in his line of work. Nagesh's true business wasn't selling pakoras—it was smuggling children to the Middle East, where they were forced into labor or worse. And here was a boy, practically walking into his net.

"You're brave, kid," Nagesh said, a smile playing on his lips. "Not many would take a step like this. But don't worry. I'll help you. You don't need to sleep on the streets tonight. I've got a place you can stay, and in the morning, I'll even give you some money for your journey. Once you've found your girl, you bring her here. I'll take care of both of you."

Pravash's eyes lit up, relief washing over him. "Really? You'll help me?"

"Of course," Nagesh replied smoothly. "What are friends for?"

But before he could seal the deal, the atmosphere shifted. A shadow fell over the small stall, and Nagesh's words faltered as he looked up. Standing behind Pravash was a man, his tall, imposing figure partially obscured by the dim light. He wore a simple dhoti and kurta, his face marked by calm but piercing eyes that seemed to see right through Nagesh's soul.

The man didn't speak. He didn't need to. From beneath the folds of his kurta, he revealed a gun, its metallic gleam catching the faint light. With a subtle shake of his head, he made his intentions clear. Leave the boy alone.

Nagesh swallowed hard, his bravado crumbling under the man's silent but unyielding presence. Pravash, oblivious to the man standing behind him, continued eating, unaware of the silent battle being waged for his future.

Suddenly, Nagesh stood up, his expression hardening as he slapped the plate out of Pravash's hands. "Get out of here!" he barked, his voice laced with feigned anger. "I'm a brahmin! I can't be helping some Muslim. Run, boy, before I lose my patience!" He spat out the word like a tool, not a belief.

Pravash stared at him, stunned and confused. "But you just said—"

"Run!" Nagesh shouted, raising his hand as if to strike again.

Fear surged through Pravash, and he stumbled backward, his eyes wide with shock. He turned and ran, his heart pounding as Nagesh's shouts faded behind him.

Pravash ran until his legs ached, his breath coming in ragged gasps. Eventually, he slowed, his surroundings blurring in the dim streetlight. The city was quiet, the bustling crowds of the day replaced by the stillness of the night. A small group of beggars lay huddled on the side of the road, their thin forms wrapped in tattered blankets.

Exhausted and overwhelmed, Pravash lay down among them, clutching his bag tightly to his chest. The pavement was cold and unforgiving, but he didn't care. His mind clung to the thought of Saira, her image the only thing keeping him from breaking.

As he closed his eyes, his body trembling with fatigue and fear, the city seemed to hold its breath around him. In the distance, a faint wind whispered through the trees, carrying with it the weight of an uncertain future.

The cold night enveloped the city of Ahmedabad, its chill seeping into the cracked pavement where Pravash lay on the footpath. His thin clothes did little to shield him from the biting air, and his small frame curled instinctively as if to protect itself. Around him, the muffled sounds of the sleeping city filled the silence—the occasional bark of a stray dog, the rustle of leaves, and the faint skittering of rats.

Pravash, exhausted and deep in sleep, didn't stir as the rats grew bold. Their sharp teeth nibbled at his exposed ankles, the tender flesh of his ears, and his shoulders. Somewhere in his mind, the pain translated into a dream—a vivid, harrowing scene where he found himself in the middle of a chaotic battlefield.

The battlefield stretched endlessly before him, a chaotic scene of blood and steel. Pravash found himself surrounded by men with twisted faces and fierce, unrelenting eyes. Each one held a weapon—a gleaming dagger or a rusted sword—and their intent was clear. They lunged at him from all sides, their blades striking at his legs and arms, their snarls echoing in the chaos.

Pravash cried out, desperate to escape. The ground beneath his feet felt sticky and unstable, as though it threatened to pull him under with every step. "Let me through!" he screamed, his voice raw with terror. His hands pushed against the bodies pressing in on him, his mind racing with fear and confusion.

Through the suffocating crowd, a glimmer of light caught his eye. His heart surged with a faint hope as he fixed his gaze on the source of the radiance. He clawed his way forward, each step a battle against the suffocating mass of attackers. Their blades sliced at him, leaving searing trails of pain, but he pushed on, the light growing brighter with each labored step.

Breaking free at last, Pravash collapsed to his knees before the divine figure that awaited him. Sitting atop a massive beast unlike any he had seen was Maa Shakti, her presence radiating both fury and grace. Her tiger, golden and without stripes, exuded an otherworldly power, its sabre-like teeth gleaming as it let out a low, bone-shaking growl.

Maa Shakti's many arms bore celestial weapons, her fierce gaze scanning the battlefield with unwavering authority. Yet when she looked down at Pravash, her expression softened, and a divine smile graced her lips.

Pravash clasped his hands together, tears streaming down his face as he trembled before her. "Hey Maa," he whispered, his voice quivering with emotion. "Please guide me… please help me. I'm your son, your child. I don't know where to go or what to do. Protect me, Maa. Please…"

Maa Shakti's tiger roared once more, and the swarm of attackers dissolved, scattering into nothingness. The battlefield melted away, replaced by a golden light that enveloped Pravash. For the first time in days, a deep sense of calm settled over him, as though the chaos within his heart had been stilled by her divine presence.

In the waking world, the rats that had been biting Pravash scattered in a sudden frenzy, startled by the silent approach of a snake. The creature slithered toward him with fluid grace, its smooth scales reflecting the faint moonlight. With a precise strike, it attacked one of the rats, sending the rest fleeing into the shadows. The snake coiled briefly near Pravash, as if standing guard, before disappearing into the darkness as quietly as it had arrived.

Not far from the sleeping boy, Kalaha watched silently. His tall, lean frame was draped in a saffron dhoti and shawl, his face calm but intense as he observed the scene. Stepping closer, he knelt by Pravash's side, his sharp eyes filled with a quiet determination.

Reaching into the folds of his shawl, Kalaha pulled out a single bead of rudraksha—a rare nine-faced bead, its intricate surface glinting faintly in the dim light. With care, he slipped the bead into Pravash's pocket, his movements gentle and deliberate.

"This will protect you, my boy," Kalaha murmured softly, his voice carrying a note of both reassurance and resolve. He placed his hand lightly on Pravash's head, as though to calm the storm raging in the teenager's mind, before standing and melting into the shadows.

The first light of dawn painted the city in soft hues of gold and grey, stirring Pravash from his uneasy sleep. He sat up slowly, his body aching and covered in irritated rashes and bite marks. His ankles throbbed, and the tender skin of his ears stung where the rats had bitten him. He rubbed at the welts absentmindedly, wincing as he moved.

Yet despite the physical discomfort, his mind felt uncharacteristically calm. A sense of warmth had taken root within him, as though the chaos of the night had been replaced by a quiet certainty. He stood, shaking off the stiffness in his limbs, and made his way back toward the station.

The bustling energy of the morning crowds was beginning to fill the air. At the ticket counter, Pravash pulled out his crumpled money and purchased a ticket in the unreserved coach of the train to Kolkata. To him, unreserved coach was the realm of the poor and the desperate—those who couldn't afford the luxury of a reserved seat. Pravash knew what to expect: overcrowded compartments, bodies pressed together in suffocating proximity, and the floor serving as a makeshift bed for those who couldn't find a place to sit. It didn't matter. He was going home.

With the few coins he had left, Pravash wandered the station and spotted a hawker selling bananas. For two rupees, he bought a dozen, carefully tucking them into his bag for the journey. Nearby, he saw another vendor selling menthol cigarettes. For fifty rupees, he purchased a pack, the familiar scent reminding him of simpler, carefree days.

Finally, Pravash settled onto a bench on the platform, pulling out his most cherished possession: a small Walkman and a cassette of *Dil Se*. The album, composed by A.R. Rahman, was a lifeline to the promise he had made with Saira. They had vowed to watch the movie together when they reunited in Kolkata, and the thought of it filled him with bittersweet hope.

Placing the headphones over his ears, Pravash pressed play. The haunting melodies washed over him, filling his mind and silencing his fears. As he waited for the train, a faint smile tugged at his lips. What felt like an eternity, he felt like he was moving closer to something—closer to her. But as the seconds ticked by, a thought struck him—a sharp realization that sent a shiver down his spine.

His family.

By now, they would have discovered his suicide note. Panic gripped him as he imagined his father's commanding voice echoing across Howrah Station, orchestrating a search for every train arriving from Gujarat. His uncle's network of contacts would surely stretch far beyond Vadodara, and Pravash knew how resourceful his family could be.

A wave of fear broke through his momentary calm, and he leapt to his feet, clutching his bag tightly. He scanned the platform frantically, his mind racing for a solution. Then his eyes landed on a street barber, seated under a makeshift shelter just outside the station. The man was hunched over a customer, deftly shaving his head while a few others waited on battered stools nearby. The barber's tools glinted in the morning sun, and Pravash's heart thudded with sudden determination.

He ran to the barber, nearly tripping over a loose stone as he reached the small setup. The barber, an older man with a thick moustache and a stained white kurta, looked up in mild irritation.

"Wait your turn, boy," he grumbled, gesturing to the waiting line.

"No, please," Pravash said urgently, his voice trembling. "I'll pay you extra. Just shave my head—right now!"

The barber raised an eyebrow but shrugged, waving the boy to sit on the creaking stool. "Five rupees," he said as he wiped the blade clean. "And extra means two rupees more."

Pravash nodded quickly, reaching into his pocket to pull out the coins. As the barber adjusted his tools, Pravash glanced around nervously, the weight of his decision settling in. He watched as clumps of his dark hair fell to the ground, the blade scraping against his scalp in even strokes. The cool morning air prickled his newly exposed skin, and Pravash felt an odd mix of relief and anxiety.

When the barber finished, Pravash stood, rubbing his smooth scalp. "Do you have *kajal*?" he asked, his voice still laced with urgency.

"Kajal?" the barber asked, narrowing his eyes. "Why would you need that?"

"Just—please. I need it," Pravash insisted, fumbling in his pocket for another coin.

The barber, shrugging in bemusement, pulled out a small tin of kajal from his bag of miscellaneous items. Pravash took it gratefully, unscrewing the lid and dipping his fingers into the black paste. He smeared it across his face, darkening his complexion with quick, uneven strokes.

The barber watched in confusion, his moustache twitching as he suppressed a laugh. "What are you doing, boy? Trying to look like a street performer?"

Pravash didn't answer. He was too focused on his task, spreading the kajal over every visible inch of skin. His reflection in the barber's cracked mirror revealed a transformation—a boy who no longer looked like the polished son of a well-to-do family but a ragged, dark-complexioned kid who could easily blend into the unreserved coach of any train.

Pravash nodded in gratitude, pressing a few more coins into the barber's hand before grabbing his bag and hurrying back toward the platform. As he walked, he glanced at the reflection of his new appearance in the glass panes of a tea stall. The boy staring back at him looked like a stranger—a disguise that he hoped would carry him through unnoticed.

He knew the risks were still high, but his resolve was stronger than ever. Saira was waiting, and nothing—not even the looming shadow of his family—would stop him from reaching her.

THE DIVINE BALANCE

1998 – Himavanta Mountain Range-Himavanta Realm, Jambudveep

Far away from the turmoil of Bharath Kshetra, in the pristine yet untamed landscapes of Himavanta Kshetra, Maa Shakti sat upon a rock overlooking a vast valley bathed in twilight. Her divine form shimmered with an aura of unyielding power and maternal grace. The golden light of the setting sun danced across her features, but her attention was fixed elsewhere, her focus spanning realms and time itself.

Two figures occupied her thoughts. One was a young boy, Pravash, lying curled on a cold pavement in Ahmedabad. In his sleep, he had cried out to her, his prayers brimming with desperation and innocence, piercing through the barriers of the matrix around Bharath Kshetra. His call reverberated through the cosmos, tugging at her heart with a force she could not ignore. Her fingers curled unconsciously against the cold rock beneath her, as if she could anchor herself against the pull of that fragile voice.

The other was Tejomayi, her daughter in every sense that mattered, kneeling before a small temple in Solan. Tears streamed down her face as she whispered her plea. "Why won't you talk to me, Maa? Don't you miss me? I miss you so much…" Her voice, filled with yearning, bridged the chasm between the mortal and divine.

Maa Shakti's hands trembled slightly as she watched them both. Her eyes brimmed with tears, her lips quivering as she whispered, "My children…"

Behind her, Shiva stood silently, his serene smile belying the intensity of the moment. His presence was like the mountains around them—steadfast and eternal, offering solace in the face of storms. "Looks like Narada's play of sending messages already reached you"

Shakti turned to him, her voice trembling with both frustration, confusion and longing. "Why are you smiling, Mahadev? Who is this boy? And why does his pain pull at my heart so strongly? My daughter calls me on one side, and now this boy…" She paused, her gaze returning to Pravash. "Why do I feel so much for him? Like I feel I have to go to him right away"

Shiva stepped closer, his eyes filled with infinite calm as he regarded her. "If it is meant to happen, Parvati, no force in the cosmos will stop you from going to them," he said gently. "But there is a reason you feel this way. Let me explain who he is."

He gestured toward Pravash's image, now glowing faintly in the divine light. "That boy is Pravash. Narada, in his ever-playful but purposeful way, has given him one of my most precious rudraksha beads—nine-faced, carved from my tears, which I shed only for you."

Shakti's eyes widened slightly as Shiva continued, his voice steady and deep. "That bead, slipped into Pravash's pocket by Narada, was a call. It is why you appeared in his dream, why his prayers reached you so clearly. Narada has a reason for everything he does, and in this case, he seeks our attention for this boy."

Shakti's expression softened, though confusion lingered. "But why this boy, Mahadev? What is so special about him?"

Shiva's gaze grew contemplative, his tone tinged with both reverence and caution. "Because he is extraordinary," he said. The word seemed to hang in the thin mountain air between them, heavy enough to still even the restless wind. "Pravash's heart holds the highest capacity for emotion of any human in Bharat Kshetra today. His love is boundless, and his hate equally unmatched. In his previous lives, his hatred was so powerful that it even tested the penance and virtues of Lord Parshvanath."

At the Tirthankar's name, Shakti's gaze dipped. For a moment she did not see the valley before her, but a still figure beneath a raging storm, coiled hoods spread wide above him like a living crown. "Yet, in the very same cycle, he embodied the profound paradox of human existence—capable of unspeakable cruelty and unimaginable saintliness within a single lifetime. And now, his focus is as unbreakable as it was then. When Pravash's mind is set on something, no force—mortal or divine—can sway him."

Shakti's brows furrowed as she listened, her emotions swirling. "And this makes him a danger?" she asked softly.

Shiva nodded solemnly. "It makes him a force unlike any other. In Bharath Kshetra, if there is anyone alive who could achieve divine powers through sheer penance, it would be him. And that is what Indra fears. Far below, beyond the last line of snow peaks, a faint curve of light shimmered into view—an invisible dome only their eyes could see, like a second sky stitched together from trapped lightning. It is why he created the unbreakable veil around the South-Center Khand of Bharat Kshetra where all the sixty-three Salaka-Purus once lived, the matrix that keeps humans trapped in a carefully controlled reality. Indra fears what someone like Pravash could become if he broke free of it."

Shakti's gaze grew more intense, her grip tightening on the trishul she held. "And Narada gave him the bead to force our hand?"

"Not entirely," Shiva replied, his voice quieter now. "Narada wants us to see Pravash for who he is. But helping him is not so simple. Pravash is still trapped within the matrix, and I cannot interfere directly while he remains there. His path must unfold naturally."

Shiva turned to her fully, his voice heavy with emotion. "What happened to him during the war between Bharat and Bahubali was not right, but it was meant to happen."

As Shiva spoke, the twilight around them seemed to darken. Between them, the air rippled with ghostly echoes—war drums, the clash of steel, the hiss of serpents coiling around banners that snapped above endless ranks of warriors. "Pravash—then known as Mahendra—was the most brilliant commander and strategist in your daughter's Naga army, fighting on *Chakravarti* King Bharat's side." Shakti flinched.

In the shifting vision, Mahendra's face turned toward her—eyes alight with fierce clarity, Padmavati's serpent crown blazing just behind him. Padmavati's scream, the one she had buried deep when his body fell, seemed to tear through her chest all over again.

"It was almost impossible to defeat Bharat's army as long as Mahendra was part of it. Bahubali's commanders knew this well, and it was his removal that turned the tide of that war."

Shiva's voice softened further. "His brilliance, his devotion, and his emotions are his greatest strength. But they are also his greatest danger. If Pravash gains great power, the question is whether he will be able to control it—or whether his emotions will consume him."

A thin crack of fear passed through her resolve—not fear of the boy, but of the storm she could already feel building inside him.

Shakti straightened, her eyes burning with resolve. "Then let me go to him. I will bring balance to his storm. I will guide him, as only I can. And perhaps…" She paused, her voice trembling. "Perhaps it will give me the chance to be with my daughter again. It has been so long, Mahadev."

Shiva looked at her with a faint smile, his voice calm yet profound as he repeated his earlier words. "If it is meant to happen, Parvati, it will. No one can stop what is destined."

He turned his gaze toward the horizon, his expression darkening slightly. "Bharath Kshetra is nearing the final decline of this cycle of Avsarpini. The end will bring untold chaos, and what lies ahead is uncertain. Currently *Simandhar Swamy (Living*

Tirthankar in Mahavideh) truly knows the future and every detail of it—while the rest of us contend with possibilities"

At the mention of the name, Shiva's hands came together in reverence, his eyes closing as he bowed.

In her mind's eye, their images overlapped for a heartbeat—Tejomayi's small fists clenched in lonely prayer, Pravash's eyes raw with love and hurt. Two storms, racing toward the same shore.

Shakti's gaze flickered with both determination and hope. She turned back to Pravash's image, her voice steady as she whispered, "I will go to him as Arya, Mahadev, and will bring balance to his life."

CHAPTER 12
The Blooming Poison

SEEDS OF DECAY

1994 – Ghaggar-Nagar, Rajasthan

In 1994, nature—resplendent and generous—rarely came without consequence. Rivers that nurtured life could also seed ruin. The same water that created could destroy; the same soil that fed generations could hide poison.

In the hills of Solan, Himachal Pradesh, the Saraswati River was revered as divine, its flow blessing the land with vitality and abundance. Yet as the river descended toward the plains, its purity became tainted by human greed, fuelling an empire of darkness.

In the fertile lands of Ghaggar-Nagar, where the Saraswati was known as the Ghaggar-Hakra, its waters nourished more than just crops. They irrigated the vast 500-acre estate of Gurpreet Kandola, a man whose power reached far beyond his title as MLA. Gurpreet wasn't just a political figure—he was the mafia don of the region, a man whose word was law and whose hands controlled a thriving heroin empire.

Gurpreet was a man of few words, but his presence spoke volumes. To the public, he was the embodiment of a traditional village leader—dressed in his crisp kurta-pyjama and a white turban, his bald head gleaming beneath the fabric, and his long moustache curling upward, giving him the appearance of affable authority.

Yet, beneath this facade lay a different man entirely. Behind closed doors, Gurpreet was ruthless and calculating, his shady beard and shrewd eyes betraying the underworld ties that had propelled him to unimaginable wealth.

He exuded a quiet, commanding power—one that made it clear to all that opposing him was akin to vanishing without a trace. His influence stretched far beyond his immediate domain, controlling elections with the ease of a seasoned puppet master. With money filling the pockets of top politicians and his growing empire fuelling his ascent, Gurpreet was well on his way to becoming one of the most powerful men in the entire country. The state government could be toppled with a mere whisper from him.

The secret to his empire lay in the rich, fertile soil of Ghaggar-Nagar, where the ever-flowing Saraswati nourished poppy fields that were the envy of the region. Gurpreet's opium was of unmatched quality, its purity elevated further by his ingenuity. Leveraging his connections in Pakistan, he had established a state-of-the-art heroin lab across the border, a hub that transformed raw opium into the finest heroin the underworld had ever seen. Smuggling the finished product back into Punjab through well-oiled networks, Gurpreet became a name whispered in fear and respect within the global underworld market.

His most sinister innovation came from his obsession with snakes. Years earlier, his son Vikram Kandola had met a gruesome end, killed by snakes and eagles in what Gurpreet believed was a freak act of nature. Vikram's death was vengeance for his attempt to harm young Tejomayi, though Gurpreet never learned the truth. Driven by grief and hatred, he began capturing snakes in large numbers, turning their venom into a potent ingredient for his heroin. The venom-infused heroin became Gurpreet's signature product, its unmatched purity and strength making it the talk of the underworld and catapulting his empire to new heights.

Gurpreet's palace in Ghaggar-Nagar was a fortress in every sense. Guarded by a private army, the sprawling estate exuded wealth and power. No one dared enter without his permission, and no authority could touch him—he had the local police and politicians firmly in his pocket. From this stronghold, Gurpreet operated with impunity, his network of enforcers ensuring that his business thrived without interference.

Within the palace walls, Gurpreet's family led lives as complex as his empire.

His wife, Kajal, was a commanding presence. Always clad in vibrant sarees with her pallu draped modestly over her head, she exuded traditional elegance. Yet, within the household, she was anything but submissive. Kajal ruled the family with an iron will, her sharp tongue and strong demeanor leaving even Gurpreet with little choice but to follow her lead.

Their youngest daughter, Harshpreet, was a mirror of Gurpreet's ambition. At fifteen, she flaunted her father's power with pride, bullying those around her with an air of entitlement. Her fitted salwar kameez and tight kurtas accentuated her striking beauty, but her sharp eyes revealed a ruthless determination. Harshpreet was eager to take over her father's empire, relishing the idea of becoming its queenpin.

Arvind Kandola, Gurpreet's younger son, was her opposite. Twenty-two and introspective, Arvind had no interest in his father's empire. Always dressed in simple kurta-pyjamas, he spent his days reading and dreaming of escaping to a life abroad. Unlike Harshpreet, Arvind was deeply uncomfortable with the violence and corruption that surrounded him. He longed for a quieter, more meaningful existence, far from the shadow of Gurpreet's legacy.

Years earlier, Gurpreet's heroin operation had been modest, catering primarily to local markets and spiritual centers like Baba Maheshwarand's ashram. The self-proclaimed godman had been one of Gurpreet's most loyal customers, mixing the drugs into his prasad to control his devotees. But with Baba's death—at Tejomayi's hands—Gurpreet had been forced to expand his business.

Though poppy fields and venom-laced powder were only half of his empire.

The other half did not grow in the soil.

It grew in cradles. In classrooms. Behind bright signboards that said *"Hope Home"* and *"Future Care Foundation"* in cheerful fonts.

Across India, Gurpreet quietly funded a chain of "charitable" orphanages and hostels. The faces on their brochures were always the same—smiling children in clean uniforms, volunteers holding steel plates, visiting film stars crouching in carefully arranged poses of compassion. Local newspapers loved them. Politicians posed beside them.

On paper, they were places where abandoned children were "given a second chance."

In Gurpreet's ledgers, they were **inventory.**

Newborn boys—especially those without names, without records—were quietly marked as "high cost." They cried too much. Fell sick too often. Required milk, medicine, endless care. The world rarely asked about them.

On the edges of small towns, in empty lots behind bus stands or near waste grounds where street dogs roamed, tiny bundles of little angels sometimes appeared at dawn.

The staff member who placed them there never stayed long. He didn't have to. By the time the sun rose, the bundles would be gone completely, or tiny bloody limbs would be all that is left.

The reports never changed:

"Child arrived in critical condition. Could not be saved."

The files were closed. No one came to reopen them.

Girls, though—

Girls were never written off.

From the moment they arrived, they were assessed the way Gurpreet assessed the quality of his opium resin. Quiet notes were made in the margins of admission forms in neat, tidy Hindi.

"Fair, sharp eyes."

"Picks up English quickly."

"Obedient. Smiles easily."

"Good posture. Can be presented."

They were sent to "grooming centers" in bigger cities—Delhi, Mumbai, Kolkata—under the pretence of "special education programs". There, they learned computer basics and English phrases, yes. But they also learned how to sit, how to laugh at the right moment, how to pretend they were comfortable when they were not.

"Modern women," the brochures called them. "Confident. Independent. Global."

By twelve or thirteen, most of them had already been chosen.

Some were shipped out on forged documents as "domestic help" to wealthy families abroad. Others were sent to "cultural troupes," "hospitality training programs," or "hostess jobs" in foreign hotels and cruise ships. The paperwork was clean. The reality, kilometres away, was anything but.

Every girl had a file. Sometimes that file included an amount circled in red ink.

The circle was the only halo the world ever gave them.

The names of the orphanages changed when they attracted too much attention. So did their logos. But the pipeline did not.

Years earlier, when Gurpreet was still building his heroin routes, human beings had not been his primary commodity. Drugs were easier. Less noisy. They didn't cry at night.

But as his empire grew, his partners began to ask for more. Drugs opened certain doors. Those doors wanted "entertainment" on the other side.

The connection to spiritual centers came through Baba Maheshwaranand.

While the godman lived, Gurpreet supplied his ashram with opioids and stimulants disguised as "herbal prasad" and "special tonics." In return, the Baba's inner circle sent him lists—names of "devotees" who had "offered themselves to seva."

They were always the same kind of people.

Women with no family left. Widows. Orphans. Girls from far districts whose parents had once come seeking blessings and never visited again. Boys who had "lost interest in studies" and now worked behind the ashram kitchens out of sight.

On the lists, they were described with gentle words: *"disciplined," "simple," "detached."*

In Gurpreet's spreadsheet, they were numbers.

After Maheshwaranand's death, nothing really stopped. Gurpreet simply shifted routes. He began expanding into the northeastern states of India, then Bangladesh, Thailand, and Vietnam—places where conflict, and quiet desperation made people easy to recruit, easier to disappear, and easiest to sell.

In Ghaggar-Nagar, a quiet proverb began to spread among the men who sat in Gurpreet's courtyard, men who believed the world existed for their appetite alone:

"If it breathes, it can be bought."

They did not see the full map.

They did not see that in Bombay, late-night television was teaching teenage boys to look at women as moving posters. That in Delhi, new music videos and magazines sold the idea that desirability was the highest currency a girl could hold. That in small towns, billboards showed photo-edited bodies under the word *"freedom."*

They did not know the name of the woman who was arranging those images, one broadcast after another, tuning a whole generation's gaze toward **lust without consequence**.

Menaka's hand never touched their contracts. Her signature never appeared on Gurpreet's paperwork. She never sat in his palace, never walked his poppy fields.

She didn't need to.

Her world taught them what to crave; his world supplied what her world promised.

Between them, a quiet, invisible trade was taking shape: From screens to streets. From fantasies to flights. From "modern grooming" to cargo holds and closed rooms in cities whose names the girls had never learned to pronounce.

With an unlimited supply of water and a perfected venom-based formula, Gurpreet's heroin started to dominate the underworld market, particularly in Punjab, where addiction ran rampant. The same river that brought prosperity to farmers in Solan and Ghaggar-Nagar also flowed through the veins of countless addicts, binding them in chains of despair.

Nature's gifts, when harnessed with greed and malice, often bore a double edge. The beauty of the Saraswati's flow masked the poison it carried downstream, where it fed both crops and corruption. Gurpreet Kandola's empire was a dark testament to the duality of creation—a reminder that even the most divine blessings could be twisted into tools of ruin.

And above it all, unseen, the cycle of Avsarpini ticked one step closer toward its final stage.

Dukham-Dukham.
Pain that forgets it is in pain.

Gurpreet believed he was just expanding a business.

He never stopped to wonder what, or who all, were using him as a tool.

—⚬✎▭✡—

THE SEARCH OF HIDDEN LIGHT

1994-1998 – Vallabhipur, Gujarat; Bangalore, Karnataka; Delhi, India; Tibet, USA, China, South Africa; Sweden

In 1994, shortly after his quiet meeting with Ved Vyas, Kalaha grasped the gravity of the situation. Ved hadn't needed many words; his caution was subtle but unmistakable, veiled beneath the warmth of friendship. The Council of Nine was restless. Their growing suspicion of Kalaha's movements signalled that mere concealment was no longer enough.

Kalaha needed to live a life so ordinary, so inconspicuous, that not even the Nine would find a reason to look twice.

Adopting the humble identity of *Vasudev Bhai Shah*, he retreated to the small village of *Vallabhipur* in Gujarat. It was an ideal choice—a place close enough to be casually monitored by the Nine yet too mundane to raise suspicion. Vallabhipur was on the verge of transformation, as the foundation of the *Ayodhyapuram Jain Temple* had just been laid. The temple, destined to become a significant spiritual sanctuary for Jain devotees, provided the perfect cover.

Blending seamlessly into the quiet rhythms of village life, Kalaha embraced the role of a small-time temple pundit. Day after day, he tended to the temple grounds, recited prayers, and guided villagers through rituals. To the outside world, he was merely a humble servant of faith, contributing to the rise of a sacred temple.

But beneath this mask of simplicity, Kalaha remained vigilant.

In his role as *Vasudev Bhai*, he grew well-liked among the temple workers and other pundits. Every evening, they would gather around him, eager to hear his captivating stories—tales of the *Tirthankaras*, of great souls and the *Salaka-Purushas*, their legends spun with such depth that they seemed to come alive in the flickering lamplight. Yet, for all his charm and warmth, Kalaha was always calculating, always watching.

More importantly, he had taken Ved's most crucial advice to heart: Soham had to be kept far away. The Nine could never know of the boy's existence.

And so, Kalaha quietly sent Soham to *Jain Vidyalaya*, a disciplined boarding school tucked away in the heart of Bangalore. It was a perfect sanctuary—respected, serene, and far beyond the reach of anyone who might be searching for Kalaha.

The city welcomed Soham with its cool breezes and sprawling canopies. Bangalore was a city alive with natural lakes and ancient trees, where the air carried the soft hum of life. The stone walls of Jain Vidyalaya, blending seamlessly with the earth and sky, became both his refuge and his cage.

Soham adapted swiftly, but deliberately. He knew he could not draw attention to himself. Though his mind was far sharper than his peers, he made sure to stay in the shadows. He never topped his classes, never spoke too much, and never excelled beyond what was necessary. His brilliance remained hidden behind a quiet, unassuming demeanor.

Yet, in the stillness of Bangalore, Soham found comfort.

It was during a school trip that he first encountered *Shri Parshva Labdhi Dham*, a Jain temple nestled among the city's green heart. The moment he stepped into the temple grounds, something ancient and familiar stirred within him. The white marble gleamed under the afternoon sun, the scent of incense hung thick in the air, and distant chants echoed softly in the vast silence.

From that day on, whenever he could, Soham would quietly slip away from the school. He would board a local bus, journey through the winding streets of the city, and return to the temple. There, he would sit for hours in the marble courtyard, watching the flickering lamps, letting the low hum of prayers wash over him. It was the only place where he felt truly at peace, as though the silence itself was embracing him.

On some weekends, Soham would escape with his school friends to *VV Puram Food Street*, a short walk from the boarding school. The aroma of sizzling dosas and the chatter of vendors filled the air. There, amidst the rustic stalls, he would indulge in the simplest pleasures—crispy vadas, spicy chaats, and sweet jalebis.

For mere rupees, he tasted moments of ordinary life, fleeting instances of joy in a life that was anything but ordinary.

Back in Vallabhipur, Kalaha continued his quiet life as *Vasudev Bhai Shah*, the temple pundit. The *Ayodhyapuram Jain Temple* slowly rose, stone by stone, a beacon of faith and devotion. He performed his duties with precision.

When Ved Vyas eventually returned to the Nine, his report was carefully measured.

"Kalaha is merely aiding in the construction of a Jain temple," Ved's encrypted message said "A temple that will become important for Jain followers in the years to come. Nothing more."

The Council accepted his explanation without question. Except for one.

Karthik.

Karthik knew all too well that wherever Narada moved, something deeper always stirred.

About Soham, no one suspected a thing.

The boy was hidden well.

And for now, that was enough.

—◇—

Across distant lands and within the highest seats of influence, the Nine moved in silence, each entangled in their own pursuits to uncover the growing disturbance they could sense but could not define. Scattered across continents, they worked relentlessly, leveraging their vast networks. Yet the world remained deceptively still.

And so, the shadows grew deeper.

—◇—

Karthik lived far from his origins, quietly operating from the cold serenity of Sweden. The peaceful coastal winds of Gothenburg cloaked the quiet storm brewing beneath his composed exterior. In the isolated stillness of *Styrsö Bratten Island*, Karthik worked methodically, piecing together fragments of scattered intelligence.

By his side, Devasena remained his quiet strength—a constant presence anchoring him through the silent war he waged. Their secluded villa offered the illusion of refuge, but Karthik's mind was never at rest.

Restless, he delved deeper into the dark corridors of global intelligence, sifting through endless reports of arms smuggling, political unrest, and covert operations. The world, as always, seemed to be unravelling in places. But nothing connected to the unease gnawing at him.

Then, something small caught his eye—a report buried beneath layers of routine intelligence. A sudden, unexplained surge in the heroin market across northern India. It wasn't the smuggling itself that struck him but the *scale* of it. The trade had expanded too rapidly, with enormous sums of money flowing unseen beneath the surface.

Karthik pulled harder on the threads, tracing shipments that crossed the border from Pakistan. His sources confirmed it: Pakistan was fuelling this flood, another veiled attempt to weaken India from within. Drugs had always been a weapon in this quiet war—a poison meant to rot a nation from the inside.

But to Karthik, this felt *too* systematic, too intentional.

He reached out to Jay and Vijay, hoping to find something more.

Jay, deeply entrenched within the United Nations Office in Geneva, was dismissive. "It's Pakistan's old game. Flood the streets, rot the foundation. This is nothing new."

Vijay, stationed nearby, worked quietly from the shadows outside the World Trade Organization. He understood the nuances of global supply chains better than anyone, but even he saw no deeper plot.

"It's economic sabotage, sure," Vijay admitted, "but not our fight. Governments have tools for this."

And so, the thread was left dangling. Neither thought to trace it deeper. Not into Ghaggar-Nagar. Not to the man whose fields bloomed with poison.

—⚲✐▭✡—

Anasuya, cloaked in a simple identity, operated from China. Embedded within the China National Space Administration, she had access to the most sophisticated satellite data and global monitoring systems. She meticulously scanned for disturbances—shifts in climate, energy patterns, and even subtle cosmic anomalies.

But nothing emerged.

The Saraswati River's steady, unnaturally strong flow through northern India slipped past her watchful eye. It seemed like a seasonal anomaly, easily dismissed amid countless other natural fluctuations. For months, its waters swelled and fed lands far beyond their natural means. Yet, it appeared as nothing more than nature's whim.

Nature often whispers before it roars.

This time, its whispers went unheard.

—⚲✐▭✡—

Menaka, the master of influence, remained in India, her hands full with the rapid expansion of multiple television networks. She was tightening her grip on the media landscape, shaping narratives and silencing opposition. Her charm and cunning kept her at the forefront of India's entertainment empire.

Her networks were vast, but her focus was scattered. Rumors of rising drug networks were buried beneath a flood of celebrity scandals and political noise. Nothing that crossed her desk seemed more than the usual underworld chatter.

Across the mid and late 1990s, the world was preoccupied.

In the United States, headlines were consumed by President Bill Clinton's scandal, a spectacle of politics and personal failure that dominated media cycles.

In South Africa, Nelson Mandela wove fragile peace into a continent scarred by division.

And in Europe, the tragic and mysterious death of Princess Diana held the world in mourning.

Amidst the noise, no one heard the quiet rise of the storm.

Chitragupt and Ved Vyas worked discreetly from Johannesburg, South Africa. Chitragupt moved like a shadow through the halls of the World Health Organization, quietly sifting through global mortality data. Ved Vyas, blending seamlessly into his position at UNESCO, monitored cultural and societal shifts.

Chitragupt and Ved—though pretended, searched for unnatural spikes in sickness, death, or suffering.

Yet, the rising deaths in Punjab were easily dismissed—another grim statistic of poverty and drug addiction. Nothing more.

Vishwakarma, meanwhile, focused his energy on shaping the future. Operating quietly from California under the name of Jon Watson, at the heart of the rising Silicon Valley, he hid behind the facade of silent investments and innovation.

"If the world will be ruled by technology," he had once murmured, "then we must be the architects of its foundation."

He subtly guided the rise of one of the world's largest technology companies—an entity designed to embed itself in every corner of modern life. His silent hand shaped the gears of the digital age, understanding that future battles would be fought with data, not swords.

Yet, even with his vast network of digital oversight, Vishwakarma failed to catch the creeping poison spreading silently through northern India.

For about four years their efforts stretched across the globe—methodical, relentless, but ultimately misguided.

The fields of Ghaggar-Nagar, fed by the ever-flowing Saraswati, quietly bloomed under Gurpreet Kandola's empire. His venom-laced heroin moved undetected, poisoning the land from within.

Yet, Karthik remained unconvinced.

The story of Kalaha—the supposed temple pundit—and the sudden, inexplicable rise in heroin smuggling felt like two disconnected threads. But something within him refused to dismiss the coincidence.

His instincts whispered that if he dug deeper, examined the details more closely, he might uncover a hidden connection.

And perhaps, in doing so, he could finally honor the silent promise he had made to his father-in-law, Indra.

To protect the balance.

To uncover the truth.

Early January 1998 – Delhi – Broadcast Tower Complex

The studio lights cooled one by one, fading from harsh white to a dull, sleepy glow.

On the main set, cameras rolled back on their tracks as crew members unhooked mics and coiled cables. The science anchor shook hands with a visiting physicist from IISc, both of them still blinking under the afterimage of the spotlight.

From the shadows just behind the camera line, **Dr. Ananya Rao** watched them with a faint, polite smile.

To the channel, she was a consultant producer for "Science & Sky," the weekly show that made complex physics palatable for families after dinner. To the world, she was a quiet name on the credit roll.

To the Nine, she was **Anasuya**.

Her salwar-kameez was simple—soft grey with a pale maroon dupatta draped neatly around her shoulders. A few silver strands threaded through the black of her braid. Nothing about her screamed "power." But the crew had learned, without quite knowing why, that when Dr. Rao walked into the control area, glitches behaved and live feeds stopped misbehaving.

"Good segment, ma'am," a junior producer said, hurrying past with a clipboard.

Anasuya smiled. "The guest was good. We just pointed a camera at him."

The red "ON AIR" sign dimmed. Someone shouted for chai. Monitor walls shifted to a low hum of standby graphics.

A production assistant appeared at the doorway, slightly breathless. "Ma'am, Ms. Kapoor has asked if you can drop by before you leave."

The name needed no clarification.

Meera Kapoor—network head, ratings queen, the face behind half the channels that lit up Indian living rooms.

Also known, when doors were closed, as **Menaka**.

Anasuya nodded. "Tell her I'm on my way."

She took the back corridor—away from the bustle of studio floors and into the deeper arteries of the tower, where the air smelled of dust, cold AC, and old wiring. Posters of past shows lined the walls, faces smiling too brightly under peeling tape.

At the end of the corridor, outside a door marked **PROGRAMMING & STRATEGY – AUTHORIZED PERSONNEL ONLY**, Menaka was waiting.

"Dr. Rao," she said, voice smooth, lips quirking. "Burning more starlight on these mortals, are we?"

"Ms. Kapoor," Anasuya replied, equally formal for the benefit of the cameras in the ceiling. "Trying to make sure your viewers know the difference between a comet and a satellite."

Menaka laughed softly. "Come in. We'll see if they still know the difference between a saint and a sponsor."

She turned, keycard flicking at the lock. The red light turned green. The door hissed open.

Once it shut behind them, the noise of the studios vanished as if cut with a blade.

Inside, the room was another world.

It was dark but for the glow of screens—dozens of them, stacked floor to ceiling, each one broadcasting a different feed. Indian news channels. European business tickers. Japanese tech programs. American music videos. Scandinavian public networks.

A few streams had no logos at all, raw satellite pulls of regions no TV schedule cared for.

In the center of it all stood Menaka, no longer just Ms. Kapoor of Delhi Broadcasting Consortium, but something older peering through the skin of a media mogul.

She wore a saree of deep emerald silk that seemed to drink in the light, the border whispering gold with every movement. Her hair flowed loose in dark waves, too glossy to be an accident. Diamonds at her ears and wrists caught the flicker of the screens and answered with tiny, cold stars.

She was, as ever, almost painfully beautiful.

Anasuya, in her muted cotton, looked like a schoolteacher by comparison. It never bothered her.

"Better," Menaka said, dropping the corporate tone as she moved toward the hub of consoles. "I like you more when you're not pretending to care about ratings, Anasuya."

"And I like you more when you're not pretending you don't," Anasuya replied gently.

Menaka's fingers danced over a panel. One of the screens—top row, second from the left—suddenly expanded across the central wall.

A Swedish news channel. The caption at the bottom read:

INVIGNING AV STOCKHOLMS VÄRLDSBARNHEM

(INAUGURATION OF STOCKHOLM WORLD CHILDREN'S HOME)

Snow drifted lazily past the camera. A small crowd stood outside a freshly painted building, its sign gleaming under winter lights. At the front, flanked by local officials, stood a familiar figure.

Gurpreet Kandola.

Gone were the kurta-pyjamas and white turban of Ghaggar-Nagar. Here, he wore a heavy charcoal overcoat over a high-necked sweater, a dark wool cap pulled over his bald pate, a scarf wrapped fashionably at his neck. He smiled broadly for the cameras, hands joined in a namaste that now looked like a PR gesture more than a blessing.

On either side of him stood two men.

They wore long black winter coats, crisp shirts, narrow ties. Their faces were handsome in a way that was almost generic—symmetrical, smooth, clean. Too smooth. Skin that had never known a sleepless night. Eyes an unremarkable dark brown if you glanced quickly…

But not if you looked properly.

Anasuya took a step closer.

From a distance, the men looked like any European fixers or security detail. But their stillness was wrong. The way their pupils didn't quite react to the flash. The way their breath didn't show on the air while everyone else's did.

Her brows knit.

"Freeze that," she said.

Menaka tapped a key. The frame paused—Gurpreet mid-smile, scissors in hand, the ribbon taut between his fingers. The two men at his shoulders, perfectly composed.

Anasuya studied them, eyes narrowing, seeing past pixels into behavior.

"Vampires," Anasuya said, the word quiet but certain. "Raktans from Airavat. The ones who learned to hide in boardrooms instead of caves."

She lifted her hand lightly, not quite touching the glass, as if feeling for heat that wasn't there.

"See the skin," she went on. "No pores. No flush. And the eyes... no micro-movement. Human gaze jitters. Theirs just... lands."

Menaka's lips curved. "You always did enjoy spotting your little anomalies."

"These are not 'little'," Anasuya replied. "They know how to pass unnoticed for decades." Her gaze slid to Gurpreet. "And he is standing between them like a bridge he doesn't realize he is."

Menaka shrugged, silk whispering softly.

"To the world's cameras, it's a generous Indian MLA opening an orphanage in Stockholm," she said. "New home for 'global children.' The Swedes love a multicultural story."

Anasuya's mouth tightened.

"And we both know what he does with orphanages," she said. "They're not homes. They're loading bays. Input here, export somewhere else. Now he's added vampires to his guest list."

"I didn't invite them," Menaka said lightly. "Before you sharpen your tongue. I didn't assign them this MLA either. Your law-and-order darling can chase that thread."

"Brett should see this," Anasuya answered. "I'll send him the feed. If Devasena is still in Sweden, she will know what to do."

Menaka smiled faintly at the mention of Devasena, but said nothing.

Anasuya tore her gaze away from the frozen image and nodded toward a different cluster of screens showing Indian channels.

"Switch to national," she said.

Menaka flicked another control.

The Swedish winter vanished, replaced by the flicker of an Indian prime-time news broadcast. A stern-faced anchor sat behind a desk, the graphic beside him showing blurred faces and the words:

DELHI SHOCKED AGAIN – BRUTAL GANG RAPE IN CAPITAL

FOURTH CASE THIS MONTH

Footage cut between angry street protests, women shouting slogans, candles held aloft, and a police van forcing its way through a crowd.

Anasuya watched for a long moment.

Then she turned to Menaka.

"You see what your doings are leading to," she said quietly. "Everything in media is being sexualized. Every frame, every jingle, every late-night show. You know what this man"—she nodded toward where Gurpreet's paused face still sat in the corner feed—"is also doing with his 'homes' for children. And still your entire media industry is putting people like him on a pedestal. Sponsors, philanthropists, 'social workers'."

Menaka didn't flinch.

"I'm only giving them what they already desire," she said, almost lazily. "I don't put lust in their hearts, Anasuya. I only give it a language. A mirror. They look into it and reveal themselves."

"A mirror?" Anasuya's brows arched. "A mirror doesn't shout in stereo and follow them into every room. You tilt it exactly where you want them to look, and you know it."

Menaka's smile thinned, but she held it.

"DukhamDukham is inevitable," she replied, tone cooling. "We're already in the last stage of Avsarpini. Pain that forgets it is in pain. The war of Kali and Kalki is inevitable too. I'm not doing anything but letting the cycle arrive on schedule."

Anasuya gave a short, unbelieving laugh.

"On schedule?" she said softly. "You're sprinting toward it. Why are you in such a hurry? Don't you remember Vishnu's conditions?"

For a heartbeat, something old flickered in Menaka's eyes.

"I remember every condition," she said. "I also remember that for Kalki to ride, Kali must finish his work. I'm not the one who decided the choreography. I'm just supplying the music."

"People were selling bodies long before my first satellite uplink," she said. "I didn't invent Heera-mandi. I just added color grading. You can't blame the river for where the boatman steers."

Anasuya's eyes flashed.

"I've seen your work in Japan," she said quietly. "Four years ago already. Those 'research projects' on online communities. Prototype chat rooms nobody asked for. Latenight phone boards and pager networks. You're laying the stage for a digital Heera-mandi, and you know it. A brothel without walls, without doors, without shame. People baring themselves—mind, body, everything—to anyone who'll look, and calling it liberation."

Menaka laughed, a low sound without much humor.

"That's Vishwakarma's arena," she said. "Servers, code, protocols, network diagrams. I just put faces in the boxes once he builds the grid. You should scold him if you're worried about 'platforms'."

"I will," Anasuya said. "But you're the one already planning what to flood them with. Don't hide behind him."

"When this breaks," she said softly, "the ones you helped descend won't just drown each other. They'll reach for you too. And don't tell me you didn't see that in any of your mirrors."

For the first time, something like annoyance—perhaps pain—flickered across Menaka's face.

"We are already losing track of an anomaly in Bharat Kshetra," she said, deflecting. "Some soul or power has slipped past Indra's veil; everyone in the Council is restless about it. You want to spend your time scolding me because my presenters show a bit of leg?"

"It is exactly because we can't see the anomaly clearly that your noise worries me," Anasuya replied. "When every channel screams, it's easier for real danger to whisper past unnoticed. Raktans in Stockholm. Don't know how many Ghraaks are breaking out of Magog."

A small, grim smile touched Menaka's lips. "You still think there's a difference between human vice and demon hunger."

"There is," Anasuya said. "Humans still have the option to be ashamed."

Menaka said nothing, but her jaw worked once, as if she were grinding down a response before it formed.

At the door, Anasuya paused.

"You're not evil, Menaka," she said softly. "You're impatient. You want to skip to the climax and forget that every small choice in between still matters. Just remember—when DukhamDukham fully settles in, when pain forgets it is pain—there is no guarantee even Kalki's war will look the way you imagine. Chaos does not always obey the ones who cheered it on."

For a heartbeat, the impossible queen of screens looked very much like a girl being scolded.

Then the mask slid back into place.

"Go file your reports, Maa," she said, voice light again. "I'll go fix tomorrow's primetime."

Anasuya's mouth twitched despite herself at the "Maa". Then she stepped out into the corridor. The door sighed shut behind her.

Inside, Menaka turned back toward her wall of moving light.

On one screen, Gurpreet smiled for the Stockholm cameras, two Raktans at his side, snow falling around them like the ashes of a future no one would admit to seeing.

On another, Delhi burned in outrage over another shattered girl.

And in between, Menaka's channels kept playing—songs, laughter, desire, a thousand tiny mirrors reflecting the same hunger back at a world already slipping toward Dukham-Dukham, one broadcast at a time.

THE SILENT PROTECTOR

1998 – Ayodhyapuram-Vallabhipur, Gujarat

The last hues of twilight clung to the sky over Vallabhipur. The *Ayodhyapuram Jain Temple*, still under construction, stood like a skeletal silhouette against the darkening sky. Half-chiselled marble pillars reached skyward, scaffolding wrapped around them like webs. The scent of stone dust and incense mixed in the cool evening air.

A few temple pundits and tired workers lingered near the unfinished steps, their tools set aside, finding comfort in the stories often shared by the humble temple priest, *Vasudev Bhai Shah*.

Kalaha, seated calmly on the rough, unfinished stone steps, let his eyes drift over the scattered audience. Yet, beyond the familiar faces of workers and caretakers, his sharp gaze caught a figure standing still in the distance, shrouded in shadows.

Karthik.

Kalaha recognized him instantly. His presence was deliberate.

But Kalaha betrayed no reaction. His expression remained composed, his tone steady as he spoke.

"Tonight," his voice carried softly through the dust-laden air, "I will tell you a story not often heard. A story of protection, of life, and of battles that go unseen."

The workers leaned in closer, their fatigue forgotten. Kalaha's voice grew richer, deeper, weaving the ancient tale into the growing night.

"This is the story of Naigamesha, the divine guardian of life. Known by many names—some know him as Kartikeya, the valiant son of Lord Shiva, but in Jain tradition, he is also remembered as the protector of children, the silent force that shields life at its most fragile."

His eyes flickered briefly to Karthik, then back to the crowd.

Long ago, when the fabric of the universe trembled in delicate balance, a soul destined for greatness was preparing to enter the mortal world. This soul would become Mahavir, the twenty-fourth Tirthankara, the beacon of liberation for countless souls.

But not all welcomed this divine birth.

Across realms, dark forces stirred. Shadows of ignorance and pride, karmic bonds of hatred and deceit—forces that thrived on keeping souls chained to the cycle of birth and death—awoke. They feared what Mahavir's birth would bring: a path to freedom, a light piercing the endless night of suffering.

These dark energies sought to disrupt his coming, to taint the sacred process before it could begin.

In the heavens, Indra, the king of celestial beings, foresaw this danger. The balance could not be risked. And so, he summoned the one protector who could guard this fragile spark of life.

Naigamesha.

With the swiftness of wind and the gentleness of rain, Naigamesha descended to the mortal realm. His form was both fierce and compassionate—a divine being with the head of a ram and the body of a man, embodying the perfect balance between strength and care.

But his task was not one of battle.

Under Indra's command, Naigamesha carried out a sacred act.

The embryo of the Tirthankara was delicately transferred from the womb of a Brahmin woman to Queen Trishala. This divine shift was not simple—it required the utmost care, for even a whisper of imbalance could unravel the destiny of the soul meant to liberate countless beings.

This was the battle Naigamesha fought—not with weapons, but with unwavering precision and boundless compassion.

Yet his duty did not end with the transfer.

For the months that followed, as Queen Trishala carried the unborn Mahavir, Naigamesha stood as an unseen shield. The dark forces that wished to corrupt the birth found themselves repelled at every turn. Her vivid dreams—of elephants, divine lakes, and golden mountains—were signs of his vigilant protection.

But Naigamesha's guardianship was not only for Mahavir.

For countless ages, he had answered the silent prayers of mothers and fathers alike. In Jain temples even today, his form is worshipped by those yearning for children, by parents seeking the safety of their young. In every flickering lamp lit in his honor, in every whispered prayer for protection, his spirit endures.

In our other ancient stories, as Kartikeya, he led celestial armies, but even in war, his true strength was in his compassion. Though he held a spear forged from cosmic fire, his greatest power lay in his relentless love for life, in his duty to shield those who could not shield themselves.

Strength and tenderness. Power and compassion.

This was the eternal legacy of Naigamesha.

Kalaha's voice softened, letting the story linger in the cool air.

"Many gods are worshipped for their might. But Naigamesha is remembered for his protection—not of kingdoms, but of life itself. His strength was never in destruction but in the preservation of what is most delicate."

A quiet stillness hung over the gathering.

The soft hum of distant tools faded as the last light of day slipped beyond the horizon. The workers sat motionless, holding onto every word that had just been spoken.

Slowly, Kalaha's gaze drifted back to the man in the shadows.

To Karthik.

Their eyes locked.

In that moment, something ancient stirred within Karthik.

The story was not just a story.

It was a mirror, reflecting something buried deep within him—an echo of a truth he had long forgotten.

A flicker of memory.

Not of battles, but of *warmth*. Of a role once held, not as a destroyer, but as a *guardian*.

Karthik's chest tightened, and before he could stop it, his eyes grew misty.

His heart, long hardened by the weight of duty and war, softened.

A warmth he thought lost returned, faint but real.

Kalaha said nothing. He didn't need to.

But after a long pause, his voice, steady and calm, broke the silence.

"I can only hope," Kalaha said softly, his gaze still lingering on the horizon, "that in northern India, where the youth are drowning in the grip of addiction… he would return again. To protect them. To save the children from poison."

The words hung in the air like a quiet prayer, weaving through the dust and the cold wind.

But they were not meant for the workers.

They were meant for *him*.

Karthik's breath caught for a moment.

In that instant, clarity struck.

Kalaha knew nothing about the surge in heroin smuggling. Nothing about the connection between growing empire of poison blooming in Punjab and Tejomayi. His words were genuine—a subtle nudge, perhaps, but free of deceit.

He isn't involved.

Karthik's shoulders eased slightly, his mind piecing together the final thread he needed.

He had seen and heard enough.

Before the workers could rise and the evening scattered them back to their routines, Karthik was gone.

Vanished into the fading light.

Kalaha did not look for him. He simply stared into the distance, the flicker of a knowing smile hidden beneath his calm expression.

And so, the story of Naigamesha lingered in the air, but Karthik had already carried its weight with him into the coming storm.

HUNGER IN THE SNOW

1998 – Village in Northern Sweden

Early January 1998 – Northern Sweden – Polar Night, the sun had abandoned this land.

For weeks, the sky over northern Sweden had known only twilight—a deep, bruised blue smeared with faint strokes of green aurora. Snowfields rolled out in every direction, broken only by black lines of pines and the frozen glint of lakes locked in ice.

Rudra stood on a ridge of windcarved snow, boots half sunk in the crust. The cold clawed at exposed skin, the air so sharp it could have cut a human's lungs.

He barely felt it.

A matte black tactical jacket strained against his shoulders, layered over dark thermals that clung to his powerful frame. His hair was pulled back, a few strands lashing his forehead in the wind. Amberbrown eyes scanned the valley below, catching details that normal eyes would never see.

The research outpost crouched at the edge of a frozen inlet—low metal buildings, a tall radio mast, satellite dishes rimmed in ice, a scatter of wooden cabins.

No lights.

No exhaust from generators.

No movement.

Just silence.

"Mathew."

The voice in his earpiece was smooth, low, utterly steady. Desiree. To the world, an elegant ghost drifting through Scandinavian diplomatic circles.

To him, always—his mother, Devasena.

"I'm here," Rudra murmured, not taking his eyes off the station.

"Last transmission from the team was at 02:17," she said. "Panic, screaming, then nothing. No distress signal. No evacuation. Satellite shows no warm bodies inside. No vehicles leaving."

Another voice slid in—lighter, quick, threaded with familiar mischief.

"I've got the southern approach," she said. "Snowmobile tracks go in. None come out. Classic."

Rudra smirked faintly. "Usha—sorry, Isha—you're late."

"You start without me, I'll break your nose," she shot back.

He could almost see her grin.

"Thermal?" Devasena asked.

"Eight signatures total," Usha replied. "One in the main building, seven scattered around the cabins. None at human body temp.

Everything normal out here is... cold. Except your son. He's glowing, as usual."

Rudra's jaw tightened.

A whole outpost didn't go dark by coincidence.

"Maybe they were evacuated," he said, though he didn't believe it.

"Evacuations leave tracks," Devasena replied quietly. "Footprints. Tire marks. Radio traffic. We've got none of that."

She didn't add the rest: *what we have are bodies.*

Faces drained of all colors. Bodies twisted midmotion, as if time had stopped in a scream.

Veins empty. Skin slack. No clean wounds.

Just... emptied.

Rudra reached up, unslung the rifle from his back, and checked the magazine by touch.

The rounds inside were not ordinary metal.

They were dull, almost black, etched with faint, curling lines like miniature yantras. Vishwakarma had named the alloy Vajraneel—a mix of fallen starmetal, a whisper of Indra's shattered vajra, and something from below the earth that didn't have a name in any human language.

"Vajraneel rounds loaded," he muttered.

"Confirmed," Usha said. "Those should break the Rakhtline. At least, that's what the old tests say."

He remembered the briefings:

These weren't human vampires turned by bite.

They were pure breed orcs, *Ghraaks*.

Descendants of Rakhtbeej's spilled blood, carried through time by the cursed currents of the Rakt River in Airavat Kshetra. They had learned to clot themselves into bodies, wear almosthuman faces when it suited them—and tear those faces apart when it didn't.

"Mathew." Devasena's tone sharpened slightly. "We go in hard if we have to. But I want eyes first, not blind fire. Understood?"

He exhaled. "Understood."

He started down the slope, every sense stretching ahead of him.

As he drew closer, details emerged from the softness of snow.

A sled halfburied, its rope lying across the path, cut cleanly in two. A cabin door hanging open, beaten crooked against its hinges. A mitten, small and blue, lying fingersup in the snow.

Rudra paused.

The mitten was dusted with white, but the cloth beneath was stiff, edges darkened.

His throat tightened.

"They had children here?" he asked quietly.

"Two families registered," Usha said. "One with a baby. The boy was five. The girl was eight."

Rage stirred, low and familiar, in his chest.

He stepped over the mitten and moved on.

The first cabin door creaked when he pushed it. No lights. No movement. The smell hit him first.

Not rot. That would have taken time.

Something older. Stale metal. Damp stone.

Inside, a table lay overturned. A chair broken. A plate shattered on the floor. Long, clean gouges marked the wooden walls, like claws had traced their way down with absentminded pleasure.

On the floor, near the center of the room, lay a shape under a blanket.

Rudra didn't pull it back.

He had seen enough of these in the photos. He knew what looked like sleep and wasn't.

He stepped out, jaw clenched so hard it hurt.

"Anything?" Devasena asked, already knowing the answer.

"Innocents," he said, voice low. "Emptied. No survivors."

A beat of silence.

When she spoke again, her voice had changed. The warmth was still there—but there was iron inside it.

"Then we don't contain," she said softly. "We cleanse."

Rudra didn't reply.

He didn't have to.

He moved toward the main building.

The station grew larger as he approached. Metal siding, doors rimmed with ice, windows fogged over. The main door hung crooked, bent in at the lock as if something had pushed from outside with casual force.

"I'll thin the ones outside," Usha murmured. "The seven around the cabins. You take the central one."

"Copy," he said.

He stepped through.

The smell hit him again, heavy and intimate.

Metallic. Thick. Fresh.

Blood soaked into metal, into snow dragged inside on boots, into fabric and hair.

He moved along the main corridor, boots clicking softly on the floor. Fluorescent tubes overhead flickered, some dead, others stuttering in sickly yellow pulses. Doors on either side gaped open or hung broken on their hinges.

The first body lay near a fallen chair.

A young man's face turned up, eyes glassy, mouth frozen midshout. His skin was drawn tight, lips darkened. His throat was a torn crater, jagged, no clean cut—ripped out in chunks. His hands were shredded where he'd tried to fight something off. Blood had sprayed the wall in a wide fan, then frozen in glossy streaks.

Rudra's jaw set.

He moved on.

In one dorm, the door had been barricaded from inside with a bunk bed. The bed was now splintered. The door lay inside the room, broken clean from the frame.

Three people huddled against the far wall. A man, his arms spread as if to shield. A woman slumped into his side. Between them, something smaller.

Rudra stepped closer.

A small boot. A small hand.

That was all that remained visible of the child between them. The rest was hidden under their bodies, as if their last act had been to cover what they couldn't protect.

A purple mitten lay a few feet away, tiny, with the knitted face of a cartoon reindeer grinning blindly through a crust of dried blood.

Heat flared in Rudra's chest, hot and unforgiving.

"Mathew," Devasena's voice was softer now. "Breathe."

He forced his lungs to obey.

"This is not feeding," he said, voice low. "This is cruelty."

"That's what they become when no one stops them," Usha replied quietly. "They learn to enjoy the screams."

His grip tightened on the rifle.

He followed the blood.

It grew thicker near the main lab.

The door here wasn't broken. It was wedged open with a shoe.

Inside, equipment lay scattered—stainless steel tables shoved aside, instruments shattered, glass underfoot making a faint crunch with every step. A microscope lay on its side, lens cracked. A computer screen flickered nonsense.

At the center of the room, a long table was almost completely obscured by a dark pool on the floor. Blood. It had spread, thinned at the edges by time and cold, thick in the center where pieces still floated.

Something moved behind the table.

Rudra heard it—the wet, ugly sound of flesh being pulled free. Chewing. A low, satisfied clicking.

He rounded the table.

It was crouched on its haunches, back to him, spine too long, jutting sharply under skin that looked like old snow. Its shoulders were narrow, arms unnaturally long, fingers sunk deep into the body beneath it.

The woman beneath was still alive.

Her eyes were wide, fixed on some point beyond him. Her mouth opened and closed soundlessly. Her shirt had been pulled aside at the collar. The thing above her had torn a ragged hole in the side of her neck and shoulder, not neat, not precise—gnawed. Flesh was missing in uneven chunks.

The monster tore off another piece with its teeth and chewed loudly, blood running from its mouth down its chin. It tossed its head a little, almost in pleasure.

Rudra tasted iron at the back of his own throat.

"Get off her," he said.

The creature stopped.

Slowly, it straightened.

It turned its head.

Its face was a mockery of human form. Skin too tight over sharp bones, cheekbones like blades. No whites to its eyes—just deep, wet black, like pits full of oil. Its mouth was wrong. It opened wider than it should, jaw unhinging slightly, revealing not two long canines but rows of small, pointed teeth, each one filed like a needle.

It smiled.

Not with kindness. With recognition. With interest.

When it spoke, the sounds were jagged, harsh, a tangle of consonants that scraped the air. But meaning slid under the sounds, straight into Rudra's spine.

"Himavant's runt," it hissed. "Abraham's cub."

Rudra steadied his breath.

"You know me and how do you know my father's current code name?"

"We smell you," it said, inhaling exaggeratedly. "Dev Lok stink. Veil blood. Child of the one who breaks armies."

Its head tilted, eyes narrowing.

"You've done enough," Rudra said. "Let her go."

The thing looked down at the woman pinned beneath it.

Then, very deliberately, it sank its fingers deeper into her shoulders.

Her lips trembled. A sound finally escaped—a broken, tiny whimper.

The ghraak's black gaze never left Rudra's face.

"There," it said softly. "Now watch."

It twisted its hands.

The woman's neck snapped with a sharp, small crack.

Her body jerked once, then went slack.

For a second, everything in Rudra went silent.

Then it broke.

"Under stone," it went on, as if nothing had happened. "Under desert. Beneath a small mountain where your people plan to test their little suns." Its black eyes gleamed with something close to pleasure. "There is a hollow there. A Pit. It breathes beneath the sand. Our brothers found it. We like what it dreams."

A map flared unbidden in his mind—classified files Brett had shared with them in hushed briefings. A barren range in Baluchistan the world knew only as a weapons test site.

Ras Koh.

That was enough.

He closed the distance in a heartbeat.

One hand clamped around creature's right forearm, the other locking onto its shoulder.

He pulled.

The arm tore free at the socket with a dry, cracking sound. No spray, no scream—just a choked, shocked noise as the creature staggered, staring at the limb in his hand as if the world had broken a rule.

Before it could recover, he seized its other arm and ripped that one free too.

"Mathew," Devasena's voice murmured in his ear. There was no command in it—just presence.

Ghraak dropped to its knees on the blood-slick floor, chest heaving in short, ragged breaths. It tried to lunge at him, mouth wide, teeth snapping for his throat.

He caught its jaw with both hands.

"You don't touch children," he said.

He wrenched.

The lower jaw tore loose with a horrible, dry crack and hung in his grip like a broken piece of bone. Its tongue flopped uselessly, black eyes wide with animal panic now, soundless.

He let the jaw fall.

Then he set his hands on either side of its skull.

It scrabbled at his chest with the stumps of its arms, but there was nothing left in those movements.

He squeezed.

Bone resisted. For a moment.

Then it gave.

The skull caved under his hands like thin stone under a hammer. The body shuddered once and collapsed sideways, head broken, face ruined, finally still.

Silence rushed in, thick and heavy.

Rudra stayed there, kneeling, fingers still dug into the fractured skull, chest heaving.

"Two outside just moved," Usha's voice cut in. "They heard that."

He stood, stepped to the doorway.

Through the lab's small window, he saw them—two pale shapes loping between the cabins toward the main building, movements jagged and too fast.

He raised his rifle, but a sharper crack beat him to it.

One of the creatures' heads snapped back midstride and exploded against the snow outside, courtesy of a Vajraneel round from the telecom tower.

The second one spun toward the sound.

Rudra fired. The bullet took it clean through the temple. It dropped, skidding across ice, limbs twitching uselessly.

"Try not to let them hug you next time," Usha said, breath fogging slightly in his ear. "Your face is too pretty."

He huffed once, a sound almost like a laugh, but there was no humor in his eyes.

"Seven," she added softly a moment later. "Area clear."

Rudra walked back out into the open.

The outpost was a ring of silence and wrong bodies—pale limbs sprawled between cabins, heads at broken angles, dark stains soaking into white. No one was left to scream now.

Or to feed.

Snow crunched behind him.

Devasena walked into the circle of cabins, coat tight against the cold, hair pulled back, grey eyes taking in the scene in a single sweep. Her gaze lingered on the blue mitten by the first door. The emotion that crossed her face was sharp, but it passed quickly, buried beneath purpose.

She stopped near the rotten demon he had killed in the lab, now dragged halfway into the snow outside, its skull crushed, arms torn away.

"Any last words?" she asked, meaning the creature.

"He said there's a Pit under a desert mountain where people plan to test little sun," Rudra replied, standing, wiping his hands on his torn jacket. "Something breathing beneath the sand. Said their brothers 'like what it dreams.'"

A muscle in her jaw tightened.

"We'll get that to Brett," she said quietly. "Let Abraham and the others pull the thread. If something is breathing under Ras Koh, I want eyes on it."

Rudra nodded, but his eyes were on the cabins, on the silent doors.

"It still feels like we're late," he said.

"We were," Devasena answered, no lie in it. "For them, we were. For the next outpost…" She glanced at the bodies in the snow. "Maybe not."

Usha joined them a moment later, rifle slung, cheeks flushed from the cold. She looked at the ring of corpses, at the tiny mitten, then at her brother's bloody knuckles.

"Next time," she said, voice tight, "we get here before they start playing."

Rudra didn't answer.

He just looked once more at the shattered station, at the heap of monsters who'd thought no one would come, and let the hatred settle into something cold and useful.

Far to the south, under rock and sand and plans made in war rooms, something old shifted slightly in its sleep.

It did not wake.

But it had heard.

And now, so had they.

As the long polar night closed back in, three dark figures walked away from the ruined station in silence, their footprints fading into the snow while behind them piles of demon bodies burned high and slow—the only light left in the frozen dark desert.

—⚲⁄⌨✡—

FIRE BENEATH THE MOUNTAINS

1998 – Ras Koh Hills-Balochistan, Pakistan

The sun blazed over the Ras Koh Hills of Balochistan, Pakistan, casting sharp shadows across the rugged mountains. The afternoon heat clung to the arid air, thick with the scent of sand and stone. Beneath this desolate landscape, something far more sinister thrived within the heart of the mountains.

Nestled deep within the hills was a fortress of terror—a hidden heroin laboratory, guarded not by mere criminals but by the full weight of Pakistan's military. Reinforced iron doors gleamed under the harsh daylight, framed by flickering security lights and watched closely by guards armed to the teeth.

But today, they would be tested.

At 2:45 p.m. on May 28th, 1998, a lone figure stood in plain sight against the blinding light. His tight black suit clung to his frame, the top buttons of his shirt undone, revealing the solid form beneath. The oppressive heat of the desert air rippled around him, but Karthik stood unmoved.

His amber eyes burned with a quiet, smouldering rage.

Kalaha's words echoed in his mind. *"If only he could return to save the children..."*

For now, the greater war could wait. This lab—this wretched hive of poison—had to burn.

Two guards, draped in military fatigues and armed with rifles, noticed him. One barked sharply in Urdu, "*Kaun hai tu?* How did you get here?! This is a restricted zone!"

Karthik did not speak.

The silence was his answer.

Without hesitation, his hands gripped the massive iron doors barring the entrance.

And tore them apart.

Steel shrieked as the thick metal buckled like paper in his grip. The guards froze in disbelief, their eyes wide with terror. One scrambled backward and slammed his fist against the alarm.

The mountains erupted in noise.

Sirens howled. Red lights washed over the stone walls. Panic electrified the air.

Dozens of armed guards stormed forward, their boots pounding on metal floors, weapons raised and ready.

Shouts.

Gunfire thundered.

Rounds from AK-47s, Type 56 rifles, and light machine guns filled the air. The bullets hammered against Karthik's body, sparks flying where they struck—but he didn't flinch.

He did not slow. Dozens of armed guards stormed forward, their boots pounding on metal floors, weapons raised and ready. He advanced, step by deliberate step, his fury mounting with each one.

Inside, the lab was a monstrous monument to science twisted by greed. A sprawling network of sterile, glass-walled chambers and humming machinery. Fluorescent lights buzzed overhead, casting harsh white light on the gleaming steel and polished floors.

The stench of chemicals and death hung in the air.

Karthik moved deeper, his burning gaze scanning the rooms.

COBRA VENOM—Behind glass walls, complex machinery hissed and churned, distilling deadly toxins into concentrated forms.

VIPER VENOM—Rows of tanks and processing units quietly pulsed, feeding the machines that refined nature's deadliest weapons.

Then his eyes fell on the largest chamber.

KRAIT VENOM.

The room stretched endlessly, larger than any of the others. Massive containment units hummed with activity, their insides slithering with serpents trapped in endless coils of suffering. Tubes and needles drained them slowly, mercilessly.

Rage unlike any Karthik had known clawed at him, and he snapped.

Millions of snakes—creatures born of the earth—sacrificed for this filth.

His fists clenched.

And then he *moved.*

No restraint.

He tore through the machinery, metal screaming as he uprooted processing units. Massive steel vats crashed against walls, glass shattered, chemicals hissed, alarms blared louder. Sparks burst as circuitry crumbled beneath his crushing grip.

Soldiers panicked, their bullets ricocheting wildly.

But nothing touched him.

Even as a bazooka was fired in desperation, the missile screamed through the air toward him.

Karthik caught it.

Caught it the way another man might catch a pen tossed across a desk.

His fingers dug into the warhead, stopping it cold. He held it for a moment, the weapon thrumming with deadly force—before he hurled it back into one of the venom chambers.

The explosion tore through the room, flames swallowing steel and glass.

Karthik was unstoppable.

Deeper inside, Karthik found them.

A glass-enclosed conference room.

Men in lab coats—scientists, engineers, architects of this poison—stood frozen in terror. Papers slipped from trembling hands, chairs screeched as they backed away.

Karthik's voice was a low, guttural growl.

"Who is behind this?"

Silence.

No one dared to speak.

Karthik's patience shattered.

Without hesitation, he seized the nearest man by the throat and hurled him upward.

The man's body slammed into the ceiling with a deafening crack, crumpling lifelessly to the floor.

Panic erupted.

Screams filled the air as the others scrambled to hide behind glass tables and scattered documents.

But Karthik's eyes were already on the metal door at the far end of the room.

No label.

He moved toward it.

Inside, the control room was in utter chaos. Red warning lights flashed, alarms shrieked, and monitors flickered with critical system failures. Soldiers and operators scrambled to regain control, but fear had taken hold.

At the center of it all, a man in a military uniform gripped the phone with trembling hands, sweat pouring down his face. His voice was hoarse with panic, yet carried the weight of finality.

"NOW! Trigger it! I don't care what's happening! Do it! Can't you see? We can't wait any longer!"

His breath grew ragged, but his grip tightened on the receiver.

His eyes flicked to the lowest set of monitors—the ones no one was supposed to know existed. In the tunnels below the venom chambers, something moved. Not men. Not snakes. Something older.

For weeks, the readings had climbed. Heat where there should be cold. Shadows where there were no lights.

"If they breach containment and that man sees them," he thought, vision blurring. "We'll lose the last weapon we still trust."

He glanced at the screens—at the destruction rapidly unfolding within the facility—and then closed his eyes for a fleeting moment.

"Bismillah ir-Rahman ir-Rahim..."

In the name of Allah, the Most Gracious, the Most Merciful.

His lips barely moved as he whispered the words, steadying himself.

"This will be my last command!"

His voice thundered, cutting through the panic.

And then the ground began to tremble.

A deep, monstrous roar surged from beneath the earth.

And the world shattered.

The mountains erupted in fire.

The sky split as a nuclear inferno tore through the Ras Koh Hills. The ground heaved and split, swallowing stone and steel alike.

The hidden lab was consumed in an instant—its walls, its machines, its monsters—turned to ash.

Karthik was hurled like a ragdoll, the shockwave launching him miles from the blast.

His body, bare and broken, slammed into the unforgiving mountainside, carving into the rock before collapsing motionless among the shattered stones.

Smoke choked the sky.

Fire raged in the distance.

And silence fell.

The world would call it a nuclear test.

But here, on these scorched mountains, it had been something else.

The winds howled through the scorched rocks, carrying the scent of ash and ruin.

And there, far from the shattered remains of the lab, Karthik lay still.

His breath shallow. His body unmoving.

The guardian, the warrior, consumed by the storm.

And the mountains held their breath.

CHAPTER 13
Bharat Kshetra – The Untold Story

STORY OF BHARAT KSHETRA

1998 – Kolkata, West Bengal

The Rathore home in Kolkata, always a place of calm dignity, had become a whirlpool of anxiety and dread. Voices overlapped, anxious whispers rose and fell, punctuated by strained phone calls and hurried footsteps. Pravash had been missing for days—days that felt like years, each minute heavy as stone.

Meenakshi sat motionless near the household mandir, her eyes fixed but distant, fingers mechanically turning prayer beads. Around her, the room was filled with worried faces—her husband Balraj, whose calm had given way to tension, paced back and forth, phone pressed tight to his ear, his voice strained as he called everyone he knew.

Balraj's brothers, Abhishek and his wife Prabha, moved restlessly, making frantic inquiries. Their sons, Prakash and Ankit, hovered anxiously near the doorway, casting glances outside, as if hoping Pravash would appear at any moment.

Kanchan, Pravash's elder sister, sat near Meenakshi, gently squeezing her mother's trembling hand, her own eyes rimmed red from worry. Aakash, his elder brother, stood near the window, staring silently into the empty street, as if searching for a sign that might never come.

Outside, distant relatives and cousins moved restlessly in and out, their voices tangled in confusion. Each person offered a theory, each call brought either false hope or crushing silence.

The chaos was overwhelming.

Yet, amidst this noise, a single knock echoed clearly, sharply through the house.

Meenakshi looked up, startled. "Did someone hear the door?" she asked softly, but no one answered, they were too consumed by their panic to notice. She slowly rose, steadying herself against the wall, and moved towards the front door.

When she opened the door, no one stood outside.

Only a scroll lay at the threshold.

It was wrapped in ivory-colored parchment, tied with a thin red thread, and sealed with wax. The seal bore a strange symbol—three interlocked triangles within a circle, etched with an elegance that felt ancient.

Her breath caught. The air around it felt oddly still.

She bent down and picked it up. The parchment was cool against her skin, and for a moment she thought she felt a faint vibration under her fingertips, like a distant, hidden heartbeat.

Before she even opened it, some part of her knew: this carried words she needed to read.

Meenakshi slipped quietly back into the puja room and shut the door behind her, shutting out the noise of the house. Sitting before the mandir, she untied the red thread and unrolled the scroll.

The script was in soft, flowing Gujarati—letters written with such care that each stroke felt like a caress.

The first line made her throat tighten:

"*Do not worry about Pravash, Meenakshi. He will return safely into your embrace. But before that moment arrives, it is crucial you understand who he truly is— and the purpose he carries in this world.*

Yet, this story does not begin with Pravash...

It begins with the First Chakravarti of this land—King Bharat, the eldest son of Lord Adinath, eldest among hundred brothers and two sisters, sovereign over six great khands of Bharat Kshetra.

Bharat conquered them all... except Paudanapura, the kingdom of his brother Bahubali.

While the others surrendered their crowns, Bahubali refused. In his eyes, only he was worthy of ruling Akhand Bharat after his father.

Bharat's massive army—one unlike the world had ever seen—stood at Bahubali's gates. In its ranks were fearsome warriors, among them Naag Sena and the dreaded Kukur Sarp Sena—beings with the heads of roosters and the bodies of serpents.

At the head of these mystical armies stood none other than Maa Padmavati, guardian of life and protector of cosmic order. At her side, her closest advisor—Mahendra, a being of immense strategy and loyalty. He was more than a general. He was like a son to her.

Bahubali's sages knew well—victory would be impossible with Mahendra and Maa Padmavati standing beside Bharat.

So they did the unthinkable.

On a fog-wrapped dawn, Bahubali's forces attacked the heart of Bharat's camp—where Mahendra rested.

In the silence before sunrise, blood stained the earth. And there, Mahendra fell—overwhelmed by a swarm of blades.

Maa Padmavati wept. Her tears shook the heavens. Her fury lit up the sky.

Even the gods of Devlok could not watch.

They descended and pleaded—end this war through battle of honor, not annihilation.

And so came the Three Trials: Drishti Yudh – The battle of vision. Jal Yudh – The battle of water and balance. Mal Yudh – The battle of strength.

Bahubali emerged victorious in all.

Enraged by defeat, Bharat hurled his divine chakra—the most sacred of weapons—at Bahubali. But the disc circled Bahubali thrice and dropped, unable to harm a soul bound in blood.

And in that moment, Bahubali saw the illusion of pride.

In a moment of furious impulse, Bahubali lifted Bharat high above his head—but a sudden wave of shame and self-awareness overcame him, making him gently set his brother back on the ground. Ashamed of the path both had walked, Bahubali renounced the world and walked away—into silence, into sainthood.

And Bharat became the first Chakravarti of Akhand Bharat Kshetra, ruling with divine ratnas and the fourteen sacred jewels.

But the soul of Mahendra did not rest.

He returned again—this time as Kamath, the evil brother of Marubhuti in Lord Parshvanath's time.

And again... he fell birth after birth.

In his final life of that cycle, he emerged as Meghamali, a wizard of immense might and fierce pride.

Jealous of the great austerities of Lord Parshvanath, Meghamali sought to disturb his deep meditation.

He summoned a terrifying storm—clouds darkened, rains poured, rivers swelled, and a flood surged to drown the unmoving Lord Parshvanath.

But as waters rose, Dharanendra Dev appeared from the heavens—spreading his majestic twenty-seven-headed hood above, shielding Lord Parshvanath from the relentless storm.

And beneath, in fierce devotion, was Maa Padmavati, circling tirelessly around Parshvanath,

creating a whirlpool of protection, ensuring not a drop of water could disturb his sacred penance.

Meghamali watched in disbelief—his storm, his pride, his ego shattered against divine protection.

Overcome by remorse, he fell to his knees, realizing his grave mistake.

Maa Padmavati could have ended him, but in her boundless compassion, she chose mercy instead of retribution.

Her forgiveness became his liberation—softening the harsh karmas he carried, freeing his soul to journey forward once more, toward rebirth, toward redemption.

Then, reborn once more...

He came as Ashoka.

The emperor whose name is still spoken in every corner of India.

A king crowned with the title of Chakravarti, yet one who had not stepped beyond the edges of the visible world—a world that is merely a fraction of vast Bharat Kshetra.

This known world is only a single Khand among six.

Its scale—a mere tiny part of the full land that stretches beyond your oceans, beyond your satellites, beyond your memory.

Ashoka's life was a paradox.

A man of immense compassion, and a ruler of terrible wrath.

Known as Chand-Ashok, the Cruel Ashoka, his hands once dripped with the blood of conquests.

Yet those same hands folded in deep penance, shaking the very gates of Devlok.

In silence, he meditated. In silence, he rose, he started gaining immense knowledge.

And the heavens trembled—not from his violence, but from his restraint, that someone so cruel can be so saint in single lifetime.

His gaze turned inward, his soul toward fire.

What he could not conquer through war, he sought through truth.

And it was in this stillness that Indra Deva came—

Not with thunder, but with humility, for even the gods feared the depth of his awakening.

Indra Dev grew concerned.

He descended to Madhya Lok to meet Ashoka himself—afraid his penance might soon pierce Devlok.

Indra, along with eight other Devas, disguised themselves as wise sages—offering to become his Ratnas.

Together, they offered to become his Ratnas—his living jewels, his illuminati.

Not to lead, but to preserve.

They vowed to carry forward his knowledge through cycles and centuries, to become guardians of truths not meant for ordinary time.

Then, in secret, they erected a shield around the southern Khand of Bharat Kshetra—A veil, invisible to the mortal eye, so that no soul could cross it unless called upon by fate itself.

Think, Meenakshi...

Do you truly believe that people riding horses and buggies built the towering temples of Angkor Wat, the star-aligned stepwells of Gujarat, or the perfect symmetry of ancient churches and pyramids in South America—all within the last 2000 years?

No.

These were not mere monuments.

They were echoes—windows into other realms.

Markers of when the shield thinned.

Whispers left behind when the portals stirred.

But from time to time, as fate demanded, beings from Airavat, Shikarin, Rakta River Isles and other realms were allowed to enter—through portals, where space and time behaves in a way that current human mind cannot comprehend, known only to the Devas.

Some came to restore balance. Some came to rebel. Others came to flee from their karma.

These portals are rare—and old.

There are places on this Earth where space and time do not follow ordinary rules.

Some of these locations awaken the soul the moment one steps in—others, remain sealed, only to be accessed when the gods so will, and only by those destined to see beyond the veil.

These sites are not gates in the traditional sense—they are folds, creases in the fabric of existence, where the realms bleed through in whispers, visions, or sudden, impossible stillness.

Among them:

Near Kailash Parvat, at the footstep of Ashtapad—a place now hidden from human eyes by the Devas themselves.

Deep in the Bermuda region, where compasses spiral and time frays like thread.

One beneath the eternal snow of the North Pole, and three shrouded in the silence of Antarctica.

A city where millions gather to circle a structure said to house a celestial fragment… its access veiled, its gravity ancient.

Another that radiates from a throne of keys, where saints once walked, and silence cloaks the archives of light.

Not all of them are meant to be understood.

Some are remembered.

Some are dreamed.

And some were never built for mortals at all.

Some say others have opened few more, hidden from Devas.

And The Nine still try to control them.

But hear this now, Meenakshi:

Ashoka has returned.

The one who unknowingly began this matrix—must now end it.

He has returned as your son—Pravash.

He will not walk this path alone.

One will walk beside him from a bond born in the past.

Another will rise to make unbreakable bond with him in the future.

You, Meenakshi,
are chosen not just as his mother,
but as the guardian of his truth.
Your son carries a mischievous spirit,
playful yet restless, inherited from lifetimes past.
At times, he may stray, drawn to paths unseen,
distracted by the charms of the world.
It is your sacred duty to guide him back,
gently, firmly, to his destined path.
For you alone possess the strength,
patience, and love to anchor him.
Time will come when you will hear
the celestial call—the divine sound
of the Panchajanya.
At that very moment, Meenakshi,
you will understand what you must do.
Until then, remain steadfast.
Prepare yourself.
Prepare your heart.
For this is not merely the story of a son.
It is the story of Bharat Kshetra—The Untold Story.

— Thus Spoke Vyasa"

KING OF UNRESERVED COACH

1998 – Ahmedabad, Gujarat; Kolkata, West Bengal

The Ahmedabad railway station hummed like a restless beast—a mix of metal, sweat, hawkers, and urgent footsteps. Pravash sat on his modest duffel bag, his knees bobbing restlessly, elbows perched on his thighs, palms clenched together as if in prayer to time itself. His freshly shaved head gleamed under the flickering sodium lamps, the thick smears of black kajal across his cheeks making him unrecognizable even to himself.

"Attention passengers, Howrah Express will depart shortly from platform number... nine."

The announcement cracked through the station's speakers like a lightning bolt. Pravash's breath hitched, a nervous fire racing down his chest. His heart thudded as though it had only been waiting for this confirmation to come alive. He stood up so abruptly that his bag toppled behind him.

Platform Nine. Howrah Express.

Home.

Saira.

The name pulsed in his mind louder than the crowd around him. He clutched his duffel, adjusted the collar of his oversized shirt, and strode toward the platform with the urgency of a fugitive and the hope of a pilgrim.

His worldly possessions were small but precious—tucked in the side pocket was a half-empty twenty-pack of menthol cigarettes, bought with the last of his coins. Around his neck dangled his most loyal companion: a Sony Walkman, its worn casing scratched by memory and travel. Inside spun a cassette of *Dil*

Se, the soundtrack that had become the anthem of his ache, his defiance, and his yearning—music by Rahman, emotions by fire.

The train screeched into the platform, its unreserved coaches already bursting at the seams with bodies, bags, babies, and the chaos of untethered journeys. Pravash shoved his way in, heart hammering against ribs like a trapped drum.

The coach was a boiling pot of limbs and life—no place to sit, barely space to stand. The air was thick with humanity, a shared breath of a hundred strangers bound only by necessity. Pravash pressed his back against the cool metal wall near the door, balancing his duffel between his legs. He looked like nothing and no one—just another nameless boy in a crowded train.

But kings are often born in disguise.

He pulled out the menthol cigarette and lit it. The first drag hit like an icy breeze in a desert storm. He closed his eyes, letting the cool menthol twist through his chest like balm. A man sitting cross-legged beside him—wiry, sunburned, with eyes like mischief incarnate—nudged him.

"*Bhai, ek drag milega kya*?"

Pravash, without a word, handed over the cigarette. In seconds, a few others leaned in too, eyes wide with curiosity.

Another one puffed. "*Areeey... yeh toh thanda thanda hai*!"

A wave of laughter erupted. "*Yeh toh sardi waali cigarette hai bhai*! Where did you get this magic stick?"

Amused, and with nothing to lose, Pravash pulled out the pack and passed it around like royal currency. Cheers erupted like he'd uncorked champagne.

And then, something miraculous happened.

The camaraderie of smoke turned to a gesture of gratitude. The men, giddy and generous, stood up, reached for the luggage compartment above, and began unloading it—sacks, bags, ropes, tins, whatever was stored, now piled onto the floor. Within minutes, they had cleared it completely.

"*Yahan baith jao bhai. Tum raja ho aaj.*" one of them grinned, lifting Pravash's bag into the space. Another boosted him up by the arm.

Pravash, stunned, sat on the hard steel rack, his legs dangling like a boy who'd just climbed onto the throne of a moving kingdom. He removed his headphones, wound the cable carefully, and then, with the simple flick of a switch, set his Walkman's loudspeaker into motion.

The opening notes of *Chaiyya Chaiyya* soared into the crammed coach like a breeze, playful and untamed. Children perked up. Someone tapped a beat on the metal side panel. Laughter rose. Even the grumpiest faces softened.

Pravash leaned back, smoke curling from his lips, his legs swinging gently to the rhythm. For that one unforgettable night, in a train surging eastward across India's veins, inside an unreserved coach of sweat and song—he was king.

Not of land, not of riches, but of something rarer.

Of moment. Of music. Of hearts briefly set free.

The echoes of *Dil Se* had faded into distant dreams. The unreserved coach, once a storm of sound and sweat, had quieted to the hush of exhaustion. As the train snaked across the final stretch of eastern India, Pravash lay on the luggage rack, half-awake, half-afraid. His head still rested against the steel wall, sticky with the dust of a thirty-six-hours journey.

Somewhere in the depth of that endless ride, between stations, between hunger and cigarette drags, between Rahman's music and tired glances at the slipping countryside—he had begun to hope.

But hope was a dangerous companion. Because now, as the train began to slow near Howrah, reality returned.

The familiar skyline of Kolkata peeked through the smeared window pane—grey buildings, rusted railings, the pale gold of the river beyond. The massive arched roof of Howrah Station loomed ahead. Pravash's heart began pounding—not the rhythm of excitement, but the terror of being seen.

He sat up slowly, his legs trembling. He wiped his palms against his trousers and instinctively checked the kajal smeared across his face. It had faded, but his head remained bald, his clothes dirty—he looked nothing like Pravash Rathore. That was the point.

He peeked through the iron bars of the window. The platform was a sea of chaos—coolies in red uniforms, families shouting over bags, vendors hawking tea. And then, through the blur—he saw them.

His family.

His father, Balraj, stood stiff and composed near the arrival gate, eyes scanning every face.

His mother, Meenakshi, hands trembling at her sides.

And then—Aakash. His elder brother.

Leaning against a pillar, arms crossed but gaze alert, scanning the coaches with silent fury. Pravash's breath caught in his throat. He couldn't move.

He had been right. They were watching every train.

He stayed still, his back pressed into the corner by the door, until the train crawled to a full halt. Slowly, silently, like a shadow, he slipped off the luggage rack, hoisted his bag, and followed the flow of passengers.

With a practiced slouch and sunken gaze, he walked right past them. Past his brother. Past his cousins. Past eyes that had once known him better than he knew himself.

No one stopped him.

No one recognized him.

The moment his feet touched the station's outer steps, he didn't look back. Not at the station, not at the family he just evaded—not even at the city that raised him. His heart pounded like a war drum. Every second now felt like he was living on borrowed time.

He knew it: the Rathores would've searched every corner by now—every school friend, cricket buddy, tuition mate. He could already imagine Ravi being interrogated, Sumeet being called home. He needed someone they couldn't even think of.

Someone only he remembered.

And then, through the haze of fear, came the name—Ariful.

The humble fruit vendor who had once gifted him guavas for helping carry crates near Mohammed Ali Park, years ago. But there was a slip—he didn't remember that it was Shyam who had introduced him to Ariful. And if Shyam had spoken, the chain might already be broken.

But Pravash had no other choice.

He flagged a taxi and gave the address to Park Circus.

The taxi chugged through the crowded lanes of Central Kolkata, weaving between trams and buses, past honking scooters and red-brick buildings now faded into sepia. Pravash sat hunched, his shaved head covered with a thin scarf, eyes peering out of the dust-smudged window.

When they reached the modest apartment block, the taxi meter ticked to a halt. Pravash didn't move. He looked at the fare and then at his empty wallet.

Before the driver could speak, Ariful himself appeared at the gate, wiping his hands on a towel, having just stepped out for errands.

"Arey... Pravash bhai??"

Ariful froze. He barely recognized him—the bald head, sunken cheeks, kajal-smudged eyes. But the voice... it was unmistakable.

"*Bhai... paise nahi hai*," Pravash mumbled, gesturing to the driver.

"Don't worry," Ariful said quickly, fishing out his wallet. He handed the money over and gestured the driver away.

Inside, the walls were warm and welcoming, smelling faintly of roasted cumin and tea. A small fan spun overhead, slicing the silence.

Ariful stared at Pravash, disbelief still settling in his eyes. "*Tu theek hai? Itna badal gaya hai tu... kya haal bana liya hai?*"

Pravash gave a tired laugh. "*Main zinda hoon... bas.*" ("I'm alive... that's all.")

Inside, the small living room smelled of cardamom and old paint. Ariful offered him water, watching him closely. Pravash sat on the edge of a charpoy, his back hunched, hands shaking slightly.

Ariful didn't say it, but the truth hung in the room like a monsoon cloud—the Rathores had come the night before, desperate, begging, searching.

But he didn't tell Pravash.

Instead, he knelt in front of him, hands on his knees.

"Bhai," he said softly, "I don't know everything, but I've heard... your family is broken right now. They think you're gone forever. They haven't eaten. Haven't slept. You have to meet them."

Pravash looked away, jaw clenched.

A moment passed.

Then, gently, he leaned in, his voice lower. "They're dying inside. Maybe it's time you saw them... at least once. Even if things go wrong, all your friends—me, everyone—we'll stand with you. Even if it means running away with Saira... we'll make it happen."

There was no drama in his words. Just honesty. And hope.

Pravash stared at the wall. A long pause. Then—he stood up. Silent.

"Take me," he said.

Ariful smiled and reached for his car keys.

The streets passed by in silence as they drove toward Elgin Road, where the Rathores had moved after leaving the old house near Mohammed Ali Park. The afternoon sun hung heavy in the sky, the city buzzing, unaware of the storm inside the boy beside him.

The car slowed to a halt outside the familiar building. Ariful glanced at Pravash. "You sure?"

Pravash nodded.

He stepped out, walked to the door, and rang the bell.

Footsteps.

The latch turned.

Ding.

The chime echoed.

Seconds passed. Then footsteps.

The door creaked open.

And there stood Kanchan—his elder sister. For a moment, she simply stared at him. Her brows furrowed, confusion in her eyes. Then, something cracked in her chest.

"Pravash...?" she whispered.

And before he could nod—

She screamed.

"Mumma! Papa!! Pravash is here! Pravash is home!!"

The door swung wider. From the narrow crack, he saw them all. Uncles. Aunts. Cousins. Neighbors.

Every face turned in shock, then joy, then tears.

And then—the wave hit him.

Hands pulling him in.

Arms wrapping around him.

Sobs rising like thunder.

Laughter. Crying. Shouts.

As if he had returned from the mouth of death itself.

And Pravash stood there, surrounded by a sea of love he never thought he'd feel again.

Eyes stung. Lips trembled.

Prakash and Ankit—his cousins—were the first to throw their arms around him, nearly knocking him over. Then came his mother, Meenakshi, who crumbled into his chest, clutching his face as if to confirm he was real. His father, Balraj, held him silently, forehead resting on his son's shoulder, tears soaking into his shirt.

Every hallway filled. Every voice trembled. Every eye wept.

It wasn't just a boy who had come home.

It was a lost world returning.

But home—would never be the same again.

Days passed like gentle waves washing over a storm-wrecked shore.

The Rathore household slowly returned to a rhythm—meals resumed on time, the evening temple bell once again echoed through the corridors, and the sound of children laughing softened the memories of silence that had once filled every room.

But even as smiles returned, something lingered beneath the surface.

One night, the clock had just ticked past 2 a.m. The house was still, save for the occasional rickshaw bell ringing faintly down Elgin Road. The ceiling fan hummed gently in the room where Pravash and Aakash now slept side by side, like old times.

Pravash stirred lightly, then froze. He could feel eyes on him.

He turned.

Aakash was sitting upright, his eyes brimming, fixed on Pravash. His fingers trembled, jaw clenched like a dam holding back something vast.

"Bhai…," he whispered, "you have no idea…"

And then, like floodwaters breaking past fragile walls, Aakash broke down. His hand reached out, clutching Pravash's wrist with a desperate force. He began to weep—loud, uncontrollable, painful sobs that echoed through the room.

Pravash shot up, wide-eyed.

"Bhaiya... what happened?!"

But Aakash couldn't speak. His body convulsed with the grief he had buried for too long.

"I thought... we had lost you," he managed between breaths. "I used to wake up... thinking maybe you'd jumped off a train... maybe someone had robbed you... left you in a ditch somewhere... We were looking at every face at every station for days. I kept thinking: What if this world has taken my brother away?"

Tears began streaming down Pravash's own face. He clutched Aakash's hand tight.

"I'm sorry... I was stupid... but I couldn't stop missing her... I couldn't...," Pravash gasped, the weight of guilt and longing crushing him from inside.

The two brothers—one still a boy, the other growing into a man—held each other and cried like sons mourning their father. Except here, the fatherly love flowed from Aakash to Pravash, raw and divine. It wasn't just brotherhood—it was parental, protective, primal.

Aakash's hands moved through Pravash's hairless scalp as if checking again that he was truly home.

Then, as the tears settled into quiet sniffles, Aakash stood up.

He wiped his face, still breathing unevenly, and walked toward the table.

He picked up the cordless landline, pressed a number.

A moment later, he turned back to Pravash. "Here," he said softly, handing over the phone. "It's Yasmeen."

Pravash blinked in surprise, slowly bringing the receiver to his ear.

“Hello?” his voice cracked.

Yasmeen’s voice came through—warm, soft, but edged with something more.

“Pravash…” she paused for a breath, “…listen carefully. I won’t be able to speak to you again after this.”

Pravash sat still, eyes narrowing. “What’s happening?”

Yasmeen’s voice dropped, quiet but clear. “If you had gone to see Saira before coming home... you wouldn’t be alive today.”

The words landed like a blade.

“Her brothers were prepared. They would have found you. Your head… your family would’ve lost a son.”

Pravash’s grip tightened around the phone, but he said nothing.

“And… Saira,” Yasmeen hesitated, “she… she was with you for the money you spent on her. That’s what she told us. That’s the truth now.”

A long pause.

Pravash didn’t answer.

Because he knew it wasn’t true. And Yasmeen knew that he knew it wasn’t true.

But sometimes, love isn’t a matter of truth—it’s a matter of mercy.

“I know,” he finally whispered, swallowing the ache like poison. “Thank you.”

A silence passed between them, heavy and sacred. Then the line disconnected.

Pravash sat for a long time, the receiver still resting in his lap.

That night, he stood by the open window, staring at the quiet trees swaying under a sleepy moon. His throat burned with unshed tears. But his eyes stayed dry.

He made a vow.

He would never again reach out to Saira.

He would not let his family suffer that way again.

He would bury that love

And in the silence of that window, under the ghost-light of Kolkata's streets,

a boy died.

And a man quietly began to take his place.

CHAPTER 14
Fresh Seeds of Eternity

NEW BEGINNINGS

1998-2000 – Kolkata, West Bengal

A few weeks passed. The shock of Pravash's return had melted into a subdued routine. The house had grown quieter, steadier. The family clung to the fragile relief of his presence, carefully avoiding topics that could rattle the balance they were trying to rebuild.

Then came the next phase—his return to school.

Since it was already mid-term, Pravash was admitted to a nearby ICSE school, repeating Standard 9. But the city hadn't forgotten. The society, now armed with whispered judgments and smug pity, had painted a red circle around his name.

To the world outside, he was the boy who ran away. The boy who brought shame.

Parents warned their children: *"Don't go near him... he's trouble."*

And so, Pravash walked into a classroom of turned backs.

Shunned by the polished and the proper, he gravitated to the margins—the same margins that had once comforted him. The rowdies, the outcasts, the notorious boys with slicked-back hair and scarred knuckles—they welcomed him without questions. Not out of respect, but because they sensed a kindred soul—a storm barely caged.

Even the teachers—tired, wary—tiptoed around these boys. They were the untouchables of the classroom, where authority ended and chaos began.

Except for one.

Harshpreet Kandola.

The daughter of Gurpreet Kandola, a man whose empire in Pakistan had recently crumbled, forcing him to pivot fast. His visits to Bangladesh had increased tenfold, and whispers passed through the underworld: *Yaba pills were flying off the lanes of East India*. The map was changing—and Kolkata was suddenly the border worth watching.

Harshpreet had insisted on moving to the city that year, saying she wanted to "experience its education." But truthfully, she was there to prove herself—to shadow her father's dealings, to watch and learn.

Tall, sharp-eyed, and stunning in a way that felt carved from rebellion itself, Harshpreet commanded the corridors like a lioness among pigeons. Boys tried. They all tried. She'd smirk, flirt, ignore, and crush at will. And then move on.

But not Pravash.

To him, she was invisible. Or worse—boring.

This insult was unforgivable.

And so, like all stories where pride is wounded and attention is misplaced, a new axis formed—one that revolved quietly around the girl he did notice.

Priyam.

If Harshpreet was fire and fury, Priyam was quiet sunrise—a girl from a struggling home, raised in scarcity but blooming in grace. Her books were hand-me-downs, her uniforms neatly stitched and re-stitched. She rarely spoke—but when she did, her words carried intent and thought.

Where others avoided Pravash, she helped. She handed him notes, stayed back after class to explain forgotten lessons, and when he made jokes no one else laughed at, she did—softly, without mockery.

And just like that, the shadows of Pravash's past began to blur.

He joined the school cricket team, became a crowd-favorite in sports, and slowly—silently—his place changed.

At the end of that first term, he flunked every subject, along with the rowdy gang that had shielded him. But through the sports quota, he was promoted.

Only one thing had changed—Priyam was now part of his world.

She was still in the same standard. They were now, officially, classmates. And in a strange twist of grace, she stayed—not out of sympathy, but something quieter, warmer. A friendship with gentle roots.

Then came the preparation months for the boards.

In one of the extra Computer Science sessions, something inexplicable happened. Pravash, who had scored 4 out of 100 in the previous exam, suddenly stood up in front of the class and explained the entire algorithm of Bubble Sort and Binary Sort—not just the steps, but the intention behind them. Even the class toppers stared, stunned.

Computers were still a privilege back then in Kolkata. Studying programming was an elite dream, reserved for the coached and the rich.

And there stood Pravash—once a runaway, now decoding logic like it lived in his bloodstream.

When the class ended, Priyam, sitting just behind him, tapped his back and whispered with a crooked grin, "*Since when did you start studying so much? I'm impressed.*"

That single sentence lit a fire in Pravash's chest.

He walked home that evening with a vow blooming silently inside him:

"I will only study Computer Science.

Not for marks.

Not for pride.

But to teach her.

So I can spend my entire life beside her."

As the year progressed, Pravash and Priyam became inseparable—the quiet power couple of the school.

Teachers noticed. Students whispered. And so did Harshpreet.

She watched the attention shift like a throne stolen in silence. For someone used to breaking hearts and writing her name across walls, this was betrayal. She flirted with boys more recklessly, threw her weight around more loudly. But it didn't matter.

All anyone spoke of now was *"Pravash and Priyam."*

And in her fury, she snapped.

It happened on a Thursday afternoon, in the biology lab. Harshpreet had taken biology as an elective. Pravash and Priyam hadn't.

They were seated in their regular class across the corridor.

That day's lesson involved dissecting frogs and fish—something routine. But Harshpreet had brought something else. From under her coat, she revealed a snake, coiled and lifeless, its scales still glistening. Nobody dared question her.

As the teacher fumbled and pretended to be unfazed, Harshpreet sliced through the snake's body—not like a student, but like a butcher punishing flesh.

Then, in a moment that made the air curdle, she grabbed the snake by its neck, stormed out of the lab, and stood in the corridor just outside Pravash's classroom.

Her eyes locked onto his.

She held the dead snake high, its body limp, the neck crushed between her fingers.

Pravash turned toward her—and something shattered.

He couldn't breathe.

The world around him dissolved. His eyes burned as if needles were driven into them. There was no air, no voice, only silence—then blackness.

And then… flashes.

A warfield.

He saw his own body—but it wasn't human.

It was a serpent—mighty, divine, majestic.

And all around him, warriors, hundreds of them, pierced him with long, shining swords. His tail was slashed, his hood beaten down. He cried out, but no sound came.

A memory? A dream? Or something older?

He couldn't tell if he was awake or asleep. If this was a dream, it felt too physical, too precise. Too… deliberate.

He stood up.

His legs didn't want to hold him. He stumbled, gripping the wall for balance. The world swam. He didn't speak. Couldn't.

He stepped out of the classroom, one hand still dragging along the corridor wall, trying to ground himself—but his knees buckled halfway.

He collapsed just outside the door.

A few students saw him go down. Chairs scraped and footsteps hurried toward him.

Priyam was the first to reach him.

She knelt beside him without saying a word. Behind her, a few of his cricket teammates gathered, unsure what to do. He was conscious—but pale, withdrawn, and clearly disoriented. The snake was nowhere to be seen now. Only Pravash's vacant gaze remained, as though he had returned from somewhere far away.

And in his mind, one thought echoed softly:

"It wasn't a dream. Not entirely. It was something else. Something that belonged to me... but from a time I cannot remember."

—❦—

WHISPERS ON THE WIND

2000 – Bangalore, Karnataka; Solan District, Himachal Pradesh

The year was **2000. Soham**, now almost eighteen, stood on the edge of another journey.

He had just completed his final board exams in Bangalore. The last of his subjects, the final bell, the school farewell—everything had passed in a quiet haze. Not because it meant nothing, but because **his heart was somewhere else.**

It had been **six long years** since he had last seen **Appa**—Kalaha, his guide, his anchor, his mystery.

The last time they had some father-son quality time was on a winter night somewhere near **Mount Kailash**, where they had meditated in silence as snow fell gently upon forgotten stones. That memory remained untouched in his soul, wrapped in the scent of incense, firewood, and the whispered rhythm of ancient mantras. Kalaha had promised they would meet again—not in noise, but in necessity.

And now, he had written.

— —

The envelope arrived wrapped in a simple cotton cloth, sealed with the familiar swirl that only Kalaha used—**a rising conch inked in blue, encircled by a feathered spiral.**

Soham had already read the letter **uncountable times.**

The parchment had yellowed slightly. The seal had begun to crack. But the ink within felt freshly poured, as though Kalaha had only just set the pen down.

Ayodhyapuram*—a name not born of nostalgia, but purpose.*

It lies about 160 kilometers from Ahmedabad, just outside the quiet town of Vallabhipur. It is not a place found on any tourist map, but the soul of it is destined to echo for centuries to come.

A few years ago, while a group of Jain monks passed through the site, a snake was run over beneath one of the passing vehicles. It may have seemed a small event, but they understood its significance. That moment was a call. A sign. Plans that once belonged to Ayodhya—to build the idol of Lord Adinath—were moved to this very place.

You must know, Soham, this land was once under the rule of Lord Adinath himself. It is said he ruled from Ayodhya, and so, this place was named Ayodhyapuram in honor of his eternal kingdom.

The idol, to be carved from a living stone, which is yet to arrive. But the foundation must be laid in silence. You must arrive before the stone does.

You will not be known by your name.

You will blend among the worker families, carrying no identity but that of a humble laborer.

For only in that silence will your presence matter.

Probably, since Adinath's emblem is the cow, you've always been drawn to its grace, its gentleness, its strength. That is no accident.

You are connected to him in ways you have yet to understand.

Soham's eyes lingered on the last sentence. He read it again, and again. The words wrapped around his thoughts like an old song—the kind Appa used to hum while boiling tulsi leaves in the quiet mornings of Thrikkakara.

He folded the letter gently and held it against his chest.

Outside the window, the world blurred past—fields, rooftops, banyan trees, and stretches of stillness. But in Soham's heart, the movement had only just begun.

He leaned his head against the frame, the metal cool against his cheek. His breath slowed. For the first time in months, he felt the silence **settle gently inside him**, like a long-lost companion returning home.

Far away, in the mist-laced village of **Solan**, nestled in the arms of Deodar-covered hills...

A girl had just stirred from sleep.

She wasn't one to follow clocks or rules. **Tejomayi,** now eleven, was still wild with innocence—never untidy, never perfect, always real. Her mischief wasn't loud; it lived in the slant of her smile, in the skip of her feet, in the way she walked as if the mountains themselves parted for her.

Wrapped in a pale wool shawl, she padded barefoot across the cold stone floor. The morning mist clung softly to the windowpanes, blurring the pine-covered valley beyond.

She tugged the curtain open with a huff.

A sliver of sunlight spilled through, catching on a delicate corner of the glass where a light layer of **dust had gathered**.

She tilted her head, smirked, then leaned forward—and with a whisper of breath, **blew**.

A swirl of gold lifted gently into the air—dust caught in sunlight, floating like soft embers of a memory not yet lived. She watched it spin, then smiled, as if **she had just teased the world awake**.

Thousands of miles away, a train cut through the heart of western India.

Soham stirred.

A breeze brushed his face—not the stale air from the cabin vent, not the harsh wind from outside. This breeze was different.

Cooler. Smoother.

Laced with something he couldn't name.

It carried the scent of pine. Of mountain air.

Of playfulness.

He opened his eyes and turned slowly toward the window, his breath stilled. The train kept moving, but everything around him seemed to pause.

There was no sound.

No thought.

Just a feeling—as though someone far away had just brushed his cheek with a question.

He didn't know who.

And she didn't know him.

But the wind… did.

And across hills and plains, temples and trees, they found each other without ever having met in this life.

—◊⁄▭✡—

Tejomayi stood still at the window, her smile softening.

Her fingers touched the wooden sill.

She didn't know why she suddenly looked out—beyond the Deodars, past the slope of the valley, into the white curling mist.

She didn't know what had brushed past her ribs like a whisper.

She only knew that something had answered when she laughed.

—◊⁄▭✡—

They didn't speak.

They didn't search.

But the wind remembered.

And in the stillness between motion and memory, they knew.

Character Table

Character	Also Known As	Role & key connections
Tejomayi	Khindni	Fiery girl of Solan; raised in a hidden hermitage by Paramarishi and the seven ancient sages; deeply bonded with Surabhi (cow), Tarkshya (eagle) and Uluka (owl).
Soham	Leo Francis, Asif Ali, Tambi	Quiet prodigy moved between identities by KalahaDutt; seen by Yasmeen (in Asif Ali form) as a brotherly figure.
Pravash	–	Teenager from Kolkata; son of Balraj and Meenakshi; best friend of Yasmeen; first love Saira; marries his high school love Priyam; father of Arya.
Kalaha-Dutt	Mathew Francis, Baig Mirza Ali, Vasudev Bhai, Narada-Muni	Trickster, sage and cosmic messenger; appears in multiple human guises; fatherly figure and secret guide to Soham.
Paramarishi	–	Guardian and Fatherly figure to Tejomayi

Character	Also Known As	Role & key connections
Saptarishis	Seven Sages, Seven Rishis – namely – Kashyapa, Atri, Vashishtha, Vishwamitra, Gautama, Jamadagni, Bharadwaja	Each trains a different facet of Tejomayi – dharma, discipline, strategy, science, healing, etc.; Menaka is eternally linked with Vishwamitra; Anasuya with Atri.
Surabhi	Cow saved by Soham	Companion to Tejomayi
Tarkshya	Vishnu's vāhana	Snowwhite eagle gifted to Tejomayi by Vishwamitra; later grows into her aerial guardian.
Uluka	Lakshmi's vāhana	White owl gifted to Tejomayi by Vashishtha; calm, watchful presence and guide.
Indra	Frank Lewis	Head of the Secret Council; appears as a powerful Western security/intel chief; father of Devasena, father-in-law of Karthik.
Karthik	Abraham	Devic warcommander operating in the modern world; husband of Devasena; father of twins Rudra and Usha.

Character	Also Known As	Role & key connections
Ved Vyasa	Mr. Singh	Eternal scholar and strategist; appears as Mr. Singh in modern times.
Anasuya	Dr. Ananya Rao	Cosmic motherfigure in the form of a scientist/producer in Delhi media; eternally linked to Rishi Atri.
Menaka	Meera Kapoor	Enchantress wearing the skin of a media baron; eternally linked to Rishi Vishwamitra.
Vishwakarma	Jon Watson	Architect of worlds and systems; appears as a lowprofile but pivotal tech/platform investor in Silicon Valley.
Jay	Brett	Law and Order specialist of the Nine; operates through UN-type structures and global policing.
Vijay	–	Strategic/economic mind of the Nine; focused on supply chains, trade and subtle leverage.
Chitragupt	–	Keeper of karmic ledgers; quiet authority in the Council when it comes to consequences.
Rudra	Mathew	Son of Karthik and Devasena; Usha's twin; superhuman field operative fighting Raktans/Ghraaks in Nordic/Arctic regions.

Character	Also Known As	Role & key connections
Usha	Isha	Daughter of Karthik and Devasena; Rudra's twin; sniper and tactical support in polar operations.
Devasena	Desiree	Daughter of Indra; wife of Karthik; mother of Rudra and Usha; anchors the family's life in Sweden while coordinating polar missions.
Balraj Rathore	–	Pravash's father; respected patriarch of the Rathore family in Kolkata
Meenakshi Rathore	–	Pravash's mother; emotional center of the Rathore household.
Aakash, Kanchan	–	Pravash's elder brother and elder sister; hold the family together during his disappearance.
Prakash, Ankit	–	Pravash's cousins; part of his closeknit family circle.
Yasmeen	–	Sees Asif Ali (Soham) as a brotherly figure; best friend and moral compass for Pravash; later glimpsed in dreams as a staffbearing rider.

Character	Also Known As	Role & key connections
Ariful	–	Yasmeen's father
Saira	–	Pravash's first love; her family's violent notions of honor nearly cost him his life.
Gurpreet Kandola	–	MLA and mafia don of GhaggarNagar; father of Vikram (deceased), Harshpreet and Arvind; builds an empire on venomlaced heroin and orphanage based trafficking.
Kajal Kandola	–	Gurpreet's wife; strong presence inside the Kandola household.
Harshpreet	–	Gurpreet's ambitious daughter; Pravash's classmate; later glimpsed in visions leading Raktans.
Arvind	–	Gurpreet's introspective son; uncomfortable with his father's empire.
Priyam	–	Pravash's highschool love and eventual wife.
Arya	–	Daughter of Pravash and Priyam; the little hand that holds his in the dream of the coming war.

Glossary

1. 63 Salaka-purush (Great Personages)

"In Jain cosmology, the 63 Salaka Purush (Illustrious Great Personages) represent extraordinary spiritual figures who appear in every cosmic cycle, profoundly shaping human destiny, morality, and spirituality in Bharat Kshetra. According to Jain tradition, each cosmic half-cycle witnesses the birth and spiritual journey of these 63 extraordinary souls, guiding humanity toward ethical living, spiritual awakening, and liberation (Moksha).

Categories of Salaka Purush:

The 63 Great Personages are classified into distinct spiritual roles:

24 Tirthankars (Ford-makers)

Spiritual guides who attain perfect knowledge (Keval Jnana) and teach the path to liberation.

Examples: Lord Rishabhanatha (Adinath), Lord Parshvanath, Lord Mahavir.

12 Chakravartins (Universal Monarchs)

Ideal emperors who peacefully rule the world, symbolizing perfect ethical governance and righteousness.

Example: Emperor Bharata Chakravarti, son of Lord Rishabhanatha.

9 Vasudev (Narayans or Heroic Kings)

Powerful, virtuous heroes who uphold righteousness (Dharma) yet experience worldly struggles, often battling their evil counterparts.

Example: Lord Krishna (Vasudev).

9 Prati-Vasudev (Anti-Heroes)

Counterparts to Vasudev, powerful beings embodying moral challenges, violence, and pride; ultimately defeated, symbolizing the consequences of negative karma.

Example: Ravan

9 Baladevas (Gentle, Peaceful Heroes)

Peaceful and virtuous spiritual heroes who prefer harmony and non-violence, acting as moral and spiritual guides.

Example: Lord Balarama, elder brother of Krishna.

Spiritual and Philosophical Significance:

The 63 Salaka Purush symbolize the complete spectrum of spiritual existence—perfect knowledge, ethical leadership, righteous strength, moral struggle, and peaceful harmony.

Their existence highlights eternal cosmic cycles of virtue, vice, struggle, and liberation, teaching profound lessons about karma, ethics, spiritual transformation, and liberation.

These illustrious personages remind humanity of the possibility and necessity of spiritual awakening, ethical living, and ultimate liberation amidst the complexity of worldly life."

2. Acharyashri

In Jainism, an Acharyashri is a revered and honored Jain monk who has attained the esteemed rank of Acharya, the spiritual leader and head of a monastic community. The title "Acharyashri" is respectfully used by followers and monks alike to address an Acharya, acknowledging not just his seniority but also his profound wisdom, exemplary conduct, and spiritual authority. Within the Jain monastic hierarchy, an Acharya holds the responsibility of interpreting sacred scriptures, guiding other monks and nuns on their spiritual paths, and setting ethical standards through personal example. In Bharat Kshetra: The Untold Story, Acharyashri Padmasagarji is the influential sage whose teachings deeply impact Pravash Rathore, guiding him toward introspection and shaping his understanding of life's purpose and spiritual truths.

3. Anasuya

"Anasuya is a revered figure prominently described in ancient Indian scriptures, celebrated for her exceptional spiritual purity, wisdom, devotion, and virtue. She is renowned as the devoted wife of the sage Atri, one of the legendary seven sages (Saptarishis) of ancient Hindu tradition.

Spiritual and Cultural Significance:

Anasuya symbolizes the epitome of virtue, devotion, and spiritual wisdom. She is especially famed for her unshakable chastity, compassion, and the miraculous powers derived from her intense penance and spiritual practices. Due to her extraordinary devotion, Anasuya earned the blessings of the Trimurti—Brahma, Vishnu, and Shiva—and, according to sacred texts, became the mother of the divine incarnation

Dattatreya, who embodied aspects of these three supreme deities.

Connection to Sun and Moon:

Anasuya's husband, the sage Atri, is closely associated with cosmic creation. According to ancient scriptures, from Atri's profound spiritual penance emerged divine beings, including Chandra (the Moon god) and partial connections to Surya (the Sun god), symbolically linking Anasuya and Atri to celestial phenomena. Thus, Anasuya indirectly embodies the nurturing energy and spiritual purity that sustain cosmic harmony and balance, deeply connecting her character to universal cycles symbolized by the sun and moon."

4. Ashtapad

"Ashtapad, meaning eight steps, is a revered and mystical sacred mountain described prominently in Jain cosmology and scriptures. According to ancient Jain texts, Ashtapad was created by the legendary emperor Bharath Chakravarti, son of the first Tirthankar Lord Rishabhanatha (Adinath), to honor the spiritual greatness and enlightenment of his father and other Tirthankars.

Creation and Significance by Bharath Chakravarti:

Bharath Chakravarti constructed Ashtapad as an elaborate shrine, meticulously designed with eight magnificent stepped terraces. Each terrace measured precisely one Yojan (approximately 12-15 kilometers, in some texts it says 1 Yojan is about ~3600 kilometers and based model that I ran in OpenAI agent with inputs of movement of celestial bodies as written in ancient texts, it comes to around 99 to 108 miles), ascending progressively upwards, symbolizing spiritual ascent and stages of enlightenment.

Bharath's purpose in creating Ashtapad was twofold:

Tribute and Remembrance: To pay homage to the enlightenment and spiritual liberation (Moksha) achieved by Lord Rishabhanatha and other great Tirthankars who meditated there.

Symbolic Spiritual Journey: Each ascending step represented the journey of a soul toward higher spiritual understanding, purity, and ultimate liberation.

Current Mystical Location – Mount Kailash:

Jain scriptures and traditions believe Ashtapad is hidden from human perception within the mystical surroundings of Mount Kailash, a sacred mountain located in the Himalayas. Mount Kailash, revered across Jainism, Hinduism, and Buddhism, is spiritually regarded as a divine, sacred, and mysterious region, inaccessible and invisible to ordinary human eyes. According to Jain texts, only spiritually awakened beings or souls with extraordinary divine vision can perceive and reach Ashtapad."

5. Avsarpini and Utsarpini

"In Jain cosmology, time moves cyclically, much like the continuous motion of a wheel. Each complete cycle of cosmic time is divided into two equal halves: Utsarpini (ascending cycle) and Avsarpini (descending cycle). These cycles define periods of spiritual, ethical, and physical progression and regression experienced by living beings.

Each half-cycle comprises six distinct eras or Aras, characterized by varying levels of happiness (Sukham) and suffering (Dukham):

Avsarpini (Descending Cycle)

The descending half-cycle marks a gradual decline from spiritual and moral perfection to deterioration:

Sukham-Sukham (Utmost Happiness)

Absolute bliss and perfection; no suffering exists.

Sukham (Happiness)

Primarily blissful conditions: minor imperfections appear.

Sukham-Dukham (More Happiness, Less Suffering)

Gradual introduction of suffering alongside happiness; morality begins to decline.

Dukham-Sukham (More Suffering, Less Happiness)

Noticeable increase in suffering, decrease in virtue and lifespan; human conditions deteriorate significantly.

Dukham (Suffering)

Predominantly suffering with minimal happiness; ethics and morality substantially decline.

Dukham-Dukham (Utmost Suffering)

Maximum suffering, widespread ignorance, ethical collapse, spiritual darkness, and short lifespans prevail.

Utsarpini (Ascending Cycle)

The ascending half-cycle marks a gradual improvement from deep suffering to spiritual enlightenment:

Dukham-Dukham (Utmost Suffering)

Deepest suffering and spiritual darkness persist, beginning of gradual improvement toward less severe conditions.

Dukham (Suffering)

Suffering remains dominant but begins to lessen slightly; gradual moral awakening starts.

Dukham-Sukham (More Suffering, Less Happiness)

Increased introduction of happiness; moral and spiritual recovery accelerates.

Sukham-Dukham (More Happiness, Less Suffering)

Happiness starts becoming more dominant, suffering steadily diminishes, noticeable progress in morality and spiritual awareness.

Sukham (Happiness)

Significant spiritual and ethical improvement; society experiences great joy, long lifespans, and minimal imperfections.

Sukham-Sukham (Utmost Happiness)

Absolute virtue, spiritual enlightenment, supreme peace, and perfection prevail; peak of spiritual and moral progress."

6. CHAKRAVARTIN

"Chakravartin, often translated as Universal Monarch, refers to an ideal and sovereign ruler whose authority, virtue, and influence extend across the entire world. This revered title carries deep significance and distinct meanings within both Hindu and Jain scriptures.

In Hindu Scriptures:

In Hindu tradition, a Chakravartin is an ideal emperor or king characterized by extraordinary valor, righteousness (Dharma), wisdom, and compassion. Such a monarch rules ethically, harmoniously uniting all kingdoms under a single righteous rule, maintaining cosmic order and justice. Chakravartin symbolizes the pinnacle of temporal authority guided by spiritual insight and moral integrity. Examples from Hindu texts include legendary kings like Bharata (ancestor of the Bharata dynasty), whose name later defined the region as Bharatvarsha (India).

In Jain Scriptures:

In Jainism, a Chakravartin specifically denotes an ideal universal emperor who conquers all lands through peaceful means rather than violence, guided strictly by the principles of non-violence (Ahimsa), truth, compassion, and righteousness. Jain tradition outlines precisely 12 Chakravartins in every cosmic time cycle, each embodying ethical perfection and ultimate secular authority. Notably, Bharata Chakravarti, son of the first Tirthankar Lord Rishabhanatha (Adinath), is the most revered Chakravartin, after whom Bharat Kshetra itself is named.

In Jain tradition, while Chakravartins attain unmatched worldly success and prosperity, they ultimately realize the transient nature of worldly authority, seeking liberation (Moksha) beyond material accomplishments."

7. CHITRAGUPT

"Chitragupt is a significant celestial figure prominently described in Hindu scriptures and cultural traditions as the divine record-keeper of human actions.

In Hindu beliefs, Chitragupt serves as the meticulous keeper of records, responsible for accurately documenting the actions (Karma) of every living being throughout their lifetime. According to sacred texts, he assists Lord Yama, the deity of death and justice, in evaluating souls after death, determining rewards or consequences based upon their recorded deeds. Symbolically, Chitragupt represents justice, moral accountability, and karmic precision.

Symbolic and Cultural Significance:

Chitragupt's role emphasizes the concept of karma, accountability, and cosmic justice, highlighting the belief that every action—good or bad—is precisely noted and influences one's spiritual journey and subsequent rebirths."

8. **Devasena**

"Devasena is a revered celestial figure prominently described in ancient Hindu scriptures as the divine daughter of Indra, king of the celestial beings (Devas), and as the beloved consort of Lord Karthikeya.

Spiritual and Cultural Significance:

Celestial Heritage: Born as Indra's daughter, Devasena symbolizes divine grace, celestial beauty, purity, and spiritual nobility. Her origin links her directly to cosmic authority, power, and celestial splendor.

Wife of Karthikeya: As the consort of Karthikeya, Devasena represents the complementary spiritual energies of wisdom, courage, purity, and devotion. Their divine union symbolizes the harmonious integration of strength with gentleness, valor with grace, and authority with compassion."

9. **Dukham, Dukham-Dukham, and Kaliyug**

"The terms Dukham, Dukham-Dukham, and Kaliyug collectively represent the current cosmic era characterized by spiritual and moral decline, suffering, ignorance, and diminished righteousness. These concepts, found within Jain and Hindu scriptures, describe the challenges and difficulties of the present time within the larger cyclical structure of cosmic existence.

Dukham and Dukham-Dukham (Jain Cosmology):

In Jain cosmology, each cosmic half-cycle is divided into six eras (Aras). The current descending cycle (Avsarpini) is characterized by increasing spiritual degradation:

Dukham (Suffering): Predominantly characterized by suffering, with limited happiness or spiritual insight. It symbolizes declining morality, spiritual ignorance, shorter lifespans, and increased material attachment.

Dukham-Dukham (Extreme Suffering): The most degraded era, marked by intense suffering, minimal spirituality, moral collapse, and profound ignorance. It represents the culmination of spiritual decline before the ascending cycle (Utsarpini) begins again.

Currently, as per Jain cosmology, humanity is in the Dukham era, rapidly moving toward Dukham-Dukham, the darkest period of moral and spiritual decay.

Kaliyug (Hindu Scriptures):

In Hindu tradition, Kaliyug refers to the final and darkest era in the four-age cycle (Yugas): Satya Yuga, Treta Yuga, Dwapara Yuga, and Kali Yuga. Kaliyug is characterized by widespread moral corruption, materialism, spiritual ignorance, greed, violence, shortened lifespans, and declining virtues.

According to Hindu scriptures, we currently live in Kaliyug, an age of spiritual darkness and profound moral challenge, ultimately to be followed by spiritual renewal in the next Satya Yuga.

Dukham, Dukham-Dukham, and Kaliyug are different descriptions of the same current cosmic condition, emphasizing universal decline in virtue, spirituality, ethics, and happiness.

These eras highlight the necessity for spiritual awakening, moral resilience, compassion, and ethical responsibility amidst profound adversity and challenge.

Both Jain and Hindu scriptures emphasize that even during these difficult times, individual spiritual awakening and liberation (Moksha) remain attainable through sincere practice, devotion, ethical living, and self-awareness."

10. Durga Puja

"Durga Puja is a vibrant and deeply cherished festival celebrated predominantly in Kolkata, marking the homecoming of Goddess Durga, who embodies the divine feminine power (Shakti). Celebrated annually during the autumn months (typically September or October), Durga Puja commemorates Goddess Durga's victorious battle over the demon king Mahishasura, symbolizing the eternal triumph of good over evil.

In Kolkata, Durga Puja transcends mere religious rituals and becomes a grand cultural spectacle that binds the entire city together. For five joyous days, the city comes to a celebratory standstill. Intricately designed *pandals* (temporary structures) housing magnificent idols of Goddess Durga and her divine family—Goddess Saraswati, Goddess Lakshmi, Lord Ganesha, and Lord Kartikeya—transform the streets into vibrant exhibitions of art, creativity, and devotion. Amidst the resonant beats of *dhaks* (traditional drums), the aroma of festive delicacies, and the radiant glow of lights, families and communities unite, dressed in their finest attire, to visit pandals, offer prayers, and enjoy cultural performances.

In Bharat Kshetra: The Untold Story, Durga Puja represents more than a festival; it symbolizes family bonds, nostalgia, and a deep-rooted connection to tradition and heritage for

Pravash Rathore and his family. It serves as an emotional anchor, pulling him back to Kolkata, to a world filled with memories, laughter, love, and a sense of belonging."

11. Gandiv

"The Gandiv Bow is a divine and legendary weapon of immense spiritual and historical significance, deeply revered in ancient Indian scriptures and epic literature. According to revered sources such as the Mahabharata, the Gandiv was originally crafted by Lord Brahma, the creator, and later bestowed upon the heroic archer Arjuna by Lord Varuna, the deity of cosmic order and water. Known for its extraordinary strength, impeccable accuracy, and unmatched power, this celestial bow is described as unbreakable, invincible, and resonating with universal energies.

Adorned with sacred engravings and crafted from celestial materials, the Gandiv's string was said to vibrate with the very breath of the cosmos. The bow's arrows could pierce through any armor, destroy formidable barriers, and vanquish even the most powerful adversaries, symbolizing the victory of righteousness (Dharma) over injustice (Adharma).

In Bharat Kshetra: The Untold Story, the Gandiv Bow is wielded by Tejomayi, symbolizing her cosmic authority and her profound role in confronting and breaking the matrix of illusion (Maya). When she releases the bowstring, the powerful resonance of the Gandiv sends vibrations rippling across realms, marking the initiation of transformative events that weave together the destinies of multiple lives and echo the eternal struggle between truth and deception, virtue and vice."

12. **Ghraaks**

Fictional creation by author, word derived from **Ghran** (Sanskrit: "rot") and **Raak** (from *Rakshas*, meaning "demon"), symbolizing beings of decay and demonic ferocity.

Definition:

Ghraaks are mythic, bloodthirsty entities said to dwell in the shadowed realms beyond human reach. They embody corruption and destruction, thriving on chaos and decay.

Author's Context:

Habitat: Reside in the forbidden lands of **Magog** (linked to Yajuj and Majuj), restrained by a colossal divine barrier that is periodically repaired after their relentless attempts to breach it.

Origin: Believed to have emerged near the **Rakt River** in the mountainous region of **Airavat Kshetra**, a place steeped in primordial energy.

Access Points: Possess subterranean portals enabling incursions beneath **Bharat Kshetra**, infiltrating the mortal world from hidden depths.

Prophecy: Ancient lore warns that during the final decline of cosmic order, their overwhelming numbers will surge forth, heralding an apocalypse that will obliterate the earth as we know it.

13. **HEERA-MANDI**

Means "Diamond Market."

Historically, **Heera Mandi** refers to a famous district in **Lahore, Pakistan,** known during the Mughal era as a hub for **courtesans, classical dance, and music.** It was a cultural center where elite patrons enjoyed art forms like Kathak and ghazals.

Over time, the term became associated with the **red-light area** of Lahore, though its roots were in refined performing arts rather than prostitution.

In modern usage, it often symbolizes a place of **sensuality, brothels**, but also carries connotations of exploitation and social stigma.

14. Indra

"In Hindu Scriptures:

Indra, prominently mentioned in Vedic texts, epics, and Puranas, is revered as the king of celestial beings (Devas). Known as the god of thunder, lightning, storms, rain, and warfare, Indra symbolizes strength, valor, and leadership. He is famously depicted wielding the powerful thunderbolt (Vajra), and his kingdom is the heavenly realm known as Svarga. Indra's heroic battles against demonic forces, such as Vritra, emphasize the eternal triumph of righteousness (Dharma) over chaos and evil (Adharma).

In Jain Scriptures:

In Jain cosmology, Indra denotes a prestigious title rather than a single deity. Multiple beings hold the title Indra, each ruling over different celestial realms (Swarg Lok). They are powerful celestial rulers endowed with extraordinary wealth, knowledge, and powers but remain bound by karma, thus subject to rebirth and the cycle of existence. Jain scriptures emphasize that despite their divine authority and luxuries, these celestial beings still strive ultimately toward spiritual liberation (Moksha), underscoring the transient nature of worldly power."

15. Jai Jinendra

"Jai Jinendra is a revered and auspicious greeting commonly used within the Jain community, embodying deep spiritual significance. Literally translating as 'Victory to the Jinas', this phrase respectfully honors the enlightened spiritual teachers known as Jinas (or Tirthankars), who have achieved complete spiritual victory over their inner passions and attained liberation (Moksha).

Spiritual and Cultural Significance:

Victory over Inner Passions: 'Jinendra' signifies spiritual teachers who have conquered all attachments, delusions, and karmic bondage.

Respectful Greeting: It serves both as a respectful salutation among Jains and as a profound reminder of the ultimate goal of spiritual liberation.

Invocation of Virtues: By greeting each other with 'Jai Jinendra,' Jains affirm their aspiration toward spiritual purity, non-violence (Ahimsa), truthfulness, and compassion, which are central teachings of Jain philosophy.

In daily life, Jai Jinendra reinforces mutual respect, humility, ethical living, and spiritual awareness, cultivating a sense of spiritual community and shared purpose among Jains."

16. Jambudveep

"Jambudveep is a significant and sacred cosmological term that appears prominently in both Jain and Hindu ancient scriptures, though depicted differently in each tradition.

According to Jain Scriptures:

In Jain cosmology, Jambudveep refers to the central continent of the middle realm (Madhya Lok), one of numerous continents within a complex cosmic structure. Shaped in a circular form, Jambudveep is divided into several regions (Kshetras), including Bharat Kshetra, Airavat Kshetra, and Mahavideh Kshetra, among others. Ideally only these 3 Kshetras are the region inhabited by humans—being the only place where souls can attain liberation (Moksha). The continent is symbolically surrounded by the great salt ocean and encircled by towering ice walls, and it represents the realm of spiritual opportunity, karmic action, and the journey toward ultimate enlightenment.

According to Hindu Scriptures:

In ancient Hindu scriptures like the Puranas, Jambudveep is also described as a continent, but with different geographical and cosmological dimensions. Positioned at the center of the cosmic structure, it encompasses the known human world, surrounded by oceans, mountains, and lands inhabited by various divine and earthly beings. Among these, Bharat Varsha (ancient India) is a prominent region. Hindu scriptures portray Jambudveep as the earthly plane where Dharma (righteousness) thrives, divine incarnations manifest, and sacred rivers like Ganga flow, sustaining spiritual life and cosmic balance."

17. Jambudveep - Important Lakes

"In Jain cosmology, Jambudveep hosts several sacred lakes, each uniquely located within the majestic mountain ranges (Parvats). These lakes symbolize purity, spiritual insight, and serenity, enhancing the sacredness and cosmic balance of their respective locations.

1. Padma - Location: Himavanta Parvat

2. Mahapadma - Location: Maha-Himavanta Parvat

3. Tingiccha - Location: Nishadh Parvat

4. Mahapundarika - Location: Rukmani Parvat

5. Pundarika - Location: Shikharin Parvat

6. Kesar or Kesarin - Location: Nilavanta Parvat"

18. Jambudveep - Important Rivers of Jambudveep

"In Jain cosmology, Jambudveep features several sacred rivers that flow across its various Kshetras, nourishing the land and symbolizing spiritual purity, prosperity, and cosmic balance. Each Kshetra is graced by two prominent rivers, typically originating from majestic mountains and flowing eastward and westward, enriching the regions they traverse.

Rivers by Region:

1. Bharat Kshetra

Sindhu (सिन्धु)
Ganga (गंगा)

2. Haimavat Kshetra

Rohitamsa (रोहिताम्सा)
Rohit (रोहित)

3. Harivarsha Kshetra

Harikanta (हरिकान्ता)
Harit (हरित)

4. Mahavideh Kshetra (Central Region)

Sitoda (सितोदा)
Sita (सीता)

5. Ramyak Kshetra

Narakanta (नरकान्ता)
Nari (नारी)

6. Hiranyavanta Kshetra

Rupyakula (रूप्यकूला)
Suvarnakula (सुवर्णकूला)

7. Airavat Kshetra

Raktoda (रक्तोदा)
Rakta (रक्ता)

19. Jambudveep - Seven Kshetras and Six Mountains

"Jambudveep is the central circular continent within Jain cosmology, measuring exactly 100,000 Yojan in diameter. It comprises seven distinct regions (Kshetras), separated by six prominent mountain ranges (Parvats). Each region is a horizontal strip extending from east to west, arranged symmetrically from the southernmost Bharat Kshetra to the northernmost Airavat Kshetra, with the largest Mahavideh Kshetra precisely at its center.

Below are the exact dimensions and brief significance of each region clearly outlined:

Southern Regions (from south towards the center):

Bharat Kshetra (भरत क्षेत्र)
North-South: 526.31 Yojan
East-West: 10,246.22 Yojan
Significance: The primary inhabited region of humans, uniquely enabling souls to attain liberation (Moksha).

Himavanta Parvat (हिमवन्त पर्वत)
North-South: 1,052.62 Yojan
East-West: 20,411.17 Yojan

Haimavanta Kshetra (हैमवत क्षेत्र)
North-South: 2,105.24 Yojan
East-West: 32,014.37 Yojan

Maha-Himavanta Parvat (महा-हिमवन्त पर्वत)
North-South: 4,210.48 Yojan
East-West: 46,708.62 Yojan

Harivarsha Kshetra (हरिवर्ष क्षेत्र)
North-South: 8,420.96 Yojan
East-West: 65,237.38 Yojan

Nishadh Parvat (निषध पर्वत)
North-South: 16,841.92 Yojan
East-West: 86,296.21 Yojan

Central Region:
Mahavideh Kshetra
North-South: 33,683.84 Yojan
East-West: 100,000 Yojan (Full Diameter)
Significance: The largest and most spiritually pure region, eternally graced by the presence of living Tirthankars and continually conducive to spiritual liberation.

Northern Regions (from center towards the north):
Nilavanta Parvat (नीलवन्त पर्वत)
North-South: 16,841.92 Yojan
East-West: 86,297.50 Yojan

Ramyak Kshetra (रम्यक क्षेत्र)
North-South: 8,420.96 Yojan
East-West: 65,239.93 Yojan

Rukmani Parvat (रुक्मिणी पर्वत)
North-South: 4,210.48 Yojan
East-West: 46,712.78 Yojan

Hiranyavanta Kshetra (हिरण्यवन्त क्षेत्र)
North-South: 2,105.24 Yojan
East-West: 32,020.88 Yojan

Shikharin Parvat (शिखरिण पर्वत)
North-South: 1,052.62 Yojan
East-West: 20,421.72 Yojan

Airavat Kshetra (ऐरावत क्षेत्र)
North-South: 526.31 Yojan
East-West: 10,267.55 Yojan

20. Jay and Vijay

"Jay and Vijay are revered celestial gatekeepers prominently mentioned in ancient Hindu scriptures, notably the Vishnu Purana and Bhagavata Purana. They serve as the divine guardians of Vaikuntha, the heavenly abode of Lord Vishnu, responsible for protecting its sanctity and restricting entry to those worthy.

Spiritual and Cultural Significance:

Jay and Vijay's role emphasizes unwavering devotion and the complexities of divine destiny. According to scriptural accounts, due to a curse, they were born multiple times on Earth as adversaries of Lord Vishnu, famously appearing as Hiranyaksha and Hiranyakashipu, Ravan and Kumbhakarna, and Shishupala and Dantavakra. In each incarnation, their confrontations with Vishnu's avatars ultimately led to their liberation, demonstrating that divine grace can manifest even in apparent adversity.

Their story symbolizes profound truths about karma, spiritual redemption, divine justice, and the mysterious workings of cosmic destiny, underscoring the belief that even souls temporarily distanced from divinity remain within the compassionate reach of divine salvation."

21. KARTHIKEYA

"Karthikeya, also known as Skanda, Murugan, or Subrahmanya, is a revered figure appearing prominently in ancient Indian scriptures, depicted distinctly within Hindu and Jain traditions.

In Hindu Scriptures:

In Hinduism, Karthikeya is the divine son of Lord Shiva and Goddess Parvati, and the younger brother of Lord Ganesha. Widely worshipped as the deity of war, courage, wisdom, and victory, he embodies youthful energy, valor, and spiritual insight. Often depicted riding a peacock and wielding his divine spear (Vel), Karthikeya symbolizes the triumph of spiritual knowledge over ignorance and evil forces.

In Jain Scriptures:

In Jain tradition, Karthikeya is not worshipped as a god but recognized as a powerful celestial being (Deva) residing in heavenly realms (Swarg Lok). Specifically, in Jain cosmology, he is known as Naigamesha, a guardian deity associated with childbirth, fertility, and protection of children. Naigamesha holds a revered position, symbolizing auspiciousness, prosperity, and divine protection, yet he remains bound within karmic cycles, subject to rebirth until achieving liberation (Moksha).

The depiction of Karthikeya as Naigamesha highlights Jainism's focus on compassion, nurturing, and safeguarding the innocent and vulnerable."

22. Lokas - Adho Lok

"Adho Lok represents the lower or underworld realms in Jain cosmology, encompassing seven distinct layers known as Narak or hells, namely: Ratna-Prabha (Pataal), Sarkaraa-Prabha (Rasatala), Vaalukaa-Prabha (Mahatala), Panka-Prabha (Talatala), Dhuma-Prabha (Sutala), Tamah-Prabha (Vitala), and Tamastamah-Prabha (Atala). Inhabitants here endure immense suffering and misery as consequences of severe negative karma. Unlike traditional views of eternal punishment, Jain scriptures emphasize that Adho Lok is temporary; souls endure their karmic debts and eventually move upward, continuing their spiritual journeys in other realms, guided by their accumulated karma.

Ratna-Prabha—the uppermost and least severe of the seven—is unique. According to Jain scriptures, this layer is not entirely filled with suffering; rather, it is described as radiant, jewel-like, and possessing regions inhabited by celestial beings or 'Bhavanvasi Devas', who live in opulence and comfort. Among these divine beings is King Mahabali, who rules Ratna-Prabha as its benevolent guardian, residing there with blessings from Lord Vishnu's Vaman Avatar (as described in the ancient scriptures). Unlike the other six lower realms, Ratna-Prabha combines elements of both karmic punishment and celestial enjoyment, illustrating the complexity and nuance of karmic balance within Jain cosmology."

23. Lokas - Madhya Lok

"Madhya Lok (literally meaning 'Middle World') is the central realm within Jain cosmology, inhabited by humans, animals, and various life forms. It is uniquely significant, being the only realm where souls can perform actions (karma), experience both joy and suffering, and attain liberation (Moksha). Bharat Kshetra, as depicted in Bharat Kshetra: The Untold Story, is a key part of Madhya Lok. Here, souls can engage in spiritual practices, accumulate good karma, or fall prey to negative actions, making Madhya Lok a realm of decisive spiritual opportunity."

24. LOKAS - SWARG LOK

"In Jain cosmology, Swarg Lok refers to the upper realm or celestial abode inhabited by divine beings known as Devas. It comprises multiple heavens—sixteen according to Jain scriptures - Saudharma, Aishana, Sanatkumara, Mahendra, Brahma, Brahmottara, Lantava, Kapishta, Shukra, Mahashukra, Shatara, Sahasrara, Anata, Pranata, Arana, and Achyuta. Devas residing here experience immense pleasure, extraordinary powers, and bliss, yet they remain bound within the karmic cycle, ultimately destined for rebirth. Swarg Lok symbolizes spiritual prosperity and elevated existence, but not the final liberation (Moksha)."

25. LORD MAHAVIR

"Lord Mahavir, also known as Vardhamana Mahavira, is the twenty-fourth and final Tirthankar of the current cosmic era according to Jainism. He is revered as one of the greatest spiritual teachers who attained complete enlightenment (Keval Jnana) and ultimate liberation (Moksha), profoundly influencing Jain philosophy and spirituality.

Life and Enlightenment:

Born as Prince Vardhamana in 599 BCE in the kingdom of Vaishali (modern-day Bihar, India), Lord Mahavir renounced his royal life, adopting a path of rigorous asceticism. After twelve years of deep meditation and spiritual discipline, he attained Keval Jnana—perfect and infinite knowledge—thus becoming a Tirthankar (ford-maker) who established a spiritual path leading to liberation.

Teachings and Philosophy:

Ahimsa (Non-Violence): Central to Mahavir's teachings is unconditional non-violence, compassion, and respect for all life forms.

Aparigraha (Non-Possessiveness): Emphasizing detachment from material possessions and worldly attachments, fostering spiritual purity.

Satya (Truthfulness): Upholding absolute honesty in thoughts, speech, and actions.

Anekantavada (Non-Absolutism): Encouraging respect for multiple viewpoints, tolerance, and understanding the complexity of reality.

Legacy:

Lord Mahavir's profound teachings shaped Jain ethical conduct, spiritual practices, and philosophy. His life exemplifies the highest spiritual ideal—complete self-realization and liberation from karmic bondage."

26. Maharishi Bhrigu

"Maharishi Bhrigu, one of the revered Saptarishis (seven great sages), was a Manasputra (mind-born son) of Lord Brahma and is regarded as the father of astrology (Jyotish Shastra) and a pioneer of Ayurveda. Bhrigu is famously known for testing the Trimurti (Brahma, Vishnu, and Shiva) to determine the supreme deity, during which he experienced Vishnu's humility and compassion. His wisdom and teachings emphasized dharma, spirituality, and the path to liberation, while his contributions to Vedic sciences highlights his enduring legacy. Bhrigu's stories symbolize humility, patience, and the pursuit of divine truth."

27. Menaka

"Menaka is a celebrated celestial figure prominently described in ancient Hindu scriptures, particularly the epics and Puranas, as one of the most beautiful and skilled celestial beings known as Apsaras. Apsaras are divine celestial dancers renowned for their extraordinary beauty, grace, and artistic abilities, often associated with the heavenly court of Lord Indra.

Spiritual and Cultural Significance:

Menaka famously appears in ancient literature as a symbol of divine beauty, allure, and enchantment. Most notably, she played a central role in the story of sage Vishvamitra, whom she successfully distracted from deep meditation, leading to the birth of their daughter, Shakuntala. Through such episodes, Menaka symbolizes the complex interplay between spiritual asceticism and worldly desires, representing temptation, beauty, and the powerful influence of emotions on spiritual journeys.

Her character often emphasizes the subtle balance between attachment and detachment, reminding individuals of the challenges encountered on the path toward spiritual growth and enlightenment."

28. Naigamesha

"Naigamesha is a revered deity prominently described in Jain scriptures and ancient Indian traditions, closely associated with childbirth, fertility, and the protection of children. He is especially venerated within Jainism as a guardian deity, embodying benevolence, nurturing compassion, and divine protection.

Spiritual and Cultural Significance:

Guardian of Children: Naigamesha is traditionally invoked for the safe birth, well-being, and protection of infants and children, symbolizing divine guardianship and parental compassion.

Symbol of Prosperity and Fertility: He embodies fertility, abundance, auspiciousness, and the flourishing of families and communities.

Celestial Warrior Aspect: Often depicted with the head of a goat (or ram) and a powerful, robust physique, Naigamesha also signifies courage, strength, and the protective aspect of divine energy.

Relation with Karthikeya:

In Jain tradition, Naigamesha is sometimes identified as Karthikeya or recognized as a distinct yet related celestial being. As a guardian figure, Naigamesha complements Karthikeya's warrior-like symbolism, emphasizing protection, compassion, and auspiciousness rather than solely martial attributes."

29. Nalukettu

"Nalukettu is a traditional style of Kerala, India architecture used primarily for building ancestral homes of well off, joint families. The term 'nalukettu' literally translates to 'four blocks' (nalu = four, kettu = blocks/structure) and refers to the layout of the house, which is built around a central open courtyard.

30. **Narada-Muni**

Narada-Muni is one of the most revered sages in Indian scriptures, known for his unparalleled wisdom and mastery of music. However, his persona is far from solemn—he is often depicted as playful and mischievous, a messenger who bridges realms and delivers divine counsel while stirring events with his clever wit. Known as the ultimate guide, Narada-Muni's actions, though sometimes misunderstood, always align with the greater cosmic order. He is considered the divine son of Brahma, the Creator of the Universe, and is said to have been born from Brahma's mind (Manasputra). His mother is Saraswati, the goddess of wisdom, music, and learning, further cementing Narada's association with knowledge and devotion. Narada-Muni is a beloved figure in scriptures like the Mahabharata, Ramayana, and Puranas.

31. **Narayan Narayan**

"'Narayan Narayan' is the iconic chant often repeated by Narada-Muni, the revered celestial sage known across ancient Indian scriptures and Puranic literature as a divine messenger, storyteller, and cosmic wanderer. This chant is Narada's distinctive invocation and a humble salutation to Lord Narayan (Vishnu), symbolizing his devotion and constant remembrance of the Supreme.

Whenever Narada-Muni enters a scene or delivers a profound yet playful insight, he joyfully utters 'Narayan Narayan', reflecting his unwavering devotion and also subtly signifying that his presence and actions are guided directly by divine will. More than just a simple invocation, the repetition embodies his spiritual identity—constantly connected with, and serving as an instrument of, the divine plan.

In Bharat Kshetra: The Untold Story, Kalaha Dutt (Narada-Muni's earthly form) often murmurs 'Narayan Narayan' during moments of revelation, deep insight, or when he senses the divine unfolding of destiny. This invocation acts as a playful reminder of Narada's dual nature—both mischievous sage and profound teacher—as he weaves subtle lessons and cosmic truths into the fabric of human lives. It signals that seemingly ordinary events are guided by a larger spiritual purpose, gently nudging Pravash, Soham, and other characters toward their ultimate paths."

32. Navkar Mantra

The Navakar Mantra is one of the most important mantras in Jainism. It's also known as the Namokar Mantra or the Namaskar Mantra. This mantra is unique because it doesn't refer to any specific gods or goddesses but instead pays respect to the virtues of different types of spiritual beings.

33. Om Sohum

"Om Sohum is a profound spiritual mantra derived from ancient Indian scriptures, deeply embedded in Vedantic philosophy and Jain spiritual tradition. Composed of two Sanskrit terms—Om and Sohum—the mantra signifies the fundamental unity between the individual self (Atman) and the universal consciousness or supreme reality (Brahman).

Om: The sacred primordial sound, symbolizing the universal vibration, cosmic creation, and ultimate reality.

Sohum: Means 'I am That', asserting the profound realization that one's true inner essence is identical to the supreme universal consciousness."

34. PANCHAJANYA

"Panchajanya is the sacred, divine conch shell (shankh) associated prominently with Lord Krishna, as described in revered ancient scriptures, including the epic Mahabharata. According to these texts, Krishna acquired Panchajanya after defeating the demon Panchajana, who resided in the depths of the ocean, inside a conch-shaped shell. The conch hence symbolizes victory over evil and the triumph of righteousness (Dharma) over darkness.

In ancient scriptures, the resonant, powerful sound of Panchajanya is said to dispel negative energies, invoke courage, and awaken divine consciousness among listeners. It is famously blown by Krishna at the onset of the great Kurukshetra war, described in the Bhagavad Gita, signalling the victory of justice and truth."

35. RAKTAN

Fictional creation by author, word derived from *Rakt* (Sanskrit meaning blood), signifying their intrinsic link to blood, and echoing vampiric traits in modern mythos.

Raktan are fictional beings akin to modern-day vampires—immortal predators who subsist on blood and possess extraordinary physical prowess.

Characteristics:

Sun Aversion: They despise sunlight, surviving only when adorned with enchanted rings or jewellery crafted by **Yakshas, Yakshinis, witches, wizards, or elves**, which absorb solar heat.

Immortality: Do not age and can seamlessly blend among humans.

Physical Abilities: Exhibit superhuman strength and exceptional agility.

Vulnerability: Can only be killed by extracting their heart.

Feeding: Thrive on blood, sustaining their vitality through consumption.

Origins:

Believed to have emerged near the **Rakt** or **Raktoda River**, regions steeped in esoteric lore.

Claim to be descendants of **Maa Kali**, born when her blood—spilled during the annihilation of Raktabeej—mingled with river waters and was unknowingly consumed by humans in the vicinity.

Symbolism:

Raktan embody primal hunger and forbidden power, representing the shadow side of immortality and the peril of divine remnants mingling with mortal realms.

36. Rudra and Usha

"Rudra and Usha are celestial figures recognized in certain ancient Indian traditions as the divine twin children of Karthikeya (Skanda or Murugan), the god of war and wisdom, and his consort Devasena, the daughter of Indra.

Symbolic and Spiritual Significance:

Rudra:

Symbolizes strength, courage, valor, and divine intensity.

Named after Lord Rudra, an aspect of Lord Shiva, signifying fierce spiritual energy, protection, transformation, and renewal.

Embodies spiritual courage, protection of righteousness, and the powerful energy required to overcome negativity.

Usha:

Represents dawn, renewal, beauty, grace, and spiritual illumination.

Named after the Vedic deity Usha (the goddess of dawn), symbolizing new beginnings, hope, enlightenment, and the awakening of spiritual consciousness.

Embodies the gentle yet profound force of spiritual awakening, purity, and compassion.

Together, Rudra and Usha embody the harmonious integration of powerful and gentle spiritual energies, balancing strength with compassion, valor with grace, and intensity with wisdom.

Cultural Context:

Though Rudra and Usha as twin children of Karthikeya and Devasena appear in select regional traditions, they encapsulate profound symbolic meaning representing the eternal balance between masculine and feminine energies, fierce strength, and gentle grace."

37. Rudraksha

"Rudraksha is a sacred seed traditionally revered in ancient Hindu scriptures, widely recognized as divine beads symbolically linked to Lord Shiva. The term 'Rudraksha' is derived from Sanskrit words 'Rudra' (an aspect of Shiva) and 'Aksha' (eyes), thus meaning 'the eyes of Lord Shiva.'
General Significance:

Spiritual Protection: Rudraksha beads are believed to protect wearers spiritually, emotionally, and physically, removing obstacles and enhancing inner peace.

Meditation and Clarity: Used extensively for meditation and chanting (Japa), Rudraksha enhances spiritual clarity, concentration, and self-realization.

Symbol of Shiva's Compassion: It symbolizes Shiva's tears of compassion for humanity, signifying universal empathy, divine grace, and spiritual awakening.

Special Significance of 9-Faced Rudraksha (Nau-Mukhi Rudraksha):

The 9-faced Rudraksha holds special spiritual significance, directly associated with Maa Parvati, the divine consort of Shiva:

Relation to Maa Parvati: Represents the energy, power, and blessings of Goddess Durga (a form of Parvati), symbolizing divine feminine strength, protection, and nurturing compassion.

Spiritual Blessings: Wearing a 9-faced Rudraksha bestows courage, fearlessness, self-confidence, and enhanced mental strength. It is traditionally recommended for overcoming fears, obstacles, and adversities.

Feminine Energy: Embodies the supreme nurturing energy (Shakti), providing emotional balance, harmony in relationships, spiritual purity, and blessings from Maa Parvati."

38. Samayak

"Samayak is a practice of achieving equanimity and spiritual purity for a fixed duration, traditionally 48 minutes, by focusing on self-discipline, meditation, and reflection. It has been considered as one of the six essential daily duties for both lay followers and monks, and involves abstaining from sinful activities, contemplating core Jain principles like ahimsa (non-violence), and performing repentance for past actions."

39. Saptarishis (Seven Great Sages)

"The Saptarishis are revered ancient sages celebrated in Hindu scriptures such as the Vedas, Puranas, and epics. Symbolizing supreme spiritual wisdom, cosmic harmony, and ethical principles, they have profoundly shaped Indian spiritual traditions, guiding humanity toward spiritual and ethical enlightenment.

Detailed Significance of Each Sage:

1. Kashyapa

Fathered numerous celestial beings, gods, demons, humans, and creatures.

Known for profound compassion and cosmic harmony.

Symbolizes creative power, fertility, and universal balance.

2. Atri

Father of sage Durvasa, Moon god Chandra, and linked to solar (Sun) and lunar (Moon) dynasties.

Husband of virtuous Anasuya, praised for their joint spiritual power and purity.

Represents compassion, sincerity, and spiritual devotion.

3. Vashishtha

Spiritual advisor and revered Guru to Lord Rama and the kings of the Solar dynasty (Suryavansha).

Author of the profound text Yoga Vashishtha, emphasizing the importance of self-realization and cosmic truths.

Known for embodying serenity, deep wisdom, and spiritual insight.

4. Vishvamitra

Originally a warrior-king (Kshatriya), he became a Brahmarishi through rigorous penance.

Composer of the powerful Gayatri Mantra, one of the most sacred mantras in Hindu scriptures.

Guru to Lord Rama and Lakshmana, imparting divine weapons (Astras) and spiritual teachings for their quest.

Symbolizes courage, determination, spiritual transformation, and discipline.

Known for his encounters with Menaka, emphasizing the balance between ascetic discipline and worldly attractions.

5. Gautama

Husband of Ahalya; their story symbolizes forgiveness, redemption, and divine grace.

Credited with numerous Vedic hymns and profound spiritual insights.

Represents ethical purity, justice, and profound spiritual knowledge.

6. Jamadagni

Father of Lord Parashurama, an avatar of Vishnu, known for re-establishing righteousness.

Symbolizes unwavering discipline, integrity, righteousness, and inner strength.

Renowned for simplicity, austerity, and adherence to truth.

7. Bharadwaja

Celebrated for extensive scholarship and contributions to spiritual and scientific knowledge.

Renowned for immense compassion, generosity, and teaching thousands of disciples.

Associated with the ancient scripture Bharadwaja Smriti, providing ethical and spiritual guidelines.

Known for his encounter with Lord Rama during Rama's exile, offering guidance and blessings.

Spiritual and Cultural Significance:

The Saptarishis correspond astronomically to the Ursa Major (Big Dipper) constellation, symbolizing cosmic significance and spiritual eternity.

They represent eternal cosmic guides preserving and transmitting profound spiritual wisdom, ethical conduct, and divine knowledge across generations."

40. Seven Immortals/Cheeranjivi's

"In ancient Indian scriptures, particularly Hindu tradition, the Seven Immortals (Cheeranjivi's) refer to legendary personalities blessed or cursed to remain alive through ages until the end of the current cosmic cycle (Kalpa). Each immortal embodies specific spiritual principles, virtues, or cosmic duties.

The Seven Immortals:

Ashwatthama

Son of Guru Dronacharya, cursed to roam eternally due to his misdeeds in the Mahabharata war, symbolizing consequences of anger, vengeance, and uncontrolled emotions.

Bali (King Mahabali)

Demon king granted immortality and eternal rule in Patal Lok (underworld). He symbolizes generosity, justice, humility, and devotion to duty.

The Story of Mahabali and Vaman

Long ago, in an age defined by unmatched valor and profound wisdom, a noble king named Mahabali ruled over Bharat Kshetra. Born into the lineage of the Daityas—often misunderstood as demons—Mahabali defied the stereotypes of his clan with virtue, fairness, and compassion. Under his reign, the kingdom flourished, blossoming with prosperity, peace, and an unwavering adherence to dharma. Above all else, Mahabali's boundless generosity defined his very being.

Yet, his rise to extraordinary power did not go unnoticed in the celestial realms. As Mahabali's benevolent influence expanded across the three worlds—Swarg Lok (Heaven), Madhya Lok (Earth), and even portions of Adho Lok (Netherworld)—unease stirred among the devas, celestial beings who feared the balance of the cosmos might soon be disrupted by his unparalleled supremacy.

To restore equilibrium, Lord Vishnu, the preserver of cosmic harmony, intervened—not from envy, but from divine necessity. Assuming the humble form of Vaman, a dwarf brahmin boy, Vishnu descended gently onto the earthly realm and approached Mahabali during a grand yajna—a sacred ritual where the king generously bestowed gifts to anyone who sought his favor.

The radiant yet unassuming brahmin approached the mighty king. "O great king," he said humbly, "I seek only a small gift from you: three steps of land, measured by my own feet. Grant me this modest wish, and my heart shall be content."

Mahabali, known far and wide for his generosity, laughed warmly. "Only three steps? My dear boy, ask for kingdoms, wealth, or whatever you desire. Why limit your wish?"

Yet the boy merely smiled serenely. "Three steps of land are all I require."

Without hesitation, Mahabali agreed. But as soon as he granted the request, the dwarf began to transform. Before the astonished eyes of all present, Vaman grew grander, his form stretching toward infinity, until he towered across the cosmos itself. With his first step, he effortlessly measured all of Swarg Lok. With the second, he spanned the entirety of Madhya Lok. Now, with no space left for the third step, Mahabali grasped the divine truth before him.

Filled with devotion rather than fear, Mahabali humbly knelt and offered his head to the divine visitor. "O Lord," he whispered, his voice resolute, "place your third step upon my head. Allow me the honor of remaining eternally true to dharma—and to you."

Moved by Mahabali's humility and unwavering devotion, Vaman gently placed his foot on the king's bowed head—not to crush him, but to guide him gracefully into Adho Lok, specifically into Ratna-Prabha, the uppermost of its seven layers. There, Lord Vishnu bestowed upon Mahabali a boon:

"You, Mahabali, embody true righteousness and devotion. Henceforth, you shall reign eternally as the guardian of Ratna-Prabha, cultivating its hidden treasures and spreading harmony throughout its realm. As my immortal devotee, you shall remain here until the cosmic balance requires your presence again. When the universe calls upon your spirit, you shall rise and return to Bharat Kshetra."

From that moment, Mahabali assumed rule over Ratna-Prabha—a realm of indescribable beauty, radiant jewels, and shimmering rivers of celestial luminescence. Under his benevolent guardianship, the realm prospered, emerging as a beacon of harmony within the vast expanses of Adho Lok.

Yet Mahabali's bond with Bharat Kshetra endured. Deeply touched by Mahabali's undying devotion and love for his people, Lord Vishnu granted him a special grace: the opportunity to return to Madhya-lok once each year during the sacred festival of Onam. On the full moon night preceding Onam, Mahabali rises from Ratna-Prabha to revisit his earthly kingdom, blessing his people and joining their joyous celebrations. His annual presence brings prosperity, unity, and joy, forever reminding humanity of the profound selflessness and unwavering dharma that once defined his rule.

Ved Vyas

Renowned sage and compiler of the Vedas, symbolizing eternal wisdom, literary brilliance, and spiritual guidance.

Hanuman

The divine devotee of Lord Rama, symbolizing unwavering devotion, strength, humility, courage, and spiritual service.

Vibhishana

Brother of demon king Ravan, known for righteousness, loyalty, devotion to Lord Rama, and adherence to Dharma despite adversity.

Kripacharya

A wise sage and revered warrior who fought in the Mahabharata war, symbolizing impartial wisdom, integrity, loyalty, and dedication to righteousness.

Parashurama

The warrior sage, incarnation of Lord Vishnu, symbolizing justice, discipline, divine retribution against injustice, and moral order."

41. Shantakaram Bhujagashayanam Shlok

The Shantakaram Bhujagashayanam Shloka is a revered Sanskrit prayer from ancient Indian scriptures, praising Lord Vishnu's divine attributes. It vividly describes Lord Vishnu's serene form, resting peacefully upon the cosmic serpent Shesha (Ananta), symbolizing infinite time and the cosmic order. The shloka emphasizes the divine tranquillity, universal compassion, and cosmic authority of Vishnu, portraying Him as the supreme protector and sustainer of the universe.

42. Simandhar Swamy

"Simandhar Swamy is a revered living Tirthankar prominently described in Jain cosmology and spiritual teachings. According to Jain scriptures, he currently resides in Mahavideh Kshetra, the eternally pure and spiritually advanced region of Jambudveep, where living Tirthankars continuously exist.

Spiritual Significance:

Living Tirthankar: Simandhar Swamy actively teaches and guides souls toward liberation in the present cosmic cycle.

Gateway to Liberation: He represents a direct, living connection to spiritual enlightenment, providing guidance and teachings for souls sincerely seeking liberation during this current cosmic era.

Significance in Jain Cosmology:

Jain scriptures emphasize that Mahavideh Kshetra, where Simandhar Swamy resides, remains eternally pure, spiritually vibrant, and unaffected by cyclic declines (Avsarpini) that affect regions like Bharat Kshetra. Therefore, establishing spiritual connection with Simandhar Swamy is considered profoundly beneficial for spiritual aspirants striving toward liberation."

43. Tarkshya

"Tarkshya is a significant celestial figure described prominently in ancient Indian scriptures, widely recognized as another name for Garuda, the divine eagle. Garuda is renowned in Hindu mythology as the majestic mount (Vahana) of Lord Vishnu, symbolizing supreme power, speed, courage, and spiritual freedom.

Spiritual and Cultural Significance:

Symbol of Strength and Courage: Tarkshya (Garuda) symbolizes immense strength, courage, and speed. His powerful flight represents spiritual elevation, liberation from worldly attachments, and transcendence of limitations.

Divine Mount of Vishnu: As Vishnu's sacred mount, Tarkshya signifies devotion, service, and unwavering loyalty, highlighting the eternal relationship between the divine and devotees.

Enemy of Serpents: Tarkshya is traditionally portrayed as a formidable enemy of serpents, representing victory over lower instincts, negativity, ignorance, and spiritual darkness.

Messenger and Protector: Tarkshya often serves as a divine messenger, protector of righteousness (Dharma), and defender of cosmic order, embodying justice and integrity."

44. Tirthankar

"In Jainism, a Tirthankar (literally 'ford-maker') is an enlightened spiritual teacher who establishes a Tirtha, a metaphorical ford or crossing, guiding souls across the river of worldly existence and suffering toward liberation (Moksha). Jain scriptures describe twenty-four Tirthankars in each cosmic era, who illuminate the path of spiritual purification through profound teachings, personal example, and unwavering compassion.

Each Tirthankar attains supreme enlightenment (Keval Gyan), conquering all karmic attachments, delusions, and passions. They become omniscient, perceiving the true nature of reality and the workings of karma. Among the most revered Tirthankars are Lord Rishabhdev (Adinath), the first Tirthankar, and Lord Mahavir, the twenty-fourth and last Tirthankar of our current cosmic cycle.

In Bharat Kshetra: The Untold Story, Lord Parshvanath, the twenty-third Tirthankar, plays a pivotal role. His life story and spiritual teachings profoundly inspire Pravash Rathore, shaping his understanding of compassion, forgiveness, and karmic redemption. The presence and references to Tirthankars in the narrative symbolize the eternal pursuit of truth, non-violence (Ahimsa), and liberation, serving as spiritual beacons guiding the characters toward their higher purpose and ultimate enlightenment."

45. Uluka

"Uluka is the sacred owl prominently associated with Goddess Lakshmi, the divine goddess of wealth, prosperity, fortune, and auspiciousness in Hindu scriptures. The owl serves as her celestial mount (Vahana), symbolizing unique spiritual and philosophical meanings.

Symbolic Significance:

Wisdom and Insight: Uluka, as an owl, symbolizes spiritual wisdom, keen observation, and the ability to perceive truth in darkness, representing discernment and enlightenment beyond superficial appearances.

Wealth and Prosperity: As Lakshmi's mount, the owl embodies careful management, vigilance, and thoughtful utilization of wealth and resources, indicating prosperity balanced with wisdom and prudence.

Balance of Dualities: Traditionally, the owl is associated with darkness, while Goddess Lakshmi embodies radiant abundance and fortune. This pairing symbolizes a harmonious balance between contrasting elements—spiritual and material, dark and light, ignorance and wisdom—highlighting the deeper spiritual principle of balance and harmony.

Overcoming Ignorance: The owl's nocturnal nature represents overcoming ignorance (symbolized by darkness), guiding devotees toward spiritual clarity and awakening."

46. Ved Vyas

"Ved Vyas, also known as Krishna Dvaipayana Vyasa, is a celebrated sage revered prominently in ancient Indian scriptures, with distinct representations in Hindu and Jain traditions.

In Hindu Scriptures:

Ved Vyas is highly respected as the compiler of the Vedas and the author of the epic Mahabharata, including the sacred philosophical discourse, the Bhagavad Gita. Known as a partial incarnation of Lord Vishnu, he symbolizes profound wisdom, spiritual authority, and cosmic guidance.

His contributions serve as foundational pillars for Dharma (righteousness), Karma (action), and spiritual liberation (Moksha).

In Jain Scriptures:

In Jain tradition, Vyasa is acknowledged primarily as a respected sage and scholar rather than a divine figure. Jain scriptures mention Vyasa as an esteemed historical personality who compiled and preserved important spiritual and ethical knowledge. However, Jain texts emphasize that despite his scholarly prominence and literary contributions, Vyasa, like all souls, remains subject to karma and the cycle of rebirth until he attains liberation (Moksha). This reflects the Jain principle that spiritual liberation requires personal realization and detachment from worldly accomplishments."

47. Vishwakarma

"Vishwakarma is a celebrated figure appearing in ancient Indian scriptures, known as the divine architect, engineer, and craftsman who creates and sustains the structures of the universe.

In Hindu Scriptures:

In Hindu mythology and sacred texts, Vishwakarma is revered as the celestial architect and divine craftsman of the gods (Devas). He is credited with constructing magnificent celestial cities, weapons, chariots, and palaces, including Indra's heavenly abode (Svarga), the city of Dwarka for Lord Krishna, and the legendary Lanka for the demon king Ravan. Vishwakarma symbolizes supreme creativity, craftsmanship, and cosmic order, highlighting the divine aspect of creation, architecture, and engineering.

In Jain Scriptures:

In Jain tradition, Vishwakarma similarly represents a celestial architect or divine craftsman residing in the heavens (Swarg Lok). Though not worshipped as a deity, he is respected as a powerful celestial being (Deva) who builds and maintains heavenly palaces, structures, and beautiful celestial abodes for divine beings. His role emphasizes perfection, creative energy, and karmic reward—yet, like all celestial beings, he remains bound within the karmic cycle until achieving spiritual liberation (Moksha)."

About the Author

Vipul is a son, brother, friend, uncle, beloved, husband, and father to a beautiful family.

Along with that he is also a digital transformation leader with over 20 years of global experience across Retail, Automobile, Fintech, Infrastructure and Supply Chain technology. Having begun his journey as a Pizza Hut cashier and freelance techie, he now leads merchandising and AI platforms for Retail Tech Giant. He represented India at the Indoor Cricket World Master Series in Sri Lanka (2024).

With the Jambudveep series, he channels his lifelong passion for storytelling into an epic saga, beginning with his debut novel, *Bharat Kshetra – The Hidden Matrix*.

Echoes on the Ninth

09/09/99

There are nights when darkness is just the absence of light.

And there are nights when it feels like a curtain being drawn back.

By then, the ***threads of destiny*** *had long since begun their quiet work around three young lives. They did not know it; they had no words for it. Somewhere, those threads were already weaving themselves into something older, something that would one day be remembered as* ***echoes of eternity****.*

On the ninth night of the ninth month of the ninetyninth year, three clocks ticked in three different rooms.

Nothing special happened when they turned to that minute.

But almost together, like three sparks falling on three different pools of oil, the first flashes found them.

Mist pressed its cold face against the windows of the hermitage.

Far below, the Saraswati River whispered through the valley, its voice softened by distance and night. Deodar trees stood guard around the stone buildings, their branches heavy with the memory of snow.

Inside one small room, the fire in the hearth had sunk to dull red embers.

Tejomayi slept curled against Surabhi, her cheek pillowed on the cow's warm flank, one arm flung across her as if she was hugging a mountain disguised in fur. Surabhi's breath rose and fell in slow, peaceful waves. Above them, Tarkshya roosted along a beam, white wings fluffed, head tucked. Uluka watched from the rafters, one luminous eye halfopen.

Tejomayi's fingers twitched in Surabhi's hair.

The feel of stone and smoke thinned under her.

The sounds of the hermitage faded like someone turning down a radio.

She was standing barefoot on sand.

Not the cold dust of Solan, but the soft, warm grains of ***Raman Reti*** *near Vrindavan. The night there was gentler—a dark blue bowl with a few scattered stars, the air warming her skin instead of biting it.*

Narrow lanes unrolled ahead of her, lined with small houses and ashrams washed in faded blue and yellow. Courtyards with tulsi plants. Low walls. The smell of incense, cow dung, frying pakoras and old stone mixed together into something strangely comforting.

Voices drifted past—bits of laughter, fragments of bhajans, the jangle of bangles, the distant ring of a temple bell.

And over it all floated a sound she had never heard before and yet, deep inside, felt she had been waiting for her whole life.

A flute.

The first note slipped into the lane like a thin thread of silver. Another wrapped around it. Then another. Soon the melody was winding between the houses, curling around her ankles, tugging gently at her chest.

Her feet started to move before the thought did.

She pushed past smudged faces—men in dhotis, women in saris, children racing each other. In the logic of dreams, none of their features stayed long enough to matter; every time she tried to focus, they blurred, as if the dream refused to waste detail on anyone who wasn't part of what she had come here for.

Only the flute stayed sharp.

It drew her toward a small temple at the end of the lane.

Whitewashed walls. An archway with a bell hanging from a wooden beam. Beyond it, a courtyard lay in a soft, strange halflight—not quite dawn, not quite dusk. A tulsi bed. Fading rangoli on stone. Steps leading up toward a sanctum where an idol sat in shadow, thick with flowers.

The flute was coming from inside.

She stepped under the bell.

The courtyard was full. Women sat crosslegged near the pillars, lips moving silently. Old men leaned on sticks. Children slept with their heads on laps. Lamps burned in tiny clay circles, their flames steady and golden.

She slipped through gaps between bodies.

Through shifting shoulders and backs, she finally caught a glimpse:

A hand lifting the flute. Brown skin under simple cloth. The slope of a neck. The edge of a cheek. And, caught in a single beam of dreamlight, the soft sway of a **peacock feather**, *blue and green and impossibly alive.*

Her heart jolted so hard it almost hurt.

You, a word rose in her, though she had no idea why.

She tried to move faster.

A woman stood. Someone shifted a basket. A child clambered into a lap. For one thin second the flute player vanished, hidden completely behind a wall of bodies.

She wove around them and reached the gap—

Empty.

The spot where the player had been was just air and lingering sound.

The flute cut off midphrase.

Silence followed—not empty, but ringing, like the air after lightning.

She spun, searching for any flash of white cloth or blue feather. The faces around her smeared further. The walls wavered. The bell at the entrance wobbled in her vision.

An ache bloomed in her chest, sharp and bewildering—the ache of being shown something from her future and then having it snatched away before she could even touch it.

The courtyard dissolved.

Light and color slid sideways and peeled away. The last fragments of flutesong stretched thinner and thinner until they snapped—

And somewhere, hundreds of kilometres away, a pencil rolled off a boy's hand and never hit the floor.

The dormitory smelled of iron cots, chalk, soap, and the faint, sour edge of tired boys.

Rows of beds lined the long room. A ceiling fan clacked rhythmically, barely disturbing the heavy air. Outside the barred windows, a dog barked twice at nothing in particular, then settled down again.

Soham lay on his back near the window, notebook open on his chest, compass and pencil balanced loosely in his right hand.

He had meant to finish one last geometry problem before sleep.

At some point between one angle and the next, his eyes had closed.

The pencil slipped from his fingers.

It never made a sound.

He was sitting with her, shoulder to shoulder, their ankles in the river.

Mountains rose around them in a wide, protective circle—their shoulders dark, their peaks capped in soft white. The sky above was a pale, clean blue. The river that cut through the valley was so clear he could see each stone beneath its surface, every shifting pattern of light as it flowed over them.

The air tasted like cold sunlight and rock.

They sat side by side on the same smooth stone at the river's edge, leaning into each other just enough that he could feel the gentle weight of her head against his shoulder. The rest of the world felt distant, blurred, as if the mountains, the sky, even the sound of the water had all stepped back to make room for this one small circle of time.

He could have stayed like that forever—breathing when she breathed, watching the light move on the surface, feeling time gather itself around this one quiet moment and stay.

He still couldn't see her face clearly.

For once, he didn't want to try.

The moment felt so delicate that even the smallest shift might break it. So he sat, and he let himself simply exist beside her.

And yet, the river tugged at him.

His hand slid down almost on its own, fingers slipping over the edge of the stone and into the water. The current was icy, but it welcomed him, swirling around his wrist, then his forearm, guiding rather than pushing.

For a few heartbeats he felt only smooth pebbles and the soft glide of the flow.

Then his fingers brushed a curve.

Hard. Ancient. Waiting.

The instant he touched it, a faint light stirred under the surface—threads running along an unseen arc, waking after an age of sleep. He closed his grip and pulled.

The bow rose from the river like something remembered.

Water slid off its limbs in silver sheets. Symbols along its length shimmered softly, then settled into a calm, steady glow. It felt dense in his hands, not heavy—full. Complete.

Its name rose in his chest like a memory returning.

Gandiv.

It had been hidden for so long that stories had turned vague and maps had gone quiet. Kings, sages, warriors—countless hands had reached for it across centuries.

None of them had been the ones it waited for.

He knew, with absolute certainty, that the bow had not been calling to him. It had been calling through him.

He was the one the river allowed to find it.

She was the one it belonged to.

He turned to her.

She was still watching the water, as if she had known something would rise from it long before he moved. Light from the river climbed softly across her features, just enough to hint at a profile the dream still refused to fully reveal.

With both hands, he offered Gandiv to her.

This is yours now, something in him said without words. It has been waiting for you for ages.

She raised her hands as if she'd heard him.

Slender fingers closed over the grip from the other side. For one suspended heartbeat, their hands and the bow were all that existed—skin touching skin over cool, ancient power.

A quiet shock ran through him.

Deep. Clean. Like finally recognising a song when you've only ever heard its echo.

The bow changed the moment her palms fully settled around it.

Completion bloomed in his chest—a steady, grounding joy, the kind that comes from finally finishing something you did not know you were born to do.

The urge to see her face flared painfully strong.

He turned, lifting his gaze.

Mist rolled in, soft and stubborn.

Her features hovered at the edge of focus—a hint of eyes turned toward him, the ghost of a smile—

The mountains smeared.

The river broke apart into brightness.

Gandiv faded from between their hands.

—⚘✎💻✡—

The night over Kolkata hung low and heavy, smeared with old smoke and neon.

Trams had mostly stopped. Taxis nosed their way through late streets, horns muted at this hour. Somewhere, a drunk laughed too loudly. Somewhere else, a radio played an old Kishore song to an empty lane.

Upstairs, down a narrow corridor that smelled of incense, old paint and frying onions, two brothers slept on one bed.

Aakash lay on his side, arm flung over his eyes. Pravash lay on his back, one hand loosely resting near the dead Walkman on the pillow beside him. The ear pads had left faint marks on his skin.

In the silence after music, something else slipped in.

—⚘✎💻✡—

He was high above a world that looked like it was about to snap.

There was no sense of a body—only the sure knowledge that he hovered somewhere above the ground. The air was thin and sharp, laced with the scent of ash and metal.

Below him stretched a plain so vast it seemed to curve with the world. The ground was dark, churned, broken. And it moved—not like earth, but like a living thing.

An army.

Not of humans.

Creatures covered the land from horizon to horizon, packed so close they were a single heaving mass. Hulking bodies, thick with muscle and bone. Skin the color of old bruises and dried blood. Jaws crowded with teeth. Eyes burning dully like embers smothered in ash.

Their armor wasn't crafted; it looked grown—from bone, from horn, from something that had never been alive but refused to die.

They roared, but the sound didn't rise like voices. It was a vibration, a low, endless thunder that shook the air where he floated. Spears and crude blades jutted upward, a forest of steel and stone catching a light source he couldn't see.

From this height, they should have seemed small.

They didn't.

Every single one felt huge, and there were millions. Enough to swallow cities. Enough to drink seas.

A cold sweat he didn't physically have prickled across his dream-skin.

Then, abruptly, everything went quiet.

The army below him froze mid-roar, mid-stride.

A warmth curled around his right hand.

A giggle.

He looked down.

His fingers were no longer empty. They were being gripped—tightly, possessively—by a much smaller hand. Soft. Tiny. The fingers didn't even close all the way around his; they just clung to one side, stubborn and sure.

The landscape had changed.

No battlefield now. Just a patch of soft, sun-warmed ground he couldn't fully place. Maybe a park. Maybe a village yard. The light was gentle, the kind that made everything look like an old photograph.

Beside him, out of his line of sight, a toddler walked.

He could see only the edge of her dress, the swing of it around stocky knees. A flash of anklets. A curtain of hair that bounced with each step, dark and slightly wavy. Her hand never loosened around his finger.

For the first time he could remember, he felt like the one being steadied.

Everything in that touch said, as clearly as any promise: I'm not letting go. I'll take care of you.

A strange calm spread through him.

Not the calm of numbness, but the calm of suddenly knowing that somewhere in this vast, dangerous world, a tiny hand had already chosen him as its person.

Behind her, just at the edge of sight, shapes waited in the haze.

Big heads. Bright eyes. Fur ruffled by a wind the lane didn't feel. Wolves—many of them—silent and watchful, their presence more like a vow than a picture.

He wanted to ask who she was. Ask where they were. Ask why he could suddenly breathe more easily than he had in years.

Before he could form the first word, the scene dissolved.

The feel of her hand lingered longest.

Then that too slipped away.

Tejomayi hit the ground hard.

Heat slapped the breath out of her.

No Himalayan chill, no river song. Just an endless desert under a burning white sun. Sand slid under her palms, hot enough to sting. The air shimmered, turning the horizon into a mirage of wavering lines.

She pushed herself up onto her knees, spitting grit.

Across from her, on the crest of a dune, a man stood.

He was dressed as if he had taken a wrong turn out of a city boardroom.

A fitted black suit traced clean lines over a strong frame—jacket buttoned, dark shirt beneath, shoes half sunk in the sand yet somehow not dirty. His hair was combed back, and in that harsh light she caught glints of silver along the sides.

The heat made his face restless; every time she tried to clearly see his eyes, the air between them wavered, smudging the details. She caught angles—a firm jaw, the tilt of a mouth that knew how to stay quiet, the suggestion of cheekbones.

He lifted one hand slightly.

Sand answered.

It rose around him in a circling veil, grains spinning upward and outward as if weight had stopped mattering. In the whirling curtain she thought she glimpsed things that did not belong to this desert at all—armies kneeling, oceans bucking, skies split by light—and then they were gone before they could settle.

Something in her blood thrilled.

Till now, every trial the Saptarishis had set her had eventually bent to her will. Stones had cracked, targets had shattered, enemies—real or conjured—had fallen.

This one did not feel like it would fall easily.

A grin, sharp and entirely her own, tugged at her mouth.

She surged forward.

The hot sand that should have dragged at her feet seemed instead to coil and spring, helping each stride. Her body moved with the ease of long practice—pivots, spins, leaps, every muscle singing with joy at being unleashed.

Her hands opened and closed.

No weapon appeared.

She didn't need one.

Her body was the weapon—fists, elbows, knees, the whipcrack precision of her legs. The dream let her be exactly what she was born for: velocity and impact, wrapped in a girl not yet grown.

She closed the distance in a blink and drove a strike straight at his chest.

For the briefest moment, his eyes came into focus.

They were not cruel. Not soft, either. They held a depth she recognised in a way she couldn't explain—a weariness that had made peace with continuing anyway.

His arm moved almost lazily.

His forearm met her punch.

The world exploded in her bones.

The shock of the block travelled up her arm, down her spine, through her hips. Her feet left the sand. She flew backward as if the air had suddenly turned into a wall. The dune caught her, then gave way, sending her rolling down its slope in a spray of hot grains.

She slid to a halt on her back, the sky a blinding sheet above her, lungs refusing to work for a moment.

Pain flared bright and electric along her ribs and shoulder.

She had been hit before. Never like that.

How can someone standing on the same ground as me do that?

The thought came not as defeat, but as astonished respect.

Gritting her teeth, she dug her hands into the sand and pushed herself upright again.

Somewhere across the dunes, a low sound drifted on the wind—not quite a laugh, not quite a sigh. She couldn't tell if it came from him or from the desert itself.

For the first time in her young life, she felt a wild, delighted certainty:

Finally.

She had found someone whose strength met hers head on.

Before she could launch herself at him again, the dunes behind him split open.

Light from another world rushed in.

This flash was special. From this shared vantage point, the three of them saw it together.

Each believed the vision belonged to them alone. But the scene was the same, drawn from angles that barely differed, as if someone had tilted a mirror a degree this way and that.

Snow.

Endless, gleaming snow.

Mountains rose, jagged and white, their peaks lost in cloud. The sky above was a bruised twilight—neither day nor night, streaked with colors that did not exist on any painter's palette. The air hummed with a tension that was almost a sound.

In the heart of a wide valley, armies gathered.

The desert peeled away from beneath Tejomayi, and suddenly she was high above a vast white plain. Mountains ringed it on all sides, their slopes and peaks buried entirely under ice, like silent watchers in white armor.

Wind roared past her ears.

Something huge and alive moved beneath her feet.

She looked down.

She was standing on the broad back of a gigantic owl, feathers white and silver, wings cutting through the air in slow, powerful strokes. Each beat sent ripples through the clouds.

Beside her, for a fleeting moment, something dark streaked past—another great shape in the air. An eagle, white, enormous and proud, wings spread wide, tips catching stray shards of light. On its back stood a boy—older than the one in Bangalore's dorm, but his gaze, the way he leaned into the wind, belonged to the same soul.

From this height, the world below unfolded like a terrible, beautiful map.

On the snow plain, a wolf ran.

Far below, the snow broke.

A single white wolf leapt into view.

It was huge—large enough that a human atop it looked perfectly at scale. Its fur shone with a light that wasn't reflection, a light from within. Its paws barely seemed to touch the ground as it ran, each stride devouring impossible distances.

On its back, a young man rode, cloak snapping behind him. His face wasn't clear in the dream—always turned slightly away, always halfobscured by movement—but the set of his shoulders, the way his hand rested on the beast's neck, spoke of someone who had finally found where he belonged.

He didn't know the names of those above him.

They didn't know his.

Yet some part of each of them recognised the others—like three notes in a chord that had not yet been fully played.

Behind the wolf-rider, the earth trembled.

An army of wolves followed.

White, grey, black, silver—hundreds, thousands—racing across the snow, paws barely making a sound. Their formation was loose and free, yet somehow perfectly coordinated, as if they had once been part of something single and divine and had only recently agreed to be many.

On the right flank, the snow exploded into fire.

A lion bounded into sight, bigger than any story had ever dared to make it. Muscles rippled beneath a coat the color of molten gold. Its mane seemed woven from sunrises. On its back rode a teenage girl clad in red and gold—an Angrakha-style top, a warrior's dhoti, fabric snapping like banners in a silent wind.

Her hair flew wild behind her. Behind her came more lions, more tigers, their roars a chorus the dreamers heard not with their ears but with their bones.

On the far edge of the sky, three serpentine shadows coiled and dove.

They were not snakes, not exactly. Their bodies were too vast, their scales caught the light like armor, their forms moved with a power closer to dragons than anything that slithered. Fire licked from their mouths, searing paths through the thin air, not to destroy, but to mark the boundaries of some invisible formation.

Even from this height, the three dreamers could sense it:

One was a man, tall and steady, the kind of presence that felt like a drawn sword kept in its sheath out of courtesy, not necessity.

One was a young woman about their own age—stance sharp, hair whipping behind her, every line of her body angled toward the battle below.

The third was a fierce, slightly older woman, posture straight as a spear, a strength in her that had clearly chosen what it would spend itself on.

From the ground's edge, another force advanced.

At its front rode a figure on a fierce white horse, wrapped in a long dark cloak that billowed behind her like a banner. In one hand she held the reins; in the other, a tall staff topped with a small cluster of shapes that pulsed softly—as if some piece of the night sky had been folded into metal.

Behind her rode others.

Dozens of riders on horses of every shade, robed in garments that flickered at the edges with symbols—wizards, or something very like it. The air around them shimmered faintly whenever they moved, reality bending to make room for whatever they were holding back.

From his eagle, Soham stared.

Her face was turned briefly upward, eyes assessing the sky.

He knew that profile.

Her features came into focus just enough for two of the dreamers to recognize her.

Yasmeen.

Pravash's breath caught in his sleep. Soham's did too.

She looked older now, sharper, wrapped in power instead of just courage. But it was her. The same voice that had once saved his life over a crackling phone line now carried a staff that made the very air listen.

He couldn't call out to her here.

He just rode beside the echo of her and felt, for the first time since childhood, that he wasn't charging alone.

Higher still, something not made of flesh cut across the sky.

A craft—sleek, metallic, edges limned with pale light. It looked like a thought that had slipped out of a draftsman's mind before its time: part aircraft, part temple, part impossible. At its open ramp stood a broadshouldered figure, scarf snapping, one hand braced against the frame as he looked down like a builder studying the bridge he'd laid across a chasm.

Not far from him, suspended in the open air, a woman hovered.

No wings. No machine.

Her hands moved in slow, complex patterns, fingertips trailing streams of iridescent blue and green, like the colors of blinking stars in a clear night. Wherever those threads touched the warriors below, armor brightened, wounds sealed, paths opened through chaos. Waves of power pulsed outward from her, bending the air itself.

With small, precise gestures, she twisted space.

And before them all, filling the far horizon, came the enemy.

The tide of creatures Pravash had seen earlier—multiplied. Wave upon wave of bulking forms. Between them stalked things with too many limbs, things that flew without wings, things that crawled with mouths where their faces should be. Above them, darker shapes glided, vast and ridged, like living fortresses.

Between those grotesque ranks, another column gathered: pale faces, toostill movements, the cold elegance of those who had learned to hide among humans. Raktans.

At their head, astride a black horse, rode a girl in dark armor.

Her jaw, her eyes, the tilt of her head—all were painfully familiar to the boy on the wolf. Once, she had prowled school corridors in salwar kameez and entitlement. Here, that arrogance had been forged into command. Orders left her mouth; the monsters around her obeyed.

From the wolf's back, Pravash's stomach lurched.

He knew that face.

From the arrogant tilt of a chin that had once promised to own the world.

Here, she was something else.

But she was not among the monsters.

She rode with them.

Somewhere between the wolves and the giants, between the lions and the pale riders, the field held its breath.

Snow trembled.

Something vaster moved.

Beyond the first ranks, a shape began to rise.

First came legs, thicker than towers, pushing up from cracked earth. Then a torso like a mountain trying to stand. Arms spread out, each finger long enough to crush whole streets. Horns curled from a shadowed skull. When its eyes opened, the dim light of that sky seemed to flinch.

It straightened slowly, until its head scraped the low clouds.

Easily a thousand feet tall.

It took one step.

The white plain quivered.

Against that height, the wolves and lions and horses, the serpents, the flying craft, even the great owl and eagle all suddenly looked impossibly small, like miniatures painted on the edge of a scroll.

The giant stretched out an arm.

Its hand rose, palm open, fingers loose, reaching down with the lazy certainty of something that had crushed countless lives and never remembered a single one.

Its shadow swept across the snow—over wolves, over riders, over lions and tigers, over the owl and eagle and the racing wolf.

In three different dreams, three young hearts hammered as that hand reached straight toward where they stood.

On the owl's back, the girl grabbed at a feather, legs bracing, every muscle coiling to leap.

On the eagle's back, the boy's fingers curled, searching instinctively for a bowstring that wasn't there.

On the wolf's back, the rider's grip tightened in snowy fur as the strange gun in his hands thrummed with energy he had never been taught to control.

The giant's hand descended, filling the sky.

Darkness dropped over everything.

All three jolted awake—in Solan, in Bangalore, in Kolkata—as if pulled from the same fall.

Three chests heaved in three different rooms. Three sets of eyes stared into the dark, ears straining for sounds that weren't there, skin still buzzing with cold wind and distant roars.

On three bedside tables, three clocks glowed the same time.

04:09 a.m.

An hour old storytellers say is when true dreams are given.

The night of 9/9/99 slid into the past like any other date.

The threads of destiny had been tugged again.

From here on, whether they realized it or not, their lives would move to the rhythm of those echoes of eternity.